# AN ECHO OF EARTH

# AN ECHO OF EARTH

## CHILDREN OF EARTHRISE, BOOK III

## DANIEL ARENSON

## CHAPTER ONE

Tom moved silently through the forest, hunting scorpions.

The trees rose tall and dark and dank around him, their bark like the burnt skin of corpses, their leaves as pale as bones. Secrets haunted this forest. Ghosts moved through the mist, whispering and creaking the branches, and dead beasts rotted under layers of rancid leaves and black moss. This was not a green, peaceful forest like those on Earth. Nor was this some enchanted alien forest, filled with exotic life and luminous wonders. This forest was a place of decay. This was a cathedral to the gods of death.

This was a world of death, Tom thought, and this was a war of death, and they were the last members of a dying species. Stubborn. Clinging to the last remnants of life like a beggar clinging to a tattered blanket as the cold wind moaned.

A shadow fluttered. Wings thudded and a caw split the air, shrill like rusty metal hinges. Tom aimed his wheeled cannon, a weapon cobbled together from the plasma gun of a fallen warship. There above—one of the foul vultures that lived on this godforsaken planet. Few species survived on Morbus, this hellhole in the dark corners of the galaxy. Fewer thrived. The vultures thrived, for they fed on decay and death, devourers of their very world.

"We're picking up more chatter," said Nathaniel. The old graybeard stepped closer to Tom, hauling a rusty transmitter. "Trouble at the gulock all right. Prisoners rising up again."

Tom nodded. "We'll be there soon. They'll need help."

His chest tightened. It was hard to forget. Hard to stop the pain. Most of them here—Tom, Nathaniel, the fifty others who followed him—had survived enclaves, deathcars, the destruction of their homes. The destruction of their humanity. They had been born human, the most cursed of creatures. Every one of them had passed through nightmares to come here, to become warriors of Earth's Light.

But among the rebels, only Tom Shepherd had survived a gulock.

Only he had seen the terror. The flayed bodies—still alive. The crematoriums—burning the remains. Humanity—beaten, tortured, made to crawl and beg before the mercy of slow death.

*My wife burned,* he thought. *I begged them. But I burned her. I—*

He inhaled sharply. He clenched his jaw.

*No time for pain now. Be dead inside, Tom. Be dead like this world, and maybe you can give others life.*

"You all right, Tom?" Nathaniel placed a hand on his shoulder.

Tom looked at the old man. Nathaniel was his second-in-command, his friend, a man as dear as a brother. They had met only months ago.

He nodded. "Come on, Nathaniel. We're close." Tom looked at the other rebels. "We're almost there."

They looked back at him. Twenty-five had come on this mission, half their force. Half of this army they called Earth's Light. Weary men and women. Haggard. Starving. They wore shabby uniforms, and most were barefoot. A year ago, they had shot down a striker, one of the scorpions' warships. Chunks of its jagged black hull now formed their armor. They had mounted the striker's plasma guns onto wooden wheels; they dragged three of these makeshift cannons through the forest. Their eyes were sunken, their skin ashen. They were hungry. They were dying.

*But we will die fighting,* Tom thought. *We won't die twisted, tortured wretches. We will die human.*

He had heard rumors, perhaps only legends, of a great human rebellion beyond the stars. They said that the Heirs of Earth was a true fleet, an army of thousands, all human. That they commanded warships. That they led companies of marines. In the gulocks and deathcars, prisoners whispered of them, prayed to them. Tom and his men had no starships, no marines, no power to even leave this planet, let alone fight in great battles among the stars. They were fifty survivors, only half of them strong enough to fight. They were Earth's Light, the rebels of this forsaken planet deep in Hierarchy space. Here in the darkness, there were no Heirs of Earth with their shiny warships. Here it was only Tom and his people. Here they were the only hope of humanity.

One rebel pushed a heavy communicator in a wheelbarrow. Tom caught his reflection in the black monitor. He looked no stronger than the men who followed him. Just another haggard soul, a dying wretch in a forest of death. Tom was only forty, but he looked a decade older. His hair had turned gray during this war. His cheeks were sunken, and deep grooves framed his mouth. His shoulders were broad but knobby. Only a few years ago, he had been a shepherd on a grassy, peaceful world many light-years from this place. His hair had been brown, his face smooth.

What had happened to that joyous young man, full of life and dreams? That life had ended. The cosmos itself was ending. The Hierarchy was spreading across the galaxy like a cancer. Humanity was fading.

*Most die in the gulocks,* Tom thought. *Like my family died. Like millions died. Like I almost died. But not us. Not Earth's Light. We will fight. We will die free. For a memory of Earth.*

They kept moving through the forest. The trunks closed in around them, so cluttered the cannons could barely roll through.

Red sap bled from the boles, sticky and hot, smearing the rebels with every step. Serpents coiled around the bone-white branches, tongues flicking, crimson eyes glaring. On the forest floor, vultures looked up from a mangy dead animal, its ribs tugged open, the last of its organs dangling like bloated leeches. The scavengers stared, silent, eyes following the humans as they trudged by.

At the sight of the dead animal, at the sickly sweet stench of it, Tom's stomach growled. He was so hungry. Yet the carrion was rancid, swarming with maggots, and Tom had not forgotten the last disease that had swept through his camp, not forgotten the eight warriors who had shivered, vomiting and shitting themselves to death in a cave. There would be food another day. Or there would be death. But there would be death in battle. Not in a foul cave in a puddle of disease.

Not in a gulock.

Not flayed and begging for death. Not burning alive like his wife, like—

Tom bit down hard. He tasted blood. It drowned the memories.

He began to walk faster now, wheeling the cannon over roots and stones. The canopy was thick, the shadows deep, but his eyes were still sharp, his pace confident. He knew these woods, knew every hill and valley and snaking river of acidic water. For seventeen hundred and fourteen days, he had survived here. Perhaps today was his last.

From ahead—a clattering.

Tom froze.

He reached for his pistol.

Behind him, the other rebels raised their rifles.

Silence. Nothing but the creaking trees, the caw of some distant vulture, a buzzing insect.

Then, from the distance—a scream.

A human scream.

Tom glanced at Nathaniel. "Somebody escaped. Somebody—"

A screech tore through the forest.

A scorpion burst between the trees and leaped toward the rebels.

Tom fired his pistol.

The bullet hit the creature, barely denting its shell. The massive scorpion, twice his size, slammed into Tom and knocked him onto the ground.

These were not like the scorpions from Earth, mythical creatures no larger than a man's palm. These were Skra-Shen. Intelligent. Cruel. Masters of the Hierarchy. The creatures who had butchered Tom's family, who were butchering humans across the galaxy. The beast pinned him down, saliva dripping, sizzling, burning Tom's chest.

"An escaped maggot," the scorpion hissed. "Are you ready to burn with your brothers?"

Beside them, Nathaniel grunted and thrust an electric prod. A bolt slammed through the scorpion—and into Tom.

Both screamed.

The alien arachnid fell.

Tom rose to his feet, crackling with electricity, clothes smoking. Within a heartbeat, he swiveled his cannon toward the twitching monster. He pulled the trigger.

As the scorpion lunged toward him, a turret of plasma washed over the beast.

This cannon had once been mounted on a striker. It was built to shatter starships. The fury melted the scorpion's shell and cooked the soft innards. When Tom released the trigger, the scorpion thumped onto the ground, a sizzling, molten lump. A few trees burned behind it. The damp, moldy air would soon extinguish the flames.

"So much for stealth," Nathaniel muttered, brushing sparks off his long gray beard.

Tom stared down at the burnt scorpion, and he remembered his family and friends burning, the countless thousands dying in the Skra-Shen factories.

*I will burn every last one of you foul scorpions,* Tom thought. *Not because you killed everyone I love. Not because you brought humanity to its knees. Because of what you turned me into. Because you turned a shepherd into a killer.*

He reached into his cloak, and he closed his fingers around his old wooden flute. For a moment Tom stood silent and still, feeling the familiar wood.

Years ago, Tom had lived on a world of endless grasslands. A shepherd. A joyful man. He would roam the hills under a pale gold sky, herding his flock, playing his flute. The flock was gone. That grassy world had burned. But he still had his flute. And Ra's mercy, he still had his memories, even if he no longer had his soul.

The rebels moved onward through the forest, guns drawn, cannons hot. The trees began to thin out. Soon the rebels would reach the rocky plains of Morbus, wastelands bereft of life, windswept desolation where even the vultures dared not fly. The trees became stunted, and the canopy no longer hid the gray sky. The sun was a pale patch like a sore behind the clouds. Tom felt exposed. Naked. He had become a creature of caves and twisting trees and decay. Open spaces now scared him. They held more danger than the dark. He was a creature of the dark now. He was the beast who lurked in shadows.

From ahead—creaking. Heavy breathing.

The rebels froze and raised their guns.

Footsteps thudded. Claws? A deep pant. A shadow racing ahead. Tom bared his teeth and aimed his cannon.

*I will kill you all.*

He saw it now—a creature moving closer. Pale. Ghostly.

A scorpion? No, too small. Perhaps one of the twisted creatures the aliens created, sewing monsters from human flesh and bones, forming decaying nurses to torture their victims. Killing such a creature was a mercy.

The creature moved forward, faint in the darkness, breathing heavily. Tom would not waste plasma on it. His pistol was full of bullets. They made their own bullets in their cave, melting metal from the hull of the fallen striker. Bullets were cheaper than plasma, and deadly enough when they hit a scorpion's eye. When they hit a tortured man begging for death.

She came racing between the last few trees, ghostly white and naked, mouth wide open, crying out. She was terror taken flesh. She was misery. She was the innocence that shattered in war. No, this was no twisted creation of oozing, stitched flesh.

This was a human.

A child.

She was naked, bald, and bruised. Her feet bled, leaving red prints.

Tom and his rebels lowered their guns.

The girl ran toward them, panting, trembling, bleeding from many cuts. She skidded to a halt ahead of Tom, spun around, raced toward Nathaniel, froze again. She turned from side to side like a trapped animal, hissing, shaking.

"It's all right," Tom said, voice gentle. "You're safe with us. We're friends."

She had come from the gulock, he knew. He had never met anyone else who had fled a gulock, who had survived the butchery.

*Nobody but myself. And this girl.*

She stared at him with wide, damp eyes.

"Human?" she whispered.

Tom doffed his cloak and wrapped it around the girl. "We're humans, yes. We're humans who fight the scorpions. We're here to help. What's your name?"

"Ayumi," she said.

Tom leaned forward, placing his hands on his thighs, bringing himself to eye level with the girl.

"Ayumi, my name is Tom. I lead this group. I've come to help people like you. Others from the bad place you fled." She began to shake violently, and Tom gently touched her arm. "I too was once a prisoner there. We're going to free more people. What can you tell me? We heard about an uprising. How many are fighting?"

Tears rolled down Ayumi's cheeks.

"You're too late," she whispered. Then she lowered her head and would say no more.

Tom glanced toward the back of the group, beckoning Shae, a dour boy of fourteen. The young rebel approached and gently took the girl's hand.

"Should I take her back to the camp?" Shae said.

Tom shook his head. "No. I need you with me. I need every man who can fight. We'll take her with us. Let's keep going."

The forest thinned even more, and soon the trees were gone. They trudged across rocky open plains. Canyons carved up the land, and boulders and mesas rose toward the clouds, black monoliths like burnt limbs. Pillars of smoke rose in the distance, blanketing the sky.

*The smoke of the gulock,* Tom thought.

He paused for just a few heartbeats.

*The place where they broke me. Where my family died.*

He inhaled sharply and moved onward, traversing the plains. The gulock was still kilometers away, but this was the closest Tom had been in years.

For the past five years, he had been fighting in the wilderness. He had shot down a striker. He had ambushed scorpions moving among the trees. He had destroyed two deathcars crammed with prisoners, granting them a quick death.

But he had never stormed the gates of Morbus Gulock. Not since fleeing them five years ago.

He walked faster, shoving the plasma cannon.

Faster still.

He began to run.

Behind him, the others followed.

They were twenty-five. They were the rebels of Morbus. They ran across the open plain.

"For Earth!" Tom cried.

"For Earth!" the others echoed the call.

They were no Inheritors, fabled warriors of might. They were just weary, dying wretches. But they charged with the courage of heroes.

Before them, the gulock was burning. Corpses covered the electric fences, blackened. Scorpions were scurrying, destroying the huts, feasting upon remains.

Ayumi's words echoed in his mind.

*You're too late.*

But not too late to die. To die in battle. To die as heroes. To die and hurt no more.

"Kill the scorpions!" Tom shouted. "Revenge for humanity!"

From behind the electric fence, it ascended. A god of dark metal, triangular like the head of a viper, rising upon a column of smoke and fire. A starship. A striker. A deity of smoke and fury.

Tom stopped outside the gates of the gulock, breathing heavily, and aimed his cannon.

The striker roared out its fury.

Tom fired his cannon, then leaped aside.

Plasma bathed the plain beside him. But his cannon fired true. And the other cannons of Earth's Light joined the assault.

Bolt after bolt of human fury pounded the striker.

And the enemy starship cracked open and fell and slammed into the gulock with an explosion that shook the plains.

The electric fence shattered, spilling corpses.

"Charge!" Tom shouted.

They charged.

Guns firing, they leaped over the carnage and stormed into the gulock.

Screaming.

Dying.

The last stand of Earth's Light.

Scorpions swarmed toward them. Claws ripped through Nathaniel. A stinger crashed through Shae's chest. More warriors fell.

Tom stood in the center of the gulock and fired his cannon.

He blasted his fury into the Red Hospital, the wretched building where the scorpions tortured and mutilated their victims. He fired upon the crematorium, upon the tannery where they turned human skin into leather. Around him, the gulock burned. The scorpions burned.

But Ayumi had been wrong.

Tom was not too late.

Some still lived.

A few last prisoners emerged from huts, skeletal, crying out. They lifted the weapons of the fallen warriors, and they fired, and they fought, and they died, and their weapons passed on to new heroes.

Tom fought through the inferno.

He fought as ash rained from the sky.

As walls fell down. As creatures crawled through the flames, melting, reaching out claws and hands, fading.

Fading.

His mind, his heart, his life—fading.

A vision of grassy fields. Of a younger man. Hair brown. Eyes joyous. No pain or hunger. Only dreams. A man upon green hills, playing his flute, guiding his flock with old songs. Lost but not forgotten.

The ash glided like snow, hot and white, the remnants of burnt life. The organic clouds parted, and for the first time in years, Tom felt sunlight on his skin.

He blinked, looking around, dazed as if woken from a fever dream. The battle had ended. Around him, the gulock was gone, fallen to smoldering ruin. A few survivors limped toward him. A few dozen, no more.

Ayumi stood at Tom's side, gazing at him. The ash fluttered around her bare feet, and her cloak billowed. A tattoo of a serpent glowed on her hand, Tom saw. A serpent forming an infinity sign, eating its own tail. An ouroboros, symbol of eternity and rebirth. Her eyes glowed purest platinum, the shine hiding her irises and pupils.

*She's a weaver,* Tom realized. *A wielder of ancient power.*

"You will see grass again, Tom Shepherd," Ayumi whispered, and a tear rolled down her cheek, filled with luminosity. Then the light in her eyes faded, and she fell.

Tom caught her, held her in his arms. She weighed almost nothing, so fragile, drowning in her cloak. The others gathered around them—a few warriors of Earth's Light, a few prisoners, the last few leaves of a once-mighty tree.

*You will see grass again.*

Tom looked behind him. The fallen striker was there, smoldering on the rocky ground.

But it was still in one piece. And Tom could repair it.

He could fly again.

He could fight another day.

"Ayumi," he said, "we're going to fix this starship. And we're going to leave this world." He inhaled the hot, ashy air. "We're going to find the Heirs of Earth."

## CHAPTER TWO

Corporal Rowan Emery knelt in her cage, a sea of scorpions spreading out below her.

The creatures hissed beneath the dangling cage. The beasts covered the striker's deck in a carpet of spikes and claws and venom. They leaped up, snapped their jaws, lashed their claws. They scuttled across the bulkheads around Rowan, cackling, leering. They clattered across the ceiling, drooling, staring with burning red eyes. On the outside, the *Venom* was a mighty dreadnought, a warship powerful enough to devastate worlds. On the inside she was an arachnid den, a hell of claws and stingers and toothy jaws ravenous for flesh.

The scorpion voices rose around her, shrill and raw.

"Rip her hands off!"

"Flay her skin!"

"Slice her bones!"

"Drink her marrow!"

"Human, human, make her scream!"

The scorpions jumped and knocked into the cage. It swung on the chain. Claws reached between the bars, lashing at Rowan. Jaws snapped at her. Tongues licked her. Eyes leaked pus, and toothy grins dripped saliva.

Rowan huddled inside the swinging gibbet. As evil swarmed around her, as the monsters cackled and cut her and laughed, she remained silent.

She had not come here for them. These were just lowly soldiers.

She was here for their leader.

For her sister.

Rowan peered between the bars. Past the chasm of scorpions, she saw the *Venom*'s bridge.

A viewport stretched across the prow, semicircular, affording a view of space. A throne rose before the screen, upholstered with human skins, hands and faces still attached.

There, upon that throne, she lounged. One leg tossed over an armrest. One hand holding a human skull filled with blood-red wine.

Jade.

The Blue Witch. The Huntress. The commander of this fleet. The monster who had butchered millions, who had placed Rowan in this cage.

*My sister*, Rowan thought.

Jade's hair, burned in a recent battle, had already grown long again. It flowed, blue and bright like fiber optic cables. Her skin was a shimmering white shell, hard enough to stop bullets. Half her head was shaved, and implants buzzed there, embedded into her skull. The scorpion emperor had broken her, rebuilt her, turned her into this machine of war.

"But deep down inside, you're still human," Rowan whispered. "You're not a scorpion. You're not one of these monsters. You're still the sister I love."

The scorpions laughed. They banged against her cage. They thrust their jaws between the bars, snapping at Rowan, licking her, coating her with sizzling saliva.

"Please, mistress!" they cried down to Jade. "She tastes so sweet. So delectable. Let us skin her! Let us snap her crunchable bones and drink her juicy marrow! Let us lap her hot blood and guzzle her living organs!"

Jade rose from her throne and spun toward the cage. She wore tall boots, a bodysuit of black webbing, and a cloak of human leather, dyed crimson with real blood. She leaped up, soared through the bridge, and grabbed the cage bars. The gibbet swung, and Rowan fell.

"Back, my fellow scorpions!" Jade said, clinging to the outside of the cage. "This one is not your morsel. Have I not fed you many humans, and have you not grown fat on the flesh of humanity?"

"We hunger still, mistress!" said a scorpion.

"This one is sweeter than the others," hissed another.

A scorpion reached between the bars and grabbed Rowan's arm. "This is the human who killed so many of our brothers. Let us toy with her."

Jade snarled. "This one is not your toy! This one is for Emperor Sin Kra. Our glorious emperor will hurt her, flay her, eat her, savor her screams. If you so much as scratch her soft, supple skin, I will crack open your shells and drink your soft innards with a straw."

The scorpions backed away, crawling across the ceiling and bulkheads, leaving the gibbet to dangle. Their drool still coated the cage and the thick chain suspending it.

Only Jade remained, clinging to the bars, staring between them at Rowan.

"Do not think this a mercy, pest," Jade said. "I saved you now because these scorpions would be too kind. They would try to eat you alive, but you would not last an hour. The suffering you'll endure at the claws of my emperor will last for years."

Rowan's heart pounded. Her limbs trembled. Her breath shook. But she managed to stare steadily into Jade's green eyes.

"I can see your humanity," Rowan whispered. "You know I'm your sister. You knew it inside the *Jerusalem*. You embraced me. You forgot but you will remember. You're still a human, you—"

Jade gripped two bars, bent them as easily as drawing curtains, and entered the cage.

She grabbed Rowan's throat, snarling.

"Enough of your lies!" Jade shrieked.

Her fist tightened. Rowan couldn't breathe. Her neck creaked. The pain shot through her, as if scorpion claws were digging down her throat into her chest. But she kept staring steadily into Jade's eyes.

*I won't abandon you, Jade,* Rowan thought. *You are my sister. You are hurt. I will always fight for you.*

Finally, when blackness was spreading across Rowan's vision, Jade released her grip.

Rowan inhaled a deep, shaky breath. She collapsed onto the cage floor, breathing raggedly.

"You know it's true," Rowan rasped.

Amazingly, Jade's eyes dampened. Her lips trembled. Her face softened, looked almost human.

Then the implants in Jade's skull came alive. Gears whirred inside them. Blue lights shone. Mechanical hums rose from the devices. Fury filled Jade's eyes, searing away the brief glimpse of humanity.

"We'll be at Ur Akad soon." Jade spat on Rowan. "Soon your pain will begin, liar."

Jade slipped between the bars, then bent them back into place. She jumped down, landed with barely a thump on the deck far below, and returned to her throne.

Rowan curled up on the cage floor. She wriggled, trying to find a comfortable position, but the cage was too cramped. She pulled her knees to her chest, placed her cheek on her palms, and gazed between the bars at the viewport. The stars spread out before her, streaming by like snow on a midnight highway. The *Venom* was flying many times faster than light, far faster than any human ship could fly. They were heading deep into Hierarchy space, far from the battles, far from her friends.

She thought about the others. Was Bay still alive, flying somewhere aboard little Brooklyn? Rowan had not seen her friend since the devastating scorpion assault above Helios, the forested moon on the front line. Was Leona still traveling to Earth, seeking humanity's mythical homeworld, or had the enemy ambushed her?

And what of Emet? Over the past few months, Emet Ben-Ari, commander of the Heirs of Earth, had become like a father to Rowan. Had he survived the Battle of Helios, and if so, was he mad at Rowan? She had disobeyed him. He had called for her to retreat. After failing to capture Jade, she could have fled with Emet, ran into the tunnel, lived to fight another day.

*I'm sorry, Emet,* Rowan thought. *But I had to surrender to Jade. I had to see her again. I know she's not evil. It's just the implants in her skull. I know that I can save her. That I can save us all.*

She lay still for a long time, remembering her friends. For most of her life, Rowan had lived in the ducts on Paradise Lost, hidden away from the galaxy. But for a brief, shining year, she had lived among other humans. Humans she loved. Rowan ached for Jade's madness, for the suffering of humanity, but also for the loss of her friends.

*I want to save you, Jade, and I want to save all humans. But I also want to see you again, Bay. To read you my movie scripts and model while you draw me. I want to talk to you again, Emet, about old legends and songs. I want to learn from you, Leona, how to be a warrior and a woman. I miss you all so much.*

The lights dimmed in the *Venom*, mimicking the circadian rhythm of Ur Akad, the scorpions' homeworld. The arachnids curled up to sleep, stingers draped across their heads. Rowan closed her eyes but found no rest. Soon they would arrive on Ur Akad. Soon Rowan would be brought before the emperor. The fear kept her awake.

*I won't let the emperor hurt me,* Rowan thought. *I didn't surrender myself to die. I came here to fight.*

She looked around her. The scorpions came from a binary star system, and a dim red lamp shone above, emulating their cooler star. Everyone on the bridge was sleeping. The scorpions slept in burrows or piles. Jade lay curled up on her throne, eyes shut, chest rising and falling with deep breaths.

Rowan furtively reached into her vest pocket. She pulled out a small golden charm on a chain. From the outside, it looked like a pocket watch, but when she pressed a button, wings and limbs and a head emerged. Fillister, her dear robotic dragonfly, stood on her palm.

He blinked his glowing blue eyes. Rowan placed a finger on her lips, hushing him. She glanced around again, ascertained nobody was watching, then brought Fillister close to her lips.

"Fill," she whispered.

"Oh, Row," he whispered back. "It's dreadful, ain't it? Them nasty beasts catching us, and—"

"Shh." She winced. "Speak even softer." She placed Fillister up against her lips, whispering so quietly her words were barely more than breath. "Listen, Fill. I have an idea."

He nodded, fluttered up to her ear, and whispered. "I'm all ears."

She cradled the dragonfly in her palms, whispering between her fingers. "When Jade was near me, I saw a glimmer of sanity. She was human again, if only for a second. She recognized me. I know it! Then the implants in her skull did something. They turned on, buzzed, glowed, and crushed the real Jade. Those implants are trapping Jade as surely as these bars trap me."

"You reckon they're hijacking her noggin?" Fillister whispered.

"You got it," Rowan said. "The real Jade is still inside, afraid, hurt. When her implants were near me, the hackles rose on my neck, and my teeth ached. Those implants are receiving and sending signals. I could feel it. Maybe the emperor can control Jade remotely. Can you detect the signals from her implants?"

Fillister frowned. He looked toward the sleeping Jade and cocked his head. "Very slight. Just a distant hum. It could just be the striker's machinery. Hard to tell from this distance."

Rowan took a shaky breath. "Listen to me, Fillister. I want you to fly closer. To hover around Jade as she sleeps. Record any bits of data her implants are emitting."

The dragonfly glanced down at the sleeping Jade, then at Rowan. "It'll be encrypted."

"So we'll crack the code," Rowan said. "We're good at that. Remember how we cracked the encryption on the Earthstone? We'll crack this code too." She took a deep breath. "And once we understand Jade's code, we can hack it. We can disable it. We can save Jade."

Fillister nodded. "Right-o, Row. We'll get out of this mess. Chin up!"

The dragonfly took flight, fluttered between the cage bars, and glided down toward Jade. The tiny robot vanished into the shadows beside the throne, secretly recording.

*I'm in a cage*, Rowan thought, *alone, far from my friends, far from the Heirs of Earth, being shipped toward torture and slow death. But I'm not helpless.* She clenched her fist. *I'm still an Inheritor. And I still fight.*

## CHAPTER THREE

*My son is missing.*

Emet stood on the battered bridge of the ISS *Jerusalem*, fists shaking.

*My daughter might be dead.*

Enemy fire pounded his warship, shaking the old frigate.

*The enemy took Rowan.*

The strikers flew all around. Thousands of them. Before them, the Concord forces—human and alien—were falling. Burning warships crashed toward the churning gas giant below. Jade's dreadnought, the *Venom*, was gone, taking Rowan with it. The rest of the scorpion fleet pounded the Heirs of Earth and their allies.

The galaxy was burning. But Emet's innards seemed frozen.

*My children—gone. Rowan—captured. Humanity—falling.*

A striker flew toward them, plasma firing, and the *Jerusalem* jolted, spun, nearly cracked open.

Emet tossed back his head and howled.

His men sometimes called him the Old Lion, referring to his beard and long golden hair, though his mane was now more white than blond. And now Emet roared like the fabled lions of Earth.

He gripped the throttle, a heavy lever. He shoved it down.

The *Jerusalem*'s engines roared, blazing on full afterburner, and the frigate charged.

The warship stormed toward the enemy.

Emet roared as he plowed into a formation of strikers.

The *Jerusalem* shook.

Monitors cracked.

Smoke filled the bridge, and the hull screeched, shields ripping off, cannons firing.

The Old Lion roared again, and he shoved the throttle with all his strength. The afterburner bellowed, overpowering even his own cry. They rampaged forth, ramming the enemy, knocking them back, tearing through the strikers' formations.

Countless strikers flew before him. Many were small starfighters. Some were warships as large as the *Jerusalem*. One was a gargantuan dreadnought, a ship the size of a town. The words *Pestilence* shone upon its mighty hull. With the *Venom* gone, the *Pestilence* now commanded the scorpion assault.

"Tear them down!" Emet cried to the rest of his fleet. "Sons and daughters of Earth—burn the enemy!"

He was mad with fury, with grief, with fear. Perhaps he should retreat, fall back, live to fight another day.

Yet to what end? His plan to capture Jade had failed. The Earthstone was gone. Rowan was gone. There was no news from Leona or Bay. Across the galaxy, Concord worlds were falling. Millions of humans were perishing in the slaughterhouses.

*So let me make my final stand here.*

He turned toward his lieutenant on the bridge, a green officer barely into his twenties.

"The *Jerusalem* is yours," Emet said.

The young man faltered. "Sir?"

Emet left the bridge.

He marched through the ravaged hull. Marines stood there, gripping rifles, ready to fight any invaders who might board the ship.

*No,* Emet thought. *In this battle, we do not wait. We do not defend. We attack.*

"Inheritors!" Emet said to the company of warriors. "Are you ready to fight for Earth?"

"For Earth!" they cried.

He grabbed an armored suit, helmet, and jetpack.

"Tonight we show the enemy Earth pride!"

They marched toward the airlock, two hundred warriors, helmets on heads, rifles in hand. The *Jerusalem* shook madly, careened, tumbled, rose again with a roaring burst of the engines.

Emet tugged the airlock open and dived outside.

Silence.

Silence flowed across him.

He glided through space, viewing the battle. Thousands of starships were battling around him. A few dozen human starships—the Heirs of Earth in all their might. A few hundred cylindrical ships filled with water—the fleet of the Gouramis, sentient fish. A few hundred round, rocky ships with crystal centers—the geode-ships of the Menorians, benevolent octopuses. Before them—the endless fleets of the Hierarchy. Thousands of dark, craggy starships filled with scorpions, spiders, slugs, and the other vicious races of the Hierarchy.

It flew directly ahead now, dwarfing all other ships, drowning a hundred strikers in its shadow.

The *Pestilence*.

Emet activated his jet back.

It thrummed on his back, blasting out fire, and he stormed toward the dreadnought.

Behind him, his company of marines followed. Two hundred trails of fire stretched through space.

Emet stared ahead, eyes narrowed, flying closer to the *Pestilence*.

Jets of plasma flew toward them.

He swerved, dodging one flaming pillar. A blast hit a lieutenant behind him. Another blast took out two sergeants. Emet and the others kept flying.

Three small strikers, so small they could fit only a single scorpion, stormed toward the humans. Enemy fire took out several more marines. Emet fired his railgun, destroying one of the strikers. Firebirds swooped, the starfighters of humanity, machine guns pounding the enemy, knocking them back.

Emet flew faster. He approached the enemy flagship.

He raised Lightning in his left hand—his electric pistol. He raised Thunder in the other hand—his heavy railgun.

*I die today.*

He fired both weapons at the *Pestilence*'s airlock.

Around him, the other marines fired with him, hammering the enemy airlock with blast after blast until it tore open.

Scorpions spilled out into space.

The aliens rolled into the formation of human marines, ripping them apart, tearing off limbs. Emet fired left and right, slaying scorpions, but kept flying forward—toward the shattered enemy airlock.

He dived through the airlock and into the dreadnought, guns blazing.

Scorpions fell before him.

Hundreds of the creatures filled the *Pestilence*, racing toward him, screeching.

Emet took step after step across the alien hangar, firing both his guns, clearing a path into the ship. Behind him, his warriors flew into the *Pestilence*, guns thundering. Two marines knelt at Emet's sides, raised flamethrowers, and blasted forth torrents of crackling death. Scorpions fell before them, screeching as they melted.

Emet moved through the dreadnought, the fire crackling around his boots. Smoke filled the cavernous halls of this cathedral of murder. Scorpions leaped from dark columns, from a vaulted ceiling cloaked in shadows, and Emet kept firing, knocking them back. His men moved with him, flamethrowers roaring, filling the dreadnought with melting exoskeletons and bubbling alien flesh.

Claws cut Emet. Fire burned him. But he was beyond pain now. A madness had taken over his mind, a bloodlust like a parasite, burning through him.

The marines reached the dreadnought's bridge, the tip of the triangle. Viewports rose ahead, affording a view of the battle. Through them, Emet saw the remains of his fleet.

*So few ships remain,* he thought. *So many fell.*

Several scorpions were operating levers and pulleys, piloting the *Pestilence.* They turned toward Emet and his warriors, screeched, and charged to battle. Blood splashed the floor. Stingers sprayed venom. Inheritors fell, screaming, helmets melting. Emet walked forward, dodging the sprays of venom, firing his rifle again and again, blasting scorpion shells.

As men and scorpions battled around him, he reached the helm and grabbed two levers.

Emet had never flown a striker, but he had seen their designs in intelligence reports. He had flown simulators. Now he flew the real thing—a massive striker that dwarfed any human warship.

He saw the *Jerusalem* ahead. She was badly damaged, leaking air. The mighty Inheritor flagship seemed so small from here, dented and burnt and falling apart. Just a clunky box of metal.

*I rammed strikers with that old frigate,* Emet thought. *Now let's see how they handle an imperial dreadnought.*

He turned the mighty striker, tugged the throttle, and roared toward the enemy lines.

A hundred strikers flew before him, bombarding the Concord ships. They didn't engage the *Pestilence*, not realizing Emet had commandeered the dreadnought.

Emet grabbed a pulley and yanked down hard.

The dreadnought's cannons fired.

Plasma pounded the formation of strikers ahead, melting the scorpion ships.

Emet fired again. Again. The strikers ahead burned. Others flew in confusion, realizing too late that their flagship had been compromised.

Before they could return fire, Emet plowed through the Hierarchy lines.

He tore through them like a cannonball through a line of infantrymen. Strikers careened before him, cracking open, slamming into other ships, exploding. Fire and metal shards filled space.

Emet had taken down thirty strikers or more before the rest turned on him.

They flew from every direction. Blast after blast slammed into the *Pestilence*.

The bridge shattered.

Fire blazed toward Emet.

Shards of metal slammed into him.

He fell, and the inferno roared above him, and the cosmos was burning, and the cosmos was dark, and Rowan was gone.

*And I failed. And I'm sorry, my children. I'm sorry, Rowan. I'm sorry, Earth.*

Hands grabbed him. Soldiers pulled him.

"Sir!"

"The admiral is hurt, get him up."

"Muck me, his leg!"

"Move, men, damn it, to the airlock!"

Emet felt consciousness slipping. He blinked and gasped for air. His vision cleared enough to see the hull of the dreadnought. His men were carrying him, and his legs bled, and a white bone rose from the skin, broken, crackling with pain like a live wire.

"We gotta set the Old Lion's bone, Sarge."

"No time! Put a bag around his leg. Get some tape."

"He'll lose the leg! Just give me a moment to find a splint, dammit, we—"

"The hull is breached, we gotta jump—now!"

His soldiers carried him toward the airlock, and more scorpions pounced. With a shaking hand, nearly blind, Emet raised his pistol. He fired. Even as he lay dying, he fought, and he fell, tumbling out into space, spinning, and everywhere around him—streams of fire, darting starfighters, crashing warships, the pulsing fear and plastic around his exposed bone and raw nerves and screaming, throbbing, demonic pain. And a whisper. His wife's face before him, eyes kind, fading into shadows.

He floated into nothingness … and was gone.

# CHAPTER FOUR

Bay sat in Brooklyn's cockpit, gazing at the photograph on his monitor—perhaps the most important photograph in the galaxy.

"There it is," he said. "In this photograph from seventeen years ago. The sword that was lost. The doomsday weapon that can win the war. The Godblade."

Brooklyn's camera swiveled on its stalk to face the monitor. "Are you sure, dude? Looks like the little girl is just playing with a toy sword. Looks like cheap plastic to me."

"It's aetherstone," Bay said. "Solid aether. The most valuable material in the galaxy. And that little girl is Jade Emery, scorpion princess."

Brooklyn scoffed. "First of all, the most valuable material in the galaxy is ant poison. With ants wreaking havoc in starships large and small, it's priceless. What can aetherstone do to compare?"

"Destroy entire fleets, save Earth, and win the largest galactic war in history," Bay said.

"And second," Brooklyn said, pointedly ignoring him, "that little girl in the photo looks nothing like a princess. She looks more like an ugly little boy with a runny nose."

Bay bristled. "You're looking at the wrong kid. That little boy is me! And my nose wasn't runny. That's just a trick of the light."

The starship scoffed. "Dude, if your nose ran any faster, it would win the Kentucky Derby."

He sighed. "Stop being obtuse, all right? I've explained this before. Jade used to live among us—among the Heirs of Earth.

We were friends. Well, mostly she was friends with Leona. Those two girls would drive me mad, always tugging my clothes and messing my hair. I remember that sword. It was Jade's toy. She used to drill with Leona, pretending to be a knight." He spoke more softly, lost in memory. "But it wasn't a toy. Even now, I can remember marveling at that sword, touching it once. It was smooth like crystal. Like a beam of moonlight taken solid form. Brooklyn, it's the same blade I saw painted in the Weeping Weaver Guildhall. The Godblade. The greatest weapon in the galaxy."

Brooklyn sighed too, vents rattling. The starship had no lungs, of course, but she often mimicked Bay's mannerisms.

"Dude, I dunno. You seem to be grasping at straws here. It just looks like a toy sword to me. There must be millions of toy swords in the galaxy. I know you're disappointed somebody beat you to the guildhall, that somebody else got the Godblade. But do you really think Jade has it? If she did, you'd know. Or, well, not know, because you'd be dead, and the galaxy would be destroyed. But you'd know for a second, at least. When Jade began to destroy the galaxy with the sword. You'd probably see a giant explosion and all your friends dying and stars collapsing and—"

"I get it." Bay cringed. "No need for the gory visuals. I've thought about this. And I can think of three explanations. One: Jade is waiting to use the Godblade and will unleash its power any day now. Two: Jade lost the weapon years ago, maybe even before the scorpions kidnapped her. Three: Like you, Jade thinks it's just a toy."

"Smart woman," Brooklyn said.

Bay ignored that last remark. "Brook, zoom in on the photo. Specifically, on the sword's pommel. Increase the contrast, bring up the brightness a bit ... there." Bay tapped the monitor. "See that symbol?"

Brooklyn stared at the zoomed-in photograph, her camera's shutters narrowing. "It looks like an infinity symbol carved into the pommel."

"It's an ouroboros," Bay said. "A serpent eating its own tail. An ancient sym—"

"An ancient symbol originating in Egyptian iconography," Brooklyn interrupted him. "The ouroboros entered western tradition via Greek magical tradition and was adopted as a symbol in Gnosticism and Hermeticism, and most notably in alchemy. Via medieval alchemical tradition, the symbol entered Renaissance magic and modern symbolism, often taken to symbolize introspection, the eternal return or cyclicality, especially in the sense of something constantly re-creating itself. It also represents the infinite cycle of nature's endless creation and destruction, life and death."

Bay rolled his eyes. "Well, look at you, Miss I-Have-A-Built-In-Wikipedia-Galactica-Library. You wouldn't be so smart without your database."

"I'm a frikken genius," Brooklyn said. "Even without my database. Just like Isaac Einstein."

"You mean Albert," Bay said.

"I mean—" She tilted her camera for a moment, and her monitor flashed through Wikipedia Galactica articles, then quickly went dark. "Shut up."

Bay slapped his head. "Anyway. You described the origin of the ouroboros symbol. But it's also used in the Weavers Guild. Weavers use runes to draw power from aether, and the ouroboros is the most powerful rune around." He tapped the photograph. "And right there—it's engraved onto the sword. That's the Godblade all right. When Coral and I arrived at the guildhall, somebody had already taken it. And I bet I know who. The same person who stole the Earthstone. David Emery. Rowan and Jade's dad."

Bay looked again at the photograph. David stood behind the children, drowning in shadows. Bay had vague memories of the man. David had traced his ancestry back to Marco Emery, the Poet of Earth, a famous author from the twenty-second century. When Bay was a child, David had been like a beloved uncle to him.

But David had betrayed the Heirs, Bay remembered. He had stolen the Earthstone and fled. He must have stolen the Godblade too, this time robbing an old mummy.

Bay never knew why David had defected. Emet was always reluctant to speak of it, only muttering something about differing visions. For years, Bay heard how David was a thief, a traitor, a monster.

And indeed, David had fathered a monster—the creature they called Jade.

*But he also fathered an angel,* Bay thought. *He fathered Rowan.*

Rowan was not in this old photograph. She hadn't even been born yet. Bay turned to look at the drawing he had hung in the cockpit. A drawing of Rowan.

*I miss you, Row,* he thought. *That day you posed for me, when I drew you, when we laughed … That was a good day. That was my best day.*

Brooklyn began to sing in a mocking voice. "Bay loves Rowan, Bay loves Rowan."

He bristled. "I do not."

"You've sure been goggling her drawing a lot," Brooklyn said.

"Do you mean ogling?" Bay said.

She flashed through Wikipedia articles again, then glared at him. "Shut up."

He snorted. "Besides, even if I do ogle my drawing of Rowan, it's better than looking at you all day."

"Well, maybe you should look at Coral," Brooklyn said. "She's pretty, right? What's she been up to anyway?" Brooklyn craned her camera toward the doorway and peered into the small hold. "Hey, Coral, what—"

Brooklyn fell silent.

Bay frowned. "What is it?"

"Coral!" Brooklyn shouted. Her vents rattled in fear.

Bay rose from his seat, stepped into the hold, and gasped. His heart thudded.

"Coral, what the hell are you doing?" he cried.

The young weaver wore an Inheritor uniform—brown trousers, black boots, and a blue overcoat—but she had embroidered the symbols of her order into the fabric. More runes, thin and silvery, were tattooed onto her dark skin. Despite her youth, her hair was pure white, flowing down to her hips like rivers of molten moonlight. She was mysterious, wise, and beautiful, a woman who had taught Bay the secrets of aether, who had made love to him, who had fought with him against armies of scorpions.

And now she stood on that same bed where they had made love, facing a dangling noose.

"Coral!" Bay rushed toward her.

She looked at him. Her eyes filled with tears.

"I have to, Bay. I have to die. To die and come back. Like the mural said."

He jumped onto the bed, stood beside Coral, and pulled her into his arms. She embraced him, weeping softly.

"Coral," he whispered, holding her close. "Why?"

She looked at him through her tears. Her lips trembled. "To gain an ouroboros rune. I saw the inscription in the Weeping Guildhall. Every rune requires an experience. To gain my skylock rune, I needed to make love to you. But to gain this rune, I must die and rise again. Only the weaver who knows the pain of death may gain the power to kill."

"Coral!" Bay looked at the noose, then back at her. "You can't help anyone if you're dead."

"You can revive me, Bay!" she said. "I wasn't going to hang myself yet. Not until you were here, waiting next to me. I'll die. You'll wait a few seconds, then revive me. You can pound on my chest until my heart beats again, blow into my lungs until they breathe anew. I'll return to you from death—an ouroboros rune on my palm. I'll be able to wield the Godblade." She gripped his shoulders, and a strange light filled her eyes. "Bay, imagine the *power*. The power to decree life or death! I will grant death to the scorpions—and life to humanity! I can save us, Bay. All of us."

Bay placed a hand on her cheek and looked into her eyes. "Coral, we don't even have the Godblade yet. Why don't we hold off on the noose for now, all right? We'll cross that bridge when we come to it."

But Coral still shed tears. "Bay, all that we went through—fighting the scorpions, finding the planet Elysium, battling our way through the guildhall ... all for nothing. All to learn that Jade, our enemy, has the Godblade. I'm scared, Bay. How can we win this war? How can we stop the enemy?"

"I don't know," Bay confessed. "But if anyone knows what happened to the Godblade, it's Jade's sister. Rowan. So we're going to fly back to the Inheritor fleet, find Rowan, and show her this photograph. Maybe she remembers something from her childhood. Until then, let's be hopeful. No more nooses. All right?"

Coral nodded. "All right."

Bay kissed her forehead. "We'll find a way, Coral. I promise. Don't lose hope yet."

Yet was he lying?

In his memories, Bay could still see it. The scorpions swarming the fleet. Starships falling like burning leaves. Seohyun's skeletal hand, reaching out from the ashes. The battles blended in

Bay's mind, becoming a single, sprawling nightmare. He had known nothing but this war all his life. Hope? What hope was there now?

He turned to look at the bulkhead, where he had hung his drawings of dragons, wizards, elven warriors, and Rowan. But one piece of paper was not a drawing. It was a photograph. A single blue pixel, magnified into a square, on a black background. It could have passed for abstract art, but Bay knew its meaning. Rowan had taken this photo with her telescope.

An photo of Earth.

"So long as Earth is out there, there's hope," he said. "So long as Earth calls to us, we'll dream."

He untied the noose and hid the rope; later he would cut it into many pieces. He accompanied Coral into the cockpit. They sat side by side, gazing out at the stars. The Milky Way's spiral arm shone before them. Earth was still too far to see with the naked eye. But their distant world called to them. They had not forgotten home.

CHAPTER FIVE

Light fell upon her eyelids, and screeches filled her ears.

Rowan moaned. Her eyelids fluttered. She felt too weak to open them.

She lay inside her cage, curled up. Her belly ached. So empty. Starving. Twisting. She licked her dry lips, but her tongue was like sandpaper. She tasted blood, and she eagerly swallowed the liquid. How long had she been lying here in the cage, dangling inside the *Venom*? Days? Weeks? Time lost meaning here.

She reached out, hand shaking, pawing for her bowl. She found the dish and tried to drink. It wasn't easy. The scorpions gave her no water, only a foul, viscous brew that tasted like blood. Rowan forced down a mouthful, shuddered, and gagged. Her eyelashes were sticky, her throat tight, her skin hot.

*I'm sick,* she thought. *I caught something. From the scorpions licking me, or from this bloody pudding they feed me.* She coughed, and her ears pounded. *Why do they keep screeching?*

The scorpions were louder today, bustling around her cage, scuttling up and down the *Venom*'s bulkheads, deck, and ceiling. The light was different. Brighter. Searing. She had never seen it this bright. Rowan coughed, pushed herself onto her knees, and leaned against the bars. She blinked, rubbed her eyes, and gazed toward the viewports at the prow.

Two suns blazed outside, crackling and washing the dreadnought with radiation.

Rowan squinted. She was weak, feverish, terrified. But still curious.

She recognized these two stars from the stories. One was small, white, and hot—Shamash Karan. It provided the scorpion homeworld with most of its heat and light. In the scorpions' mythology, Shamash Karan was a goddess of war and conquest. The second star was larger, cooler, and red, a bloated giant like a stain of bubbling blood. Here shone Kali Karan, the Bloodied God, the mythological deity of death and afterlife. It so large, it could have engulfed Earth's entire solar system.

Rowan had read about these binary stars. She had seen pictures of them. Now, seeing them before her, she shuddered. How different it was to see a place in real life! One could view a thousand photos of a place, never getting a true sense of it, not until actually visiting the location. It was the difference between dreams and reality.

*Someday, may I see Earth rise before me,* Rowan thought. *May the light of Sol—smaller and gentler than these cruel deities—shine upon me.*

The scorpions were still bustling across the *Venom*. They gazed at the light of their stars, raised their claws, and cried out in exaltation. Some knelt and prayed. Jade stood before the viewports, head tossed back, arms wide open. The *Venom* flew toward the binary stars, and light and heat flooded the starship.

Rowan blinked, rubbed her eyes, squinted, and saw a speck ahead. As the *Venom* flew, that speck grew larger, becoming an orb, then a planet. A dry desert planet. Cracked. Parched. If Rowan hadn't known better, she would have thought it a dead world.

But she did know better.

She saw, even from here, the countless starships orbiting that world. Saw the military might gathering in the darkness. A swarm of strikers flew ahead like bees around a hive, guarding their homeworld.

Here before Rowan it floated, bathing in the light of its two stars.

"Ur Akad," she whispered. "Homeworld of the Skra-Shen. Planet of the scorpions. The center of the Hierarchy."

Rowan lowered her head.

*When Emet picked me up from Paradise Lost, I hoped to be flying toward Earth, to see my blue homeworld rise before me. Not this place. Not this cruelty.*

As the *Venom* flew closer, many other strikers appeared around them. Countless warships filled this star system. Starfighters streaked by, jagged black triangles like arrowheads, leaving trails of fire. Hulking warships rumbled above them, each so large it could have swallowed any human ship. Space stations hovered everywhere, shaped like sea urchins the size of cities, their piers stretching out like spines, lined with docking starships. Typical star systems were mostly empty space, just billions of kilometers of vacuum sprinkled with a handful of tiny worlds. Not this place. Here was a star system like a massive military base. Rowan didn't know how many scorpion starships flew here. Thousands. Probably millions.

*We cannot win this war,* Rowan thought. *They are too many. Every civilization in the Concord, fighting united, cannot defeat such power.*

As they flew closer, the desert planet grew. Soon the planet consumed the viewports, hiding the last stars. Leaning against her bars, Rowan watched the desert roll by below. It was a painting in ocher, burnt orange, and dirty yellow. Canyons, volcanoes, and rocky plains formed a cruel surface like scabby skin.

Rowan had studied this planet. Every Inheritor had. This world was larger than Jupiter—a gargantuan rock, almost large enough to become a star. Entire Earths could have fit into its deepest canyons.

Rowan frowned. The world seemed dead. No vegetation. No roads. No cities. No signs of life at all. Yet as they flew closer, as the planet's gravity began rattling the *Venom*, her eyes widened.

There *were* cities here, but nothing like Rowan had ever seen. Sandstone towers soared like termite hives, craggy and twisting. Holes peppered cliffs. Mountains had been carved with gargantuan arachnid faces, each larger than a dreadnought. Quarries sank into the ground, filled with steam and molten metal. The scorpions built no cities of shimmering glass or verdant gardens, no metropolises of light and splendor. They had deformed the living rock of their homeworld, carving cities of canyons, holes, towers, and caves, extensions of the dry, cracked landscape.

*Is this where I die?* Rowan thought. *On this desert world so far from home?*

Light reflected on metal.

Rowan winced.

Fillister, her loyal dragonfly, was flying back toward her. Rowan caught her breath, sure that the scorpions would see the robot. But the aliens were staring through the viewport, bowing and rearing and bowing again, screeching for their planet.

Undetected, Fillister shot between the bars of Rowan's cage and landed in her hands. She hid him between her fingers, heart thumping.

"Did you manage to detect the signals from Jade's implants last night?" she whispered.

"Indeed I did," Fillister whispered back. "It's just as you suspected, Row. Her implants are constantly sending and receiving data. Busy as a chimney sweep on Boxing Day, they are. I've recorded as much data as my memory chips will store."

Rowan winced. "And? The encryption?"

"A doddle, Row," said Fillister. "I cracked it within two hours."

A huge grin spread across Rowan's face, and a weight lifted off her shoulders. "That's wonderful, Fill. And the code? What did you find?"

He peeked between her fingers, eyes blue and sad. "You were right, Row. The real Jade—the human Jade, your sister—is still in there. The implants have hijacked her brain, are holding her captive. The real Jade is still trapped inside, as surely as you're trapped in this cage. And she's crying for help."

Tears flooded Rowan's eyes. "I knew it." The teardrops fell. "I knew I didn't lose my sister. That I can save her. Tell me we can save her, Fill. That we can hack the implants, disable them, and free Jade's mind."

The robotic dragonfly winced. "Well, there's the rub, Row. I understand her encryption now. I understand some of her source code. But I'm still missing a piece of the puzzle. I need to see how the implants' algorithms react to Jade trying to break free. I need to see Jade's mind make a real attempt to remember her past, to act like a human—and then I need to see the implants kick into gear to stifle her. I need to record that algorithm in action. Until I see it, I can't learn how to disable it."

Rowan nodded. "All right. Stay in my pocket. Stay hidden. And keep recording. I'll get you the data you need. Now hush! Hide! We're entering orbit."

Fillister retracted his head and limbs, and Rowan placed the pocket watch into her vest pocket.

The *Venom* entered orbit and hovered over the giant desert world. The viewports gazed upon the canyons, mountains, and a hazy yellow horizon. Countless other starships orbited with them, gathering for war.

Jade turned away from the view, her leather cloak swishing, and stared up at Rowan's dangling cage.

"We're home, sweet pest!" Jade said. "Soon your torment will begin."

*Get ready, Fill,* Rowan thought.

Jade jumped from the floor with inhuman strength. She soared and caught the gibbet, sending it into a swing. The huntress clung to the bars, grinning, eyes mad.

"You don't have to do this, Jade," Rowan whispered from inside the cage.

Jade tore out a bar, reached into the cage, and grabbed Rowan.

"Silence, pest!" Jade pulled Rowan toward her, pressed her nose against Rowan's neck, and inhaled. "Oh, the sweet scent of your skin! Soon it will upholster my new throne."

As the cage swung, Rowan stared into her sister's mad green eyes.

And for just an instant, Rowan saw sanity. She saw her sister's soul, trapped, peering out, afraid.

*You better be recording, Fill,* she thought. She placed her hand atop her pocket, feeling him there.

"Jade, don't you remember me?" Rowan said. "Think back to our childhood. You were a girl once. A human like me. Do you remember playing with toy swords? Do you remember our parents? Our life in a glittering cave, and—"

Jade struck her. Hard. So hard the blow knocked Rowan against the bars and bloodied her lips. Her head rang.

"Enough of your lies!" Jade shrieked, voice like a typhoon. "Soon I will rip your tongue from your mouth."

Jade's powerful hands nearly crushed Rowan's arms. The huntress tugged Rowan from the cage, pulled her close, then leaped to the floor. She landed with a soft thud. But Rowan, held in her sister's arms, felt every bone in her body rattle. Her head spun, and blood dripped from her mouth. She tried to speak again, but coughed and nearly choked.

"Sister," Rowan managed. "Listen to me. I—"

Jade shoved Rowan onto the floor, then pulled her hair, yanking her head back. Before Rowan could say more, Jade gagged her with a cloth.

"I tire of your whimpering," she said.

Rowan tried to speak through the gag, but she could barely even breathe.

Smirking, Jade handcuffed and collared Rowan, then attached a metal leash to the collar. She tugged the chain, yanking Rowan to her feet.

"Walk, pest! Heel! We go to see the emperor."

Rowan rose, choking, dizzy. Jade began to march across the starship, pulling the leash. Rowan stumbled after her, her handcuffs jangling.

*I hope you recorded what you need, Fill,* she thought. She felt the robot in her pocket, round and hard and comforting. *Let's hack her code the way we hacked the Earthstone. We can't defeat this enemy with warships or armies. But maybe we can with a little cleverness.*

Jade dragged her down a shaft and into a cavernous hangar. Dozens of black, triangular shuttles were docked here. Cannons thrust out from them like claws, and metallic tails rose behind them like stingers. One shuttle was finer than the others, trimmed with gleaming red metal, and its tail was gilded. It looked to Rowan like an ancient chariot built for some vain, vampiric pharaoh.

Jade marched toward the shuttle, pulling Rowan on her leash. They entered the small ship, and Jade shoved Rowan onto the floor. She fell, banging her knees. Jade took the helm, tugged levers and pulleys, and the shuttle's engine rumbled. They stormed across the hangar toward an airlock, then dived down—out of the *Venom's* belly and toward the planet below.

The shuttle sliced through the atmosphere with a blaze of fire. Wind shrieked around them. They plunged down like a comet.

Rowan knelt on the rattling floor, bloodied and bound, her jaw clenched around her gag. She stared up at her sister. Jade stood at the controls, her back to Rowan. But Rowan could see the implants on her skull—shining, churning, spinning.

*I have the code I need,* Rowan thought. *I will save you.*

The fire blazed across the viewport, then flickered away, revealing the desert landscape below. The shuttle flew toward the surface of Ur Akad, homeworld of the scorpions.

## CHAPTER SIX

"We're only a few light-years from Earth, and we're stuck." Leona stared through the viewport, fists clenched at her sides. "We cannot stop here. We will not!"

Captain Ramses "Pharaoh" al Masri sat at the helm of the ISS *Nazareth*, the last surviving starship of the Inheritor's expedition to Earth. He lifted his tiny porcelain cup, pinky finger extended, and sipped his black coffee, a drink so thick and strong it could serve as engine oil.

"Well, Commander," he said, "without a fleet of flying chariots worthy of a pharaoh like myself, it seems like we're stuck."

Leona glared at the captain, second-in-command of the mission. Ramses claimed to be descended of ancient Egypt's pharaohs, and he looked the part. He had aristocratically arched eyebrows, a meticulous pointy black beard, and a noble bearing.

*You may look like a genteel cat, but you're not a goddamn pharaoh!* she wanted to tell him, but she bit back the words.

Earth had fallen two thousand years ago, and no human had set foot there since. For eighty generations among the stars, humanity had mingled, forming new races on distant colonies. Leona doubted anyone today who claimed to be descended of any specific Earth nationality.

And yet—some still clung to ancient traditions, old ethnicities or famous dynasties, even now, so long after the fall. Captain Mairead McQueen, one of Leona's best officers, proudly called herself a pagan, descended of the wild Scots of old. A few warriors harked back to Feudal Japan, maintaining shreds of their lost culture in poems and stories passed from generation to generation. Many warriors, like Ramses, worshiped the sun god Ra. Other Inheritors clung to other ancient faiths, praying to old gods whose memories they had carried into space.

And was she herself, Leona Ben-Ari, any different? Her family claimed to be descended of Einav Ben-Ari, the legendary leader of Earth, the lioness of humanity's golden age. Her father had raised Leona and Bay in their family's ancient Jewish faith, lighting candles, braiding bread, singing old songs. They had worshiped separately from the other Inheritors, a ritual of sacred isolation. Leona did not believe in a creator, in any supernatural deity or force. The God of Abraham was a stranger to her. Her father too lacked faith, Leona knew. Yet they had worshiped nonetheless. They had clung to traditions, to an ancient way, and her childhood memories were poignant, a tie to her family's past. To their homeworld.

And was Rowan any different? She claimed to be descended from Marco Emery, the famous poet, and from Addy Linden, the legendary alien slayer. Rowan too claimed proud ancestry, the blood of heroes. Perhaps only a legend, yes. But a legend that gave Rowan, that gave all of them, strength and courage.

*We all still carry a piece of Earth within us,* Leona thought. *A song, a tale, a family name, a shred of ancestry. These are the strings that connect us to our homeworld. Who am I to sever them?*

Leona turned to face the viewport again. The stars spread out before her. One star, right ahead, was Sol. The star Earth orbited. From here, Sol was clearly visible to the naked eye. It was one star among millions. It did not stand out, merely one more dot of light. But to Leona, it was the most important star in the universe.

"It's home," she said, looking at that star. "It's close. It's so close. And thousands of basilisk ships guard the path there."

Ramses set down his mug and shuddered. "Basilisks. A nasty bunch. The blasted serpents destroyed my dear *Rosetta*, the best starship in the galaxy."

Leona struggled not to shudder too. She didn't want to show weakness. But her insides roiled.

The memory of the basilisks had never left her. The giant, sentient snakes had nearly killed them all. Leona had heard legends of this serpentine species, tales whispered in the darkness, used to terrify children. Behave or the basilisks will strangle you! As a youth, Leona would scare Bay with such stories.

Yet the monsters were real. She had seen the basilisks— serpents large enough to swallow men whole, intelligent and cruel, flying starships through the darkness. The monsters from the stories, mere cryptids, had built an empire.

An empire that included Earth.

She examined the charts on her monitor for the hundredth time. For several days now, the *Nazareth* had been hovering here on the fringe of the Basiliska Empire, scanning the darkness, collecting data. They had scanned only a fraction of the space around Earth, and just that fraction swarmed with basilisk ships. Hundreds of them. When Leona had moved the scanner to another coordinate, examining another narrow funnel of space, she had found hundreds more.

If her calculations were correct, the damn snakes were flying a hundred thousand starships across their empire. Navigating to Earth would be like trying to run through a minefield. While wearing concrete shoes. And dribbling a basketball. With each hand.

"Damn it," Leona said. "How the hell do we get past them?"

The door to the bridge banged open.

"What's up, bitches?"

Captain Mairead McQueen strutted into the room, her boots banging against the metal floor. She held a bottle of grog in one hand, a cigar in the other. She wore a blue jumpsuit, and a bandoleer jangled across her chest. Her helmet hung askew, the words *Hell's Princess* scrawled across it. Strands of her hair stuck out from under the helmet, as red and wild as flame.

"The commodore was lamenting our stalemate," Ramses said, and took another sip of his coffee.

Mairead snorted. "I don't know the meaning of stalemate."

Ramses raised an eyebrow. "You believe there's always a way through?"

"Huh?" Mairead tilted her head. "I mean I literally don't know what the word stalemate means. But muck yeah, there's a way through this shit! We fight our way through." She placed the cigar in her mouth and punched the air. "We pound those Ra damn snakes and crush their skulls!"

Leona placed her hands on her hips. "Nobody is pounding anything or crushing anyone's skulls. We can't fight our way through this. We'll have to use stealth."

Ramses raised his eyebrow even higher. "Stealth? Commodore, to remind you, we're flying a clattering, rusty old frigate that emits an electric signal louder than Mairead's snoring."

Mairead puffed smoke his way. "I'm gonna agree with the pharaoh here. No use being stealthy in this hunk of junk. We fight our way through. With cannons, with missiles, with good old-fashioned guts. Muck, I'll fly out in my spacesuit and wrestle the buggers to death if I must. I've always wanted to wrestle a snake."

"You wrestled snakes back on Helios!" Ramses snapped. "You even smuggled a few onto my starship."

Mairead snorted. "Yeah, but those were tiny ones! No longer than I'm tall. I wanna wrestle some big-ass basilisk!"

"A giant constrictor wrapped around you might be the only way to shut you up," Ramses muttered.

"I'll show you constrictor!" Mairead leaped onto him and began to wrestle, ignoring his cries of protest.

Leona tuned them out. She paced the bridge, hands clasped behind her back. She had a hulking warship filled with two hundred warriors. No stealth technology. No other ships but the Firebirds inside her hangar. No way to fight, no way to sneak through.

She looked back at Sol. She bit her lip.

Damn it! She had come so far. She was so close. She could not turn back now.

"How do we cross a field of snakes?" she said softly.

She gazed out into the darkness. A darkness swarming with serpents. The *Nazareth* was a sizable frigate, but some of those basilisk warships were large enough to swallow them whole.

*Like a snake devouring an elephant,* she thought, remembering the famous drawing in *The Little Prince,* a book she loved.

"That's it," she whispered. She turned toward her two captains and smiled. "We can't fight our way through. We can't sneak our way through. But we can wear a disguise."

The two finally separated, winded and battered.

Mairead tilted her head. "What, plastic nose, fake mustache, big glasses, that kinda thing?"

Ramses rose to his feet and smoothed his uniform. He nodded slowly. "I think I know what the commodore means." He winced. "It won't be easy."

"Nothing worthwhile is ever easy," Leona said.

"I am," said Mairead. "And I have no mucking idea what you two are talking about. Can somebody please fill me in?"

"The basilisks fly huge, elongated ships," Leona said. "Many are larger than ours. And many are cargo hulls, only lightly armed. We're going to hijack one of their ships. We're going to squeeze the *Nazareth* right into it. And we'll fly onward—hidden inside a giant snakeskin."

Mairead spat. "I ain't gonna sneak around like a coward."

"You will do as you're commanded," Leona said. "We are humans. We have no homeland, no empire of our own, barely any weapons. But we have our ingenuity. Our resourcefulness. We'll win this war with cleverness. With sneakiness. That's not cowardice, Captain McQueen. That's pragmatism."

Mairead sighed. "My old da always did say I have more balls than brains. Fine! Muck it. At least I'll get to fight one battle when we hijack a ship." She puffed her cigar. "I'm game. And speaking of games, anyone for a round of poker after the battle? How about snakes and ladders?"

Ignoring the redheaded pilot, Ramses stepped toward Leona. His eyes were somber, and he spoke softly.

"Are you sure we can do this, Commodore?" he said. "We have only two hundred marines and a handful of Firebirds in our hold. It's probably enough to hijack an alien frigate, yes. But if we're discovered, it won't be enough to fight off the basilisks. Are you sure we shouldn't return home, report to your father what we've seen?"

Leona placed a hand on the tall man's shoulder. "Ramses, we *are* returning home." She pointed to the distant star. "That's our home. And that's where we're going."

Ramses tightened his lips. He nodded. "Then I'm with you, Leona. We all are."

Mairead pulled them both into a crushing embrace. "All for one, and one for all! We're the Mucking Musketeers."

Leona freed herself from the embrace and scanned the monitor. Hundreds of potential targets showed up—the basilisk ships patrolling the border. She tapped a dot.

"This ship is isolated," Leona said. "It's large and heavy and slow. I'm guessing it's a cargo barge, not a warship. This is our target." She turned toward Ramses. "Pharaoh, I want you to fly the *Nazareth* on this mission."

Ramses saluted, slamming his right fist into his left palm. "Gladly."

Leona turned toward Mairead. "Firebug, we have seven Firebirds in our hangars, but we're missing a pilot. Too many died on the way here. You used to fly Firebirds, right?"

Mairead placed a fist on her hip and cocked an eyebrow. "Baby, I commanded the entire Firebird fleet. But you already knew that."

Leona nodded. "Ever miss flying them?"

"Ra yes!" Mairead said. "Flying warships is a mucking drag. Too heavy and slow."

Leona smiled thinly. "Well, you're being demoted. You're back to Firebirds. You'll lead the squadron we have. While the marines raid the enemy hulk, you and your Firebirds will cover them."

Mairead bristled. "Hang on. *Cover* the marines? I wanna fight!"

Leona sighed. "I have a feeling you'll have a fight on your hands. This place is swarming with snakes. The basilisks have just joined the war, swearing allegiance to the Hierarchy. They're on edge and antsy for battle. Any freighter will have its own starfighters accompanying it. You'll get your share of fighting, Firebug."

Mairead nodded. "Excellent. And what of you, Curly? You gonna dip your beak?"

Leona looked back toward Sol.

*I didn't want to fight,* she thought. *Not the scorpions. Not the snakes. All I want to do is go home. But for you, my homeworld, I will fight. For an old song. For a dream of blue skies. For an echo of Earth.*

She looked back at her captains.

"I will lead the boarding party into the enemy ship," Leona said. "We're going to invade them. Our entire marine force. We'll fight room to room if we must, slaying every basilisk who doesn't surrender. I don't enjoy killing any creature, not even monsters who've joined the Hierarchy, who fight alongside the scorpions to destroy us. But for Earth, I will kill, and I will die if I must. Are you ready, my captains? It's time to go home."

They did not need to answer. She saw the dedication in their eyes.

Ramses took his seat at the helm and nudged the thruster. The *Nazareth*'s engines rumbled, and the warship flew forward, entering the Basiliska Empire, inching closer to a distant pale light.

## CHAPTER SEVEN

Emet woke up in a hospital bed, took half a second to moan, then pushed himself up and reached for his pistol.

His holster was empty.

His heart burst into a gallop.

"Damn it, why aren't I on the bridge?" he rumbled. "Where are my weapons? Give me a status report! How long was I out? Are our lines holding? Give me the enemy positions, now!"

He could barely see. His eyes were blurry, and his head spun. When he blinked, he could make out a tall figure in pale blue. A woman, he thought. She placed her hands on her hips, and he heard her voice, muffled and distant.

"Lie down, Emet, or I will strap you down! The battle is over. The enemy is a light-year away. Now calm yourself! Your heart is galloping like a Ra damn muler with its ass on fire."

Emet blinked again, struggling to process all that. He felt weak. His head kept spinning. He ached to fall onto his back, but he forced himself to sling his legs across the bedside.

"I need to be on my bridge," he said, pushing himself up. "I—"

"You do not leave this bed until I say so," said the woman.

She shoved him back down. She actually shoved him—an admiral, the commander of the Heirs of Earth.

And he was so damn weak he couldn't resist her.

"Damn it," he said, still struggling to focus. "Why can't I see right?"

The blurry woman huffed. "Because I pumped you full of enough painkillers to stun a starwhale." She raised a blurry sliver that looked disturbingly like a needle. A very large, sharp needle. "Try this."

She slammed the needle into his thigh.

Emet bellowed.

"Ra dammit, woman!" he roared.

His heart was pounding again. But his head stopped spinning. His eyes cleared. He no longer felt like he was swimming in cotton.

He could finally see his tormentor clearly. She was a tall, striking woman in her late forties, dressed in blue scrubs. Her eyes were sharp, blue, and intelligent. Her black hair was just long enough to reach her chin. As the fog cleared from his mind, Emet recognized her.

"Cindy," he said.

She nodded, hands on her hips. "While you're in my sick bay, you may call me Nurse Cindy or ma'am. I don't care if you're the admiral of this fleet. You're my patient."

Emet couldn't help but smile wryly. He remembered when Duncan, his old friend, had promoted Cindy to head nurse. The very same day, Cindy had flown a shuttle to the ISS *Jerusalem*, marched onto the bridge, and demanded to teach every Inheritor a first aid course. She then made Emet vow to never send anyone into battle without a personal first aid kit. Not just a platoon medic—a first aid kit on every soldier.

*You send them into battle with weapons that kill and maim,* Cindy had said that day. *So send them with tools to heal.*

"How long have I been out, Cindy?" Emet said, then winced as she raised the needle again. "*Nurse* Cindy. Ma'am."

She glowered at him, one hand on her hip, the other holding her needle. "You've been here on the hospital ship ISS *Kos*, unconscious, for over two days. Some stunt you pulled, mister, jumping into a Ra damn scorpion dreadnought like that. You nearly left us without an admiral."

"The battle—" he began.

"It's over," Cindy said. "We lost. I called the retreat myself after the scorpions drained you of half your blood."

He pushed himself back up. "You *what?*"

She shoved him back down. "Lie down! You need to rest. Don't make me tie you down. With you unconscious, and with Commodore Leona on her expedition, the chain of command moves to the medical ship. And since Duncan is no longer with us, I assumed command. I pulled the fleet back. We retreated into Concord territory. And we're going to stay here until you recover."

Finally, Emet looked down at his body. Bandages covered his legs, the side of his torso, and an arm.

"Ra damn," he muttered.

"You lost a lot of blood," Cindy said, voice softer now. "And a lot of skin. You nearly lost your life. You got here just in time. I covered your burns with stem cell therapy. Your skin is already regrowing, and it won't leave a scar. But you were close. Another moment, you'd have been beyond my skills. That was a damn foolish thing you did."

Emet sighed and let his body relax, sinking into the mattress. "Perhaps all soldiers are fools. Fools and madmen make the best heroes and villains."

"And we sensible folk clean up after you," Cindy said. She approached a shelf, picked up a tray, and placed it by his bed. "Here. I got you some coffee and cherry pie. Both were made from powder. But one is hot and the other is sweet, and maybe they'll return some color to your cheeks. And wait, lie down! You need to *stay in bed*. I brought you a minicom, so you can chat with your generals while you drink, eat, and rest."

For a moment, Emet was torn between racing out of bed, barking orders into his comm, inquiring about his wounds, and a thousand other concerns. And for that moment, weariness and gratitude drowned those worries. He looked at the tall nurse with the blue eyes.

"Cindy, thank you," he said.

Her eyes softened—a rarity for Cindy. She patted his arm. "Drink your coffee. You need it. Now if you'll excuse me, I have twenty other wounded soldiers to patch up."

He took a sip of coffee. It was hot, black, bitter, and wonderful. It was synthetic, of course. Nobody had brewed coffee from true beans in two thousand years. Not even Ramses.

*As soon as we get home, we'll grow true coffee,* Emet thought.

He turned on the minicom. He spent a few moments, coffee and pie forgotten, reading logs, speaking to his officers, catching up on the past two days.

The news was bad.

They had lost the Battle of Helios—the battle where Emet had hoped to capture Jade, to end this war.

Hundreds of Concord starships—many Inheritor vessels among them—were lost.

Hundreds of human warriors had fallen.

It was perhaps the greatest blow the Heirs of Earth had ever suffered.

The Hierarchy had claimed Helios, an important base of operations. Across the galaxy, the scorpion forces had been sweeping across systems, conquering world after world. The Concord fleets were crumbling before them. Planet after planet burned. Civilization after civilization joined the enemy—or perished.

Rowan—captured.

His children—missing.

Hope—all but gone.

*We are losing this war,* Emet knew.

Cindy had ordered him to remain in bed. But damn it, he could not lie here as the galaxy burned. He forced himself out of bed, ignoring the agony from his wounds. His body protested, screaming in pain. Let it scream.

Perhaps Cindy had known he would disobey her. He found his uniform on the bedside table, stitched up and freshly laundered. Brown trousers heavy with pockets. Black boots. A buttoned shirt. A sturdy blue overcoat with brass buttons. Cindy had even remembered his cowboy hat. His weapons were there too: dear old Lightning and Thunder, his loyal companions. Emet dressed slowly, stiffly, and strapped on the pistol and rifle.

He took a step, groaned, and winced.

He saw then that Cindy had also left him a cane. Grumbling, Emet grabbed it.

He limped out of the hospital room. The *Kos*, the fleet's hospital ship, was small and cluttered. A few years ago, she had been a scrapped cargo freighter, cracked and rusty. The Heirs had converted her into a floating hospital, and today she was brimming with patients. As Emet walked down the central corridor, nurses and medics raced by him, wheeling patients into operating rooms. He passed by rooms where soldiers lay on beds, on cots, some on the floor. They were bandaged, burnt, some missing limbs, others missing faces. Some screamed. Others wept. Some lay dying. Others were already dead.

Emet recognized them all. Some were the warriors who had invaded the *Pestilence* with him.

He entered their rooms. He shook their hands—those who still had hands. He joked with them. He patted their shoulders, told them to be strong, told them they were brave.

But inside him, ice spread over the fire of pain.

*I could have retreated earlier,* he thought. *The instant the scorpions captured Rowan, I should have realized the battle was lost. But I fought on.*

Around him, they screamed.

A man wept, begging for his mother, as a nurse sawed off what remained of his leg.

A man writhed in a bed, burnt, blisters covering his skin.

Emet stared around him, barely able to breathe. His head spun again. They all spun around him. The faces of men and women. Boys and girls. Some of these warriors were only fourteen or fifteen years old.

*They followed me. They suffer for me. So many died for me. I made a mistake.*

Emet wanted to turn away. To hide from the faces of this war—faces screaming. Faces gone, eyes and noses and mouths taken by fire and claw. But he forced himself to look, to meet them, to talk to them, comfort them. And all the while the guilt filled him.

*I stayed too long. I should have fallen back sooner. This is on me.*

And he knew, too, that sooner or later—perhaps in a few years, perhaps in only a few months or even weeks—there would be no more fleeing. The scorpions would be everywhere in the galaxy. And this war would end.

*If we must die, we will die fighting, not in gulocks,* Emet thought, standing among the wounded and dying. *But there is no nobility to death in battle. This is what it looks like. A hell of blood and burns and shit and screams.*

Finally, when he was dizzy and leaning heavily on his cane, a nurse arrived to give Emet another shot of morphine, and a second nurse practically forced a meal down his throat. With his head clearer, Emet limped into the hospital's hangar, entered a shuttle, and flew into space.

The remains of his fleet hovered around him, battered and burnt. Several warships had not made it back from Helios. Hundreds of warriors would never see Earth. Even those ships that had survived showed their scars. Some were missing shields and cannons. Others were missing entire decks. Some warships barely flew.

Emet flew toward the *Jerusalem*. The once-mighty warship was now dented and cracked. Mechanics were already flying around her, soldering, patching her up, preparing her for the next battle.

And suddenly it hit him again.

Rowan was not waiting on the *Jerusalem*. She had fallen into Jade's hands.

His daughter, Leona, was not waiting there either. She had flown off in search of Earth, dozens of strikers in pursuit, and Emet had not heard from her since.

His son, Bay, was not there. He was missing in action, had vanished during a scorpion assault months ago, presumed dead.

The grief, the fear, the tragedy hit Emet like a ramming striker. He gasped for breath.

For a moment, he let it crush him.

The he raised his chin. He took a deep breath. He squared his shoulders. The galaxy was falling apart. But he didn't have to.

"So long as I draw breath, I will fight," he vowed. "If everyone that I love is dead, I will fight for those who still live, and I will love them as I love my children. Every human who still lives is my child, and I will never stop fighting for them."

He flew the shuttle into *Jerusalem*'s hangar, then marched across his flagship and back onto his bridge.

Several officers stood there. As he entered the bridge, they saluted.

"Welcome back, Old Lion," said Commodore Crane, a grizzled warrior who had fought with the Heirs of Earth since its founding.

Emet walked toward the controls, cane tapping. He wanted nothing more than to lie down, to sleep, but he forced himself to move, to work, to press buttons, to pull levers, to frown at monitors. To keep busy. To be useful. Maybe to redeem himself. To save a life for all those he had led to death. To hold back the terror.

He summoned a holographic map of the Milky Way Galaxy. The spiral hovered above a control board, as wide as his arm span. His officers gathered around the hologram, gazing upon the galaxy.

"The blue stars represent Concord territory," Emet rasped, his voice even hoarser than usual. "The red stars represent the Hierarchy, at least the systems we know they've conquered so far."

They all stared, grim.

Most of the galaxy was painted red. As they watched, the map kept updating itself. Every moment, another star turned from blue to red—another world fallen to the Hierarchy. Helios. Akraba. Vaelia. Paev. Thousands of others. So many planets where the Heirs of Earth had fought—fallen to the enemy. The Hierarchy was spreading like blood across the galaxy.

Emet looked at the Orion Arm, where Earth was located. His homeworld lay within the Basiliska Empire, a rising power which had sworn allegiance to the Hierarchy. Earth was deep in the red. He looked away.

"The enemy is closing in on Aelonia, center of the Concord," Emet said, zooming in on another sector of the galaxy. "At this rate, the scorpions will be there by the end of the year."

Thousands of sentient civilizations formed the Concord Alliance, ranging from single-world species to empires spanning many stars. The Aelonians were the mightiest among them. The tall, graceful humanoids had transparent skin and glowing innards. Duncan had once called them living lava lamps. Humanity had clashed with the Aelonians before; humans were treated as pests in their empire. And yet Admiral Melitar, a powerful Aelonian, had been kind to Emet, had praised humanity's courage in the fight against the Hierarchy. Melitar had even recognized Earth as humanity's birthright.

"Aelonia is our closest ally," Emet said. "The only civilization that acknowledges our connection to Earth. They're also the mightiest of the Concord races. If Aelonia falls, humanity falls. The galaxy falls. Civilization falls."

They all looked at Aelonia in the hologram. The Aelonians had built a Dyson sphere around their home star—a massive sphere of metal enclosing their entire solar system. Here was a gargantuan fortress in space, a center of science, wisdom, and might.

And all around, the Hierarchy was tightening like a noose.

"Admiral," said Commodore Crane, voice low. "Emet. Maybe we must accept that the war is lost. We should take what remains of our fleet and fly to Earth. Join Leona. Raise our homeworld again. This war, this chaos—it's an opportunity to build a new order in the galaxy. To restore our ancient home. This?" Crane gestured at the holographic galaxy. "This isn't our war."

"Isn't it?" said Emet. "Do millions of humans not live in exile, scattered across this galaxy? Do they not burn in the inferno of the gulocks? This *is* our war, my friends. We're humans. We suffer like none others at the claws of the scorpions. If we cannot defeat them, there will be no Earth. The scorpions will move on from Aelonia and destroy every world in their path—Earth included. Above all else, our loyalty is to humanity, to Earth. But we also fight for life in general. For civilization across the galaxy. For freedom. This is a war between light and dark, between good and evil. This is a war we will not shy away from."

"And what of Earth?" said Crane. "How long can we fight the scorpions while Earth cries out for us?"

"I never forget Earth, not for a second." Emet stared at the hologram. "My heart yearns to fly there. But not yet. My friends, we must fly instead to Aelonia. All species who still fight must fly there. At Aelonia we will face the great battle of our time. At Aelonia the fate of Earth, humanity, of the galaxy itself will be decided."

An alert flashed on a monitor.

An incoming ship.

Emet stared, fearing another scorpion attack. But their systems detected only a single vessel. A small ship. A starfighter, perhaps just a shuttle.

"An enemy scout?" said Crane, frowning at the monitor.

Emet stared at stats coming through. The computer recognized this ship.

Its name appeared on the monitor: The ISS *Brooklyn*.

Emet hit his comm. "Hangar, this is Admiral Ben-Ari. Send out three Firebirds. Escort the *Brooklyn* back to the *Jerusalem*."

Brooklyn.

Bay.

Emet watched the Firebirds fly out, not sure if Brooklyn was flying back with his living son or a corpse.

Finally, when Brooklyn was close enough, his comm buzzed.

Bay's voice emerged.

"Dad?"

All the day's horrors parted like curtains. Emet took a deep, relieved breath.

"I'll meet you in the hangar, son," he said, struggling to keep his voice steady.

He limped with his cane, cursing his slowness, back toward the *Jerusalem*'s hangar. He arrived covered in sweat, his legs shaky with weakness, to see Brooklyn glide through the airlock and dock. The small ship looked like she had flown through hell and back.

Brooklyn's hatch opened, and Bay emerged.

The young man's uniform was dusty and tattered, and his limbs sported more than a few bandages, but he was alive, and he was smiling.

Emet stepped forward and stood before his son.

Bay stared back, tightened his lips, and saluted.

Emet pulled the young man into an embrace.

"Thank goodness," Emet said, voice hoarse. "I thought you were gone, son. I thought the scorpions got you."

Perhaps it was the painkillers, his exhaustion, his grief—but suddenly, for the first time in years, tears filled Emet's eyes. He blinked them away quickly, daring not to let anyone see.

"I'm back, Dad," Bay said, his own voice choked. "I didn't mean to go. Coral wanted to find the Godblade in the guildhall. She took me with her. We found clues, but—"

Emet pulled back from him. He stared at his son, frowning.

"Coral the weaver?" he said. "The woman I locked in the brig, who escaped during the battle?" His eyes widened. "She stole Brooklyn to seek that myth, didn't she? And she stole you with her. Of course."

Bay winced. "Dad. I didn't believe it at first either, but Coral was speaking the truth. We didn't find the Godblade, but we saw murals. I think I know where it is. I think that Jade—"

"Son." Emet gripped Bay—not unkindly, but firmly. "I want you to report to the *Kos*. Have Cindy look at your wounds. I could use more painkillers myself. We have more battles facing us, and we must be strong. I don't want to hear any more about ancient myths, magic, or enchanted temples, all right?"

A voice rose from inside Brooklyn. "Do not mock the Weavers Guild, Admiral, for there is power in the aether you do not understand. The Godblade is real—and Jade Emery possesses it. Or did, years ago. We must find this weapon ... or the galaxy will fall."

She stepped out of the Brooklyn—a woman with long white hair, dark skin, and silvery tattoos.

Coral Amber.

Emet hit the comm on his lapel. "Security—send a squad down to the hangar."

Bay gasped. "Dad!"

Coral only smiled thinly. "You need an entire squad to deal with me?"

Guards burst into the hangar, and Emet pointed at Coral.

"Arrest this woman. She's an escaped prisoner. Return her to the brig and keep guard." As the guards stepped toward Coral, Emet stared at the weaver. "You will stand trial, Corporal Amber, for escaping the brig, stealing an Inheritor ship, and going AWOL during a battle."

"Dad!" Bay said again, voice louder now. "She's telling you the truth about the Godblade. You have to listen."

The guards grabbed Coral. She put up no resistance, only smiled as the guards began dragging her away.

"He'll listen, Bay," she said. "He'll listen to you. Tell him. Tell him about Jade. About what we saw."

Before Coral could say more, the guards pulled her out of the hangar. She left without a struggle, giving Emet a last look, small smile, and nod.

Emet shook his head with a sigh. Ancient temples? Magic swords? It was all nonsense. He was an admiral. He dealt with steel and fire and blood. And he had a battle to prepare for.

*Aelonia*, he thought, icy claws digging into him. *The heart of the Concord. The great battle of the war draws near. We'll make our final stand in Aelonia—but we'll be fighting for Earth.*

"Dad?" Bay said, tearing him away from his thoughts. "Where's Rowan? I want to see her."

Emet turned toward his son, and his heart broke.

*My son already lost one woman he loves,* he thought. *This will break him.*

"Dad?" Bay whispered, and fear filled his eyes.

Emet placed his hand on Bay's shoulder.

"Bay, I am so sorry."

His son stared at him in horror, eyes wide and damp. "Rowan? Oh Ra. Did Rowan die?"

Emet shook his head.

*Her fate is worse than death,* he knew.

"The enemy captured her, son," Emet said. "I'm sorry."

Bay blanched. He tried to speak, but no words emerged, and Emet had a sudden memory of Bay as a baby, crying so hard he could make no sound, not even breathe.

Again tears filled Emet's own eyes, and his heart broke for Rowan, for his son, for his soldiers. For humanity.

He pulled Bay into his arms, and the two men stood in the hangar, embracing, silent as the galaxy burned.

## CHAPTER EIGHT

Bay stood in the *Jerusalem*, staring through a porthole into space, feeling helpless. The terror was searing ice in his belly.

"Rowan," he whispered.

His eyes narrowed, stinging. His lips shook.

*The scorpions captured Rowan.*

His knees shook. Bay placed his hands flat against the bulkhead. He stared out the porthole at the stars.

*They have Rowan. They have her. They're going to torture her. Oh Ra.*

Bay spun back toward the war room. The generals of the Heirs of Earth were there. Emet, his father. Commodore Crane, commander of the *Jaipur*. Other officers, stern and shabby, eyes hard. Most of them were aging, hair graying, and they wore blue cloaks that had survived many battles, the fabric torn and singed. Their weapons, rifles of brass and iron and wood, had slain many. Bay was only a corporal, lowly among the Inheritors, barely more than a green private. He was twenty-five, old for a corporal, but had spent years lost in a haze of booze and drugs.

*After Seohyun died, I vanished for a decade*, Bay thought. *I won't let Rowan die too.*

"We must save her," Bay said. "We must attack Ur Akad, homeworld of the scorpions, and bring Rowan home."

The officers looked at one another, eyes dark.

Emet turned toward his son. "Bay, we don't have the power to attack Ur Akad."

"The Concord does!" Bay said. "If we get the Aelonians to help us, a few other species too, we can beat them."

Commodore Crane scoffed. "The Concord? They're retreating as fast as they can fly. Nearly all their territory is gone. Their fleets are fleeing back to Aelonia." The grizzled general shook his head. "No, Corporal Ben-Ari, we can't contemplate assault now. Right now, we must be on the defensive."

"But Rowan—" Bay began.

"Corporal Rowan Emery is a single soldier," said another officer, a tall and gaunt man with sunken cheeks. "And she is lost. I'm sorry, Corporal Ben-Ari. I know she was dear to you. But sometimes we must leave a soldier behind."

Bay stared from one officer to another. They all stared back.

*I won't abandon you, Rowan. I won't.*

"This single soldier has the Earthstone," Bay said, changing tactics. "An artifact that contains Earth's cultural heritage. If you don't care about Rowan's life, surely you care that—"

"Bay!" Emet said, rising to his feet. "Don't accuse us of callousness. We care about Rowan's life. Every officer here grieves that we lost her. But if we attack Ur Akad, more will die. All of us will die."

Bay lowered his head. "I know. I misspoke. I apologize." He looked up again, his insides roiling. "If we can't attack Uk Akad, we mount a secret rescue mission."

Emet sat back down, sighing. "Bay, millions of strikers fly between us and Ur Akad. Their homeworld is the most defended place in the galaxy. We can't get close without them seeing. Jade will have taken Rowan to the imperial palace. If we could reach that place, we would have assassinated the emperor long ago." He shook his head. "I am deeply sorry. Truly I am. But Rowan is beyond our reach. Our best hope is to face the Hierarchy at Aelonia, fight to turn the tide, and slowly drive the enemy back— star by star, year by year. This will not be a short war. But Rowan is strong. She is brave. She can survive captivity, and maybe someday—"

"They're going to kill her, Dad," Bay said. "They're going to execute her publicly, a soldier of the Heirs of Earth, entertainment for the crowd. Or worse—they'll turn her into a creature like Jade. We can't wait out this war."

The officers glanced at one another again, silent.

Emet approached his son. He placed a hand on Bay's shoulder.

"Bay, I know it hurts," he said. "I can't even imagine the pain you're feeling now. But we are soldiers. We cannot let our pain determine our actions. Rowan understands this. She understood the risks when she spoke the vows. She knew she might have to sacrifice her life. We must think of Earth. Our loyalty is to our homeworld."

Bay stared into the taller man's eyes. He saw kindness there. Compassion. Wisdom.

Nothing that would save Rowan.

"I understand," Bay said. "Sir."

He saluted stiffly, then turned and left the war room.

He walked down the *Jerusalem*'s central corridor, his soul shaken.

Coral was imprisoned in the brig, here in this very ship. Rowan was imprisoned on Ur Akad, facing torture, execution, or both. The Concord was crumbling. Leona had been gone for months now, possibly dead, and the basilisks were flying around Earth.

Bay had never felt so hopeless.

*How did this happen?* he thought, marching down the hallway. *Only a year ago, we had so much hope. Now everything is falling apart.*

A voice inside him cried out for grog. For drugs. For lost hours in a casino or brothel. He wanted to flee this place, this war, to find another sin hive. To sink again. To drown in the depths of forgetfulness, to wither and die.

*I should never have left Paradise Lost,* he thought. *I should never have come back. I should never have fallen in love.*

He returned to his cabin and stared at his reflection in the mirror. A stranger stared back. He had changed over the past year. His dark blond hair was neatly cropped now. Instead of a shaggy, hooded cloak, used to hide drugs and hide himself, he wore an Inheritor uniform—brown trousers with many pockets, tall boots, and a navy blue overcoat with shiny buttons. A rifle hung across his back, its stock wooden and trimmed with brass. But the biggest change was his carriage. He no longer stooped, shuffling like a thief. He stood tall, shoulders squared.

He was no longer the vagrant, the junkie, the boy lost in the darkness. He was a man. He was a soldier.

Bay looked at the wall, where hung a black cowboy hat. His father always wore such a hat. Bay hesitated, then lifted the hat and placed it on his head. He looked back at his reflection. And he saw his father's son.

*I'll make you proud, Dad. I promise.*

"No, I won't abandon this war again," Bay said to his reflection. "I won't sink into that old pit. But neither can I abandon Rowan. She's in her own dark pit now. And I will save her—if I must burn the whole galaxy down."

He raced to the hangar. Brooklyn was docked there among ten Firebirds. The souped-up shuttle seemed bulky, slow, and crude compared to the slick starfighters. But to Bay, she was the best ship in the fleet.

He entered Brooklyn, sat down in the cockpit, and switched her on.

"Morning, Brook," he said. "We're flying out. Don't bother checking the flight logs. We're not scheduled."

Her camera swiveled toward him. "Are you stealing me again, Bay? *Again?*"

He nodded. "Yep."

Brooklyn groaned. "This will be the third time somebody's stolen me from the *Jerusalem*, you know."

He patted her dashboard. "Then you should be used to it."

She rolled her camera lens. "Fine! Are we going to almost certainly get killed again?"

"Of course," Bay said. "That's all the fun."

"Fun for you maybe," Brooklyn muttered. "I'm the one who gets hit with all the plasma bolts."

She ignited her engine and rolled into the airlock. Bay typed in the code, and the outer door opened to the stars.

Several guards noticed. They began pounding on the airlock's inner door.

"You know the drill," Bay said.

Brooklyn heaved a sigh. "I hate you, Bay Ben-Ari."

She blasted out into space, engines roaring.

The *Jerusalem* was flying at warp speed, heading with the rest of the fleet toward Aelonia. With the combined power of their azoth crystals, the warships formed a massive bubble of warped space around them, which the entire fleet shared. Within moments, Brooklyn fell out of the bubble. Mere seconds later, the fleet was millions of kilometers away.

Brooklyn and Bay floated in empty space—alone.

"So, Bay old boy, where are heading this fine morning?" Brooklyn said. "What splendid adventure do you have planned for us today? A trip to the singing waterfalls of Lerinia? The diamond towers of Mazil? Perchance the fairy forests of Alisium, to see the rainbow birds?"

"We're going to fly to Ur Akad, homeworld of the scorpions and heart of the Hierarchy, and infiltrate the imperial palace."

Brooklyn stared at him, camera shutters narrowing. "I hate you."

"Yes, you mentioned," Bay said.

"Well, they better not have any ants," Brooklyn muttered. "Scorpions I can handle, but if there are any ants, I'm turning right back."

She fired up her own warp engine. They blasted into the distance, flying toward the heart of the empire.

## CHAPTER NINE

Rowan knelt in the alien shuttle, chained and collared and gagged, gazing down upon Ur Akad.

Below, the desert sprawled into the horizons, a wasteland of canyons, volcanoes, mesas, and rocky plains. Rowan had never seen a planet this large. Intellectually, she knew that that Ur Akad was larger than Jupiter. It was a planet so large it shouldn't even exist. She knew that Earth could fit into some of these canyons. But her eyes could not comprehend the sheer size of this place.

If the landscape seemed dead, the yellow sky was certainly not. Thousands of other vessels flew everywhere, ranging from shuttles only large enough for a single scorpion to warships that could carry thousands. The ships were rising from the deep canyons, soaring across the sky, and heading into space.

*They're heading to war*, Rowan knew. *There's a big battle coming. Maybe the final battle.* She nervously chewed on her cloth gag. *I must save Jade before then. I must return her to sanity—and to the cause of Earth.*

She looked up at her sister. Jade stood at the controls, flying the shuttle. Her back was turned to Rowan.

*If Emet were here, he would have fought her*, Rowan thought. *Even handcuffed and collared, he'd have fought. And he'd have died. I cannot defeat Jade with my strength; I have none. We cannot defeat the Hierarchy with our fleets; we are too weak. But maybe, as cliché as it sounds, I can win with love.*

It did sound terribly cliché. And almost hopeless. Yet what other hope did Rowan have?

She wriggled and felt Fillister shift in her vest pocket. The tiny robot was still hidden, recording the signals from Jade's cybernetic implants.

*Jade is arrogant,* Rowan thought. *She took my gun, but she never bothered to empty my pockets.*

"Stop wiggling around back there!" Jade said and laughed. "You can't escape, pest. Very soon, the emperor will see you. I'll enjoy watching him peel your skin. Look! Look below, pest, and behold the imperial city."

Rowan shuddered.

*The emperor will skin me alive.*

Sudden terror burst inside Rowan like a geyser. She had to flee! She had to fight! She had to kill herself if she could. Anything to avoid this. Her heart pounded. Cold sweat washed her. Why had she surrendered herself? She could have run. She could have fled with Emet! She could have been with her friends now, and tears filled Rowan's eyes, and her chains rattled.

She took a deep breath.

*Focus, Rowan,* she told herself, blinking the tears away. *You faced the bonecrawlers in the ducts. You faced the scorpions in battle. You are strong. You are an Inheritor. You can do this.*

She rose to her feet and stared out the shuttle's window. Below her spread the imperial city.

Rowan had seen human cities in the Earthstone. This was nothing of the sort. There were no roads, no houses, no gardens or parks. It looked more like a giant hive, many kilometers wide. Mesas rose like skyscrapers, peppered with holes. Thousands of caves perforated cliffs and stony plains. Canyons carved the landscape, forming great spirals. Millions of scorpions scuttled below, tiny dots from up here, racing into and out of holes. Jagged black ships rose from chasms like demons from the underworld, rumbling toward space, leaving fiery wakes. The shuttle trembled as the warships soared by, and Rowan glimpsed scorpions inside them, soldiers for the war.

The shuttle flew lower and skimmed over the city. Ahead rose a towering structure of sandstone, the only thing here resembling a true building. Rowan had no frame of reference, but she could tell this tower was *tall*. Kilometers tall, maybe. Taller than any skyscraper from ancient Earth. It was shaped like a giant scorpion pincer, twin towers curving toward each other, tapering into points.

Jade tore off Rowan's gag. "It's almost time to hear you scream, pest." She laughed. "Do you recognize the palace below?"

Rowan's jaw ached. She opened and closed her mouth several times, flexing her jaw muscles, before being able to speak again.

"That's Baal Skran," Rowan said, surprised at the awe in her voice. "The palace of the emperor. I've read about this place."

"It's the place where you'll die," said Jade.

Rowan lowered her head.

*I shouldn't be here,* she thought. *I should be back with Bay. Laughing with him. He would tease me, call me a hobbit, and draw me. And I would read to him my new dinosaur script.* Tears filled her eyes. *I miss him. I miss everyone. But I must be strong. I must be brave. As soon as I have a moment alone with Fillister, I can examine Jade's code.* Rowan tightened her lips. *And I can save her.*

Jade flew the shuttle toward the claw-shaped palace and descended slowly. The shuttle thumped down with a cloud of sand.

Rowan winced. She lay on the deck, curled up, and brought her face as close as possible to her vest pocket.

"Fill?" she whispered.

"Still working on it, Row," the dragonfly whispered back. "I need a few more hours. And your help."

Damn it.

Jade shut off the engines and turned toward Rowan. Her green eyes were wide with rapture and bloodlust. Her lips peeled back in a lurid grin. She grabbed Rowan by her short brown hair, twisted, and yanked her to her feet. Rowan stood up, wincing, strands of her hair tearing.

"Come, pest." Jade moved toward the hatch, dragging Rowan by the hair.

The sisters stepped outside into the searing sunlight. Heat blasted Rowan, worse than the furnace rooms of Paradise Lost. Both suns blazed and crackled above, white and red, lashing her with radiation. Rowan gasped for breath. The air was dry, thin, and sandy.

"Kneel!" Jade shrieked. "Kneel, pest! You are on holy ground."

Jade didn't even need to shove Rowan down. She just had to release her, and the gravity yanked Rowan to her knees. She coughed, kneeling on the rocky earth. Rowan was a slender girl, but with the enormous gravity of Ur Akad, she felt as heavy as a sumo wrestler. Invisible claws seemed to stretch out from the soil, to grab her, to yank her down. Rowan struggled to remain on her knees, then finally collapsed and lay prostrate, glued to the ground.

*I used to be a hobbit,* she thought, worried that she was crushing Fillister under her weight. *Now I'm Fat Bastard.*

Jade stood over her and laughed. "Good. Crawl! Crawl like the worm that you are."

She grabbed Rowan's leash and dragged her forward. Rowan wanted to walk, but the gravity was too immense. She crawled across the ground, bloodying her knees and elbows on sharp rocks. Jade walked at a quick pace. Whenever Rowan lagged, she choked on the collar. She struggled to keep up, feeling as if she carried a backpack full of boulders.

*It's no wonder Jade can jump so high in regular gravity*, Rowan thought.

Jade pulled her toward the towering palace. Rowan crawled after her like a cur on a leash, too weak to stand upright. Her head felt like a boulder topped with anvils, but she strained and grunted, finally managing to raise her head. She gazed up at the imperial palace.

The sandstone structure soared, its curving towers tapering to points that seemed to pierce the binary suns. The red and white sunbeams sliced the sky.

"It's beautiful, isn't it?" Jade said. "Here is the glorious heart of the empire."

"It's not your home, sister," Rowan whispered, struggling to speak louder. It was hard enough to remain on her hands and knees; the ground kept trying to flatten her. "Our home is Earth."

Jade laughed. "Maybe once we defeat the Concord, I'll visit Earth, draped in a cloak of your skin."

She increased her pace, marching to the palace. A stone archway loomed before them, shaped like two scorpion stingers, their tips meeting at the keystone. Rowan crawled after her sister, and they entered a cavernous hall.

Though her neck creaked in protest, Rowan kept her head raised, gazing around her, instinctively seeking an exit. She saw none. Here was a den of scorpions, a massive hive brimming with the beasts.

The chamber was so large warships could have docked here. The floor was raw stone sizzling with saliva, venom, and blood. Countless human skins hung on the walls, forming a lurid tapestry. Thousands of scorpions scuttled across this unholy den. Burly black scorpions, the warrior class, clattered across the floor and guarded holes that led to tunnels and shafts. They wore spiky armor, and some carried crude iron cannons on their backs. Slimmer golden scorpions, the graceful females, lounged in pits of poison, their claws trimmed with precious metals, their shells painted with red lines. A handful of scorpions clustered in an alcove, their shells white and marked with silvery runes—weavers, able to access the power of the aether.

As Jade marched across the hall, the scorpions screeched, cackled, laughed, scuttled, cheered. The leash tightened, and Rowan crawled after her sister. All around, the foul arachnids spat at her, scurried close to smell her, to lick her, to trace their claws across her skin.

"Behold!" Jade said. "Here squirms Rowan Emery, the pest who slew our brothers and sisters, who thought she could defeat us. See how the worm crawls!"

The scorpions jeered. They tossed sticky filth, perhaps their excrement. The foul ooze clung to Rowan, matted her hair, and drenched her clothes. Rowan winced, hoping that Fillister stayed dry.

*I just need an hour alone with him,* she thought. *To review his logs of Jade's code. To write an algorithm to hack the implants.*

Fillister was brilliant, of course. But he had always been better at logging and analyzing data, not writing algorithms. When it came to creative programming—that had always been Rowan's forte. Dear old Fill had helped her understand how the Earthstone was coded, but Rowan had written the scripts to crack that code and access the treasures within.

*I just need an hour with you, Fill,* she thought. *Hang in there.*

She looked up at Jade, who marched before her, tugging the leash. The implants shone in the shaved side of her head, emitting blue light.

*I'm going to shut them down,* Rowan thought. *I wear a collar of metal, but you are collared by these machines. I'm going to save us both.*

In the center of the hall rose a mountain of bones. Human bones, Rowan realized with a shudder. Millions of human bones. A staircase had been formed from femurs, rising up the mountainside. Jade began to climb, tugging the leash. Rowan followed, climbing the staircase on hands and knees. The mountain shifted and clattered beneath them. Every kind of bone formed the pile: hips, hands, limbs, rib cages, skulls. Empty eye sockets gazed at Rowan. Jawbones silently screamed. There were even baby skeletons in the pile.

*The scorpions don't merely want to conquer the galaxy,* Rowan thought. *They don't merely want to kill us. They want to gloat. To delight in the slaughter. They are not mere exterminators seeking the purify the galaxy of pests. They are galactic serial killers, psychopaths who collect trophies of their victims.*

They finally reached the top of the mountain. Rowan had expected a jagged peak. Instead she found a depression like a volcano vent. She realized that the bones only shaped the outer shell of the mountain. On the inside, the mountain was filled with teeth.

Rowan stared, aghast. Teeth. Human teeth. Millions of them. They filled this bone volcano like lava. She was so shocked it took her a few seconds to even notice the scorpion atop the pile.

It was a huge scorpion, three times the normal size. It perched upon the bones like a dragon over a hill of treasure. Rather than the typical black or golden shell, it was deep crimson, the color of wounds. The beast clattered across the pile of teeth, moving with a grace that belied its size. The pincers looked large enough to tear through starships, the jaws mighty enough to swallow men whole.

Rowan knelt on the pile of teeth. She looked up at this creature and gasped.

"I know you," she whispered. "I saw you before. I—"

The memories pounded into her.

A glittering cave. Stalagmites and stalactites that shone with lavender light. A family. Parents who loved her. An older sister, kind and pure. A life of joy in shadows and light and safety.

Scorpions.

Scorpions invading the cave. Claws lashing. Guns firing. People dying.

And one among them—a crimson scorpion, towering over the others. Its pincers—cutting her parents. Grabbing her sister. Carrying Jade away, and Rowan screaming, begging for her parents to wake up, fleeing in a starship, fleeing into space, alone. Afraid. Leaving behind only blood and memories.

Though the gravity of Ur Akad weighed her down, Rowan found the strength to rise. She stood atop the mountain of bones, the teeth shifting under her feet, and stared at the gargantuan scorpion.

"It's you," she said. "You're Sin Kra, Emperor of the Hierarchy. You're the one who murdered my parents."

The scorpion stepped closer, looming above her. Two of his legs slammed down on either side of Rowan, framing her like bars in a cage. The emperor lowered his spiky head. He opened his jaws, revealing teeth like swords. When he hissed, his breath assailed Rowan, reeking of rot. Strands of flesh, perhaps human, still clung to his gums. Rowan cringed as two tongues emerged, warty and dripping, and licked her from navel to chin.

"Yes, I remember you," Sin Kra said, voice like silk over steel. "You fled me that day. I still remember your screams. I remember the sweet taste of your mother. The stench of your father soiling himself as he died. I remember taking your sister." The emperor cackled. "They say you joined the Heirs of Earth like your father. Good. Very good. That will prove useful."

Rowan clenched her fists. She trembled, she was weak and sick with fear, but she glared into the emperor's eyes.

"I will never betray my people," she said. "Torture me if you must. I will not speak."

The emperor laughed. "Oh, sweet child. I will not torture you for information. I know everything about your beloved Heirs of Earth. I know their command structure, their numbers, their location, their arsenal, their plans. Their skins will soon bedeck this hall. You are dear to them, I hear. To Bay, who loves you. To Emet, who sees you as a daughter. To Leona, who sees you as a sister." Sin Kra chortled. "Emotions! Love! Compassion! Such human weaknesses. Yet so amusing. I will not kill you, Rowan. Not yet. That will not satisfy me." The scorpion leaned closer, grinning. "But I will change you. Break and rebuild you. Turn you into a creature like Jade. And then, Rowan, you will hunt for me. You will kill those who love you!"

Rowan inhaled sharply. Her heart pounded. She spun toward Jade.

"Did you hear?" Rowan said. "You heard him! He changed you. Turned you into a creature. You're my sister, Jade. You—"

Jade struck her, knocking her down onto the teeth. "Silence, worm!"

Rowan stared up at her sister, blood in her mouth, tears in her eyes. "Jade, you heard him! Don't you remember?"

The emperor laughed. Beneath their pincers, the Skra-Shen had a set of smaller limbs tipped with something akin to fingers—long, narrow, clawed, used to manipulate tools and build starships. Sin Kra reached out these bony palps, grabbed Rowan, and yanked her to her feet.

"She can't remember, Rowan," the emperor said. "Her mind is broken. You could speak to her for hours of your childhood, and she won't hear. Her mind will eradicate the information like she eradicates humans across the galaxy. And soon you will be the same."

"I will never be like her!" Rowan shouted, tears falling. "I will never serve you!"

"Oh, but you will, sweet child." The emperor stroked her cheek with a long, cold claw like a razor. "You will become my most precious of killers. You will become a princess of the Hierarchy. Jade! Bring forth the brand."

Jade walked forward, grinning savagely, and handed Sin Kra a metal rod. The tip was red-hot and sizzling, shaped like a scorpion stinger—symbol of the Hierarchy.

Rowan took a step back, eyes wide, but Jade grabbed her, held her in place.

Sin Kra brought the brand close.

"I warn you, Sin Kra!" Rowan said. "The wrath of the Concord will—"

The emperor pressed the brand against her arm.

Rowan screamed.

The brand sizzled. Burning. Searing. Rowan struggled, tried to free herself, but Jade held her fast. It seemed ages that Sin Kra held the brand down, as if he sought to burn through the skin, flesh, and bone.

Finally he pulled it back.

Rowan gasped for air, trembling with pain.

A Hierarchy symbol now blazed on her arm.

Sin Kra hissed and grinned. He licked Rowan's cheek as if stroking it.

"You are marked," the emperor said. Teeth cascaded as he laughed.

Finally Jade released her, and Rowan fell to her knees. The pain blazed. She clutched her arm in agony.

"You son of a bitch!" she shouted at Sin Kra, ashamed that tears filled her eyes.

The emperor laughed. "Tomorrow, we will begin your transformation. I will perform the procedure myself. I will peel off your skin and replace it with a hard shell. I will drill into your skull and implant the machinery there. I will give you strength, cruelty, and loyalty. You will be glorious!"

Rowan was a fraction of his size. But she stared steadily into the emperor's eyes.

"You will die," she said, ignoring the pain. "Your empire will fall. The cosmos will forget about the Skra-Shen. You will vanish into the shadows like all those before you who tried to destroy humanity. But Earth will rise again. We are going to beat you. We are human, and we are eternal."

The emperor stared back at her, silent for a moment, red eyes narrowed. Then he began to laugh. His laughter was deep, booming, and shook the mountain of bones. Across the hall, the other scorpions cackled with him, a din that echoed through the hive.

"You are standing on what remains of humanity!" the emperor said. "Every tooth here is from a human I killed. Now yours will join them."

Sin Kra grabbed Rowan's jaw and squeezed it open. He extended the knobby digits that grew like fingers from his palp. He reached into Rowan's mouth and grabbed one of her teeth.

She struggled, unable to free herself. She looked at Jade, trying to cry out to her, but her voice was muffled.

The emperor yanked the tooth from her jaw.

Rowan screamed.

Her blood gushed. Her nerve blazed like lightning in her mouth. Her jaw felt like it was coming loose. She wanted to be strong and proud, but she couldn't help it. She screamed in agony again.

Jade watched, silent. For once, there was no smile on her face.

The emperor licked the blood off the tooth, then tossed it down onto the pile. It clinked. He turned toward Jade.

"Lead her into a prison cell, daughter," he said to Jade.
"Tomorrow at dawn, we will gather the crowds before the temple.
Spread the word. They will all watch Rowan's agony. Tomorrow,
you and I will skin and break and rebuild her, and you will have a
sister."

Jade stared at the emperor. For a moment, she hesitated.
She glanced at Rowan, eyes confused. Then her implants whirred
and buzzed and shone, and bloodlust filled Jade's eyes. She smiled
and nodded.

"Yes, Father."

Jade tugged Rowan's leash, dragging her down the
mountain of bones. Rowan followed, head lowered, blood
dripping down her chin. Every breath ached, and her jaw blazed
in agony. She couldn't even speak. Scorpions raced around her,
laughing, reaching out to poke and jab and torment her.

Jade pulled Rowan down a tunnel and toward a round
stone cell. She shoved Rowan into the dark chamber, and Rowan
fell, bloodying her knees. The gravity did the rest, tugging Rowan
facedown onto the floor. She lay, crushed, bleeding.

Jade spat on her. "You pathetic liar. I'll enjoy your screams
tomorrow." She knelt and stroked Rowan's damp hair.
"Tomorrow you'll be like me. Finally you'll get your wish. We'll be
sisters."

With that, Jade left the cell and slammed the barred door
shut, sealing Rowan in darkness.

## CHAPTER TEN

They flew through the darkness of the Basiliska Empire. Two hundred humans in a single starship. Heading to that light ahead—to Sol. To their sun. To their planet. To a pale blue dot only a few light-years away.

*We're so close to home,* Leona thought, gazing out a porthole toward her distant home star. *But I've never felt so far.*

She turned around, facing the cavernous hold of the ISS *Nazareth.* A company of warriors stood here, two hundred strong, ready for battle. They wore dark spacesuits, the fabric dented and charred from previous battles. Their helmets were dusty and scarred. Their rifles and pistols were old and prone to jam. They looked more like hungry mercenaries than a true military force. But Leona knew they were the bravest warriors in the universe.

She stood before them, wearing her own spacesuit, her helmet held under her arm. She spoke.

"The basilisks, a cruel species of sentient snakes, have risen in this sector of space. Earth lies in the heart of their empire. And they have sworn fealty to the Hierarchy. We now fly behind enemy lines."

The soldiers stared back. A few grumbled under their breath.

"Yet we will not abandon Earth," Leona continued. "Earth is where we evolved. Where we thrived. The planet our ancestors fought for, bled for, died for. For a hundred thousand years, we humans lived on that world, defended that world, and even in our exile, we have not forgotten it. All our hopes, our dreams, our heritage—all lie on that pale blue world. We're close to home now. But ten thousand basilisk ships lie between us and that home. We are the few, those chosen to lead humanity back home. And we will fulfill our task! For Earth!"

"For Earth!" the warriors cried.

"We are strong," Leona said. "Stronger than the enemy imagines. For two thousand years in exile, we humans hid, cowered, died. No more! Today we have an army. Today we can fight for our lives. Yet we cannot fight ten thousand basilisk ships. Not alone. But we can fight one ship. And right now, that's all we need to do. The *Nazareth* is flying toward a basilisk freighter. We don't know its proper name, but we've nicknamed it the *Snakepit*. Our task, soldiers, will be to board the *Snakepit*, to slay the basilisks on board, and claim the ship."

Sergeant Fox, a burly bearded man, grunted. "We're gonna fly home in an alien vessel?"

Leona stared at him. "The *Nazareth*, in which we now stand, was once an alien vessel. Our ride doesn't matter. Our destination does. We'll fly disguised as basilisks. In that freighter, we'll be safe. We'll appear as just another basilisk starship. We'll be able to fly right up to Earth before any basilisk figures out anything is wrong. We must seize this ship. It will take us home."

Fox nodded. "Aye, ma'am. We'll take the *Snakepit*. We'll crush the damn serpents inside."

Now another soldier spoke, this one a young lieutenant with a wispy blond beard. "Ma'am, with all due respect, the basilisks have done us no harm. Are we truly justified in attacking one of their ships, in killing them?"

Leona fixed the lieutenant with a cold glare. "The basilisks joined the Hierarchy, Lieutenant. They joined the effort to exterminate humanity, and before we even entered their space, they assaulted us, destroying the *Rosetta* and killing her crew of fifty humans. The basilisks have declared war against us. We will not cower from a fight! We're only moments away from reaching the *Snakepit*, and our scanners detect many explosives inside it. This is no innocent freighter. It's ferrying weapons to the enemy. And we will kill any basilisks aboard."

The lieutenant squared his shoulders. "Delivering weapons to the enemy? Yes, ma'am, these basilisks are dead."

Leona nodded. "Fight well today, my soldiers. Fight with courage and strength. Fight for your home. The enemy will be strong. Do not underestimate him. But we will overcome—in this battle and the ones after. For Earth."

She placed on her helmet and approached the airlock.

"Lionclaw Platoon," she said. "You and I will form the vanguard. The rest of you—you will form the second wave of assault."

Lionclaw Platoon—fifty of Leona's best warriors— entered the airlock. They crowded together, rifles clattering. The room was barely large enough to hold them.

"Commodore?" Captain Ramses, back on the bridge, spoke through the comm. "We're seconds away."

Leona pulled open the airlock door.

The air streamed out, leaving Leona and her platoon standing in a vacuum.

Ahead she saw it—the basilisk freighter. The *Snakepit*.

The damn thing was massive. The Nazareth wouldn't just fit inside; it could fly loops inside. The vessel ahead was no warship. It was ponderous and slow, slabs of heavy metal bolted together, dented and crude. Only two basic gun turrets defended its hull.

No, Leona wasn't worried about this ammunition ship. But a handful of smaller ships, which were escorting the *Snakepit*, gave her pause. The basilisks flew slender, elongated starfighters, their hulls coated with metal scales. The slender ships reminded Leona of discarded snakeskins. These ships could bite.

She hit her comm. "Mairead?"

The Firebug was in the *Nazareth*'s Firebird hangar on a lower deck.

"I see 'em, Curly," Mairead said. "Enemy starfighters. I count seven of 'em. They're toast."

The *Nazareth* increased speed, charging toward the enemy freighter. Leona and her platoon remained in the airlock, ready to jump out.

The alien starfighters saw them. The long, scaly starships came flying toward the *Nazareth*.

"Firebirds, attack!" Leona said.

From the *Nazareth*'s hangar, the Firebirds stormed into space. Standing in the open airlock, Leona saw humanity's starfighters blaze toward the enemy, guns firing.

She took a deep breath.

"Marines, let's seize this ship! Fly!"

She leaped out of the airlock.

She dived into open space, ignited her jetpack, and charged forth. The rest of her platoon followed.

Ahead of her, the human and basilisk starfighters clashed.

Silent explosions mushroomed across space. The Firebirds fired missiles and bullets, hammering the enemy. The basilisk starfighters undulated like metal serpents, firing lasers. One green beam sliced through a Firebird, cutting the ship—and its human pilot—clean in half.

As Leona flew through open space, jetpack thrumming, she fired her rifle.

Around her, the fifty marines fired their guns too.

The bullets streaked toward the serpentine starfighters, only to glance off the ships' scaly armor.

The enemy ships shone more lasers. Green beams strobed across the battle, slicing everything in their path. Beside Leona, a laser beam cut a marine in half from head to groin. Another laser carved a marine open from left shoulder to right hip. A third beam seared through another Firebird as if the starfighter were made of cardboard. The pilot ejected, screaming, feet severed.

For an instant, Leona stared in terror. She had seen laser weapons before, but none so deadly, none that could carve through graphene shields like katanas through silk.

*My Ra,* she thought, watching the lasers blasting from the enemy ships. *We underestimated them.*

She raised her eyes for just a split second. And she saw Sol in the distance.

*Calling us home.*

She stared at the enemy freighter ahead.

"Marines, charge at the *Snakepit!*" she cried. "No fear! Fire and fly! For Earth!"

She shoved the throttle on her jetpack, increasing it to full speed. She blasted forth. She yanked on the handles, zigzagging between the laser beams. A serpentine starfighter flew overhead, briefly revealing its exhaust. Leona fired, hit the exhaust pipe, and the scaly ship careened. She fired again and again, and her fellow marines joined her, until the starfighter exploded, scattering metal scales the size of dinner plates.

Ahead, Mairead's Firebird flew toward another enemy ship, shot over it, swerved, then unleashed its hellfire. As the scaled starfighter exploded, Mairead whooped and hopped inside her cockpit. The Firebug waved at Leona, stuck out her tongue, and flashed the devil horns.

Leona soared higher, dodging a coiling starfighter, then flew onward. She was only seconds away from the *Snakepit* now, a ship so large it was practically a space station.

The *Snakepit's* cannons pointed at her.

Fire roared out, spraying like volcanoes.

Leona screamed and swooped. Fire skimmed her back, and she howled. Above her, the flames torched several marines and a Firebird.

"Ramses!" she shouted into her comm. "Take out those cannons!"

Before she had even completed her sentence, the *Nazareth* opened fire. Its shells slammed into the ammunition ship, shattering a cannon. Mairead streamed forward in her Firebird, adding her missiles to the assault. The *Snakepit* listed, its hull breached, its guns gone. Air streamed out from a gaping hole, fueling the flames.

Damn it. Leona had wanted the ammunition ship whole. But this would have to do.

"Platoons Two, Three, Four—deploy!" she cried.

As more marines jumped from the *Nazareth*, Leona flew toward the jagged hole in the freighter. The remains of Lionclaw Platoon flew behind her.

Seared, melting metal framed the hull breach. Touching the rim could burn off her flesh, Leona knew. She narrowed her eyes, straightened her body into an arrow, and dived through the hole.

She hit the deck, rolled, sprung up, and opened fire.

Basilisks reared before her, shrieking.

At their full height, the serpents towered over Leona. In the Earthstone, Leona had seen images of giant snakes from Earth—the anacondas and pythons. These aliens looked similar, but they were not dumb animals. There was intelligence in their eyes, and forearms sprouted from their bodies, tipped with claws.

Leona peppered them with bullets.

Their scales cracked. Their blood sprayed. The creatures screeched. They lunged at her, jaws snapping.

Leona leaped aside, emptying a magazine into one of the aliens. More basilisks came swarming from chambers deep in the ammunition ship. More Inheritors dived in. The chamber was just large enough to fit them all. Soon blood and offal adorned the curving metal walls.

A basilisk emerged from a chamber above, slithering through a hole in the ceiling. This one seemed to belong to a warrior class; the huge serpent wore dark armor over his scales. When Leona fired her rifle, the bullets shattered against the iron plates. The basilisk pounced at her, and Leona sidestepped, dodging the snapping jaws.

Belatedly, she realized the basilisk wasn't trying to bite her. The serpent's head moved behind her, then snaked around her other side. The creature began wrapping around her.

Leona shouted and fired her gun, but her bullets kept ricocheting off the armor. One bullet flew back at Leona, hit her head, and cracked her helmet. She yowled. Her ears rang.

The basilisk completed another loop around her—then began to tighten.

Leona grimaced and tried to pull her legs out, but the serpent nearly crushed them. It made a third loop, now wrapping around her torso, pinning her arms to her sides. Only Leona's head emerged from the bundle. Around her, basilisks were coiling around other human soldiers.

"Human ..." hissed the basilisk constricting Leona. "We love humansss ... We've heard about you, yessss ... Delicious morselsss."

The basilisk tightened around Leona. She screamed—a hoarse, weak sound. The snake was crushing her, nearly snapping her ribs. She couldn't breathe.

Laughing, the basilisk raised one of his small arms. The arms were perhaps short, but the fingers were long and tipped with claws like daggers. The basilisk stroked Leona's cracked helmet.

"You are delectable." A forked tongue slipped between its fangs, then rose to lick the jaws. "I will enjoy devouring you. You will live for days inside me, screaming and wriggling deliciously as I slowly digest you."

Leona's arms were pinned to her sides, bones nearly snapping as the serpent tightened further. But she managed to extend her fingers, to grab the throttle of her jetpack.

She fired it up.

Flames burst out from the jetpack.

The basilisk screamed and uncoiled, freeing Leona. The beast reared, howling, jaws wide open.

"Digest this," Leona said, emptying a magazine of bullets into its open mouth.

Not her most eloquent quip, perhaps, but her bullets did the job nonetheless. The basilisk's head exploded, spraying scales, bits of skull, and clumps of brain. Its body thumped onto the floor, shaking the chamber.

Leona looked around her. Several humans and basilisks lay dead. Others still fought. But as the rest of the Inheritor company entered the ammunition ship, the tide turned, and humanity's bullets and blades tore down the serpents.

Leona gestured at a few soldiers, then pointed at three round doorways. "Guard those passageways."

She approached the shattered hull and peered out into space. She could see the *Nazareth* in the distance. The frigate had taken heavy punishment. The shields were cracked and smoldering, and fire crackled near the stern, where air was leaking out.

The Firebirds—the last few that remained—assumed a defensive formation.

Mairead's voice emerged from Leona's comm.

"All enemy starfighters destroyed, Commodore." The Firebug's voice turned somber. "But we lost some good friends."

"Keep patrolling around both the *Nazareth* and *Snakepit*," Leona said. "Don't return to the hangar yet. The basilisks might have called for reinforcements."

"How are things going in there, Leona?" said Ramses, hailing her from the *Nazareth*'s bridge.

"We're inside," Leona said. "We're gonna go exploring. Cover us in case more of those scaly starfighters show up."

Her platoon, the Lionclaw, had suffered heavy losses. Leona distributed the survivors among the three other platoons. One platoon had lost its lieutenant; Leona took command instead.

She pointed at the three passageways in the chamber.

"We split up three ways," Leona said. "Let's clear out this ship."

"Ma'am, this ship is the size of a mucking skyscraper," said Sergeant Fox. The burly marine's beard was splashed with basilisk blood.

She nodded. "So we better get to work."

For her own platoon, Leona chose the passageway in the ceiling—the one the armored basilisk had dropped through. Fox, who could probably deadlift a truck, lifted Leona toward the ceiling. She grabbed the hole's rim and climbed through. The rest of the platoon followed.

They found themselves in darkness. Leona lit a flare and tossed it forward. It hovered in midair, casting bright white light. Her eyes widened.

"Ra damn," she muttered.

They were in a chamber with rounded black walls. It was filled with explosives. Shells, missiles, grenades, mines—they covered row after row of metal shelves.

Fox whistled softly beside her. "Damn. Enough bombs in here to blow up a planet."

Leona nodded. "Nobody fire any bullets. I don't care what leaps at us." She got on the comm with the other two platoons. "Fellas, no more bullets."

"Great," Fox muttered. "How are we supposed to fight 'em? Sit 'em down and have a stern talk about their life choices?"

A lieutenant's voice emerged from Leona's comm. "You seeing this too, Commodore? Shelves of explosives?"

"Yeah," she said. "Keep searching the ship. I want this place cleared of basilisks."

"If we can't shoot, how do we kill?" Fox insisted.

Leona approached a shelf. It was topped with blades—beautiful ceremonial sabers. Apparently, the basilisks—or whoever their customers were—hadn't forgotten their preindustrial roots.

She lifted a saber and sliced the air. The handle was a bit too large for human hands, but it would do. When she pressed a button on the hilt, an electrical current raced across the blade, cracking and ionizing the air. Leona looked at her troops and gave them a crooked smile.

"Arm yourselves, ladies and gentlemen."

They all took swords, then walked between the shelves of weapons. Passageways led to more chambers; they too were filled with explosives. Room after room, shelf after shelf, bomb after bomb. Clearly, this was no simple freighter. It was a massive ammunition ship, the largest Leona had ever seen.

"This ship can arm an entire mucking army," Leona muttered. "And it was headed toward the war. We hijacked this ship so we can hide inside. But I think we just dealt the Hierarchy a serious blow. Or prevented a serious blow to the Concord, to be more accurate. If this shipment had fallen into the scorpions' claws, they—"

"Commodore!" Fox shouted.

Leona spun and saw it.

A basilisk leaped off a shelf, lunging toward her.

Leona stepped back and slashed her blade.

The electric sword slammed into the beast's head, denting a scale but not breaking through. The basilisk thrust forward, jaws snapping, fangs as long as her blade. Leona stepped back, parrying, knocking those teeth aside.

"More behind us!" Fox shouted, swinging his own sword at serpents.

Leona sneered, hopped back, then thrust her sword. She pierced the basilisk's eye, and the creature screeched. Leona twisted the blade, shoving it deeper, grunting with effort until the sword sank down to the hilt. When she pulled the blade back, the basilisk thumped onto the deck—only to reveal two more behind it. And these two wore heavy armor.

Leona groaned.

*You've got to be kidding me.*

With a sigh, she vaulted over the dead basilisk, then bounded forward, howling, blade flashing.

She stabbed a basilisk eye, then leaped aside. A massive snake's head slammed into her, knocking her into a shelf of explosives. Leona winced. Grenades fell around her, clattering against the floor.

She swung her blade again. It crackled with electricity. A basilisk pulled back, then snapped its teeth. A fang scraped Leona's arm, ripping through her spacesuit, and her blood dripped. The other basilisk began wrapping around her. Behind her, her soldiers were busy fighting the other beasts, cursing as they used blades instead of bullets.

*Ra damn it, I'm going to regret this,* Leona thought.

She grabbed a grenade.

As a basilisk opened its jaws above her, she shoved the grenade in, then grabbed the jaws and pulled them shut.

The basilisk swallowed.

The grenade exploded.

The beast's belly swelled, scales and armor cracking, and smoke puffed out.

Leona winced, for a second terrified the shrapnel would break through and bring down the whole ship.

But the snake thumped down dead, nothing but puffs of smoke escaping the corpse. Leona thrust her blade into another basilisk's jaws, then yanked back hard, slicing open the palate. As it screeched, she drove the sword deep into its brain.

Behind her, her soldiers took down the last of the serpents.

Leona exhaled in relief.

Sergeant Fox glared at her. Both human and alien blood splashed his armor.

"Commodore," said the burly marine, "that was incredibly stupid. A grenade? In a ship full of explosives?"

Leona nodded. "I know. I'm an idiot." She sighed. "But I figured if they're wearing armor, it should be safe. Well, somewhat less than dangerous. Okay, still incredibly dangerous, but maybe a breath shy of suicidal. Okay, suicidal, but it worked."

She smiled weakly. The sergeant only glared.

"If you weren't my commanding officer, I'd be chewing you out right now," Fox said. "You pull a trick like that again, and I'll do worse."

Leona nodded. "And you'd be right to."

Her comm buzzed. It was Ramses on the line, sounding anxious.

"Leona, the freighter is sending out a signal!" the captain said. "A Mayday call. You better shut that shit down!"

Leona cursed. "I'm on it."

Heart pounding, she ran.

## CHAPTER ELEVEN

Her jaw blazed with pain.

Demons seemed to be drilling into her gum.

Rowan had not imagined that a body part so small—just a few millimeters of gum—could hurt so much. But it did. The pain spun her head and clouded her thoughts.

"At least it was one of my crooked teeth, right, Fill?" she said, then winced. Even speaking hurt, and she tasted fresh blood.

Fillister stood on her shoulder. "Those beasts!" The tiny robot trembled with rage. "Sic me at 'em, Row. I'll rip 'em apart! I'll tear 'em to shreds! How dare they hurt you!" He buzzed around her head, then landed on her shoulder again and wrung his wings. "Awful, awful creatures! Oh Row. I'm so sorry. I failed to defend you."

Blood dripped down her chin. She tried to suck on the blood, but it felt like sucking up more pain from the gum. She winced.

"You can still defend me," she whispered. "Keep your voice low. And show me the code you recorded. The code to Jade's implants."

She sat in her prison cell, a round stone chamber beneath the imperial palace. The only light came from Fillister's luminous blue eyes. And even those were growing dim; he would need to recharge soon, and Rowan doubted the scorpions would provide any batteries. Rowan leaned against the craggy wall. She could barely even raise her arms, let alone stand up.

*With this gravity, it feels like a hippopotamus is sitting on me*, she thought. *A big one. After a heavy meal. And a sumo wrestler is riding him.*

Wearily, Rowan looked at the barred doorway sealing her in this cell. Between the bars, she could see a tunnel curving up toward the throne room. The scorpions were still up there, scurrying, clattering, screeching. Thankfully, they were too far to hear her and Fillister.

"They underestimate us," Rowan said. "They think I'm just a worm. That'll be their undoing. Do you have the code ready?"

Fillister nodded. "Sure do, Row. Encrypted and analyzed. Let me show you how I think it works. I need your help sorting out the last few bits."

He emitted a beam, projecting a screen full of code on the wall. The image was dim. Fillister was running low on power. Rowan would have to read quickly before the dragonfly went dark.

"See, I translated it into Monty," he said. "I know it's your favorite programming language. I gave all the functions meaningful names too. Let me run you through it."

He scrolled through several screens, showing her different algorithms, explaining how he thought they worked. Rowan nodded. The code seemed divided into two main parts: code to manage the cybernetic implants, and code to interface with Jade's biological brain. The latter was far more confusing. Most of that code—used to hijack Jade's neurons—seemed like gibberish to Rowan.

"The scorpions aren't genius programmers," she said. "A lot of this is crude, brute-force coding. Not as elegant as my own coding, if I may say so myself. What stumps me is the cybernetic machine-to-biology chunks. If I had more time, I could figure it out." She frowned. "Fill, can you show me the algorithms that activated when I spoke to Jade about her childhood?"

"Sure can, Row," he said. "Let me run it in debug mode. Follow the highlight. It'll show you what code ran and when." A highlight began to move across the code, line by line. "Here we're just scrolling through standard threads, and—there! See that function that just activated?"

She nodded. "Yeah, that's a big one."

"And it fired up seconds after you told Jade that she's your sister."

Rowan squinted, examining the code. "So this is it. An algorithm that attacks any forbidden information entering Jade's brain."

"Seems like it," Fillister said. "And guess what? The same algorithm fired up when the emperor talked about modifying you, turning you into a creature like Jade. This algorithm censors forbidden information, preventing it from entering Jade's brain."

Rowan's heartbeat quickened. Her fingers tingled. "Can you click open this module, Fill? Show me the subroutines on that function."

He expanded the function, and a new screen appeared on the wall, showing a long list of subroutines. Each subroutine had its own task. Some tapped into a database to categorize information as admissible or forbidden. Another subroutine awoke to censor forbidden information. Other functions seemed to release chemicals into Jade's brain—perhaps chemicals associated with anger and aggression.

"The implants don't only hide forbidden knowledge from Jade's brain," Rowan said. "They pump her full of crap. They make her aggressive, warlike, evil." Her eyes dampened. "She's not really evil, Fill. There's no natural evil inside her. It's just the implants pumping it into her. They're not just databases of code. They're filled with chemicals to control her actions."

"So it would seem," Fillister said. "It's a proper mess. But blimey, Row, the intricacies of this code are beyond me. I understand the basic ideas here, but the implementation is massively complex. See all these tens of thousands of lines of code here? This is the code that interfaces with her neurons. I can't make heads or tails out of it."

"Neither can I," Rowan confessed. "We'd need a neuroscientist for that. But we don't need to understand how these algorithms work on a low level. We just need to stop them from firing up. Our job is to create a hack that you can transmit wirelessly. Just a script that will crash the code."

"And that's where I need your help, Row," Fillister said. "I'm decent at understanding code. Piss poor at writing it. Hey, it's in me own code! Me programmers didn't want me modifying myself."

"Well, I can code," Rowan said. "I don't have a keyboard, but I'll dictate. Ready?"

The dragonfly nodded. "Ready."

His light kept fading. His battery was almost dead. Rowan's mouth hurt so badly she could barely speak. But she forced herself to keep dictating code, to tweak, test, correct the bugs. Normally she would need hours to code something like this. Today she had only moments.

Finally, it was Fillister who stopped her. "Row, I'm down to only 5% of me battery power. We almost done?"

Rowan cringed. "Yes. I was hoping to test the last function. But debugging this code can easily eat up three or four more percent of your power. We'll have to make do with what we've got. Not my best work, but hopefully good enough. You better shut down now. I'll wake you up when I'm ready. When Jade is here."

He shut down at once, not even saying goodbye. Rowan tucked him into her vest pocket, wishing she had another power source. Would her code work? A single bug would be enough to trip the whole thing. And Rowan always had bugs in the first drafts of her code. She winced. She would have to hope. She had done all she could for now.

She lay down on the floor, hoping for some sleep before dawn. But the pain in her jaw was excruciating, and she could barely breathe with this gravity. It was no use. She would get no sleep tonight.

From her pocket, she pulled out her old, rumpled photograph. The one she had been carrying around for years. She smoothed the plastic wrapper and gazed at the image.

The photograph showed Rowan with her family. They were back in the Glittering Cave, the place where they had hidden so many years ago. Father was there, a tall man with a mustache. Mother stood beside him, graceful and beautiful, always a little sad. Rowan was there, only two years old, a somber girl with short brown hair.

And Jade.

Jade was in that photo, standing by Rowan. She was so young, a girl with bright green eyes, with long blond hair. She held a toy sword in her hand, made from white crystal, perhaps a crystal taken from the cave. She looked happy.

*We were all happy then*, Rowan thought. Her tears splashed the photograph. She returned it to her pocket.

She closed her eyes, and she tried to imagine she was back home. Not on Earth. Earth was her birthright, yes, but not her home yet. Nor did she imagine Paradise Lost; she had spent most of her life in those ducts, but that had never been her home. She did not imagine the Glittering Caves; that place was only a faded dream by now, perhaps a nightmare. As Rowan lay in the cell, she imagined herself back on the ISS *Brooklyn*. Lying in Bay's bed.

Everything hurt. Her gum still bled. She was facing torture at dawn. But Rowan managed to smile—a shaky smile that tasted of blood and tears. She imagined Bay by her side, imagined them watching *The Lord of the Rings*, and his hand on her waist, and the comforting presence of Brooklyn flying them toward bright stars. She brought to mind his drawings on the bulkheads, the space warriors and dragons, and she imagined posing for him as he drew her, turning her into an actual hobbit on an adventure, maybe an adventure on *Dinosaur Island.*

"I miss you, Bay," she whispered. "I hope I can see you again."

And suddenly it was all too much—the war, the pain, the terror, the loss of so many. Rowan wept.

For a long time, she lay in a pool of misery.

Finally, when she could summon no more tears, she blinked and rubbed her eyes.

*Humanity is dying,* she thought. *My friends are far away, maybe dead too, and even Fillister is almost dead. I'm starving and bleeding and about to be tortured. But that's it. That's enough. No more tears. And no more feeling sorry for myself—no matter how bad things are. I might be the most miserable girl in the universe, but self-pity will make things worse. I must focus on my task. On the fight ahead. I will save Jade. I will escape this place. I will defeat the scorpions. And I will go home!*

She forced herself to sit upright, then paused for breath. Grimacing, she grabbed cracks in the wall and rose to her feet. Even on this huge planet, with the gravity tugging her, with her wrists handcuffed with heavy iron, she managed to stand straight and tall, to square her shoulders, to raise her chin.

"I am an Inheritor," she said. "And I am strong."

Dawn was breaking. Its faint light was illuminating the tunnel, even reaching Rowan's cell. As she stood, gazing at the light, she noticed a shadow moving down the tunnel. Rowan stiffened. Footfalls sounded outside, and the door creaked open.

Jade stood in the doorway, smiling crookedly. She wore an outfit of white webbings, daggers hung from her belt, and she had braided her long blue hair. The implants shone above her ear. Rowan stared at the glowing devices.

"Good morning, Rowan," Jade said. "Rise and shine! Are you ready to be broken before the cheering crowds? Are you ready to become my sister?"

Rowan was several inches shorter and far weaker, but she stood straight and stared into Jade's eyes.

"I will not become your sister in murder and death and slavery," Rowan said. "You are a slave, Jade. I came here to save you. To bring you home." She pulled Fillister out of her pocket and tossed him into the air. "Jade Emery! You are my sister. My true sister. You always were. You are human."

Fillister—down to his last drops of power—blasted out a beam of code.

Jade stared from Rowan to Fillister, green eyes wide. Her hair crackled and shone like fiber optic cables. Her fists clenched, and she bared her teeth.

"Liar!" She reached out, grabbed Rowan's throat, and squeezed. "You will pay for your lies. What is this trinket you smuggled here? How you will scream! I—"

But it was Jade who screamed.

The scream was so loud Rowan winced, thought her eardrums would tear.

The taller woman stumbled back, releasing Rowan, and fell to her knees.

Fillister buzzed around her, transmitting his code.

On Jade's head, the implants whirred, spinning faster than ever. They emitted blinding blue light, buzzing, moving so fast Rowan worried they would crack Jade's skull.

Jade screamed again, on her knees, clutching her head.

"It's working, Row!" Fillister said.

"I know it's working!" Rowan cried. "Keep doing it!"

Jade shoved herself up, reaching toward Rowan. Claws thrust out from her fingertips, gleaming.

"You pathetic little worm!" Jade screeched.

Rowan took a step back. "I love you, Jade." Tears filled her eyes, and her voice shook. "I love you, my sister. Remember the cave. Remember our parents. Remember that I love you."

Jade stared at her, and tears filled those mad green eyes. Fillister kept circling her, broadcasting the signal, growing dimmer but still flying.

"I ..." Jade trembled. Her implants spun madly, overheating, but then began to slow down. "I remember. A cave. Crystals. I ..." Her eyes widened, and she looked into Rowan's eyes. Her voice dropped to a whisper. "Rowan?"

Tears flowed down Rowan's cheeks. She took a step closer. "It's me, Jade. It's me. I came back to you."

Jade trembled. "I'm scared," she whispered. "I don't know what's happening."

Her implants went dark and fell still.

Sniffing, Rowan pulled her older sister into an embrace. "I'm here, Jade. I'm here to help you. To save you. I—"

"Row, I'm losing power!" Fillister said. "Down to 1% and ... shutting ... down ..."

The dragonfly clattered to the floor.

Rowan gasped and stared back into Jade's eyes.

"It's all right, Jade," Rowan whispered. "It's all right. You're healed now. You—"

Jade's implants began to hum again.

The madness returned to Jade's eyes.

She sneered and gripped Rowan, digging her claws into the flesh.

"You tricky worm!" Jade howled. "You thought you could deceive me! Liar! Pathetic pest!"

Jade shoved Rowan against the wall, then stomped down, crushing Fillister under her boot. Gears and chips and bulbs clattered across the floor.

Rowan wept.

Her strength vanished. She fell to her knees.

Trembling with fury, Jade grabbed her collar.

"You'll pay for this, pest." She yanked the leash. "Come, and I'll skin you myself! The galaxy will hear you scream!"

Jade marched out of the chamber, pulling the leash. Rowan dragged after her, scattering gears, microchips, and the shards of her last hope.

## CHAPTER TWELVE

Leona ran through the basilisk starship, heart pounding.

The Mayday call kept blaring, calling for every enemy warship around.

Damn it!

Her fellow soldiers ran with her. The freighter was the largest ship Leona had ever been on, labyrinthine and dark, filled with round doorways and cylindrical corridors, a place built for slithering snakes, not human feet.

"All troops, make for the bridge!" Leona said into her comm. "We got to silence that signal!"

"Where's the bridge?" asked Sergeant Fox, running behind her. The man was burly and powerful but a slower runner, and sweat dampened his thick dark beard.

"I don't know!" Leona shot down a leaping basilisk, and kept racing through the labyrinth. "Soldiers, spread out and find it!"

Eventually, it was Leona who found it first. It couldn't have taken her more than ten minutes, but it felt like an eternity. She raced into the control room, panting, covered in basilisk blood. Viewports towered across the bulkheads, gazing into space. Control panels and monitors hummed and buzzed and shone, displaying messages in alien letters.

A basilisk was waiting on the bridge, larger than the others, with three scaly heads.

All three heads turned toward Leona.

"You are too late, human," the alien hissed, speaking from all three mouths at once. "A thousand more basilisk ships are on their way. You will all die. You. Your clan. Your species. You cannot—"

Leona fired her rifle, shattering one of the three heads.

Blood showered. The two remaining heads screamed. The creature flailed. He tried to slither toward Leona, but more marines stepped onto the bridge. They raised their rifles, and the alien froze.

*There are no explosives on the bridge*, Leona thought. *And these bulkheads are thick steel. We can fill this place with fire if we must.*

"Cancel the Mayday call," Leona told the pilot.

The basilisk's scales clattered. Two heads glared at her. The third wilted, a ruin of blood and bone.

"You do not intimidate me, ape," he said. "You will beg for mercy as you are digested in—"

She shot the second head, pounding several bullets through it.

"Cancel the signal," she said, loading another magazine and aiming at the last head.

The mutilated basilisk hissed, venom in his eyes.

Leona shrugged. "Fine. Men?" She glanced over her shoulder. "Bring in the other basilisk. The one who agreed to take over the bridge. Let me just kill this one first."

The wounded basilisk screeched. "Wait. Wait!" He glowered, saliva dripping. "Very well."

Two of his heads gone, he slithered toward the control panel. He began to type.

"Tell your friends it was a false alarm," Leona said.

The basilisk kept typing, then turned toward her, hatred oozing from his eyes.

"Ramses?" Leona said into her comm.

The Pharaoh spoke from aboard the *Nazareth*. "The signal is gone, Commodore."

She nodded. "Good." She turned toward her soldiers. "Keep this one alive. Medic? Treat his wounds. We might need him again. He's the last basilisk we have."

"Trickery!" the basilisk screeched. "Lying, cheating human, I—"

When the soldiers aimed their rifles, the creature fell silent. The troops began chaining him up.

The ship was theirs.

With her adrenaline fading, Leona's knees began to shake, and her stomach churned. She took a deep breath, but her head spun, and she had to lean against a wall.

Men carved up in space. Men dying around her, crushed in basilisk embraces. Blood. Death. Fire and screams. Leona clenched her fists so tightly she cut her palms, and the old memories were rising, memories of her wedding day, and—

Her comm buzzed.

"Commodore?"

Leona started. She took a few more deeps breaths, calming herself.

*Stay in control, Leona. Be strong. You are their leader. Strength! Courage!*

Her comm kept ringing. She took the call.

"Talk to me."

"Lieutenant Legault here."

She nodded. She knew him, the commander of her third platoon. "Go on."

He cleared his throat. "I'm in the heart of the ammunition ship, standing in a hangar. Ma'am, you ... better come here. I'll ping you my location."

Leona frowned. "Snakes?"

"Not as such, ma'am."

She groaned. Whatever it was, she heard no screaming. That was good. She left a few warriors on the bridge to guard the mutilated pilot, then ran through the serpentine corridors of the freighter. Following Legault's ping, she eventually passed through a round doorway and stepped onto a mezzanine.

She lost her breath.

She was standing over a warehouse. The place was gargantuan, larger than the entire *Jerusalem*. And inside, arranged neatly on the floor ...

Leona's eyes widened. "Starfighters."

Instead of a ladder or staircase, a chute led down to the hangar. Snakes, of course, would use slides. As Leona slid down toward the warehouse, she couldn't help but laugh. Tears filled her eyes. Terror filled her belly. But still she laughed.

*If only you saw me now, Bay, trapped in a giant game of Snakes and Ladders. Just like we used to play.*

When she reached the floor, Leona walked between the starfighters. There were forty-three, cigar-shaped, all wrapped in plastic sheets. When Leona pulled back the wrappings, she revealed iron scales. The vessels looked like bloated snakes.

"New starfighters, factory fresh, heading to the front line," Leona said. "Well, they won't be killing humans now. Humans will fly them. Humans will fly them against the damn Hierarchy."

And suddenly Leona was shaking, and her eyes dampened. She had to turn aside, to face a wall, to hide her tears. She could not let her soldiers see her crying. She was the famous Commodore Leona Ben-Ari, the Iron Lioness, second-in-command of the Heirs of Earth. She could not reveal weakness. Yet humans had died out there in space, sliced apart with lasers. Humans had died here in the freighter, bones crushed like twigs. Millions of humans were burning across the galaxy. And for a moment, all Leona could do was cry.

Then she dried her tears. And she was ready to fight again.

And once more—her damn comm rang. Not a moment of peace.

"Leona?" Ramses's voice emerged from the damn contraption. "Reporting from the *Nazareth*. I'm detecting basilisk ships coming in. Three of them. Big ones. Warships."

Ra damn it! Had the basilisk pilot betrayed them?

"How long do we have?" Leona said.

"They'll be here in fifteen minutes," he said.

Leona grimaced. *Damn.*

"Ramses," she said, "we've got fifteen minutes to clear out the warehouse I'm in, hide the *Nazareth* inside, and convince our friends everything is kosher."

"Leona," Ramses said, "shouldn't we just abandon the *Nazareth*? We can all fly off in the *Snakepit*, leave our old ship behind."

"Too risky," Leona said. "If the enemy finds the *Nazareth*, they'll know we're here. Even if we blow it up, they'll find the debris. I'm standing in a giant hangar. The *Nazareth* will fit. We've got to hurry before those three warships arrive!"

Mairead joined the call. "I say we blast the bastards. Only three? We can take 'em."

"And those three will summon three hundred," Leona said. "The goal here is sneakiness, and we've already drawn too much attention to ourselves. Now come on! We got work to do."

Leona stared at the warehouse.

Yes, she could hide the *Nazareth* in here. But first, she had to move the starfighters. There were dozens of them, covering the floor, leaving no room for her frigate.

Somehow, Leona had to move the starfighters out of the way—within only a few minutes.

She saw two options. Behind her rose a huge doorway—an airlock, she surmised, one large enough to admit starships. She could try shoving these starfighters out into space, but a group of empty alien starfighters would look suspicious. Besides, Leona wanted to keep them for the wars ahead. That left stacking up the starfighters against the far wall, leaving room for the *Nazareth*.

She liked that second option.

"We need to move these starfighters," she said. "And fast!"

She raced toward one of the basilisk vessels. It was fresh off the assembly line, still wrapped in plastic. She tore the wrapping off, pulled the round door open, and crawled inside. It wasn't much larger than the chute Leona had slid down. There was only room in here to crawl. The starfighter was cylindrical, designed to allow a basilisk to lie flat, head in the cockpit, arms thrust forward to operate the controls.

Those controls looked discouragingly complicated.

"How the hell do I turn this thing on?" Leona muttered.

She must taxi it across the deck. But if she pressed the wrong button, she was likely to ignite its afterburner or release a missile, destroying the hangar. She could figure it out, she knew. But not without taking it apart first. Not within a few minutes.

She crawled out. "All right, moving these isn't going to work. Not until we find the user manual."

"Leona, we have only twelve minutes," Ramses said through the comm.

She cursed. She bit her lip. "All right, Pharaoh, we're opening the hangar doors. You'll have to land on top of some starfighters."

"You sure?" Ramses said. "Those sound like nice starfighters you got there. Would be a shame to squish 'em. Our pilots sure could use more starfighters. We lost too many of our own."

Leona frowned, chewing her lip. "We'll turn off the artificial gravity." She nodded. "Ramses, you copy? You'll float over the starfighters."

"You better turn it off quickly," he said.

Leona ran. She wriggled up the chute, raced through corridors, bounded across chambers, and cursed every second that passed. Finally she burst back onto the bridge.

The three-headed basilisk—well, he had only one head now—was chained and bandaged. He was still alive, thankfully—but barely. When he saw Leona, the creature whimpered. He pulled his last head away.

"All right, buster, you betrayed us." Leona aimed her rifle. "Three of your friends are flying over."

"I canceled the Mayday!" the basilisk said. "I swear, human. Do not shoot my last head! I beg you."

"Normally I'd love to hear you beg, but I'm in a rush," Leona said. "Get on those controls. Open the hangar doors. And shut down the artificial gravity."

"Shut down it down? But—" he began.

She fired a bullet over his head, hitting a bulkhead. "Do it!"

Three minutes.

The basilisk's long fingers flashed over the keyboards. On a monitor, Leona watched a video feed of the hangar. The airlock doors were slowly opening, revealing space. The *Nazareth* was already waiting outside.

Two minutes.

The frigate began rumbling into the hangar, thruster engines groaning, stabilizers blasting out gas from every side. Leona had perhaps overestimated the size of the hangar. Or underestimated the size of the *Nazareth*. She had been wrong—the frigate would be flying no loops inside the *Snakepit*. In fact, she barely fit.

"Ra damn," Mairead muttered, speaking through the comm. "Like squeezing into a virgin on her wedding night."

"Firebug, watch your tongue," Ramses said.

"You watch your flying!" Mairead said. "Careful, the—"

Standing on the *Snakepit*'s bridge, watching through the monitor, Leona winced. The *Nazareth* veered to the side and banged against a bulkhead. Both starships shook.

Thirty seconds left.

"Gravity off!" Leona said, jabbing her muzzle against the basilisk's last head.

The alien pressed a few buttons, and they all began to float. Including, Leona saw in the monitor, the starfighters in the hangar. The *Nazareth* kept squeezing in, hitting the floating starfighters, knocking them back.

Ten seconds.

"Close the hangar door—now!" she shouted at the basilisk.

He hissed at her.

She shoved the muzzle into his jaws.

"Now, or by Ra, your brains hit the bulkhead!"

Glaring at her, the basilisk hit a button. With mere seconds to go, the hangar doors thudded shut, hiding the *Nazareth* inside.

And through the viewport, Leona saw them emerge from warped space.

Three basilisk warships.

Leona turned toward the captive basilisk. "All right, buddy, I imagine that you're homesick. I don't need you forever. You do your job, I'll release you when this is done, and you can return to your family, friends, or whatever small animals you enjoy tormenting. But right now, I need you to tell those three warships that everything here is fine and dandy. I'll be standing behind you. If you make a wrong move, you know the drill—brains on bulkhead."

The creature hissed. "How do I explain my missing two heads?" Bitterness dripped from his voice.

"Shaving accident," Leona said. She smacked the creature's last head. "You don't, idiot! You do an audio call only. Tell them the video is busted." She pointed at a flashing monitor. "Looks like they're already calling. Oh, and my soldiers here understand your language, and they'll know what you're hissing. So no funny business."

She stood behind the creature, gun to his head. She had lied, of course. Nobody in her crew spoke Basilisk. She wasn't even sure how the damn things spoke Common Human. Were they simply scholars of language, able to speak tongues from across the galaxy? Or ...

*They've met humans before,* she thought. *My Ra.*

Her head spun. Her chest shook.

*We're not the first humans to have come this far. We—*

The basilisk started hissing into his communicator, speaking to the three warships outside. Leona pushed thoughts of language aside. The implications were enormous, but she'd have to consider them another time.

She peered out the viewport. From this distance, without a video feed, the enemy wouldn't be able to see her. The basilisk warships were shaped like giant cobras, coated with scales, their cannons thrusting out like fangs.

*A warship like this destroyed one of my warships,* she thought. *And there are thousands of them in this corner of space. Surrounding Earth.*

For long, tense moments they waited. The basilisks hissed.

Then finally the three warships turned and flew away.

Leona exhaled with relief.

"Now fly," she told the basilisk pilot. "Fly this ship. You're taking us to Earth."

There were still light-years to go. Even at warp speed, the journey would still take days, maybe weeks, maybe even months if the *Snakepit* was slow. But Leona could see Sol outside. She was hidden inside an enemy ship. She had enough weapons for an army. And perhaps most importantly—the basilisks could speak Common Human.

*There are more humans out there,* she thought. *Others who've come before us.*

Her head spun. Were those other humans dead? Was this a good sign or a bad one? She did not know. She could not think. Her mind was filled with blood and screams. She handed over command to Ramses, then went into the *Nazareth*, lay down, and slept for ten hours straight.

## CHAPTER THIRTEEN

The *Mother's Mercy* was a small striker, no larger than a human corvette. In some ways, she looked like a typical scorpion warship—triangular, black, and cruel. But gold trimmed her edges, denoting her status, and a blazing red stinger was engraved onto her hull, painted with real human blood. This was a ship of royalty.

Rowan lay inside the rocky hold, for the scorpions filled their starships with sand and boulders from their homeworld. A matching stinger, similar to the one on the hull, was branded into her arm. She shivered, chained, waiting for her torture.

Jade stood at the controls, manipulating levers and pulleys, flying the striker. She wore a rich cloak of human leather, and golden vambraces shone upon her forearms. She looked over her shoulder at Rowan.

"Cheer up!" she said. "We're almost there, pest. Soon you'll be like me. Look outside. Behold the Temple of Ishara!"

Rowan peered out the porthole, blinking in the sunlight. They were flying over the wastelands of Ur Akad. Canyons and monoliths carved up the land. The scorpions didn't build many structures aboveground, but ahead, Rowan saw a ziggurat rising from the desert. It was a trapezoid, as large as a mountain, built from bricks the size of this striker. Millions of scorpions were gathering around it and crawling up its craggy slopes. The binary suns of this world shone down, painting one side of the ziggurat white as bone, the other red as blood.

Jade pulled the controls. The *Mother's Mercy* veered down toward the ziggurat so fast Rowan gagged and her ears popped.

They slowed down, hovered above the ziggurat's flat top, then thumped down with a cloud of dust.

"Come, pest." Jade shut off the engine and grabbed Rowan's collar. "We begin."

Jade opened the airlock and stepped outside onto the rooftop. Rowan crawled after her, emerging into the blinding sunlight and heat.

She blinked in the light. Hot wind blew sand in her face, and she coughed. Her gum and jaw still throbbed from when Sin Kra had torn out her tooth. Her knees and elbows were scabbed over. Worse were the thirst and hunger. Back in her prison cell, the scorpions had given her a foul brew, a slop of crushed insects fermented in blood. Rowan had vomited on the sticky gruel.

Jade tugged the leash. Rowan wanted to stand, to walk with dignity, but the gravity was too strong, and her thin limbs were too weak. She crawled over the craggy stones, leaving a trail of blood. The brand on her arm, shaped like a stinger, still blazed with pain. Every movement felt like the brand burning Rowan anew.

Scorpions chanted around her. Millions of them. Jade was leading her across the flat top of a ziggurat, a structure of boulders and sand and mortar that soared over the desert, an edifice that would dwarf the fabled pyramids of ancient Earth.

Rowan crawled into a shadow. A bronze statue rose ahead, larger than a warship. It was shaped as a rearing scorpion, its limbs spread out like Vishnu's arms. Human spines dangled from the metal arms like broken chains. The statue's head was disturbingly humanoid, the cadaverous head of a starving woman. A bandoleer of severed heads, these clearly human, hung across the goddess's chest. She had eight breasts, heavy and spiderwebbed with cracks. Below them, the statue's belly swelled, showing the vague outline of eggs. Killer. Mother. Tormentor of humanity. Crawling beneath this statue, Rowan felt like a worm gazing upon a queen.

Jade admired the statue, eyes shining. "Behold the goddess Ishara, giver of life to scorpions, bringer of death to humans! This is her temple. Bow! Bow before her!"

She placed a boot on Rowan's back and shoved her down, forcing her to lie prostrate before the bronze idol.

*Their entire religion is centered around killing us,* Rowan thought. *Their faith, their society, the only meaning of their life—to slaughter humans. They have no art other than this statue, raised to celebrate human death. No architecture other than these crude temples and palaces, built to worship our destruction. No songs or stories or meaning to their existence. Their only purpose, their only reason to live—to murder us.*

Across the desert city, scorpions kept emerging from their holes, climbing their knobby hives, filling the canyons, and covering the plains. They all gazed toward the temple, hissing and screeching. The workers lurked in the canyons, their shells the color of sand. The warrior class, burly and black, covered the mesas that jutted up like skyscrapers. Females gathered on rocky plains, shells golden, some painted with decorative patterns, many carrying larvae on their backs.

Scorpions covered the sloping facades of the temple too. Here was the nobility. These scorpions adorned their exoskeletons with iron, copper, and platinum. Strings of gilded human bones jangled around their necks, lurid jewelry. Many of the noble scorpions were larger than the commoners—perhaps better fed, perhaps genetically modified.

The scorpions did not modify their environment as much as other species. Judging simply by their crude hives, they barely seemed sentient. But there were signs of their intelligence. Chimney vents rose across the desert, pumping out smog, hinting at underground industry. Some scorpions had prosthetic, mechanized limbs. One elder, large and cracked, rode in a motorized chariot trimmed with precious metals. The sky, especially, showcased their technology. Many of their warships hovered above, belching puffs of smoke, casting thousands of triangular shadows across the desert. Countless more strikers were flying across the galaxy now, conquering world after world, hunting human after human.

*Maybe that's why they're great,* Rowan thought. *Long ago, we humans polluted and destroyed our planet. By the time the Hydrians arrived, we were weak, suffocating in our own smog. The Skra-Shen did not repeat our mistake.*

Jade marched toward the edge of the temple's roof, tugging the leash. Rowan crawled after her. The desert sprawled ahead, rolling toward a distant yellow haze. Mountains soared on the horizon, and canyons delved deep into the ground. Millions of the scorpions spread across the landscape, maybe billions, all come to see the famous Rowan Emery. The human from the Heirs of Earth. The one who had fought them, killed them. The one who would now become their greatest killer.

A stone platform thrust out from the roof like a plank. Jade dragged Rowan along it toward the edge, where they stood a kilometer above the desert. Wind shrieked, hot and sandy. The suns blazed directly overhead. As Rowan glanced upward, wincing, she saw the small white sun crawl closer toward the red sun. They were about to align.

Two metal poles framed the edge of the stone jetty. Jade grabbed Rowan by the hair, yanked her up, and chained her wrists and ankles to the poles. Rowan stood, spread-eagled, chained. She rested her chin on her chest, too weak to raise her head. If not for the chains holding her up, she would have collapsed.

"Jade," she managed to whisper, and her gum opened again, dripping blood. "You don't have to do this."

Drones hovered up toward the platform, oval and dark like floating eggs. Cameras pointed at Rowan. Images of herself—

chained and bleeding between the poles—appeared on cliffs and mountainsides across the landscape, hundreds of meters tall. The crowd of scorpions cheered.

"Jade, please," Rowan whispered, and the scorpions cackled.

A scraping and clattering sounded. A deep breath hissed. Rowan frowned, managed to raise her head, and looked around. But she saw nobody. The scraping and huffing continued, closer now, and a foul stench like urine and rot filled her nostrils. A shadow stirred below. Rowan let her chin drop back to her chest. She stared down and her eyes widened.

He was crawling *under* the stone pier. Rowan could see his claws grabbing the edges. A scorpion. A huge scorpion, his claws red. He crept directly below Rowan, then emerged over the edge of the platform. The beast rose before her, grinning, his saliva dripping and sizzling on the stone.

Sin Kra. Emperor of the Skra-Shen.

He was even larger than Rowan remembered, and his exoskeleton was a brighter red streaked with black. He must have shed his old shell, emerging stronger than before.

*He's bigger than goddamn Jaws and twice as mean*, Rowan thought. *Where is Ellen Ripley when you need her?*

She barked a laugh, her eyes damp. Humor. She recognized the absurdity of it. Right now, with so much terror and pain, perhaps only humor could keep her sane.

"Hello, Rowan," Sin Kra hissed. He clung to the ledge, claws digging into the stone. He lowered his huge head, bringing himself to eye level with her. "Shall we begin?"

His fangs gleamed, as long as Rowan's arms. His claws tightened. Rowan winced but refused to look away. She stared into this creature's eyes.

*Be brave. Be strong. Show him no fear. No weakness. He wants me to be afraid and weak. But I am brave.*

"Go to hell," Rowan said.

The scorpion's toothy jaws widened in a grin. "Oh, my dear ... we're already there."

The emperor held a bundle of human skin. He placed it down before Rowan. He unrolled the pack, exposing tools: scalpels, blades, cables, and electronic implants similar to those in Jade's skull. Jade unrolled her own leather bundle, revealed jars of gleaming white paste.

"Your new skin," Jade explained, smirking at Rowan. "It will be hard and white and pure like mine. Your old skin will adorn my new throne."

Sin Kra raised a hooked tool.

A flaying blade, Rowan realized. She began to pant in panic.

"So, um ... just a little trim off the nose please," Rowan said, feeling faint. "Maybe bigger boobs too? Put it on my Mastercard. I need the points."

The emperor trailed the blade down Rowan's skin, applying the faintest pressure—enough to make her cringe, not enough yet to cut the skin.

"Where shall we begin?" Sin Kra said. "With your limbs?" He traced the blade across her arm. "Perhaps your face?" He brought the point to her cheek. "I think perhaps your torso." He lowered the blade to rest between her collar bones. "Yes, a nice incision, slow and meticulous. You will bloom open for me, as beautiful as a desert rose."

Rowan turned her head away from the spiky red scorpion, the creature that had murdered her parents. She looked at Jade.

"Sister, you might want to look in my pocket," Rowan said.

Jade struck her. Hard. She loosened another tooth, and Rowan tasted more blood.

"Silence, pest!" She grabbed a blade. "I will skin you myself."

Jade thrust the blade. It pierced the skin between Rowan's ribs.

Rowan refused to scream, to shake. A calmness came over her. Here before the crowd, about to be transformed, facing the greatest darkness in her life, a strange calmness fell upon Rowan, a numb haze.

"I have another robotic dragonfly in my pocket," Rowan said. "I'm about to activate it and hack into your implants again. Remember how much it hurt last time? I warn you—release me! Release me now, or I will activate my code again."

Jade scoffed. "You fool. You are chained here! You cannot threaten me." She reached into Rowan's pocket. "What's this? A piece of paper?" She scoffed. "What is this trickery?"

Jade unfolded the paper—the photograph Rowan had kept all these years.

They both stared at it. The drones zoomed in, broadcasting the photograph across the cliffs and mountainsides, large enough for the millions of scorpions to see.

A photo from fifteen years ago.

A photo of the Emery family in the Glittering Caves. Their father, thin and mustached and solemn. Their mother, willowy and beautiful and sad. Young Rowan, a toddler with large brown eyes and short brown hair. And with them—Jade, a precious child with long golden hair and green eyes, holding the crystal sword Father had given her.

"It's us," Rowan said. "It's you, Jade. Fifteen years ago. It's you."

Jade clutched the photo with both hands, staring, silent, transfixed.

"What is this?" Jade whispered.

Her implants began to whir again. Rowan knew she had only seconds before the scorpion algorithms took over.

"You remember it," Rowan said. "I know you do. Very soon, the implants in your head are going to block the memory. I tried to hack into your implants, to stop them. But I can't. You have to stop them yourself, Jade. You have to believe me. The scorpions around us? They're your enemies. You were like me once. Human. They stood you here, and tortured you, and turned you into what you are. Like they want to do to me. For a long time, I thought that I could save you. But you have to save yourself, Jade. You have to believe me. And to fight them."

The emperor leaned closer. He snatched the photo away from Rowan and tossed it aside.

"Do not listen to her, Jade," Sin Kra said. "Continue your work."

The implants spun and shone.

Jade's eyes hardened.

But the drones were still displaying the photo across the cliffs and mountainsides. The scorpions below were hissing and muttering amongst themselves. They pointed claws at Jade.

Rowan wasn't fluent in their language, but she understood enough. The scorpions were pointing at Jade and saying: "Human! Human!"

The emperor sneered, head turning from side to side. He turned toward Jade. He began hissing and clattering in the language of scorpions, speaking too quickly for Rowan to understand.

Jade stared at the emperor, comprehending the strange sounds. She had grown up speaking this harsh tongue.

"But I can remember," Jade whispered to the emperor. "The photograph she showed me." A tear flowed down her cheek. "I remember that day."

The emperor hissed and clacked and grunted.

Jade trembled. Her implants whirred so fast they threatened to detach. Her voice rose to a hoarse shout. "Was I human once? Did you bind me here, flay me, change me like you want to change Rowan? Like—"

The emperor raised a claw, and a mechanical ring shone around it.

Jade screamed.

Her implants crackled.

She fell to her knees, clutching her temples, grimacing in pain.

"Fight him, Jade!" Rowan cried. "I've seen the code in your implants. It's controlling your brain, but you can fight! You have to be strong. You can fight it yourself!"

Jade tossed her head back, howling in agony, eyes screwed shut. The implants shone so brightly the glow engulfed her head.

Sin Kra loomed above the sisters, laughing. Gears turned on his ring—perhaps controlling the implants in Jade's head.

"It's too late for her, Rowan." The scorpion leaned down, lifted a fresh implant, and raised it toward Rowan's skull. "And soon it will be too late for you. You will be like her!"

Rowan winced and turned her head aside. Sin Kra grabbed her skull and yanked her head closer. The implant he held was long and sharp like an ice pick. It could easily crack her skull. The emperor placed the tip against Rowan's head, then prepared to drive it into her brain.

"No!" Jade screamed.

Howling, she leaped forward.

Rowan gasped.

Jade barreled into Sin Kra, knocking the giant scorpion off the stone platform.

Sin Kra tumbled down, roaring, legs kicking.

The implants buzzed with electricity, shooting sparks, and Jade screamed. She grabbed an implant with her clawed fingers and yanked. It came out, its tip bloody, its cables flailing.

The emperor was still screaming, still falling down toward the desert.

Jade ripped out a second implant.

Scorpions below howled.

Jade tore out the third implant, then fell to her knees, gasping, weeping. Three small holes were bleeding on her head.

Far below, the emperor landed on the crowd of scorpions. He thrashed, roaring. Still alive. Still alive!

"Jade!" Rowan shouted. "He's still alive!"

Breathing raggedly, Jade struggled to her feet. She swayed, bleeding heavily from her head. Pain washed her eyes—but no more madness.

She pulled a key from her belt and unlocked Rowan's shackles, freeing her from the metal poles. Rowan collapsed into her arms. For a moment, the sisters held each other, embracing and crying.

A clattering din, loud as a hailstorm, shook the temple.

The sisters stared around them.

The scorpions—countless of them—were racing up the ziggurat toward the two humans.

Jade grabbed Rowan's hand.

"Come on, little sister!" she said. "To the striker!"

They ran along the stone pier, heading toward the *Mother's Mercy*. The striker was standing on the rooftop nearby, engines cold. When Rowan fell, Jade lifted her and kept running. She raced across the ziggurat, carrying Rowan. All around, the scorpions were clattering up the walls, pouring onto the roof.

A scorpion lunged at them.

Jade roared and lashed her claws. The scorpion fell, head cracked open.

Another scorpion attacked, spraying venom. Jade dodged the spray, jumped, swung her claws, and ripped off the scorpion's stinger. She landed behind the wailing arachnid and kept running.

More and more of the beasts pounced from every side.

"There are too many!" Rowan shouted.

Jade narrowed her eyes. "Hold on tight, sister."

Head still bleeding, holding Rowan in her arms, Jade snarled and leaped into the air.

She howled—a sound of pure fury, of unadulterated rage and agony and grief. The sisters soared through the air, the sandy wind flapping their hair. Below them, hundreds of scorpions shrieked.

"For Earth!" Jade cried, flying toward the statue of the goddess.

She plowed into the massive bronze idol with both feet.

Still holding Rowan tight, Jade fell back and hit the rooftop.

The towering statue of Ishara, this deformed scorpion goddess, tilted over, then fell.

The ziggurat shook.

The tower crushed scorpions, then rolled across the roof, plowing through more arachnids. The bronze goddess reached the roof's edge, swayed, then began to roll down the ziggurat's sloping wall, steamrolling over hundreds of scorpions. Finally, at the desert plain below, the statue shattered into a thousand pieces.

Jade stared for a moment, tears in her eyes, then turned away.

She ran.

The sisters reached the *Mother's Mercy*, and Jade dived into the airlock. Several scorpions, beasts who had survived the falling statue, pounced toward the striker. Rowan yanked the door shut, slamming it into several scorpion legs, severing the limbs.

"Rowan, operate the cannons while I fly!" Jade shouted, racing toward the controls. "Black lever aims, red pulley fires!"

Rowan nodded. She managed to rise despite the heavy gravity and trudge toward the bridge.

"Got it!" she said, manning the gunnery station. "I used to be the *Jerusalem*'s gunner. I've also played about ten thousand hours of *Space Invaders*. I got this."

Jade grabbed the helm controls and the striker's engines roared.

Scorpions lunged onto the striker, slamming into the hull, clawing at the metal.

The *Mother's Mercy* soared with a cloud of smoke and flame, blasting up so fast Rowan nearly blacked out.

The gravity was already immense here, and now extra G forces pressed down on her. Rowan gasped for air, finding none. It felt as if planets were crushing her, about to snap her bones. She was losing consciousness. She was vaguely aware of strikers swooping from above.

"Rowan, fire!" somebody shouted in the distance, voice muffled, and Rowan gagged, was blind, was fainting, but she yanked the pulley.

Plasma roared out as she trembled, sputtered for air, and gagged.

Metal twisted.

Explosions rocked the sky.

*Stay awake!*

Jade was shouting and Rowan fired again, and plasma bolts slammed into strikers above, and then Jade swerved madly, dodging an assault, and it was too much.

Rowan's consciousness slipped away.

She fell into a deep, dark hole.

The weight of the cosmos crushed her, then vanished, and she floated through nothingness.

CHAPTER FOURTEEN

She crawled through the ducts of Paradise Lost, desperate to escape the beasts pursuing her.

They filled this labyrinth of metal. Creatures in the shadows. Clattering, hissing, staring, calling to her. Beasts with many segments of bone. Elongated spines with heads like human skulls.

"Rowan ..."

They reached toward her with hooked blades, ready to flay her, and she bloomed like a flower.

She crawled, trying to find a way out. She could not rise. The ducts closed in, and the gravity crushed her, and then the ducts tore open, and she crashed down, and a furnace gaped open like jaws of fire.

"Rowan."

A claw touched her cheek.

Her eyes snapped open.

She lay in *Mother's Mercy*, the striker she had fled Ur Akad in. Jade knelt above her, stroking her cheek.

"Rowan, are you all right?" Jade whispered. Her head was bandaged, her eyes damp and red.

Rowan leaped to her feet so fast her head spun. She was still weak, starving, but thankfully the gravity seemed more bearable. She darted toward a porthole, looked outside into empty space, then spun back toward Jade.

Her mind raced. *We fled the scorpions' planet. Jade's implants are gone. I saw no strikers pursuing us. I'm wounded. Jade's implants are gone! Is she still evil? Will she attack me? How far away are the scorpions?*

Jade took a step closer.

Rowan retreated. She pushed herself against the bulkhead, her hands curling into fists.

Jade winced.

"Rowan," she whispered, and tears gathered in her eyes. "I'm sorry. I'm sorry."

Then Jade fell to her knees, shaking and weeping.

Rowan stood for a moment, biting her lip, wanting to embrace her sister. Instead she ran to the striker's cockpit. She looked out the viewport and saw smudged streaks of starlight. They were flying at warp speed. The control panel flashed and chirped, but Rowan could make no sense of the alien instruments.

She looked through the viewport again.

Stars.

Nothing but stars.

Rowan allowed herself a deep, shaky breath.

For the moment, she was safe. She was alive. She was still human. And her sister was sane again.

*Bloody hell*, Rowan thought. *I spent fourteen years stuck in a duct, and now the universe is changing so fast my head spins.*

She ran back into the hold and knelt by Jade. Her sister was still on her knees, head lowered, weeping.

"Jade." Rowan grabbed her arms. "Are the scorpions still chasing us? How long was I out?"

Jade raised her wet green eyes. Human eyes. Finally— human eyes.

"We're a hundred light-years ahead of them," Jade said. "I flew us through a wormhole, then nuked the portal. It'll take them weeks to catch up." She clenched her fists. "And when they catch up, I will fight them. I will kill them." She trembled. "For what they did to me. To you. What they made me do. Rowan, the things they made me do ... I'm sorry. I'm so sorry."

Her tears flowed. Jade collapsed, sobbing.

Rowan wept too, and she pulled her older sister into her arms.

"It'll be all right now," Rowan whispered, stroking Jade's synthetic blue hair. "Whatever they made you do—it wasn't you. It wasn't you."

Jade looked up, shaking with sobs. "I love you, Rowan. I'm so sorry. I love you so much."

"I love you too," Rowan whispered.

The sisters embraced tightly, crying together, never wanting to let go.

Finally, after long moments, Jade spoke again, voice soft and shaky.

"What do we do now, Rowan? I don't know what to do. How to be human. I don't know where to go."

Rowan held her firmly and stared into her eyes. "We're going to the Heirs of Earth. And together, we're going to defeat the scorpions."

## CHAPTER FIFTEEN

Bay flew toward the front line—a single man in a single shuttlecraft.

*I'm one man against a galaxy,* he thought. *But for you, Rowan, I will do this. I will fight empires. I will die if I must. I won't abandon you.*

He looked at the artwork he had pinned to the dashboard—a drawing he had made of Rowan.

*The day you posed for me, when I drew you—that was the best day of my life,* Bay thought.

He imagined the scorpions binding her, torturing her. His throat tightened. His hands began to shake, his belly to churn. He forced himself to take deep breaths, to clear his mind. Panic would not help now.

"Everyone else abandoned you, Rowan," he said to the drawing. "But not me. You're not alone."

Brooklyn sniffed. "This is terribly romantic."

"Stop sniffing!" Bay said, shifting uncomfortably. "You don't have a nose."

"But I do have a heart!" she said. "Well, actually, I have no heart either." She cackled evilly. "I'm heartless! But that's beside the point. I think what you're doing is terribly romantic."

"Brook, there's a galactic war going on," Bay said. "Billions, maybe trillions of sentient lifeforms are dying. Humanity is dying. The entire galaxy is dying. And you're worried about romance?"

"Well, so are you," Brooklyn said. "That's why you're flying to save Rowan, isn't it? Because you love her?"

"I don't love her!" Bay said. "I've only known her for a year or two."

"That's not long enough? Bay, within moments of eating your first MLT sandwich—mutton, lettuce, and tomato—you proclaimed that you were madly in love with it."

He bristled. "That's different. First of all, that was a movie reference Rowan taught me. Second, Rowan isn't a sandwich!"

Brooklyn scoffed. "Who knows with you biological things? Sandwiches, humans, you're all the same to me." Her voice grew serious. "Bay, we're only an hour away from the front line now. Maybe closer. It's moving toward us all the time. Are you sure we should do this?"

"No," Bay confessed. "But we will anyway."

"Bay! Listen to me. I have a backup of my software on the *Jerusalem*. If I'm destroyed out here, your dad can install me into a new starship. But you're organic. If the scorpions kill you, you can't come back. And I'm scared, Bay. I'm scared that they'll kill you."

"I'm scared too," Bay said. "And I know it's dangerous and foolhardy. But I keep thinking about how scared Rowan must be, how alone she must feel. If I fly back now, I couldn't live with myself. I would live in constant anxiety and guilt. So you understand, Brooklyn. I have no choice. I'd rather die trying to save her than live without her."

Brooklyn sighed, vents rattling. "I understand. Damn it, sometimes I wish you hadn't installed emotions into me. Sometimes I wish I could be a mindless starship like the *Jerusalem*. It's so hard to be scared, worried, anxious. To grieve when people die. It's better not to have emotions."

"But then we wouldn't have joy," Bay said. "And love. And all the other good emotions. Someday we'll be happy again. Maybe not you and me. But others will. If we can defeat the Hierarchy, if we can reach Earth—maybe it'll all be worth it. And hey, maybe we won't die today. Maybe we'll make it. Maybe we'll win. We'll live on Earth, find a nice beach somewhere. Leona will have the sailboat she always dreamed of, and Rowan and I can live in a cottage by the shore."

"And what about me?" Brooklyn said.

"I'll finally buy you that android body you've been asking for," Bay said. "You'll live with us." His voice was suddenly hoarse, and his eyes stung. "We'll be a family. We'll be happy."

"I'd like that," Brooklyn said. "Something to hope for."

"To look forward to," Bay said. "That sounds better somehow than hope. More optimistic."

"Bay." Brooklyn's voice was tense. "Ahead. The front line. Do you see it?"

He stared. At first he saw nothing. Then he made out a faint shimmer like a cloud of dust.

"It looks like a nebula," he said.

"It's a battle." Brooklyn shuddered. "A battle between a million starships. My scanners are detecting at least a hundred species fighting here, divided into Concord and Hierarchy camps. And the Hierarchy is winning. Every instant, I'm scanning fewer Concord ships."

"Can we fly around the battle?" Bay said. "Last time, Coral made us fly through the battle, and I damn near had a heart attack."

"Thankfully, Coral isn't here now," Brooklyn said. "So yeah. We're gonna give this battle a *wide* berth."

She began to fly higher, to rise over the battle. Bay sat stiffly, leaning forward, examining the stats on the monitor. He pulled up a graphic display of every starship in the area. Brooklyn appeared as a tiny speck of light flying over a cluster of swirling dots. The battle kept changing shape like a swarm of bees—one moment elongated, the next a compact sphere, then expanding into a wide blob, then spreading out in thin sheets, always shifting, rising, sinking. The battle was most dense in its center, but it cast out tendrils of violence. It looked to Bay like a galaxy, the starships performing a dance in the darkness.

"Brook, what's this?" He tapped the monitor. "There's a group of strikers breaking through. They're flying toward us."

He stared out the viewport, but the ships were still too far to see with the naked eye. He looked back down at the monitor. A handful of strikers were still charging right at them.

"Damn it!" Brooklyn said. "They saw us. But there's only a few."

"Think we can take 'em?" Bay said.

"No, but when has that ever stopped us?"

Bay grabbed the helm. "Better let me fly, Brook. You're good at navigation. But we might have a good ole' fashioned dogfight on our hands, and that's my forte."

"Dogfight on your *hand*," Brooklyn said. "Singular."

He flipped her off, using his one good hand. "Muck you."

He placed that good hand on his joystick. He placed his left hand, the one that couldn't uncurl its fingers, into the leather harness he had built around the throttle. He flew, trying to dodge the strikers ahead. But they adjusted course, aiming at him.

One of the strikers hailed him.

Bay frowned. "What the hell? They're calling us."

He yanked the joystick and leaned into the throttle. He tried to rise higher, to fly over the strikers. He was moving farther and farther from the battle, but the strikers ahead—he counted five—kept pursuing. And they were faster than Brooklyn.

He flipped a switch on the joystick, igniting the afterburner. Brooklyn groaned with pain. Bay knew she hated using her afterburner, but right now, he needed the extra boost of speed. The engine rumbled and fire blazed out from the exhaust, blue and white.

The strikers adjusted their trajectory, moving up to meet him.

Bay winced. He could see them now with the naked eye.

"Five strikers." He frowned. "One at the lead, and four …" His eyes widened. "Bloody hell, Brook. The nutters are fighting one another."

Brooklyn tilted her camera. "Are you being British? Dude, do you become British when you're shocked?" Her camera shutters narrowed. "Have you been speaking to Fillister?"

Bay ignored her. He rubbed his eyes and looked again. One striker was fleeing four. Plasma blazed from the pursuers, slamming into their prey.

The fleeing striker was the one signaling them.

"Is it defecting?" Bay said.

"It looks operational to me," said Brooklyn.

"*Defecting*, not defective."

"Eww," Brooklyn said.

"I said *defecting*, not—" Bay groaned and rolled his eyes. "That means it's leaving the Hierarchy. Going AWOL. You know, like we're always doing."

The strikers were only moments away now. More fire hit the fleeing vessel. It tilted, hull denting, and one of its engines burst into flame. The four other strikers pursued relentlessly. And still the fleeing warship was signaling Brooklyn, trying to reach them.

Frowning, Bay answered the call.

His video monitor turned on, displaying an image of the striker's bridge.

Rowan sat there.

Bay stared, shocked into silence.

Rowan.

It was Rowan.

Daniel Arenson

She was thinner than before, her cheeks gaunt, her eyes sunken. Her uniform was tattered and sandy.

But it was her.

Bay's mouth hung open.

"Bay!" she cried.

Finally he found his voice. "Rowan!"

A blast hit her striker. The image jolted. Rowan grimaced. "Bay, a little help?" she said.

Shock pounded through Bay. But he had no time to contemplate this. Maybe this was a dream. Maybe this was an illusion. He would figure this out later. Right now, he shoved down the throttle, roaring toward Rowan.

The strikers pursuing her rose higher, now facing Brooklyn.

Bay fired his cannons, unleashing a fusillade of explosives.

The shells were heat-seeking and hypersonic. They scattered out, streaked past the strikers, then spun back and whizzed toward the warships' exhaust pipes.

Most missed their mark and crashed against the enemy shields. But one shell made it into a striker's exhaust.

The ship exploded.

Bay swerved, dodging shrapnel, and released another volley.

The three surviving strikers fired on him.

Bay yanked the joystick, dodging several bolts, but one blast of plasma slammed into Brooklyn.

The starship screamed, her hull denting, and spun madly.

As Bay struggled to steady the ship, he glimpsed Rowan's striker turning to face her enemies.

She charged at them, cannons blazing.

Finally Bay regained control of his ship. Dented and smoldering, Brooklyn groaned in protest, but soon Bay was storming back toward the melee.

A plasma bolt hit Rowan, knocking her striker into a tailspin. Brooklyn roared over the tumbling warship, and Bay unleashed another volley of shells.

This time, he wasn't aiming at exhaust pipes. He concentrated all his fire against one striker's hull, pounding the same spot with shell after shell.

The artillery exploded against the striker. The shells couldn't penetrate the shields—but they were powerful enough to shove the striker back into its two brethren.

The three strikers collided, sparks rising between them.

"Rowan, charge at them!" Bay shouted.

They attacked together—Brooklyn from one side, Rowan's ship from the other—hammering the enemies with their cannons.

The three strikers exploded.

A fireball filled space, spraying shards of metal and exoskeleton.

The blast knocked both Bay and Rowan back and set their starships spinning.

Bay steadied Brooklyn and breathed out in relief.

"Rowan." He took a deep, shaky breath. "Rowan, can you hear me? Row?"

He stared at his monitor and saw Rowan gasping for air.

He understood at once: her hull was breached. The air was escaping her striker.

Bay ran out of the cockpit.

"Brooklyn, fly!" he cried.

"More strikers are coming at us!" Brooklyn said.

"Bring us near Rowan!" he shouted, vaulting over his piles of laundry. "Bring our airlocks together!"

Brooklyn swerved with engines rumbling. Her hull was dented and creaking, but she was still airtight. As she aligned the airlocks, Bay pulled on a helmet, then grabbed a second helmet from his cabinet.

"We're lined up!" Brooklyn said.

Bay opened the airlock and leaped into Rowan's striker.

Rowan was already waiting in her own airlock, face blue. A hooded woman stood with her, wrapped in a cloak. Her face was shadowed, but Bay heard her also gasping for air. Bay grabbed both women, pulled them into Brooklyn, then slammed the door shut.

Rowan and the hooded woman collapsed onto the deck, gulping down air.

"Bay, strikers!" Brooklyn shouted.

Bay could see them through the porthole. They were closing in, cannons blasting. A dozen or more.

"Get us out of here, Brook!" Bay shouted. "Back the way we came, full warp speed! Go, go!"

With roaring engines, they blasted away, thrumming and shaking so violently Bay thought Brooklyn would crack open. Outside the porthole, the stars streaked and blurred.

Bay raced into the cockpit and checked the monitors.

They were staying ahead of the enemy—for now. A head start at such speed would give them a few moments at least. He inhaled shakily. His fingers tingled. His head spun.

*Rowan. Rowan is here.*

He ran back into the hold and there she was, standing before him. It wasn't a dream. She was truly here. She was real.

"Bay," she whispered, eyes damp.

He pulled Rowan into his arms and embraced her so tightly she probably couldn't breathe again.

They stood for long moments, just holding each other. Rowan was so small, so thin. The top of her head barely reached his shoulders. But she was the strongest woman Bay knew.

"You can tell me what happened when you're ready," he finally whispered, holding her in his arms. "For now, I'm so glad you're here, Rowan. I missed you. And I love you."

Eyes damp, she smiled shakily. "I missed you too," she whispered. "I love you too."

"I knew it!" Brooklyn said. "I knew you loved her! Didn't I tell you, Bay? I told you that you loved her as much as a sandwich!" Her camera peeked through the cockpit door. "Oh hi, Rowan. Welcome back! Why is Jade here too?"

Bay frowned. His heart burst into a gallop.

He spun toward the back of the hold and faced the hooded stranger.

The woman pulled back her hood and looked at him with green eyes.

Jade.

It was Jade Emery. The Blue Huntress herself.

Bay drew his pistol, aimed it, and pushed Rowan behind him.

"Stay back, Rowan!" He sneered, staring at Jade. "You won't hurt her any more, beast. Hands up! Now or I fire a bullet between your eyes!"

"Bay." Rowan placed a hand on his wrist, gently lowering his pistol. "Her implants are gone. See the bandages? It's fine, Bay. She's safe. She's good again."

Bay stared at Jade, then at Rowan. He blinked.

"Poor boy looks hopelessly confused," Jade said. "Are you sure this is the famous Bay Ben-Ari?"

Bay had to sit down on his bed.

"This has been a long, strange day," he said.

Rowan sat beside him, wrapped her arms around him, and leaned her head against his shoulder. Jade joined them and slung her arm around Rowan. The three sat together in silence, just breathing, just seeking comfort in one another's warmth.

*I flew out here with no hope,* Bay thought. *I was mad with grief, a man on a suicide mission. But Rowan is back. Jade is no longer hunting us. In the darkness, I found a small light. I found a little bit of hope.*

They flew onward, leaving the front line behind, heading back toward the Heirs of Earth.

Yet when Bay returned to the cockpit and checked the monitors again, the front line was moving closer. The Concord fleets were losing. More stars fell to the Hierarchy. And Bay knew that he could never fly far enough.

"Aelonia," Bay said to the sisters. "The capital of the Concord. The enemy is moving toward it. That's where the Concord will fight its final stand."

Rowan clasped his hand. She stared into his eyes with love and fierceness. "So we'll face them there. And we'll fight them together. And if we die, we die together. Warriors."

Jade nodded. "Family."

Rowan smiled. "Humans," she whispered.

## CHAPTER SIXTEEN

Tom sat in the dark forest, playing his flute as the demons danced.

Demons had always been his companions.

Back home, on the grassy world of Seia, there had been simpler demons. Shaggy canines that lurked in the tall grass, that hunted his flock. As a child, Tom had once faced the grasswolves in a field, had stood before the heavy predators, had pelted them with stones. His father, a stern man with a white beard, had heard young Tom's cries, had scared off the beasts with a gunshot. But not before the wolves had lacerated Tom's leg. For years afterward, the monsters haunted his dreams. He still bore the scar.

There had been other demons in the Corps. The Peacekeepers had drafted him, had sent Tom to patrol distant worlds where aliens rebelled against the Concord. Tom had worn the red armor, had served with creatures from a hundred species, the only human among them. He had watched rebels firebomb a base, slaying a platoon, watched the Peacekeepers flee a building, living torches. He had watched the rebels lynch a soldier, ripping him open as he screamed, pulling out the organs and feasting.

And now there were new demons. Darker, larger, louder. The demons from the gulock. Clawed, cackling. Demons who flayed their victims. Demons from a red hospital. Demons that danced around Tom in his sleep and in his waking nights. Demons he knew would forever haunt him.

And so he sat outside on this rotten planet called Morbus, a desolate world where he had been dying for years. And he played his flute. A silver flute. A flute his father had given him many years ago. Tom had forgotten his age. Perhaps he had crossed forty. Perhaps he had crossed it by quite a bit. His hair was gray, his cheeks gaunt, his brow lined. Many years had passed since those innocent days in the fields, when the only monsters were wolves in the grass. He was no longer young, no longer innocent, no longer scared of wolves. But he had kept the flute. It could not banish the demons. But sometimes it could make them dance instead of claw him apart.

Footfalls sounded in the dark forest. A twig snapped. Tom looked up. In the campfire light, he saw Ayumi approach. The girl still wore his coat, which he had given her. For days now, since they had found Ayumi fleeing the gulock, she had not spoken. When they gave her food, she only ate a little, hid the rest in her pockets and sleeping bag. When they spoke to her, she trembled and cowered.

*She survived the gulock,* Tom thought. *I was in my thirties when they sent me there, and it broke me. She's only a child. They could not break her body. But they broke her soul.*

"Hello, Ayumi!" He lowered his flute and patted the log where he sat. "Would you like to join me?"

She wrapped her coat more tightly around her, stepped around the campfire, and sat beside him. She stared into the flames, silent. The firelight painted her pale face.

Tom looked at her, and his heart broke.

*Children should not endure such horrors,* he thought.

"Would you like me to teach you how to play the flute?" he asked.

She shrank away, daring not meet his gaze. She shook her head.

"Would you like me to play you a tune?" he asked.

She nodded meekly.

Tom raised the flute to his lips. He wondered briefly if he should play another shepherd's song from his grassy home. But no. Perhaps that had never been his true home. It was not *their* home. Instead, he played an old song called "Earthrise." A song of Earth. Of their lost homeworld.

As he played, tears flowed down Ayumi's cheeks. She had not spoken a word in days, but now, surprising him, she began to sing.

*Someday we will see her*
*The pale blue marble*
*Rising from the night beyond the moon*
*Cloaked in white, her forests green*
*Calling us home*
*For long we wandered*
*For eras we were lost*
*For generations we sang and dreamed*
*To see her rise again*
*Blue beyond the moon*
*Calling us home*
*Into darkness we fled*
*In the shadows we prayed*
*In exile we always knew*
*That we will see her again*
*Our Earth rising from loss*
*Calling us home*
*Calling us home*

The song ended. Ayumi fell silent and Tom lowered his flute. The campfire crackled. For a moment they sat in silence, awed by the lingering echoes.

Finally Tom spoke. "You have a beautiful singing voice. Not like me. When I sing, I sound like a frog." He gave a little croak.

Amazingly, Ayumi—despite all she had lived through—gave a small smile. It lasted only a second. But it warmed Tom's heart more than a thousand people laughing.

"My father used to sing me that song," she said, and her smile faded.

*Her father died,* Tom knew. *So did her mother. So did all her family. So did most of humanity. We few are among the last humans.*

"Ayumi, our mechanics have been working on the striker we shot down over the gulock. We think we can fly it soon. Some of us want to remain here, to keep fighting the scorpions, to stop them from rebuilding the gulock. But others—myself among them—want to fly. To leave this world. To seek the Heirs of Earth."

Ayumi's eyes widened. "The Heirs of Earth," she breathed. "I never knew if they were real."

"We don't know for sure," Tom said. "For a long time, I myself thought the Heirs of Earth were a myth. A human rebellion with actual starships, with uniforms, with trained marines—a real army?" He smiled thinly. "It sure beats what we've done with Earth's Light, doesn't it?"

They both turned to look at the forest camp. A wooden palisade surrounded a few tents. Farther back, survivors huddled in a cave. A handful of guards stood among the trees, rifles in hand—gaunt men in rags. At first, Earth's Light had just been Tom and a few other survivors. At one point, they had been down to five men. Today they had twenty rifles, a few cannons, and a hundred gulock survivors. These poor souls were Tom's flock. They obeyed him, fought for him. But this was hardly an army.

*We need a real army,* he thought. *Real ships. Real warriors. We need to find the Heirs of Earth and join them.*

Ayumi was looking at him, waiting for him to say more.

"I'll be leading the mission to find the Heirs of Earth," Tom said. "A handful of us will stay here. It's safe in the cave and forest. At least, safer than out in space where the war rages. But if you're willing, and if you're brave, I want you to come with me. To help me find the Heirs."

Ayumi trembled. "Why me?" she whispered.

He looked at her, this child of shattered innocence. Her hair, which the scorpions had sheared, was slowly growing back. The stubble was snowy white despite her youth. For somebody who had survived the gulock, who had survived a year or more in hiding, she looked remarkably healthy. She had a few scrapes and cuts, but she wasn't skeletal like so many gulock survivors.

There was something special about her.

There was a glowing mark on her hand.

A tattoo in silver ink, shaped like a serpent biting its own tail.

"Because of what's on your hand," Tom said.

She pulled her hand to her lap, and her cheeks flushed.

"Do you know what that symbol means?" Tom asked her.

Ayumi nodded. "A weaver's rune," she whispered. "My father was a weaver. A true member of the Weavers Guild." Finally, for the first time, she dared look into Tom's eyes. "He was a great weaver. He could weave wonderful rugs with birds that flapped their wings, and rivers that flowed, and stars that shone. He wove me a rug with images of Earth once, and the birds actually sang and flew across the fabric. He had runes on his hands too. Not like mine. His were shaped like looms, and they helped him weave his rugs. My rune is shaped like a serpent. I don't know what it means. But I know that the ancients marked me. The wise ones who live in the aether. They gave me this rune, and they gave me life, because they needed me to do something. I don't know what. I don't know how or when. But they gave me

145

this rune as a gift. And I must learn how to use it. If I can help humanity, I will."

Tom stared at her, taking this all in. Finally he laughed. "Ayumi, you have not spoken for days, and now you've delivered a beautiful speech."

She flushed and lowered her head, but a thin smile touched her lips. "I'm sorry."

"You have nothing to be sorry for," Tom said. "Ayumi, the Heirs of Earth might have weavers. Or books about weavers. They might know what your rune means. Whether it can help our cause. They might be able to teach you how to fulfill your destiny. Will you come with me to seek them? The way will be dangerous. Space is vast and dark and dangerous. But maybe there's also hope out there. For me, for you, for all of us."

Ayumi stared at her lap. She clasped her hands together and tightened her lips. Slowly, wincing, she opened one hand and looked at her rune. A snake, forming an infinity symbol, biting its own tail.

"It's an ouroboros," Ayumi said softly. "My father once told me it's the most powerful of weaver runes. But I don't know its purpose. I don't feel powerful. I feel weak and afraid." She met Tom's eyes, and he knew that took tremendous courage. "I'll go with you, sir. We'll find the Heirs of Earth, and we'll join them. And we'll find the meaning of my rune."

Tom nodded. He smiled at her.

"I have something for you, Ayumi." He pulled from his pack a wooden figurine. He handed it to her.

Ayumi took the gift. "A bird!"

"A bird from Earth," Tom said. "A dove, I believe. I saw a drawing of one long ago. Back on Earth, it symbolized peace. I whittled it for you. Maybe you're too old for toys. But I thought you might like it."

She cradled the dove to her chest. "Thank you, Mr. Shepherd. I love it. It looks like the bird from my father's tapestry. A dove." Tears sparkled in her eyes. "He wove a dove."

Others came to join them around the campfire. Rebels. Survivors. Some had been fighting the scorpions for years. Others had only recently fled the gulock, and they stared into the fire with haunted eyes. Tom played his flute for them, old songs of Earth.

*Once I was a shepherd,* he thought. *I played my flute in the grasslands of a distant world, and I guarded my flock from wolves. This is my new flock. And there are new wolves in the grass. But I still have my flute. And I still defend my flock.*

The next day, the striker was ready to fly. It was built for scorpions. There were no chairs, no beds, no keyboards. Its cockpit was cavernous, filled with levers and pulleys, and its hold was rocky and rugged, mimicking the desert world of the Skra-Shen. But when Tom fired up the engines, they rumbled and hummed.

A hundred humans crammed into the striker—the bulk of Earth's Light. Some had chosen to remain behind, to keep fighting here on this desolate world, to attack the scorpions should they rebuild their gulock.

*Someday I'll return for you,* Tom vowed.

He turned toward Ayumi, who stood beside him in the alien cockpit.

"Are you ready, Ayumi?" he said.

She nodded, holding her wooden dove. "Yes, Mr. Shepherd. I'm ready to go home."

Tom tugged a pulley. The striker soared. They crashed through the canopy of trees, rumbled through the dark sky, and breached the clouds. The stars spread out before them.

For a moment, Tom gazed in awe. For years now, he had struggled to survive on Morbus, this planet eternally cloaked in dark clouds. For the first time in a decade, he saw the universe.

"There is more out there than death and despair," he said softly. "There is more than ugliness and fear. I lost my family. But I'm here. And you're here, Ayumi. And a hundred humans are here. Earth is out there. One of those distant lights is our sun. We will return home."

Other strikers were orbiting the planet. As Tom flew by them, he caught his breath, worried that they would attack, that he'd have to fight them. But the other vessels did not acknowledge him. They just saw another striker, one of millions that flew across the galaxy.

They flew onward. Tom ignited the warp drive, and they blasted into space, leaving the dark planet and ruined gulock behind. Though even as Tom flew between the stars, he knew that he could never flee that gulock. Not truly. Wherever he went, the demons would follow, and they would dance.

## CHAPTER SEVENTEEN

Emet stood in the brig, staring at Jade Emery.

*We have her. By Ra, we have her.*

When Bay had returned to the fleet yesterday, Emet had barely believed it. Not only had his son returned home with Rowan, itself a miraculous feat, he had brought Jade Emery too!

Emet's heart was still pounding.

*Jade Emery, the woman who had butchered millions, is standing here aboard my starship.*

The Blue Huntress stood before him, wrapped in chains. Her limbs were stretched out, chained to the floor and ceiling. More chains wrapped around her torso. A muzzle secured her jaw. A collar encircled her neck, chained to the wall. The metal was reinforced with graphene, impossible to break.

Just in case, five guards surrounded her. The burly sergeants aimed pulse-rifles at Jade, ready to blast her with enough electricity to stun a brontosaurus. Outside the brig door, five more Inheritors stood with railguns, ready to hammer Jade with armor-busting bullets.

Jade had terrorized the galaxy. But right now, she wasn't going anywhere.

"I don't want you hurt," Emet said, staring at the creature. "I don't want you dead. I want to help you, Jade."

And the creature spoke, voice soft behind her muzzle. "And you want me to help you."

Emet nodded. "You stood by Emperor Sin Kra for years. He considered you a daughter. You heard his plans. You executed his plans. And now you can tell us everything you know."

Beside him, Rowan shifted uncomfortably. The buttons on her vest clanked. She stared at Emet, eyes hard.

Yes, Rowan disapproved. Emet knew this. She was a corporal in the Heirs of Earth, a brave warrior, and Emet loved her as a daughter. But Rowan was still only seventeen, too young for wisdom.

"Sir—" Rowan began.

"Hush, Corporal," he said.

Surely Rowan had known that Emet wouldn't just give Jade a uniform, a cabin on his ship, and his blessings, enlisting her into the Heirs of Earth like any other soldier. Here before him stood the Blue Witch herself, the dreaded Scorpion Princess who had led millions into the gulocks.

*The woman who …*

Emet winced. No. Even now, even after all this, that pain was too great to contemplate. That trauma was too raw, too real.

For the first time, Jade looked up and made eye contact with Emet.

And she began to cry.

"He made me do it," she whispered. Her tears fell into her muzzle. "Sin Kra controlled me. I was his puppet. His plaything. With the implants inside me, he made me do horrible things. I remember them all. Every murder—I remember. And I can't stand it. I can't stand the guilt. The pain. The visions."

Rowan grabbed Emet's arm.

"You have to free her! She's in pain!" Rowan tried to go to Jade, only for the guards to block her way. "It's all right, Jade! I'm here. Your sister. Your Rowan. I won't let them hurt you."

"Corporal!" Emet barked. "Stand back. Now."

Begrudgingly, Rowan returned to stand at his side. He felt her glare boring into him.

Ignoring her, Emet returned his eyes to Jade. She hung limply in the chains, tears on her cheeks.

"Jade, I want you out of these chains," Emet said. "I want you and your sister to be together. To heal together. Maybe to find joy together. But first, I need to know that I can trust you. That you're truly on our side."

Jade blinked tears out of her eyes. "You already scanned my body, finding no more implants. You already scanned my brain, finding no insanity. You poked and prodded me. How else can I prove my loyalty?"

"You can tell me everything you know about Sin Kra."

Jade gave a weak laugh. "I told you, Admiral. The instant I fled, Sin Kra changed all his plans. Of course he did. He knows you have me. He probably thinks you're torturing me for information. And that's not far off." She tugged the chains.

"Can't you see she's in pain?" Rowan blurted out. "This is inhuman! At least give her a chair, a bed to sleep in, some humane conditions."

Emet glared at the young soldier. "Rowan, your sister has the strength of ten gorillas. Sin Kra not only hijacked her brain; he modified her body as well. Her skin is bulletproof. Her fists can punch through steel. She could outrun a motorcycle. If she's still compromised, and set loose in the ISS *Jerusalem*, she can destroy the ship."

"But she won't," Rowan said. "She could have when we first brought her aboard! But she didn't. She stood calmly, letting the guards chain her. Sir, I know my sister. I know her heart is kind."

Emet looked at the two. The women, despite being sisters, looked nothing alike. Rowan was petite, the smallest soldier in the fleet. Her eyes were large and brown, her hair dark and short, her features elfin. Meanwhile, Jade was tall and powerful, her face sharp, her eyes shimmering green, her hair long and blue.

But Emet saw the similarity too. It wasn't physical. It was something deeper. An aura. A light in their eyes. And it was so familiar.

"I knew your mother," Emet said, speaking to both sisters. "Sarai Emery was a brave warrior in the Heirs of Earth. And a good friend. Hers was a wild heart, filled with fire and honor."

Both sisters looked at him, silent now.

Emet continued. "For years, Sarai served at my side. Her husband eventually left the Heirs. He took her—and both of you—with him. But I never doubted Sarai's honor or loyalty to Earth. I see the same honor in both of you. Rowan, you look more like your father. Jade, you look more like Sarai. To me, both of you are like family." He stepped between the guards and placed his hand on Jade's shoulder. "Jade, I want to trust you. I know that someday soon, I will. Until then, I need you to trust me."

Jade gave a weak laugh. "Admiral Emet Ben-Ari. I grew up hearing stories about you. Emperor Sin Kra talks about you often. All scorpions do. They call you King Pest. The leader of the apes. They mock you, scorn you. But they also fear you. I saw the fear in their twitching claws. I smelled it in the sizzling stench of their venom." She stared into Emet's eyes. "They hate you. And so I trust you, Admiral Ben-Ari. Fully. Completely. With my life. I will do whatever I can to help you defeat them. I swear this on my fallen parents."

Emet stared into her eyes, scrutinizing, seeking conceit.

Finally he nodded. He turned to his guards.

"Unchain her."

The head guard frowned. "Sir?"

"You heard me," Emet said. "Bring a bed, chair, and desk into this cell. Feed her three meals a day, the same as our soldiers eat. Bring her whatever toiletries she needs. Treat her as well as we treat any other prisoner." He looked back at Jade. "We'll need to run more tests. They won't be invasive. They won't hurt.

Psychiatrists, neuroscientists, and intelligence officers will still see you. Many of them. They'll question you until you want to strangle them. But no more chains."

"And if I satisfy them?" Jade said. "Will you free me? Will you give me a uniform, let me take the vows, become an Inheritor?"

"We'll cross that bridge when we come to it." Emet turned toward the door. "Rowan? Come. We're needed on the bridge."

As Emet marched down the *Jerusalem*'s corridors, the memories filled him. Memories of his old life, of so many people gone. Of his wife, the beautiful and brave Alexis, whom Sin Kra has murdered. Of David Emery, his closest friend, the man who had betrayed him. And of Sarai, wise and strong, a warrior he saw again in Jade's eyes.

# CHAPTER EIGHTEEN

"He put her in the brig." Rowan paced Brooklyn's small hold. "Bay! Your father put my sister in the brig!"

Bay winced. "Row, I know. She needs more medical tests. Neuroscientists. Psychiatrists. Cyberneticists. A whole bunch of experts needs to examine Jade, to make sure she's safe. My dad will release her when he can."

Rowan glared at him, hands on her hips. "Then Jade needs to be in the ISS *Kos*, a hospital ship! Why is your dad keeping her in a *prison cell* aboard the *Jerusalem*?"

Bay smiled wanly. "At least he removed the chains, right?"

Rowan only glowered. "Not good enough."

Bay winced. He hated to see Rowan so distraught. The past day had been a whirlwind. As soon as Bay and Rowan had rejoined the fleet, they had been quarantined. For hours, they had been poked, prodded, questioned. There had been medical examinations, psychiatric evaluations, briefings, more tests, needles, scanners.

Emet needed to know if Bay and Rowan had been compromised, converted to the scorpion cause. If they carried diseases or alien implants. The fiery Nurse Cindy had even given them full body scans, running them through clattering devices that left Bay feeling like a sock in a dryer. Perhaps Cindy was searching for alien eggs.

Only moments ago, Bay and Rowan had finally been given the all-clear. At once, they had returned to Brooklyn to recuperate.

As for Jade—Bay had not seen her since rejoining the Inheritor fleet. Guards in hazmat suits, carrying very big guns, had arrested Jade at once. Bay shuddered. If he—the son of the admiral—had undergone so many tests, he could only imagine what Jade was going through.

"She'll be all right," he said, trying to soothe Rowan. "They just need to make sure Jade is healthy. She's in good hands."

"In a prison cell, Bay," Rowan said. "She's in a prison cell! I saw her. She's suffering. She needs to be here with me."

"She will be soon," Bay said. "Look, Row, you have to understand my dad's perspective. He doesn't know Jade like you do. He just knows that Jade did ... horrible things. He has to make sure she's good now. He has to protect the rest of the fleet. He's being a responsible admiral. That's his job. To look after us."

"Jade is harmless now," Rowan said, but her voice lost some of its conviction.

"And my dad will figure that out himself," Bay said. "I promise you, Rowan. No harm will come to Jade. In a few days, she'll be here with us aboard Brooklyn."

Rowan scoffed. She looked away from him. She stared out the porthole at the *Jerusalem*, which flew nearby.

"I wish I could believe you," Rowan said. "Your dad might have finally unchained her. But he'll keep interrogating her. Jade has information about the Hierarchy. She's the most valuable prisoner Admiral Ben-Ari could have dreamed of catching. She'll never leave that cell." She turned back toward Bay. "Was I an idiot, Bay? Should I have hidden Jade somewhere, or run away with her?"

"No!" Bay took her hands in his. "Rowan, your sister won't be *interrogated*. She'll be *questioned*, yes. And Jade *wants* to help us, right? She's not really in prison. She's just in quarantine. We're all on the same side. And someday, once we win this war, we'll all live together on Earth. In peace."

Rowan sighed. She looked back outside. "Do you really think we can win, Bay? I saw the scorpions' homeworld. Bay … they have millions of strikers. More than we can defeat."

Bay attempted a smile. "But we've got the Emery sisters. That's got to count for something, right?"

Rowan laughed weakly. "You mean you have the famous Jade Emery. Little Rowan Emery isn't worth much."

"I think she's worth a lot," Bay said. "A whole lot."

She scoffed, but her body relaxed. She sat on the bed. "Yes, little Rowan Emery knows all the *Game of Thrones* and *Monty Python* quotes," she said. "I'm sure that'll come in handy in the wars ahead."

Bay caressed her cheek. "Row, you fought many battles. You marched into the very heart of the Hierarchy, the den of evil, and you brought Jade home. You are the bravest, strongest woman I know. I can think of nobody better to fight with us. With me."

Rowan looked at him, smiling thinly. "You sure seem to like my cheek. You've been stroking it a lot."

"Do you want me to stop?" Bay asked.

She lowered her eyes, then looked back up at him. "I didn't say stop."

He kept caressing her cheek, then began to stroke her hair. His fingers scattered sand.

"There's still sand in your hair," he said.

"I haven't had time to wash it," Rowan said. "It's sand from the scorpions' world. I'm probably really stinky too. But you can still kiss me, if you can stand the smell." She bit her lip and gasped. "I can't believe I said that. Oh gosh, I'm horrible at this romance stuff. I—"

Bay kissed her.

Her lips were soft and warm. They sat on the bed, holding each other, kissing. It only lasted a few seconds, but to Bay, they were the best seconds of his life. He had known pure fear. He had known pure grief. These were seconds of pure joy.

When their kiss ended, Rowan smiled shakily, and her cheeks flushed.

"I'm shy," she said. "Am I blushing?"

"Are tomatoes red?" Bay asked.

She covered her cheeks. "Great. I used to be a hobbit, and now I'm a frikken tomato. A tomato with hobbit hair?" She bit her lip. "You're a really good kisser, do you know? Oh gosh. I'm talking too much, aren't I? I do that when I'm nervous. And I'm super nervous now. And ..." She lowered her head. "And I forgot that I'm missing a tooth. Oh Ra, you kissed me, and my mouth is all messed up, and even the teeth I still have are crooked, and you must think I'm hideous, and—"

"Rowan, can I kiss you again?"

She nodded. And he kissed her again. And it was just as good this time.

"By the way." Rowan frowned and tilted her head. "I don't think I forced you to watch *Game of Thrones* yet, have I?"

"You did!" Bay said. "The one with the hobbits, remember?"

She groaned. "How can you draw so many elven warriors and not know this stuff? We watched *Lord of the Rings*! Now it's time to watch *Game of Thrones*. I must continue to work on your education."

Bay winced. "I dunno. Most of *Lord of the Rings* was just walking scenes. Does *Game of Thrones* have lots of walking in it too? I'm not sure I can handle that."

"It has boobs." Rowan waggled her eyebrows.

"All right, we're watching it!" Bay nodded emphatically. "Come on, *Game of Thrones* time!"

She rolled her eyes. "Oh, look who's so eager now?"

# Daniel Arenson

She placed the Earthstone in the rig she had built, attaching it to a keyboard and monitor. They curled up on the bed, and the show began. They lay on their sides. Rowan faced the monitor, and Bay lay behind her, his arm tossed over her waist.

As the show played, Rowan held his hand. The bad hand. The deformed one, curled up into a tight fist. Normally Bay hid that hand, embarrassed. But today he let Rowan hold it. He didn't mind her teeth; he thought she had a beautiful smile. Why should she mind his hand?

She watched the show with fascination. But Bay looked away from the monitor, and instead he admired her face. The light from the monitor washed over her, painting her blue and white. Her eyes were wide, her lips smiling.

*You're so beautiful, Rowan,* he thought, holding her close. *I love you so much.*

Suddenly guilt filled him. He thought of Coral. He remembered making love to her in this very bed. Coral too was imprisoned, languishing in a cell. The weaver was awaiting trial for stealing Brooklyn, kidnapping Bay, and going AWOL during a battle.

*I made love to Coral in this very bed,* Bay thought. *Now she's in the brig, and I'm lying here with Rowan.*

The guilt worsened.

With her dusky skin, flowing platinum hair, and wise eyes, Coral was mysterious and alluring. She was among the bravest, most beautiful women Bay had ever known, and he treasured the time they had spent together. The memory of making love to Coral would always be precious.

But that lovemaking had been for duty. To give Coral a life experience, allowing her to gain a new rune, a rune they needed for the war.

With Rowan it was different. She was not as beautiful as Coral, perhaps. At least not in the same ethereal, intoxicating way. She had never made love to Bay; they had only just kissed for the first time. And yet, Bay would have chosen to lie here with Rowan, to watch movies with her and laugh with her, rather than to sleep with Coral again. Any time.

"Bay!" Rowan groaned. "You're not watching the show! Stop looking at *me* and look at the monitor."

He laughed. "All right, all right."

She rolled her eyes. "Great, now I have to rewind it." She gave him a playful punch. "Pay better attention!"

"Yes, ma'am!"

Jade and Coral were in prison. The scorpions were moving in. The galaxy was falling apart. But for a few hours, Bay and Rowan lay together, curled up in bed, escaping into a fantasy world. For a few hours, they lived in joy.

## CHAPTER NINETEEN

The Heirs of Earth flew through the darkness, heading toward distant Aelonia, as behind them rose the tidal wave of evil.

The *Jerusalem* led the fleet. The frigate had survived countless battles, had been breached, battered, burnt, only to rise again and again like a phoenix. At sixty years of age, the *Jerusalem* was old and creaky, a ship that would normally be scrapped. Today she led the armada of humanity.

Behind her flew the ISS *Jaipur*, the mighty warship that had destroyed many strikers during the Battle of Akraba. The ISS *Bangkok* flew here too, a hulking battleship lined with cannons large enough for men to crawl into. Among these mighty frigates flew corvettes, small and fast and deadly. The *Cagayan de Oro*. The *Bridgetown*. A dozen others. Firebirds flew around them, guarding the larger vessels, ever on the lookout for a scorpion attack.

These were the warships that had been fighting with Emet for decades. But new ships had joined them this past year. Old Luther, blues player and scrap dealer, had provided a hundred more ships, ranging from hulking tankers to small pontoons. Refugees and rebels from other worlds had brought their own ships. Some flew only rusty family vessels. Others had fought their own rebellions, had built their own militias, and had joined the Heirs of Earth with true warships.

Emet stood on the bridge of the *Jerusalem*, gazing at his fleet, at the strength of humanity. Then he turned to face his people. Commodore Crane, Old Luther, Bay, Rowan, and a dozen other soldiers and officers had joined him on the bridge.

"A year ago, we had twenty ships," Emet said. "Now a thousand fly with us. Humanity has gathered in the darkness. We shine our light. We fight against those who burn our brothers and sisters. But we do not fly to Earth. Not yet. We fly to Aelonia. There, we will join fleets from across the Concord. There we will make our final stand against the Hierarchy. There the fate of the galaxy will be decided. But know this, friends. While we fight alongside other races, at a place far from Earth, this will be a battle for our homeworld. This will be a battle to stop the scorpions, the evil that seeks to exterminate our species. We fight at Aelonia, but we fight for Earth!"

"For Earth!" they thundered, fists raised.

"Sir!" A young officer turned from a control panel. "A lone striker just appeared on our sensors. It's flying right at us."

Emet stepped toward the controls. He frowned over the young officer's shoulder.

"Is it mad?" Emet said. "A single striker taking on an entire fleet?"

"It could be a kamikaze attack," said Commodore Crane. The beefy old officer came to stand by them. "A striker filled with nuclear explosives or even antimatter. Sir, I recommend we send out cruise missiles. Hit it at a distance."

Emet was about to agree. He reached toward the artillery controls.

Bay stepped forward and grabbed his arm. "Dad, wait."

A few officers scowled. Bay scowled right back at them.

"Son, you better explain yourself," Emet said.

"That striker might be defecting." Bay pointed. "Look at how it's flying. Erratically. No shields. Its cannons are cold. It's all alone, light-years away from any other scorpion ship. Dad, trust me. I saw Jade defect in a commandeered striker only days ago. There might be allies, even humans, aboard this one too."

Emet was about to argue when a light bleeped on the monitor.

"Sir, the striker is hailing us," said a young communication officer.

"A trap," said Crane. The grizzled officer grumbled. "They must be loaded with explosives."

"We'll soon find out." Emet looked at his communication officer. "Lieutenant, answer the call. Put them on the central monitor."

They all turned toward the large, central monitor. A video feed appeared, showing the striker's bridge.

Bay had been right.

Instead of scorpions, humans stood inside the striker.

One was a middle-aged man, gaunt and gray-haired. The other was a girl, her hair pure white despite her youth. Other humans huddled behind them, thin and pale, maybe starving, and wrapped in rags.

"Greetings, Heirs of Earth!" said the gaunt man in the striker. "My name is Tom Shepherd. I command a group of rebels and refugees. We have no ships other than this striker we've hijacked, but we have courage, and we've come to join your service."

Emet nodded. "Good morning, Mr. Shepherd. I'm Admiral Emet Ben-Ari, commander of the Heirs of Earth. Welcome. We're glad to have you. I must say, a striker in our service will be a first."

"Apologies for my ship, sir," Tom said. "I imagine you were moments away from blasting us out of space. I hope she comes in handy in the battles ahead."

Emet gestured at Bay, who stood nearby. "This is Lieutenant Bay Ben-Ari, my son. He'll fly out in a shuttle to examine your ship. If everything seems right, he'll accompany you into our fleet's formation. Anyone among you who can fight—

we'll swear you in, give you uniforms, and bring you up to speed. There will be water, food, and medical care too."

"Thank you, sir," Tom said.

Emet hung up, then turned toward Bay.

"Well, son?"

Bay stared at him, eyes wide. "*Lieutenant* Bay? Not Corporal Bay?"

Emet nodded. "I just promoted you. You earned your commission." He looked at Rowan. "You both did. You and Lieutenant Rowan Emery. You are both now officers in the Heirs of Earth."

Rowan gasped and saluted. "Thank you, sir." Her eyes shone.

"Bay." Emet turned back to his son. "Go welcome the new refugees. If all looks well, and they're not hiding any scorpions in there, show them the ropes."

Pride filled Bay's eyes.

*There's so much I want to tell you, son,* Emet said. *So many words I don't know how to speak. I know the darkness you traveled through. I know the struggles you faced. I know the transformation you underwent, turning from grief and grog to honor and heroism. I'm proud of you. And I love you.*

No, Emet did not know how to utter those words. But he hoped that Bay saw them in his eyes.

"Thank you, Dad," Bay whispered. He saluted, then turned and left the bridge.

Emet and his officers began discussing battle plans again, analyzing possible formations for the defense of Aelonia. Yet as they flew onward, Emet kept thinking of his son, a rising officer in the fleet, and of Leona, who had flown to seek Earth.

*I wish you could see our children now, Alexis,* Emet thought. *You would be so proud. As I'm proud.*

Yet along with his pride and love—fear.

Fear of losing his children like he had lost his wife.

Fear of losing all of humanity in the fire.

*Aelonia,* he thought. *Center of the Concord. We'll be there within weeks. And we'll know if Earth will rise or vanish forever in shadow.*

\* \* \* \* \*

Lieutenant Bay Ben-Ari entered the striker with a crew of infantrymen, medics, and nurses.

He found a nightmare.

Refugees crowded inside, so thin they were barely more than skin and bones. They cowered in the corners, whimpering, gazing at Bay and his fellow Inheritors with sunken eyes.

*They're like frightened animals,* Bay thought. *They survived a gulock. I can't even imagine the terror they've seen.*

"Welcome to the Heirs of Earth, friends!" Bay said, holding out his arms in a welcoming gesture, wishing more than ever he could uncurl his left fist. "My name is Bay. You're among friends here. Among brave warriors who are sworn to protect you. You're safe."

Many still cowered. But others shuffled forward. Some could only crawl. They grabbed Bay's hands, kissed them, mumbled to him.

"Thank you, sir."

"God bless the Heirs of Earth!"

"We are safe. Bless the Heirs!"

One of the survivors stepped forward. Bay recognized the man who had hailed the *Jerusalem.* Like the others, he was gaunt, and his eyes were sunken, but he still stood tall, shoulders squared. A rifle was slung across his back. His hair was gray, his face weathered, though Bay could not guess his age; often the survivors who came to them looked aged beyond their years.

"Tom Shepherd," Bay said, remembering the man's name. He reached out his hand to shake.

Tom shook his hand, his grip surprisingly strong.

"Lieutenant Bay Ben-Ari," he said. "Thank you. Before anything else: Would you be willing to share food? My people haven't eaten in two days."

"We have food to share," Bay said. "And water, and comfortable sleeping bags, and accommodations in a cargo hold. It's not a luxury hotel, but it'll be roomier than this striker. But first, my nurses need to examine your people, and my technicians need to examine your ship."

Tom nodded. "Of course." Tom turned toward the others. "My people! We found the Heirs of Earth. We found hope! These nurses will examine you, just to make sure you're well."

*Just to make sure they're not carrying alien diseases,* Bay knew. *Just to make sure they're not carrying hidden scorpion implants.*

He knew Tom understood—and accepted it.

As the nurses worked, a few survivors cringed. Others wept. One man kept screaming.

"No, no!" he cried as a nurse approached. "Not the hospital. Not the hospital! Please!"

Bay stood, watching the nurses try to soothe the survivors, to tend to them.

Standing at his side, Tom heaved a sigh. He turned to Bay.

"They lived through horror," Tom said. "We can feed them, maybe bring them back from the brink of starvation. We can maybe heal their bodies. Healing their souls will be more difficult. The things we still see ..." Tom seemed to stare ten thousand miles away. "The demons that haunt ..."

Bay nodded. He understood.

"I hope that someday soon, the warmth of our sun shines on them," Bay said. "On all of us. That we feel Earth's grass beneath our feet. That we grow produce in its soil. There might be some healing there."

"We never forgot Earth," Tom said. "Not even in the pits of despair."

Bay watched as a nurse examined one of the survivors. The girl seemed healthier than the others, not as skeletal, but just as frightened. She was perhaps twelve or thirteen, but her short hair was white. Bay recognized the girl he had seen in the video call.

"That is Ayumi," Tom said. "I know what you're thinking. She doesn't look like the others, not ravaged by the gulock. I can't explain it. She survived for a year in hiding, living in an attic, slowly starving, only to be captured, to endure the horrors of the gulock. But when I found her, she seemed healthy and well-fed. Her only wounds were scrapes on her bare feet from the rough ground. There was a strange mark on her hand too—a weaver's rune. Do you have any weavers among the Heirs of Earth?"

"One," Bay said. His heart sank to think of Coral languishing in the brig.

"Good," Tom said. "Perhaps your weaver can meet with Ayumi, can examine her rune, can teach her how to use it. A rune shaped like a serpent biting its tail."

Bay lost his breath.

He spun toward Tom.

"What did you say?" he whispered.

Tom tilted his head. "I said that I hope your weaver can teach Ayumi. Bay, are you all right? You look like you saw a ghost."

Frowning, Bay stepped between refugees toward Ayumi. The girl sat quietly, holding a wooden dove, letting Nurse Cindy examine her.

The tall nurse turned toward Bay, fist raised. "Now don't you be interfering with my work, Bay Ben-Ari." Cindy glared at him. "I'm with a patient."

Bay hesitated. Cindy was not physically intimidating. But her sharp needles and sharper tongue had terrorized many an Inheritor. Bay had known Cindy all his life. In fact, as a youth, he had harbored a secret crush on her. He knew her heart was kind. Cindy cared deeply for humanity, had dedicated her life to healing the hurt.

But, yes, she was also terrifying.

"Cindy," Bay tried.

"*Nurse* Cindy," she corrected him.

He cleared his throat. "Nurse Cindy, would you mind if I speak to Ayumi for a moment?"

Cindy rose to her full height. She stood even taller than Bay. She placed her hands on her hips and glared at him.

"Bay, unless this is an emergency, let me treat my patient, or I will take this needle and shove it into your neck. *Do you understand?*"

Bay couldn't help it. He felt a smile tugging at his lips, and he stifled it with effort. "Yes, ma'am."

Cindy returned to Ayumi, mumbling soothing words about rude boys interrupting the girls.

The medical examination took only moments, but it seemed ages to Bay.

"Remarkable," Cindy said, turning toward Bay. "She's healthier than you are."

"Thanks," Bay said. "You do know I lay off the grog and drugs, right?"

"That's not what I mean." Cindy pulled Bay aside and her voice dropped to a whisper. "This girl survived nearly two years on her own, fleeing the scorpions, suffering in the gulock, yet she's probably the healthiest person in the fleet. A little hungry, maybe. But that's about it."

"Weaver stuff," Bay said.

Cindy rolled her eyes. "I'm a medical professional. I don't believe in that hocus pocus."

"Neither do I," Bay said, "but it might still save the galaxy."

He turned toward Ayumi and knelt before her. The girl lowered her eyes and trembled.

*Surely I'm not scarier than Cindy,* Bay thought.

"That's a beautiful doll," he said. "Is that a bird?"

Ayumi nodded, eyes still lowered. "It's a dove." Her voice was barely a whisper. "A bird from Earth."

"You should talk to my friend Rowan," Bay said. "She has many photographs from old Earth. They're very old but still clear. I'm sure Rowan can find you photos of real doves, maybe even a video of them flying."

Ayumi raised her eyes and gasped. "Really?"

Bay nodded. "Would you like that?"

Her eyes dampened. "Yes, please, sir."

"Rowan is really nice," Bay said. "You'll like her. She can show you all sorts of movies and books, and she's really funny. I'm sure you two will be great friends."

"I would like that," Ayumi whispered.

Bay glanced at her hand, but her fist was closed. He looked back into her eyes. "Ayumi, Tom tells me that you also wanted to learn about weaving. Is that true?"

Her trembling resumed. Ayumi hugged herself and lowered her eyes. Tears rolled down her cheeks.

Bay softened his voice. "It's all right, Ayumi. You're among friends. One of our friends is a weaver, a very nice woman named Coral. If you like, she can teach you."

Ayumi bit her lip, shaking. But she looked into his eyes, her tears falling, and held out her open hand.

"Can Coral teach me what this means?"

And there Bay saw it.

A serpent rune.

An ouroboros.

The memories flowed back into Bay: discovering the Weeping Weaver Guildhall, fighting the scorpions in its halls, seeking the Godblade, learning the truth of the ouroboros rune.

*It's the only rune that will let a weaver use the Godblade,* Bay remembered. *The Godblade—the weapon that we couldn't find, the weapon that can destroy the Hierarchy.* He looked at Ayumi in wonder. *This little girl is the one who can wield our doomsday weapon. My Ra.*

"Sir?" Ayumi said. "Are you all right, sir?"

Bay remembered more. He remembered a noose. Remembered Coral trying to kill herself. Remembered the truth he had discovered in the tomb: only a weaver who had died, and who had risen again, could gain an ouroboros rune. Only one who truly understood death could wield the Godblade, a weapon that could deal death to millions.

*She died,* Bay realized. *This girl before me died—and rose again. Ra above.*

"Ayumi," he said, "will you come with me? I'd like you to meet my friends."

As they flew toward the *Jerusalem*, Bay's heart thumped and his hands tingled.

*We didn't find the Godblade in the guildhall,* he thought. *But we have a girl with an ouroboros rune. And I know who can find the Godblade.*

# CHAPTER TWENTY

Tom Shepherd stood in the conference room of the ISS *Jerusalem* with a hundred others.

Refugees.

Survivors.

Men and women tortured, haunted, risen from the brink of death.

Their eyes were sunken—but proud. Their shoulders were bony—but squared. Their hearts were broken—but blazing with light.

Today they would become Inheritors.

Tom smoothed his coat. It was woven of rich blue fabric, the color of Earth's sky. The buckles and buttons clanked, forged from brass. An Inheritor jacket. For years, fighting in the wilderness of Morbus, he had worn rags. Today he wore a uniform.

They all did.

Tom glanced over at Ayumi. The girl stood at his side, chin raised. She had just turned fourteen, a year shy of the minimum age to enlist. But she had insisted, and Emet had agreed. The galaxy was ending. They needed every last soldier they could get.

*Here, at the end, we enlist even children,* Tom thought. *As the galaxy crumbles around us, all of humanity is an army.*

Ayumi now wore the Inheritor colors—brown trousers, a white shirt, and a blue vest with silver buttons. Her hair had grown longer, the color of moonlight. She looked up and met

Tom's gaze. Ghosts danced in her eyes. But there was steel there too.

*When I met you, Ayumi, you were naked and afraid, a miracle risen from the inferno of the gulock. Today I see a young warrior.*

The others stood around them. The survivors of gulocks. In their captivity, they had been kept naked, starving, diseased. Today they all wore the brown and blue of the Heirs of Earth.

A door opened. Admiral Emet Ben-Ari entered the room and came to stand at a podium. He too wore the same colors. He was a towering man, and his overcoat hung nearly down to the top of his boots. Long hair, gold streaked with white, spilled out from under his black cowboy hat. His beard was nearly fully silver now. The Old Lion, they called him. He was approaching sixty—a good fifteen years Tom's senior—but still stood tall and strong.

*That lion can still roar,* Tom thought.

For the past decade, Tom had served no man. He had led Earth's Light, a small rebellion of hungry survivors. Many human rebellions had sprung up across the galaxy. Many had come here, willing to fight under Emet's banner. As the news spread, more humans joined them every day.

No, Tom had never bowed to another man. But here was a man he would proudly fight for. Even die for.

*What you did here is a miracle, Emet,* Tom thought. *You gathered a thousand starships; we in Earth's Light only had one. You saved thirty thousand humans; we had only a hundred. In exile, you have united humanity. You made us strong. I will proudly fight for you. Always.*

Emet gazed at them all. They stared back.

The Old Lion spoke.

"You rose from the inferno." His voice was like distant thunder, deep and comforting. "You survived while so many fell. You carry on your shoulders the burden. You carry in your hearts the pain. In your ears, you still hear the cries of the dying. You know, as I do, that the dead command us to remember them. To remember Earth. And to fight!"

Tom nodded.

To fight. Always to fight.

Tom stepped forward. He spoke. "I was a shepherd once. Sheep were my flock. But we humans will never be sheep! We will never again march meekly to the slaughter. We will fight! For you, Old Lion."

Tom took a step back. Perhaps he had broken protocol. But Emet seemed pleased. He nodded at Tom.

"You're Tom Shepherd, aren't you?"

Tom nodded. "I am."

"You led Earth's Light," Emet said. "You liberated Morbus Gulock. You saved the life of Ayumi, the child who stands beside you. You are a hero, Tom Shepherd. I'm proud to fight at your side." He looked at the others. "You are all heroes. And you all make me proud. Now repeat after me. Speak the Inheritor's Vow, and join the Heirs of Earth."

They spoke together, chins raised, hands on their hearts. A hundred voices rising as one. Even Ayumi spoke in a loud, clear voice, tears in her eyes.

"Earth calls me home. I vow to forever heed her call. I vow to cherish Earth, to sing her songs, to preserve her heritage. I believe, with all my heart, that Earth is the homeworld of humanity, and that someday I will see Earth again. All of Earth's children are my brothers and sisters. They are lost, but I will guide them home. Wherever a human is in danger, I will be there. I am Earth's child. I am ready to fight, even sacrifice my life, for my homeworld. Someday Earth's lost children will return home. I will not rest until that day."

Their vows were spoken.

They were Heirs of Earth.

Several young privates entered the room, and they poured wine. Everyone took a cup. Emet raised his drink overhead.

"For Earth," he said. "And for life."

"For life!" they repeated.

They drank.

*And for you, my fallen wife,* Tom thought. He looked at Ayumi. Even the child took a sip of wine. *And for you, Ayumi.*

Ayumi smiled at him. "We're soldiers now, Mr. Shepherd."

*My wife was pregnant when the scorpions murdered her,* Tom thought. *My daughter might have looked like Ayumi.*

Pain stabbed him. Because Ayumi was a child. Only fourteen. And yet old enough to be a soldier. Old enough to know so much about death.

"I'm sorry, Ayumi," Tom said.

"For what, Mr. Shepherd?" she asked.

"You should never suffer like this," Tom said. "Not you. Not any child. One so young should not have to fight."

Ayumi nodded. "I know. But I'm proud to fight with you, sir. For Earth."

"For Earth," Tom repeated softly. "May we all return to Earth. May the next generation of children, and every generation afterward, live in peace."

They turned toward a porthole. They gazed out into the darkness. They dreamed of a distant light. A pale blue dot. Calling them home.

## CHAPTER TWENTY-ONE

"That is absolutely the most ridiculous, nonsensical high tale I've ever heard." Emet grunted. "Is that why you called his meeting, Bay? We're days away from Aelonia. We're days away from the greatest battle of our time. We need every hour to plan, to train, and you tell me tales of magical swords and fairy tattoos."

They stood in the *Jerusalem*'s war room. Through the portholes, Emet could see the rest of their fleet—a thousand ships flying to war. Too many important people stood here, wasting their time. Bay was here, of course; he had called the damn meeting. Rowan had come with him. Tom Shepherd had come, wearing his new Inheritor uniform, accompanying young Ayumi. Nurse Cindy had joined them, wearing her scrubs, insisting that the girl was traumatized and needed her.

But worst were the two prisoners, which only an hour ago had been in the brig.

Both prisoners were here in chains. A full ten soldiers armed with guns guarded them, all officers with security clearance.

Two criminals. Coral—the rogue weaver. And Jade—the Blue Huntress herself.

*Damn it,* Emet thought, staring at the two across the wide table. *Why did I let Bay talk me into this?*

"Dad," Bay said, looking at Emet. "I know it sounds crazy. Hell, I think it's crazy too. But I saw the guildhall. And I saw Coral use the power of aether. These are not just stories."

Emet snorted. "Please. Aether? Ancient mystical beings in another plane of reality, providing power through runes? Nonsense."

Tom Shepherd cleared his throat. "Sir, if I may?"

Emet turned toward the man. Tom was looking a hell of a lot better these days, no longer the shaggy, starving rebel from the forests of Morbus. In a uniform, a rifle across his back, his gray hair trimmed and his face cleanly shaved, Tom was a new man. He struck Emet as a good soldier—and a good man. He had done well leading Earth's Light, had slain many scorpions, was loyal to the cause.

*And it's good to have another Ra damn responsible adult around,* Emet thought.

"Share your thoughts, Tom," he said.

Tom looked out the porthole, ghosts in his eyes, then back at the room. He spoke to them all. "I never thought I'd believe in magic. I was a shepherd once, a man of soil and grass and wool, not of spells or scrolls or secrets. For long years, I fought in shadows. In dark forests and decaying mountains. I fought the scorpions, and I killed many, and I saw them kill friends. And family." He had to pause, to lower his head, to take a deep breath before continuing. "For years, I thought the cosmos was nothing but darkness and despair, that there could be no more light, no more wonder. But then I saw something." He raised his eyes, and they shone, damp. "I saw something that gave me new hope."

Ayumi patted his arm. "Tell them, Mr. Shepherd," she whispered.

Tom looked at her, warmth in his eyes, then back at the others. "I saw a girl emerge from fire. A girl ran to me from an inferno of death. She had survived the gulock where hundreds of thousands had perished. There was not a mark on her body, aside from where the rocky ground had scratched her bare feet. And there was a rune on her hand, shining bright. I knew then that Ayumi Kobayashi is blessed. That the ancients are real. That the power of the weavers is true." Tom stared at them, one after the other. "You see, I was wrong that day. Ayumi had not survived the gulock. She had died in that wretched place. Died in pain and given new life. The ancients resurrected her to fulfill a purpose. And I believe her purpose is to win this war."

Emet scrutinized the man. Tom seemed earnest enough. Yet the mind was tricky. Wracked by hunger and fear, it was liable to hallucinate. Emet had never gave much credence to anecdotes. He needed evidence, not stories. Too often, men saw what they wished to see.

"You speak eloquently," Emet said. "But I'll need evidence that—"

"That weavers have true power?" Coral interjected, speaking for the first time. The woman was chained between guards, and she stared at Emet with glowing eyes. "That aether is real? Behold then, Emet Ben-Ari! The ancients are real, and aether shines true."

A tattoo on Coral's cheek glowed. And she began to levitate.

They all stared. The guards reached for their guns.

"Get down, weaver!" shouted a guard.

"Let her show us," Emet said, frowning.

Coral's tattoo still shone. Her hair flowed around her, as if she floated in zero gravity. Her cloak billowed. She rose several feet above the ground, then lowered herself again, and her tattoo dimmed. Coral slumped, looking exhausted, but managed to raise her chin.

"Do you see, Admiral?" Coral said. "No magic, no tricks. Aether. With aether, I could manipulate gravity around me. To the old weavers, it was a mystical art. But there is science to what we do. A different sort of science. A different rulebook, not the physics we use to fly these starships. But science that works. That weavers study and understand. I am but a simple journeywoman, not a weaver of great rank or worth. But this girl ..." She pointed at Ayumi. "She has the most powerful of runes. A rune that can let her wield the Godblade itself. A great weapon that can destroy fleets." Her eyes shone. "That can defeat the scorpions."

Emet wondered. Was there indeed truth here? Was Coral using parlor tricks, smoke and mirrors? Was he wise to be skeptical, or was he being close-minded, ignoring everyone's advice?

He grunted. "Yes, Bay told me about seeking this Godblade. He said you searched the old guildhall, but that somebody had taken the artifact already."

Rowan cleared her throat. She stepped forward and spoke for the first time, voice soft but firm. "My father took the Godblade from the guildhall. Like he took the Earthstone from you." She turned toward Jade, who still stood at the back of the room, handcuffed and guarded. "Do you remember, Jade? That crystal sword Dad gave you. How you loved that sword! You never put it down. We thought it was just a beautiful toy. But it was made of aetherstone. And on its pommel—an ouroboros rune. It was the Godblade, Jade. A great weapon that Dad hoped could someday help humanity."

They all turned to look at Jade.

She stared at them. The woman who had slaughtered millions of humans. Her hair was still electric blue. Her skin was still hard and white, a material impervious to bullets or bombs. But she wore an Earth-blue cloak now, and her eyes were timid, afraid.

"I remember," Jade whispered.

*She never murdered anyone*, Emet realized, looking at the young woman. *The scorpions made her do it. My Ra, the agony she must have lived through. Perhaps she's the greatest victim of this war.*

And suddenly Emet believed it.

He believed it all. That Jade had a good heart. That the Godblade was real. That Ayumi could wield it. That there was hope in this war. That they could win. That they could see Earth again.

"Jade," he said, stepping toward her. "Do you know where the Godblade is now?"

Jade smiled tremulously. "The same place Rowan last saw it. The place where Emperor Sin Kra killed my parents and kidnapped me. I tried to fight him with the Godblade that day— with what I thought was a toy sword. Sin Kra thought it was a toy too. He ripped it from my hands. He tossed it aside. I still remember watching the sword clatter away." She looked at her sister. "Rowan, the Godblade is still in our old home. In the Glittering Caves."

## CHAPTER TWENTY-TWO

The basilisk ammunition ship, a gargantuan starship filled with enough explosives to destroy a small moon, lumbered on through space.

The *Snakepit* flew slowly. But she flew steadily. She was headed to Earth.

Leona stood on the alien bridge, her rifle in hands, a bandanna covering her mouth and nose. She looked out into space. Sol shone ahead, still a distant light, but growing brighter every day. After half a year of travel, she was only two weeks away.

"You'll never get away with thisss," the pilot hissed, turning away from the controls. "Millions of my fellow serpents guard Earth. They will crack your bones. They will devour you alive. They—"

Leona poked his head with her rifle. "Shut up, Kaa, and keep flying."

The pilot hissed at her, forked tongue flickering.

"My name is not—"

She drew back the cocking handle. "Shut up and keep flying."

He kept flying.

She had given him that nickname. Kaa. The name of a snake from *The Jungle Book*, a novel she had loved as a child.

But Kaa wasn't a snake. Not truly. He was a basilisk—an alien the size of a Burmese python, scaly and sentient. His jaws were powerful enough to break bones and steel. His arms were short, but his fingers were long, filled with joints, and tipped with claws, made for ripping through flesh. Now those fingers were tugging on pulleys and levers, flying the ship.

No, not truly a snake. Kaa wasn't even a regular basilisk. Most basilisks had a single head. This creature, perhaps bred to look at several monitors at once, had once had three heads.

Leona had blasted off two of them. And the stumps were rotting.

"I need medicine," Kaa hissed. His voice was grainy. Weak.

"We gave you medicine," Leona said. She adjusted the bandanna over her nose. The bridge reeked of his decay.

Kaa spat. "Your human medicine is useless to me."

"Well, then keep flying to Earth," Leona said. "You say there are basilisks there? They can give you snakeoil and cure your ouchies."

Though Leona had to admit—these were more than mere "ouchies." She began to doubt anything could cure the serpent.

*Muck, I should never have shot him in the heads,* Leona thought. *Why didn't I just shoot him in the ass? Well, I suppose because he doesn't have an ass. But I do! And now my decision is biting me there.*

Her crew's medic had amputated the wounded heads, treated the stumps, and wrapped them with bandages. But now pus and blood stained the bandages, and the stench of gangrene filled the bridge. Rot was spreading down the two necks. They had pumped Kaa full of antibiotics, but the medicine did nothing. Soon the infection would reach Kaa's heart.

*We better reach Earth first.*

Even with the alien controls, Leona could figure out how to fly the ship herself. Flying wasn't the problem. A bit more problematic were the thousands of strikers flying everywhere around them. Only Kaa, with a gun to the back of his head, could ward off his buddies.

*Without Kaa, we're dead,* she knew.

Leona stared out into space.

It still shone in the distance. Sol. Earth's sun. From here, it just looked like any other star. It was still light-years away. Perhaps no human had been closer in thousands of years.

And there, coming in from ahead—more basilisk ships. Damn it.

Every few hours now, the damn Rattlers appeared. Leona had come to calling the basilisk warships *Rattlers*. The name seemed fitting. The ships mimicked the aliens who flew them. They were tubular vessels, covered with green and black armored plates like scales. Red portholes blazed on their prows like eyes, and their cannons resembled fangs. Their round engines reminded Leona of rattlesnake tails. Thousands had been flying toward the front line, joining their scorpion masters in the war against humanity.

The Rattlers—there were fifteen ahead—came flying toward the *Snakepit*. A call came in.

"Answer." Leona jabbed Kaa again. "Answer and give them the all clear. Do this, and I'll bring you some food."

She shuddered. She has seen the basilisks' food sources. The lower level of the *Snakepit* was filled with them—plump, hairless rodents the size of pigs, kept in cramped cages. The lower level stank almost as much as the bridge.

"Very well." The basilisk hissed into his comm, talking to his fellow pilots, glaring at Leona all the while. Finally the Rattlers turned and flew onward, leaving the *Snakepit* to continue toward Earth.

*But this won't work forever*, Leona thought later that day, watching the medics change her pilot's bandages. *Kaa is dying*.

She returned to stare out toward the stars.

Most of the time, it was just her and Kaa here on the bridge. Leona had set out on this quest with four starships and hundreds of intrepid colonists. She had only one starship left—

the frigate *Nazareth*—and it was hiding in the *Snakepit*'s cavernous hangar. She had only two hundred humans left—and they were hiding inside the *Nazareth*.

Leona understood her crew. The *Snakepit* was a shadowy labyrinth, a freighter one could get lost in for days, filled with burrows and chutes and round chambers. It was built for snakes, not humans. Most of the chambers held weapons—bombs, missiles, grenades, mines—originally meant for the war. Other chambers held gruesome surprises—snake eggs, shed skins, or the squealing rodents the basilisks ate. It was no wonder her crew remained on the *Nazareth*.

But Leona preferred the *Snakepit* bridge, even with the foul stench of the rotting, dying Kaa. A nervousness filled her. A fear that so close to Earth disaster would strike. She needed to stand here. To gaze out at distant Sol. Ever vigilant. So close to home.

And yet—she had been here for twelve hours straight now. She needed a shower. A meal. A few hours in bed. Let somebody else take a shift. She rubbed her shoulders and prepared to leave the bridge, walk through the labyrinthine corridors of the *Snakepit*, enter the hangar, and disappear into the *Nazareth* until tomorrow.

As she was walking away, the ship's radar beeped.

Leona turned back toward the controls. A monitor displayed another incoming vessel.

She sighed. "More damn basilisks."

Kaa, sitting at the controls, chortled. Saliva dripped from his powerful jaws.

"No, not this time," the dying basilisk said. "The incoming spacecraft is a human vessel."

Leona snorted. "No human has flown through this sector in two thousand years."

Kaa hissed, forked tongue flicking. "My sensors do not lie, ape. That is a simian ship. One of your pathetic relics that litter the galaxy."

Leona frowned. A relic? She stared at a monitor. Basilisk letters were scrolling by, perhaps giving information about the approaching vessel.

"Translate this for me."

Kaa growled. "I am not your slave."

Leona rolled her eyes. "I already shot off two of your heads. Do you want me to shoot off your tail next?"

The basilisk cackled. "I am nearly entirely tail, pest."

"Exactly. So translate!"

Kaa gulped. He turned toward the monitor. His eyes narrowed.

"The approaching vessel is small," he hissed. "No larger than a starfighter. Its origin is Earth."

"Earth!" Leona gasped. "This ship came from Earth?"

Her mind reeled. Did humans still live on Earth? Was that how basilisks knew the common human tongue?

"When did it leave Earth?" she said. "Calculate based on its current velocity and trajectory."

Kaa hit a few buttons, running calculations. He stared at her, eyes narrowed. "It left Earth over two thousand of your years ago, human. In what you call the year 1977."

Leona covered her mouth. "It's flying at sub-light speed." She hit the comm on her coat's lapel. "Ramses, Mairead, you there?"

Ramses's voice spoke through the small device. "Here, Commodore. Just playing a round of poker on the *Nazareth*. Firebug is cheating."

Mairead's voice sounded from the distance. "Am not! You lost fair and square, buster."

"You have five aces!" Ramses said. "That's impossible."

Mairead scoffed. "Sore loser."

"Enough," Leona said. "Mairead, take a shift on the bridge. Ramses, put on your spacesuit. You and I are going on a little spacewalk. We've got a relic to retrieve."

"What?" Mairead said through the comm. "Curly, let me go on the spacewalk! I hate the *Snakepit*'s bridge. Place stinks worse than the Pharoah's feet."

Ramses scoffed. "Please, my feet smell of lavender and frankincense."

"Sissy," Mairead said.

"Enough!" Leona said. "Firebug, that's your punishment for cheating at poker. And stop calling me Curly."

"Fine!" Mairead groaned. "But I'll put my spacesuit on too. At least I won't have to breathe that basilisk stink."

Moments later, Leona met Ramses in the airlock. The tall Egyptian was pulling on his spacesuit. He paused to hand Leona a thermos.

"Coffee?" he said.

She let out a sigh. "You're a lifesaver." She took the thermos gratefully and sipped.

"I hope it's not too hot," Ramses said.

"It's mucking wonderful," said Leona. She yawned.

"How long have you been awake?" Ramses zipped up his spacesuit.

"Can't sleep," Leona said, pulling on her own suit.

Too many memories. Too many worries. Whenever she lay in bed at night, Leona relived the battles. The basilisks destroying her other ships. The scorpions slaughtered the millions. Over and over, her mind turned to Earth. To a planet so close. A planet Leona worried she would never reach. She kept imagining disasters—aliens attacking, or Kaa dying, or a disease spreading among the troops. At other times, she worried about what she would find on Earth. Would she land on a clement world? Or would she find a wasteland overrun with mutants and monsters? Perhaps more than anything, she worried about her family. About her father. About Bay. About them fighting the scorpions a thousand light-years away.

"Well, the coffee will help you sleep," Ramses said, tearing her away from her thoughts. He winked.

Leona smiled wryly and placed on her helmet. "Let's go for a starlit stroll."

They strapped on their jetpacks and flew out. Leona breathed in relief. It felt good to be out in space, free from the confined corridors and chambers, from the stench of the place, from the rumbling engines and hissing serpent. There was beauty out here. The Milky Way's spiral arm flowed before her, glittering like purest silver. Sol shone ahead, bright and welcoming. Leona wished she could float out here forever.

She turned around and looked at the *Snakepit*. The basilisk ammunition ship was lumbering forth, huge and dark and ugly. Within it—the hope of humanity.

Leona looked away. And she saw it in the distance, moving closer.

The relic.

She and Ramses ignited their jetpacks and flew. They reached the relic and flew around it. Leona frowned. She had never seen any vessel like it. There was a large dish on top, about the size of a dinner table. There were various antennae and sensors attached. It seemed primitive, barely able to fly, something from the dawn of a technological era. There was no faster-than-light capability. Barely any shields. The communication system seemed to use radio waves instead of quantum mechanical transmitters. There was a certain beauty to it. Here was a vintage piece of early tech, endearing and graceful. A relic from an earlier, more innocent age.

"Leona!" Ramses said. "Come, look at this."

She flew toward him. They stared together. Leona's eyes widened.

"A record," she said. "A golden record."

The disk was attached to the relic. There were symbols engraved onto it—a pulsar map, a hydrogen atom, and other symbols Leona didn't understand. Ancient symbols.

But next to the golden record, engraved onto the space probe itself, were human letters.

A word written in Middle English. It was an ancient dialect, but one Leona spoke well; much of the Earthstone was in that old tongue.

*Voyager.*

"This space probe is the *Voyager*," she whispered in wonder. "Humans built this. Over two thousand years ago. This is a wonder from ancient Earth." She smiled, tears in her eyes. "Like your pyramids, Ramses."

"I heard of the *Voyager*," Ramses said. "A spacecraft launched by an ancient civilization called America. My father told me about this empire and its technology. They were almost as impressive as Egypt. Almost."

Leona smiled through her tears. "My father told me of *Voyager* too. It was among the first spacecraft humanity launched into the cosmic ocean. All the way back in 1977. It's been flying for twenty-two hundred years." She sighed. "It didn't get very far."

Ramses chuckled. "No it didn't. When you don't have faster-than-light engines, two thousand years doesn't get you very far."

Leona gently ran her fingers over the golden record. "The ancient humans sent this as a message. They hoped an alien civilization would find it, would learn about humanity. We were so innocent then, weren't we, Ramses? If we knew the terrors out there, we would have hidden."

"Leona, this isn't just a space probe," Ramses said. "This is a time capsule. There's data on the Golden Record. Like the Earthstone, it contains information from Earth. We should bring this aboard."

"Agreed."

They tugged the relic, guiding it into the *Snakepit*, and placed it on the hangar floor. The entire crew gathered around it, eyes wide, reaching out with reverence to touch this treasure from their past.

They got to work, rigging an interface that could read the data on the *Voyager*'s Golden Record. Within a few hours, they were able to access the data.

On the record was music. Photographs. Films. Recordings of Earth sounds. Human voices.

The humans gathered around, listening to Mozart, Bach, and Chuck Berry. They listened to babies crying and laughing, the songs of whales, and waves breaking on a shore. There were recorded greetings from ancient humans, both leaders and commoners, their voices speaking across the generations. And there were photos. Many photos of humans from old Earth. Humans who had died millennia ago, who lived on in memory.

"This is holy," Leona said. "This is proof." Tears rolled down her cheeks. "This is evidence that we humans are indeed from Earth. That we originated on that world. For thousands of years, aliens called us pests, demons born in black holes or hatched from eggs in rotting carcasses. The Golden Record proves beyond doubt that we were always right. That we are indeed from Earth. That Earth is our birthright. This isn't just a space probe. This isn't just a time capsule. It's evidence. It ties us home."

"Should we take it with us?" Mairead said. She sat on a crate of grenades, puffing on a cigar.

"Put that out!" Leona said. "And no. We won't take it with us. We'll release the *Voyager* back into space. We'll let it continue to fly."

Ramses gazed at the *Voyager*. He spoke softly. "Old tales of many faiths tell of a flood on ancient Earth. A flood that covered all lands. A man named Noah built an ark. He sailed for many days, desperate to find land. Finally one day, a dove flew to him, holding in its beak a sprig of olive. There was land ahead. There was hope." Ramses placed his hand on the *Voyager*. "This is our dove. She will fly on, and may she bring hope to a galaxy in despair."

Leona embraced her dear captain and kissed his cheek. "Well spoken, my Pharaoh."

"Go, Johnny, Go!" Mairead said, slapping the *Voyager*.

They released it back into space. They stood at the airlock door, watching the space probe fly on, then vanish into the distance.

*Go, Johnny, Go,* Leona thought. *Fly on and bring hope to the hopeless.*

That night, she lay in her bunk, but again she couldn't sleep. Again the worries rose—for her family, for humanity. Again the terrors danced behind her eyelids.

Finally she rose from her bed, giving up on sleep. She wrapped a bed robe around her, passed a hand through her mane of dark curls, and stepped into the corridor.

*Stupid, stupid,* she told herself as she padded barefoot down the hall.

She knocked on his door.

For a moment there was silence. Leona wanted to turn back. But then Ramses opened the door. He nodded to her.

"Leona."

"Your damn coffee," she said.

He took her hand in his. "I told you it would keep you awake."

He took her into his chamber. And into his bed. And as Leona made love to him, she imagined that they were outside in space, floating among the stars. At peace. In beauty.

"You are beautiful," Ramses whispered to her, kissing her naked body, his hands in her hair.

Leona straddled him, tossed her head back, and closed her eyes. She swayed atop him, and he cupped her breasts in his hands. She had not made love to a man since her husband had died. It had been a decade of celibacy, of war, of the nightmares.

*Let this be a night of pleasure,* she thought. *Of warmth and comfort. Of hope. A night of doves.*

After their lovemaking, she lay by him in bed, and he wrapped his arms around her.

"Stay the night," Ramses said to her.

"I should return to my cabin," she whispered. "People will talk."

"Let them."

She wanted to get dressed. To go back to her cabin. But the bed was warm, and his arms were warm, and when she closed her eyes she saw no nightmares.

She slept.

The *Snakepit* flew onward, heading toward Earth. Behind them, the *Voyager* continued its journey, heading toward distant flaming stars, carrying the voices of lost innocence.

## CHAPTER TWENTY-THREE

"Did we really have to fly in the striker?" Rowan shuddered. "This place gives me the heebie jeebies."

Jade turned from the controls. She frowned at Rowan. "The heebie-what-now?"

"You know," Rowan said, "the heebie jeebies. The willies. Ants in pants."

Jade tilted her head. "Are there ants in your pants, sister?"

"God, I hope not, or Brooklyn will never speak to me again." Rowan looked around her at striker's bridge. "Why couldn't we fly in Brooklyn again? She could have taken us to the Glittering Caves to find the sword. Brooklyn is actually comfortable. There's a bed. There are controls made for hands, not claws. There's artwork on the walls. This place looks like an abandoned bug hive."

The sisters were flying aboard the *Mother's Mercy*, the striker they had fled Ur Akad in. The bulkheads were forged from craggy black iron. Boulders—actual boulders of real stone—rose across the hold. Two lanterns shone above, one small and bright and white, the other large and dim and red, mimicking the binary suns of the scorpion homeworld.

Rowan did not appreciate the ambiance.

A shudder passed through her. Since fleeing Ur Akad a few weeks ago, the nightmares had never left Rowan. Her days were always exhaustingly busy. Emet had commissioned her, naming her a lieutenant, an officer of the Heirs of Earth, and she had not rested since. She trained for battle with the best sergeants. She attended meetings in the war room, listening to generals discuss battle plans. She joined video calls with alien admirals, learning about diplomacy and alliances. Rowan had even been learning to fly starships, ranging from starfighters to frigates. The days seemed endless, crammed with activity, so busy she barely had time to breathe.

The nights were a different matter.

At night, when she closed her eyes, the terrors emerged.

In her dreams, Rowan was still a prisoner, still hanging in a cage over a pit of scorpions. They cut her. Licked her. Mocked her, flayed her. Again and again, the emperor held the brand to Rowan's arm, and her skin sizzled.

*You are marked,* Sin Kra told her, laughing as she screamed.

Rowan awoke in cold sweat several times a night, panting, struggling for air.

For the first few nights, Rowan had slept in a cabin aboard *Jerusalem*, one she shared with other junior officers. Eventually, faking allergies to the *Jerusalem*'s mattresses, she received permission to spend her nights aboard Brooklyn. In the small shuttle, she shared Bay's bed, seeking comfort in his embrace.

Rowan didn't enjoy lying about allergies. But Bay was worth a little dishonesty.

Sometimes he even kissed her goodnight. A nice little perk.

Yet even there, even in his arms, the dreams haunted Rowan. She would wake up screaming, drenched in cold sweat, scorpions crawling over her. Bay would soothe her, kiss her tears away, and she would sleep close to him, her head against his chest. And dream of scorpions again.

"Nope," Rowan said, looking around her. "Being inside a striker definitely isn't helping my anxiety."

Jade paused from working the starship controls, a complex system of levers and pulleys.

"Little sister, I know how hard this is," Jade said. "But we must fly in a striker, not a human starship. We're behind enemy lines now. In this striker, we're disguised. We're safe. We can reach the Glittering Caves and find the Godblade that I dropped there fifteen years ago. If we had flown here in Brooklyn, we'd be more comfortable, yes. But we'd alert every striker within range."

"I know," Rowan said softly. She lowered her head. "It's just that ... being here, with the boulders, and the two lights, and memories, it ..." Her voice caught, and she could say no more.

Jade embraced her. She stroked Rowan's short brown hair. "I know, little sister. I know how much it hurts. I too have been having nightmares every night."

Rowan laid her head against her sister's shoulder. "I'm sorry. I was thinking about myself, being selfish. I can't even imagine how hard this is for you. I survived a few weeks in captivity. You survived fifteen years."

Jade's eyes hardened. "We will have our revenge. We will defeat the Skra-Shen." Her lips peeled back in a snarl, her cheeks flushed, and for an instant she almost looked like the old Jade, the Blue Huntress. "We will find the Godblade, and we will kill them all."

Rowan took a step back, suddenly afraid. "We don't need to kill them all. We just need to kill Sin Kra."

Jade stared into Rowan's eyes, gaze hard and cold. "You don't understand, Rowan. Even now, you don't understand. You did not see what I saw. You were never ..." Pain twisted her face. "One of them. But I was. The scorpions are not like humans. Humanity is a mix of good and evil, an array of infinite grays. But the scorpions are not. The scorpions are pure evil. Every one of them, from the newly hatched to the oldest warriors. They are evil incarnate. There will be no peace so long as a single one lives."

"Isn't that exactly what they say about us?" Rowan whispered, trembling.

Jade looked aside. She scoffed. "You have a good heart, sister. But my heart was burned long ago."

"No it wasn't." Rowan placed her hands on Jade's shoulders. "You have a heart. A good, kind heart. Just ... a heart that knew much pain. A broken heart. You're a good person, Jade. You are innocent of any crime."

"But not innocent about the wretchedness in the cosmos," Jade said, and her eyes dampened.

Rowan looked outside at the stars. *Mother's Mercy* was flying light-years behind enemy lines now, and battles raged around many of the nearby stars, but the interstellar medium was a peaceful black ocean. They were only several days away from Harmonia, the world where the Emery family had hidden so long ago.

"I barely remember anything from the cave," Rowan said softly. "A few vague images. Our parents. The glowing stalactites. Maybe those aren't even memories of the cave, just memories of me looking at my photograph. Do you remember it, Jade? I don't mean the day the scorpions came. I mean the days before that. Were we happy?"

Tears flowed down Jade's face. "We were happy." She smiled shakily. "I remember the first time I saw you. You were just about an hour old. Mom placed you on the bed, and you pooped. Right there on the bed. It was a weird black and green color. I remember. I was horrified! I thought you would ruin my life."

Rowan cringed. "Lovely memory."

Jade actually laughed. "Oh, but later that day, they let me hold you. I was only four, and I was scared that I'd drop you. But Mom and Dad let me hold you, and I knew then that I love you, Rowan."

"Love you too, sis." Rowan leaned against her, and they gazed out together at the stars. "What were they like? Mom and

Dad. I can hardly remember them. Just fuzzy half-memories, a few images, flickers like photographs in my mind."

"To be honest, I don't remember much either," Jade said. "I was six when Sin Kra killed them. Old enough that I should have more memories than this. But ..." She winced and touched the scars on the side of her head. "The implants hurt me. I think they killed most of my memories. But I can remember a little. Flickers, blurry images. Mom smiling, hugging us, helping us arrange crystals in decorative patterns. Oh, and I remember storytime with Dad! We would lie in bed, both us girls, while Dad read us books. Those were good times. I was happy then. We were all happy. That's what I remember most. Happiness." Jade lowered her head. "I don't know if I've been happy since."

"We'll be happy again." Rowan squeezed Jade's hands. "I promise you, Jade. We'll be happy."

"How can there still be happiness after so much pain?" Jade whispered. "How can we ever forget?"

"We never can," said Rowan, "and we never should. I don't want to forget anything. Not the good things or the bad things. We need to remember bad things too. They help us appreciate the good. And we'll have a good life. On Earth. We'll build a beautiful house in a forest, with a path that leads to a lake. We'll have a garden with grass and flowers. On warm days, we'll sit on the dock, and we'll fish and listen to the frogs and birds sing. On days when it rains or snows, we'll sit by the window, staring out at the cold garden, feeling warm by the fireplace. We'll read books and watch movies and play board games. You and I, my sister. We'll be happy again. On our homeworld. Together."

Jade wiped her eyes. "I'd like that. I don't know what frogs or birds sound like, or what fish tastes like, and I've never seen the snow or rain with eyes that weren't blind with madness. But I'd like that."

They embraced. For a long time, they stood silently, holding each other as the stars streamed by outside.

They kept flying. Hours went by, then days. At times, they'd see flights of strikers in the distance. Sometimes only a handful of strikers on patrol. Other times, they saw thousands of the warships traveling toward Aelonia, toward the great final battle to crush the Concord. Most of these ships ignored the *Mother's Mercy*. One time, when somebody hailed them, Jade answered with a series of hisses, clicks, and clatters she could emit flawlessly from her human throat. The scorpions inside the other strikers accepted her as their own. They flew on, leaving the *Mother's Mercy* to continue unmolested.

"I told them we're a Skra-Shen scout on a top secret mission," Jade said. "They believed it."

Rowan looked at her sister in wonder. "How do you make all those clicking sounds?"

"When Sin Kra modified me, he enhanced my vocal cords, enabling me to speak in the language of Skra-Shen. The scorpions communicate with hissing from their throats, but also clatters from their claws and pincers. I can make the clattering sounds with my tongue."

Rowan lowered her gaze. "I'm sorry."

Jade raised an eyebrow. "Why? It came in handy when I was a child. I was able to talk to the other juvenile scorpions."

Those words cut Rowan like icy blades. "It must have been so hard for you. I forget sometimes that you spent most of your childhood there. What was it like? My God, it must have been so alien. I mean, you don't have to tell me. Not if it hurts."

"It hurts now," Jade said. "It hurts to look back, to realize how blind I was. But then? No, it didn't hurt when I was growing up. I thought I was a scorpion. The implants made me think so. Oh, I knew my body was different. Sin Kra told me that he shaped me this way, made me look human, so that I could become a spy. He told me that I still had a scorpion heart. That he was my father."

"Did the other scorpions pick on you?" Rowan asked. "Human children pick on those who are different. At least, that's what I've seen in the Earthstone."

"I was stronger than the other scorpions," Jade said. "And they knew it. You see, the Skra-Shen have no art. No music. No literature or poetry. Their entire society is dedicated to violence. Even the juveniles fight. The instant a mother's eggs hatch, the larvae battle one another. Most are slaughtered right there in the nest. Of those who survive that first day, most never survive the next few years. In our nurseries, education hives, and training yards, they encourage juveniles to butcher one another. Only one in a hundred reaches adulthood." Jade smiled wryly. "I had to kill many scorpions as a child. It readied me for this war."

"That sounds horrible!" Rowan said. "To grow up like that, without any children to play with, the only one of your kind ..." She bit her lip. "Well, I suppose I grew up like that too. After the scorpions killed Mom and Dad, Fillister flew me on the family starship. Pirates grabbed us on the way. They took the ship. They sold me to a pet shop."

Jade's eyes widened. "A pet shop?"

Rowan nodded. "Yeah. A pet shop on Paradise Lost, a space station near Terminus Wormhole."

"I destroyed that space station," Jade mumbled.

"Can't say I blame you, to be honest." Rowan smiled bitterly. "I escaped the pet shop pretty early, I think. Or maybe nobody wanted to buy a human, so the owner just released me. I don't remember. I spent the following fourteen years hiding in the HVAC ducts."

Jade's eyes softened. "Oh, Rowan! I'm so sorry. I can't even imagine ... I grew up far from other humans, but at least I had sunlight, open spaces, even something akin to companionship."

Rowan's smile trembled. "It was hard. Especially when I became a teenager. I got so angry, so depressed. Sometimes I was suicidal."

Jade hugged her. "I'm so sorry."

"The Earthstone took me to another place," Rowan said. "It got me through those times." She smiled wistfully. "The Earthstone took me away to Earth—with movies, books, shows, and music. For thousands of hours, I lay in a duct, curled up, staying home alone with Macaulay Culkin, or exploring New Zealand with Frodo, or fighting the Demogorgon with Eleven. I read countless books. My favorites were those by Marco Emery, our ancestor, who wrote stories of fantasy and science fiction, but also the books by the famous Einav Ben-Ari, the legendary leader of Earth, who wrote several volumes of her memoirs. And I watched concerts too! I danced around—as much as I could in a duct, at least—while watching Rolling Stones and AC/DC concerts. Bon Jovi was my imaginary boyfriend for a year. But mostly I liked K-pop. That's stuff you can really wriggle around to! I must have shaken the ducts so much I scared half the guests."

Jade laughed. "I like music too. The little I've heard. The song you sang to me once, that Mom and Dad used to sing. Earthrise, it's called."

"Earthrise is a good song," Rowan said. "It's the song of humanity. Our anthem. But wait until you hear K-pop!"

Jade patted her hand. "I'm glad you had the Earthstone during those years."

"And I had Fillister," Rowan said. "He kept me company too. Without him, I'd have gone mad. That dear little robot! He was even better than the Earthstone. When I was sad, he cheered me up. *Chin up, Row!* he'd say with that funny cockney accent of his. I miss him."

Jade covered her mouth. "Oh dear. Fillister! The dragonfly that I—"

"You crushed him." Rowan nodded. "Don't worry! I have a backup of his software. I'll install the backup once I find him a new body. He's safe and sound now, resting in the *Jerusalem*'s database. Probably getting up to all sorts of trouble in there, flirting with maintenance subroutines, picking fights with antivirus software, and raiding the entertainment vaults. I was tempted to store his backup in Brooklyn, but those two would kill each other."

"Robots have it easy," Jade said, gazing out into space. "They can't feel pain. And if they die, they can just come back. I'm jealous."

"Yeah, but we human can eat, and kiss, and have sex. That's gotta be worth something, right?" Rowan blushed. "Not that I'd know personally about sex, of course."

Jade laughed. "Nor would I."

"Maybe someday," Rowan said. "When we're on Earth."

Jade raised an eyebrow. "With Bay? You fancy him, don't you?"

"What?" Rowan bristled. "I do not."

Jade shrugged. "He's quite good looking. For a human."

"That's beside the point!" Rowan's cheeks burned hotter. "He's too old for me. He's twenty-five."

"Oh yeah, he's positively ancient," Jade said. "Needs a cane, probably."

"Well, to me he's ancient! I'm only seventeen, you know." Rowan frowned. "Wait, am I eighteen already? I can't keep track with all this flying around, time dilation, and all the busyness. I think I'm eighteen now? To be honest, I don't even know what my birthday is."

"May 3rd, 4135," Jade said. "Now you know."

"Some good that does me." Rowan snorted. "Meaningless. Dates only mean something on Earth. Time dilation. It speeds up or slows down, depending on how fast you fly, how warped spacetime is around you, how much gravity affects you, and so on. For me, this war has been going on for only a year or two. But for humans languishing in gulocks, not flying up in space, it's been going on for many years. Decades for some." She gave a weak laugh. "For all I know, Bay could be ninety years old by the time we fly back."

Awkward silence filled the striker. Besides, who could think of romance during times of war and despair? Rowan cared about saving humanity. Defeating the scorpions. Finding Earth. Yes, she had kissed Bay—and her cheeks flushed to remember that. But she could not pursue a proper romance with him. Not like this. Not with all this death around her.

"On Earth," Jade said softly, gazing out into space. "On Earth we'll be happy."

Rowan stared out with her. They were silent for long moments. Distant explosions flashed in a nearby solar system. From here, they looked like fireflies.

"A battle," Rowan said. "Thousands of ships fighting. Thousands of aliens dying." She pointed. "There. At that star too. Another battle. The war is all around us. The great Second Galactic War. Star after star burning away. Planet after planet— gone. Civilizations crumbling. Billions dying." She heaved a sigh. "I want to be hopeful. I want to believe we can win, that we can go home, see Earth. But here, flying in the darkness, with genocide all around us—it's hard. It's hard to be hopeful. Even the lights in this darkness are the lights of death."

Jade frowned. She pointed ahead. "What are those lights?"

Rowan leaned toward the viewport, squinting, struggling to bring the distant lights into focus. "They're moving fast. Enemy ships?"

"Our sensors detect no electromagnetic radiation," Jade said.

"They're moving toward us." Rowan raced toward the gunnery station. "It's a battle."

Jade grabbed the navigational pulleys, prepared to fly while Rowan fired. The sisters stared out into space, watching the approaching lights.

Rowan stepped away from the gunnery station.

"Rowan!" Jade said. "Man the cannons!"

But Rowan walked closer to the viewport and pressed her face against the glass. She stared outside, eyes wide.

"They're ..." She gasped. "They're whales! Starwhales!"

The animals flew closer, gliding through space. An entire pod. The adults were larger than the starship Jade and Rowan flew. Silver lines flowed across their deep blue skin. Barbels grew around their mouths like catfish whiskers, tipped with bioluminescent beads. Their eyes shone, gold and lavender, lighting the darkness. The adults flowed gracefully and calmly, but the cubs frolicked, flying rings around the pod, sometimes somersaulting, then floating toward their mothers to nurse.

Jade's eyes widened. "I've heard of starwhales. The scorpions hunted them long ago. I thought they were extinct."

"They're fleeing the battles," Rowan said, voice soft. "In a way, they're like us humans. Lost. Homeless. Doomed to wander the galaxy forever. Even in old legends, they have no world of their own. Einav Ben-Ari wrote about them in her memoirs. Their story is a sad one. But they're beautiful."

The starwhales came to fly around the striker. At first, Rowan feared they would attack; after all, strikers were warships that had hunted these graceful aliens. Yet the whales gazed into the ship, saw the sisters inside, and extended tendrils. They touched the portholes, and beads of light ran across the barbels.

Rowan laughed, tears in her eyes. She raced toward a porthole and placed her hand against it. A starwhale placed the tip of his tendril against the other side.

"We're holding hands," Rowan whispered.

Then the starwhale sang, a deep, sonorous sound that passed through the barbel, through the porthole, and filled the starship. Rowan's tears fell. It was beautiful. It was so beautiful.

"Is this ... music?" Jade asked.

Rowan nodded, tears on her cheeks. "It's music."

The starwhales flew with the *Mother's Mercy* for a long time. The adults glided around it, as if they were protecting the ship. The cubs frolicked around the starship, spinning, cavorting, gazing inside with curious eyes.

"They're protecting us," Jade said. "They somehow understand. They somehow know we're on a mission to fight the scorpions. They want to help." A sob fled her lips. "They want to help."

Rowan guided her sister toward a porthole. "Place your hand on the window, Jade," she whispered.

Jade hesitated. Her eyes hardened, then softened again. Her legs trembled. Finally she placed her hand against the porthole, and a starwhale reached out a barbel, bringing its tip to Jade's hand. Once more, beads of light shone, and the starwhale's song filled the cabin.

"I think he just said hi to you," Rowan said.

And Jade began to weep. Her body shook with sobs.

"It's beautiful," Jade whispered. "It's so beautiful. And I'm so sorry. I'm so sorry, Rowan. For everything I've done. All this death. Because life is so beautiful. Life is *so* beautiful."

The sisters stood together, but now their tears were tears of joy—for the beauty that still remained, the beauty they still fought for.

Finally, after hours of flying together, the starwhales rose and glided away. The sisters stood, watching until the animals faded into the distance, continuing their own quest for life.

"May you find peace in the darkness, friends," Rowan said softly, then turned to look at Jade. "I was wrong, Jade. Not all lights in the darkness are lights of death. There are lights of beauty and hope too."

Jade pointed out the viewport. "There is another light of hope. The whales guided us here."

The indigo world floated ahead, growing larger by the moment. A shimmering, crystal planet like a jewel in space.

Harmonia. The world where Rowan had been born. Where her parents had died. Where Jade had dropped the Godblade in a glittering cave. A light in the dark—a place where they would find hope or despair, life or death.

## CHAPTER TWENTY-FOUR

After weeks of travel, after two years of war, Emet saw it ahead.

Aelonia. Center of the Concord. A last bastion of freedom in a galaxy aflame.

"Aelonia." Emet's voice was a low rumble like gentle thunder. "The Sphere of Dreams. The Great Light. The Hall of Starlight and Song. It has many names, and none do it justice."

Tom Shepherd stepped across the bridge and joined Emet at the viewport. The man had done impressive work with Earth's Light, had liberated a gulock, and had brought good fighters experienced at killing scorpions. Emet had made him a lieutenant commodore in the Heirs of Earth—a new rank of officer between captain and commodore, created to match the organization's swelling numbers.

Emet liked the man, trusted him. Tom was only in his forties, but years of war had turned his hair silver, had left his face deeply lined. His uniform—the polished black boots, the rich blue overcoat, the shiny brass buttons, the insignia on his shoulders—could not hide the ghosts, the gauntness of those cheeks, the weariness in that soul. Tom Shepherd had survived a gulock, and those demons would always dance around him.

Yet this man's eyes—dark, sunken, and sad—still shone with wonder as they gazed out into space.

"Poets sing of this place across ten thousand worlds." Tom patted the silver flute that hung from his belt alongside his pistol. "I myself played some songs of Aelonia in the fields of a distant planet."

Emet nodded. "Yes, here it is. The capital of the Concord. This place has lit the galaxy for a thousand years. Now we'll see if Aelonia stands or falls."

Others came to join him at the viewport. Old Luther limped forward, tapping his cane; he too wore a uniform now, serving as Chief Quartermaster. Nurse Cindy approached, still wearing her scrubs. Officers and guards. They all stared in awed silence as Aelonia grew.

Aelonia was a Dyson sphere, the last one remaining in the Milky Way. Once several such spheres had lit the galaxy. They had shattered in the First Galactic War, the great conflict that had burned the galaxy a thousand years ago, birthing the Concord and Hierarchy. From those ashes had risen Aelonia, a new center of power, a Renaissance of civilization.

Here was the largest structure in the known universe, completely surrounding a star system. From here, still far away, it looked like a fully-urbanized planet, coated with metal and lined with lights. But it wasn't the sight of Aelonia that Emet marveled at. It was its *size*.

"This place could engulf our home solar system," Emet said, "from Sol all the way to Neptune. A shield around a star and its planets. There is more mass ahead, friends, than in a million planets."

"And it's more than just a shield," Tom said. "The outside is metallic and armored. Crude, yes. But the inside layer, the bards sing, is covered with forests, grasslands, lakes and rivers, a wilderness larger than a million Earths."

"The bards are right," Emet said. "My father visited here as a child, traveling with his own father, a merchant of rare furs and stone sculptures. He told me many tales of Aelonia. Inside this sphere are the greatest institutions in the galaxy. Concord Hall, a shimmering glass tower where ambassadors gather from ten thousand civilizations. The Citadel of Peace, a fortress of stone, headquarters of the Peacekeepers. The Temple of Memory, a library larger than a million Earthstones, containing the cultural heritage of a galaxy. The Cosmic Museum, safeguarding the secrets of the galaxy's scientific wonders. The Botanical Terrarium, where plants from a thousand worlds grow."

Cindy cleared her throat. "We get it. It's nice. Do they have hospitals? Because we're in serious need of more medical supplies. Especially if we start fighting soon."

Emet nodded. "Just this morning, I had a call with Admiral Melitar, commander of the Aelonian fleet. We fought side by side at Terminus. I trust him. He'll supply us with all that we need: food, water, ammunition, and yes, medical supplies. We'll be ready when the enemy strikes."

They turned to look at the holographic map of the Milky Way Galaxy, which rose behind them on the bridge. The computer had been updating the map as the war raged on. Hierarchy stars appeared in red. Concord stars appeared in blue.

The map was nearly entirely red now.

There was a single blue orb in the map—Aelonia.

"We're an island in a sea of wolves," Tom said softly.

"Or a sea of scorpions," said Emet.

Cindy looked at the map, eyes haunted. "The disease has spread across the body. If the Milky Way galaxy were my patient, I'd be tempted to pull the plug. How do we win?"

Emet raised his chin. "Maybe we won't win. Maybe we'll lose. Maybe in Aelonia we'll die. But we will fight nonetheless. This will be our final stand. The last roar of humanity."

He gestured outside at the rest of the human fleet. A thousand starships. Thirty thousand warriors and refugees. They had come here from across the galaxy, many rebellions gathering together under Emet's command. Warships. Starfighters. Infantry. The human army, prepared for its final battle.

Cindy clasped Emet's hand. "Our final stand," she whispered.

Old Luther turned his strange, starry eyes upon Emet, the irises shaped like sunbursts, eerily bright against his dark skin. "For decades, I languished in a relic, selling scraps for profit." The starling squeezed Emet's shoulder. "I'm proud to fight with you, Emet. I'm old. I'm dying already from the cancer in my belly. I'll be glad to go down fighting."

Tom was still looking at the holographic map. He turned toward them. He spoke slowly. "I've faced hopelessness before. In the gulock. I thought it was my final stand. A lost battle. Death spread all around me—thousands of bodies burning. I was in hell. Everywhere—the demons." He faced them, but he was gazing ten thousand miles away. "But in the darkness, a light shone. Hope rose from despair. Ayumi came to me, running pure and blessed from the inferno. She gave me hope. She made me believe in miracles. I survived that day. And I believe again. That Ayumi died in that gulock. That she returned to life, her hand marked. That she returned for a reason." His eyes shone. "The ancients brought her back, my friends, for this battle. For the battle of Aelonia. She will deliver us."

They all looked at him, silent. Emet saw the doubt in the eyes of his officers and friends. He himself felt such doubt.

Yes, Ayumi had a rune on her hand, perhaps even a rare rune. Yes, Jade and Rowan had gone to the Glittering Caves, seeking the mythical Godblade, a weapon that only Ayumi could wield. Bay was even overseeing a team of engineers, installing a turret atop the *Jerusalem*, a place for Ayumi to stand and point her blade at enemies like a gunner aiming a cannon.

To Emet, it all seemed pointless. Old tales.

But he allowed them to believe. The sisters. His son. Tom.

*It gives them hope,* Emet thought. *Right now, they need to believe in miracles. Let them have hope before the end.*

Emet put his hope elsewhere. If he had any hope, it lay in what he now saw outside. He pointed.

"Look, friends. We're not alone."

Other fleets were flying toward Aelonia.

Many of them.

At their starboard side, lights shone, and a fleet of Gouramis glided toward Aelonia. The sentient fish flew cylindrical starships filled with water, their lavender sails undulating like fins. Beyond them flew round, rocky ships filled with crystals—the geode ships of the Menorians, a race of benevolent mollusks with many arms. Beyond them flew a fleet of silvery, elongated starships; Emet recognized the Altairians, a race of tall, green humanoids with many eyes.

He turned toward the port side, and there he saw more fleets. Ships of crystal and wood carried the Silvans, a race of furry forest-dwellers. The Esporians had come, sentient mushrooms flying pod-ships that could sneeze out venomous spores. The Silicades were here, intelligent crystals flying huge warships like mountains of quartz. The Tarmarins joined them, a race of warlike armadillos, their oval ships covered with metallic scales.

There were many other fleets too, some from species Emet didn't recognize.

"Their worlds had fallen," he said. "They are now exiles like us humans. They all came here. To Aelonia. To make a final stand against the enemy."

Cindy raised an eyebrow. "You know, Emet, for two thousand years, these species oppressed humans. They locked us in enclaves. They hunted us for sport. Many of them butchered us like pests. These are not our friends."

"No," Emet agreed. "They're not our friends. But they *are* enemies to our greatest enemy. So we'll fight by their side. And Admiral Melitar, the supreme commander of this united force, *is* our friend. I'm proud to fight with him. We fight at Aelonia. But we fight for Earth."

They all turned and gazed together toward distant Earth.

If the scorpions won this battle—Earth too would fall.

Their homeworld was too far to see from here. But they knew it was out there. That it needed them. That Leona needed them.

*Godspeed, Leona,* Emet thought. *We'll do our best to hold them off. I hope and pray you reach our homeworld soon. If we fail, if we cannot stop the scorpions, make your stand there. Let the last humans die on Earth.*

## CHAPTER TWENTY-FIVE

The first time Ayumi saw the weaver, she fell madly in love.

"Hello, Ayumi." The weaver walked into the room, a creature as mystical and graceful as a spirit. "My name is Coral. I heard you wanted to learn about weaving?"

It had been two years since the scorpions had invaded the peaceful world of Paev, since they had slain Ayumi's parents. Since then, Ayumi had become used to cowering in corners, hiding in shadows, avoiding eye contact. In the open, in the light, there were dangers. There were scorpions. There were enemies everywhere. Her fellow humans had given Ayumi a bed. She slept under it. They gave her food. She only nibbled, hiding leftovers in her mattress, saving them for days of privation. They spoke to her. She only huddled in a ball, staring at her lap, trembling until they went away.

For months now, Ayumi had been flying with other humans—first with Tom, then with the Heirs of Earth. For months, she had hidden in shadows, too afraid to speak to anyone but Tom, sometimes too afraid to breathe.

Now, for the first time, Ayumi forgot her fear. Forgot to hide. Forgot to lower her eyes.

She looked at Coral with open wonder.

"You're a weaver!" Ayumi whispered.

Coral was only in her twenties, but her eyes seemed older somehow, wise beyond her years, filled with ancient wisdom. Her skin was dark brown, smooth, and adorned with silvery runes. Ayumi's hair had turned white in the gulock, and she had been ashamed, hiding it under a hat. But Coral too had white hair, long and smooth and gleaming like moonlight, and it was beautiful. The weaver wore an Inheritor uniform—supple brown trousers, symbolizing the brown soil of Earth, a buttoned white shirt, symbolizing the clouds, and a blue overcoat to symbolize Earth's blue sky. But unlike other Inheritors, Coral had embroidered runes into the fabric, using thread that shone like starlight.

*I want to be proud and strong like her,* Ayumi thought. *A weaver with many runes. I want to walk with my back straight. To let my white hair flow for all to see. To not be afraid.*

Then Ayumi lowered her eyes.

*But I'm not like that. I'm not a heroine. I'm small. I'm weak. I'm scared. I'm just a mouse in a world of cats.*

The scorpions rose like ghosts around her. Their claws cut her. Flayed bodies twitched, still alive. Fire ate them.

Ayumi padded toward the corner. Her bunk aboard the *Jerusalem* was small, barely large enough for her cot, but even it felt too large. She curled up in the corner. She held the wooden dove Tom had given her, seeking comfort from this offering of peace and hope.

Coral knelt before her. The weaver's face was soft and kind. She smiled.

"I'm indeed a weaver," she said. "What's your name?"

"Ayumi Kobayashi," she whispered.

"That's a beautiful dove you have, Ayumi. Can I hold it?"

Ayumi handed the dove over. "Tom Shepherd made it for me. He was the leader of Earth's Light. One of the rebel groups that joined the Heirs of Earth."

Coral took the dove. She stroked the wood. "It's beautiful. There were similar birds on the planet I'm from, a desert world called Til Shiran. The birds there were white as snow. They would flutter around the granaries, looking for fallen seeds. Sometimes I would sit by the window for hours, watching them eat and fly, imagining their lives."

"That sounds nice," Ayumi said. "I once tended to a baby bird, but ..." She lowered her head. "He died."

*And I died,* she thought. *I died in the gulock. The scorpion doctor killed me. Again and again. And brought me back with his defibrillator. Again and again. Until ...*

She began to tremble.

"Ayumi, can I show you something?" Coral said.

She looked at the weaver. That gentle face soothed Ayumi. She nodded.

Coral rolled up her sleeves, revealing more runes, and took a deep breath. A rune on her forearm shone. It was shaped like a tree, its roots winding, its branches forming a circle around its trunk. Coral cradled the wooden dove in her hands, and suddenly—

Ayumi gasped.

"It's moving!" she said. "The dove! Its wings are moving!"

The movement was subtle, but it was there. A stirring of the wings. A rustling of the wooden feathers. An opening and closing of the beak.

Coral smiled. "Would you like to hold it? The aether won't last long."

Ayumi nodded. When Coral placed the dove in her hands, Ayumi nearly dropped it. Her heart pounded. The bird scared her. She worried it would take flight, even attack. But it moved gently in her hands like a roosting mother hen. It slowed down, then fell still, just a wooden sculpture again. The rune on Coral's arm dimmed.

"Can you teach me how to do that?" Ayumi said. "Please."

Coral smiled. "I used a tree rune. It's normally used by gardeners to guide the roots and branches of trees, though also by carpenters who form those trees into new objects. It's a semi-advanced rune. But I can teach you simpler runes first."

Ayumi mustered all her courage and made eye contact with Coral. "How can I not be ready for a semi-advanced rune? Bay says I have the most advanced rune in the universe." She hesitated, then took a deep breath and opened her palm. "A rune shaped like a serpent eating its own tail."

Coral stared. She lost her breath. Her eyes dampened.

"So it's true," she whispered. "An ouroboros. You're a Godweaver."

And Ayumi was afraid again. She didn't want to inspire such awe in anyone. She didn't want to be special or important. She just wanted to go home. To see her parents again. To leap from roof to roof in Palaevia Enclave, to eat the sweet rolls Mister Hiroji baked, to return home and curl up in bed between her parents, to feel safe and warm and loved.

*But Palaevia is gone,* she thought. *The enclave is gone. My parents are gone. The scorpions destroyed it all. They destroyed the galaxy. If there's a new home for me, it's on Earth. So I must fight for Earth. However I can.*

"What is a Godweaver?" Ayumi said.

Coral embraced her. "It's you, little one. The most precious weaver in two thousand years. Not since the days of Sage Gadriel has any weaver earned an ouroboros rune."

"What can I do with this rune?" Ayumi asked. "Can I make a bird move?"

Coral grew somber. She held Ayumi at arm's length and stared into her eyes.

"With an ouroboros rune, you can grant death to worlds. To empires. To civilizations that span star systems. With this rune, you can defeat the Hierarchy and save humanity."

Ayumi bit her lip. "But no pressure, right?"

Coral laughed. The tension left the room.

"I'll be with you, Ayumi," the weaver said. "Every step of the way. I'm not a Godweaver. I don't have an ouroboros rune. But I've been weaving for years, and I've dedicated my life to the art. We're flying to Aelonia. To the center of the Concord. There we'll take our final stand against the Hierarchy. Until we arrive, I will train you."

Ayumi lowered her head. "I want to learn. To be a weaver like you. But I don't understand." Her knees began to tremble. "What can my rune do? How can it kill so many people?"

Coral sat on the bunk and patted the mattress beside her. Ayumi sat down, and Coral wrapped an arm around her.

"A long time ago," Coral said, "there was a man. A human. His name was Gadriel, and he was very wise. This was when humans still lived on Earth. But cruel aliens came from the sky. They were called Hydrians, monsters that looked like squids."

"I've heard of them," Ayumi said. "The Hydrian Empire destroyed Earth."

Coral nodded. "They did. This was only a generation or two after the Golden Lioness, the legendary leader of Earth, had died. Without her strength and wisdom, humanity faltered and fell. The squids murdered billions. They destroyed our cities. Only a few humans escaped. Some historians believe that only a few thousand made it out of Earth. Gadriel was one of them. Humanity scattered across the stars, seeking refuge on alien worlds, treated like pests. Gadriel led his followers to a distant planet named Elysium, and there he founded a guildhall. Gadriel was a mighty weaver who forged many artifacts from aetherstone. Do you know what an artifact is?"

Ayumi nodded. "My father had one. A lume. It had a rune engraved into it. With that lume, he could weave magical rugs. He wove me a rug once with scenes of Earth. The fabric stars shone. The rivers flowed. There was even a bird embroidered onto it, and its wings flapped—like the wings of the wooden dove."

"There was aetherstone inside that lume," Coral said. "And there was a matching rune on your father's hand. There are thousands of runes, Ayumi, but they all fall into two types. The

213

most common type are called *power runes*. With power runes, we can do many things—fight, heal, even alter reality. They all use aether, a luminous substance that flows from a higher plane of reality called the Empyrean Firmament."

Ayumi nodded, remembering her experience after dying in the Red Hospital. Her soul had risen to a higher plane, a realm full of light and shadows but no solid figures. She had heard a kind voice, the voice of an angel. That must have been the Empyrean Firmament.

"What is the second type of rune?" she asked.

"Aether also has a solid form," Coral said. "We call it aetherstone, and it's exceedingly rare. With it, we can forge artifacts. The first weavers discovered the power of runes when embroidering designs into their fabrics. When they discovered aetherstone, they used it to forge looms that could weave beautiful fabrics some called magical. They could capture starlight and weave it into satin, and the stars would shine. They could weave flowers into dresses, and the flowers would bloom and send forth sweet scents. Later on, weavers discovered they could also forge other artifacts. Farm tools. Machines. Engines. And weapons."

Ayumi glanced at the dagger that hung from Coral's belt. Its blade was short, its pommel as large as an apple. A rune was engraved there.

"Is that ..." Ayumi began, then lost her courage.

Coral nodded. "I bear a runeblade. Do you see the rune engraved into the pommel?"

"Yes," Ayumi said. "It looks like a sunburst."

Coral opened her hand, revealing a matching rune on the palm. "This is a *key rune*. While power runes connect directly from the Empyrean Firmament, key runes are different. They let us unlock artifacts. The runes on my hand and the pommel match." She drew the dagger, and its blade shone.

"It shines!" Ayumi said.

"It shines with aether," said Coral. "This blade is now mighty, able to cut through steel. Here, hold it."

She flipped the dagger over and held it out, hilt-first. Gently, Ayumi took the weapon. As soon as Coral let go, the blade went dark.

"I don't have a matching key rune," Ayumi said. "That's why I can't use it, right?"

Coral nodded. "Yes. There is a sunbeam rune on the dagger. But on your palm is an ouroboros rune. Both are key runes, but of a different type."

Ayumi twisted her lips. "How can I gain a sunbeam rune?"

"Every weaver has a mentor," said Coral.

"Will you be my mentor?"

"I can be your teacher," Coral said. "A mentor must be an ancient. Do you know who the ancients are?"

"I think so," Ayumi said. "They're very wise. And very good. I ... I think one talked to me once. Before the ouroboros appeared on my hand. Coral, I ..." The words spilled out from her. "I died. I died in the gulock, and when I died, an ancient spoke to me. He sent me back. And when I came back, my hair was white like yours. And there was this rune on my hand. And I'm scared. I'm so scared."

Coral wrapped her arms around her. "I know, sweet child. We're all scared. But the ancients blessed you. The ancient who spoke to you is your mentor. He will guide you, watch over you, grant you runes if you earn them. Often, the ancients demand different tasks, different journeys for us to take. They want us to grow as people before we grow as weavers. Your journey took you into the realms of death and back, a journey no other weaver has taken since Gadriel."

Ayumi wiped her tears away. "Gadriel, the first weaver, died and came back too?"

Coral nodded. "He did. The Hydrians killed him. He was resurrected, like you were, and on his hand was the same rune." Coral traced the rune on Ayumi's palm. "A serpent forming an infinity sign. Biting its tail. A rune that symbolizes infinity and rebirth, life and death. The ancients guided Gadriel, and he forged a great weapon. Not a mere dagger like mine but a sword. A sword called the Godblade. A sword with an ouroboros rune engraved into its pommel. The mightiest weapon in the world. My dagger can cut through steel, but the Godblade can cut through worlds."

Ayumi rose to her feet, panting. Her head spun and her heart burst into a gallop. "So I'll wield the Godblade! I'll fight the scorpions. They murdered my parents. They murdered millions of humans. I'll fight them bravely! I'm not afraid. I'll be like Gadriel. Where is this Godblade? Let me begin training."

Coral nodded and smiled. "Good. We still have a while before we reach Aelonia. I'll teach you all that I can. Maybe your mentor, the ancient who blessed you, will even grant you more runes before the battle. Runes to help you see far. To move quickly. To stay awake for days on end. You'll need to meditate, to enter a trance, to learn to speak to your mentor. I'll teach you these things. I'll be your guide to the Empyrean Firmament. But first, I want to show you something. Can you come with me?"

They left the cabin, that tiny closet of a room. Ayumi had been spending most of her time there, hiding from the bustle across the *Jerusalem*. The Inheritor flagship seemed massive to her, a labyrinth of corridors and rooms where hundreds of people served. It reminded her of the enclave back home. Tom had told her that the *Jerusalem* was actually small for a flagship, that some alien civilizations flew ships that could swallow ten *Jerusalems* with room for dessert. But to Ayumi it seemed a world.

Soldiers bustled back and forth, wearing the brown and blue. Marines trained in crowded halls, firing at targets. Starfighter pilots played poker in a rec room. The men sported curling mustaches, and the women wore their hair in braids, status symbols reserved to pilots. Officers frowned at monitors and marched between war rooms, ranging from babyfaced lieutenants to gray-haired commodores. Gunners stood at their stations, manning the warship's mighty cannons. Mechanics, navigators, engineers, computer programmers, and countless other military technicians moved back and forth, busy at their tasks. There were even robots who scurried about, just as busy as the humans.

The refugees had been moved to other ships. The *Jerusalem* was now dedicated to only one purpose: war.

As Ayumi walked between these soldiers, she was afraid. Afraid of the crowds. Afraid of the battle ahead. Afraid of the memories she knew would haunt her that night. Afraid of her task in this war. Yet with every step, seeing these soldiers, her fear eased.

She looked out a porthole and saw many other warships. A thousand human ships flew here. Humanity had rallied. From hundreds of communities. From dozens of rebel groups. They had joined here to fight. Thirty thousand humans. It was a small army, as far as armies went. It was a speck of dust by the great armadas of the enemy. But it made Ayumi proud.

"I no longer hide," she said softly. "I no longer cower in shadows. I no longer walk like a lamb to the slaughter. I fight."

Coral squeezed her hand. "And we all fight with you. For all those we lost. For their memory. And for those who still live."

They took an elevator to the upper deck, walked down a corridor to the prow, and approached a ladder. They climbed toward the roof of the *Jerusalem*. A hatch awaited here. They climbed through the opening, entering a small dome that bulged atop the *Jerusalem* like a blister.

Bay was waiting inside this turret. He was working with a screwdriver, bolting components into the transparent canopy. He turned toward them, placed his screwdriver down, and wiped sweat off his brow. Other tools, bolts, and gears lay scattered around him.

"Hello, ladies," he said. "It's coming along nicely. Almost ready."

Ayumi looked around her. Her eyes widened. Standing here in the canopy, it felt like standing in open space. She could see the rest of the fleet flying all around her.

"We're standing on the roof of the *Jerusalem*!" she said.

She gaped, spinning slowly in a circle, taking in the view. The warships of humanity flew around her, ranging from single-pilot vessels to barges containing thousands of people. On every hull appeared the same symbol: a blue planet with golden wings. The stars spread all around.

"Here it is," Bay said softly. "What remains of humanity. Lost in space all around us."

"Not lost," Ayumi said. "Going home."

Bay smiled. "That's right. Here, Ayumi! Take a look. I've been building this for you." He pointed. "See?"

Ayumi looked. She gasped.

For the first time, she noticed that a sword impaled the canopy. The hilt was inside the turret. The blade was outside in the vacuum of space. The crossguard was bolted into the transparent dome.

At first, Ayumi thought this was the Godblade. But no— Jade and Rowan were still on their quest to find the artifact. There was no rune engraved into this blade.

"It's only a placeholder for now," Bay said. "A fake sword. I'm using it to test the rig I built for you. Standing in this turret, atop the *Jerusalem*, you get a full view of space all around you. You can even aim the sword in different directions. Try it!"

Ayumi approached the hilt, hesitated, and glanced at Coral.

The weaver nodded. "You can do this. I'm with you."

Ayumi tightened her lips and held the sword hilt. She nudged it, then gasped.

The entire canopy was moving around her! The transparent dome moved as she tugged the sword hilt!

Bay grinned. "Cool, huh? The canopy around us can move along tracks. You can aim the sword anywhere you like. Forward, backwards, sideways, even directly overhead. It's the same principle as a gun turret. It just uses a sword instead of a cannon. And once Rowan gets back with the Godblade, I'll replace the fake sword. Standing here, Ayumi, you'll be able to see all around you—and aim that weapon."

Ayumi yanked the hilt sideways. The canopy moved around them, and the blade pointed forward. She spun, fast as she could, and aimed the blade behind her. The dome moved without a hitch. Ayumi tightened her lips, then raised her hand overhead. The sword pointed above her toward the distant stars.

Coral and Bay were staring at her, silent.

Ayumi stared back.

"I'm no longer afraid," Ayumi said. "I will train. You will teach me. We will find the Godblade." She thought of her parents. Of the millions of dead. Of a kind presence in a dark place. She narrowed her eyes and smiled. "We will win."

## CHAPTER TWENTY-SIX

The *Mother's Mercy* glided down toward Harmonia, a world of shimmering crystals and dark memories.

Rowan gazed down at the glittering lavender planet. A lump filled her throat. She remembered this place. She remembered standing at a starship porthole long ago, seeing the same endless plains and crystal mountains.

Last time she had been fleeing this world, a toddler, an orphan.

Now she was a woman, a soldier, a lieutenant in the Heirs of Earth. Now she was coming home.

Home? No. Perhaps not. Earth was her home. But here was the place Rowan had been born. The place where her parents had died. Her anchor and port of call.

"How do we know where the Glittering Caves are?" Jade said. "This is a large planet. Almost as large as Earth."

"I can find it," Rowan said. "I remember."

Jade raised an eyebrow. "You remember the coordinates of a cave you haven't seen since you were two?"

"Fillister knew the location," Rowan said. "He told me about it. Many times. I used to dream of someday flying home, of living in the cave again. I memorized the coordinates. I would write them over and over on napkins I stole, etch them into the walls of the ducts of Paradise Lost. Dreaming of someday flying back. Of finding my parents alive again." She gave a sad, soft laugh. "The dreams of a child."

Jade placed an arm around her. "Dreams show us the way home."

Harmonia had a thick, warm atmosphere, rich with oxygen and nitrogen. The planet had no plants or animals, but life thrived here. Bioluminescent bacteria filled Harmonia, deep blue, silver, and lavender, living inside the crystals. The planet orbited a small white dwarf no brighter than the moon, but Harmonia shone with its own light.

*Mother's Mercy* glided over crystal plains and over a deep blue sea. The waves shone with trillions of luminous microorganisms. Islands of dark rock and purple crystal, draped with silvery algae, pierced the water, soaring tall and thin toward the starry sky. A shore shone ahead, the white sand glowing, and beyond rose indigo cliffs and obsidian mountains.

Rowan pointed, the lump growing in her throat. "There."

The striker glided over the shore, circled a cobalt mountain, and descended toward a valley. Rocky tors rose all around like fortresses, but silver sand filled the valley, reflecting the starlight.

"Land here," Rowan said.

Jade pulled on chains and adjusted levers. The *Mother's Mercy* landed in the sandy valley. The mountains rose around them, a ring of black stone draped with lavender moss. The stars shone above.

And there, ahead, Rowan saw it.

A cave.

"Our old home," Jade said. "I remember! I used to sometimes run out into this valley. I would play in the sand." She looked around her. "It seems so much smaller now. I used to think this valley the size of a nation."

Rowan smiled. "It's barely larger than a football field."

Jade tilted her head. "What's a football? Is that some kind of ball made from a severed foot?"

Rowan cringed. "Yikes. No!" She shuddered. "You have a *lot* of catching up to do, sis."

They exited the starship. The air was cool and rich with oxygen, and the sand whispered beneath their boots. A breeze rustled their hair and stirred luminous lichen that hung from boulders. Rowan drew Lullaby and loaded the heavy pistol. Jade extended her claws, one of the modifications Sin Kra had given her. This was a beautiful place, a quiet and peaceful haven. But if the Godblade was truly here, it was also the most important place in the galaxy. The sisters walked warily, eyes darting, ready for enemies to spring from behind the boulders.

They reached the cave and stepped inside. A tunnel delved downward. They walked slowly, Lullaby pointing their way. The air was cooler in here, and water trickled ahead and dripped down the walls. For the first few steps it was dark, and Rowan needed her flashlight. But soon soft light glowed ahead. The sisters walked toward the light, entered a chamber, then stared around with wide eyes.

"It's beautiful," Rowan whispered. She clasped Jade's hand. "It's so beautiful."

They stood in silence for a moment, gazing upon the Glittering Caves, their childhood home.

Crystal stalagmites and stalactites filled the hall, some as small as fingers, others larger than men. The microorganisms of Harmonia filled the crystals, shining within their mineral homes, glowing in all shades of purple, silver, and blue. A stream flowed along the floor, reflecting the lights above. Rough passageways led to deeper chambers, and there too crystals shone.

"We were lucky to live here," Jade said, voice soft as if fearful to disturb this beauty. "If only for a while."

They walked between the crystals and along the stream.

"Do you remember where you dropped the Godblade?" Rowan said.

"No." Jade looked around her. "I think it was into a fissure or chasm, but my memory is fuzzy. Maybe—"

Suddenly Jade froze and let out a strangled gasp.

Rowan raised Lullaby, tensing. "What?"

Jade pointed. "Look."

Rowan looked.

A skeleton lay by a cluster of crystals. A human skeleton.

Rowan exhaled shakily and lowered her pistol. Her heart still pounded.

"Jesus, Jade, I thought it was a scorpion." Rowan approached and stared down at the skeleton. "You don't think this is our ..." She covered her mouth, feeling ill.

"No." Jade shook her head. "He's wearing a prosthetic finger. See? I remember a man with a prosthetic finger. He used to spin the prosthetic like a toilet paper roll, making me laugh." She sighed. "I don't remember his name."

Rowan took a few more steps. "Here's another skeleton. A child." She took another few steps. "More of them. God. There are a whole bunch."

The sisters walked in solemn silence, passing from chamber to chamber. There were dozens of skeletons. Some were badly damaged—limbs ripped off, ribs broken, skulls caved in. Rowan wondered which were her parents. She dared not guess. She didn't think she wanted to know.

"This battle was my first memory," Rowan said. "The night the scorpions came. Only we two survived."

Some skeletons still held rifles. One huddled over the skeleton of a baby. Two other skeletons were still embracing. The skulls' jaws hung open in silent screams.

"We need to bury them," Jade said. "On Earth. Come, Rowan, help me." She knelt and lifted a skeleton's arm. "Let's carry them back into *Mother's Mercy*."

Rowan shook her head. "No. We can't carry so many skeletons. There must be a hundred here. We won't just treat them like a pile of bones, tossing them into storage while our war continues. These people have been resting here for sixteen years. They can rest a little longer. Once we defeat the scorpions, and once Earth is ours, we'll return here. With a crew. With coffins. With leaders of faith. We'll bring them all home in dignity and bury them on Earth. That's what they deserve."

Jade winced. "I didn't mean disrespect to the dead. I ..." She lowered her head. "I still have so much to learn. About honor and compassion. About how to be human."

Rowan patted her shoulder. "No, you meant well. It was a noble thought."

"I have so much to atone for." Jade looked around at the dead. "I killed people. Not these ones. But many others. Countless others. I can never redeem myself. I can never find salvation. But maybe I can do a little good. Fix a little bit that is broken."

"You did nothing wrong." Rowan placed her hands on her hips and glared at her sister. "You murdered nobody, Jade. The emperor wielded you as a weapon. The sword isn't responsible for those it cuts. Only the hand that wields it."

"I was aware of it all." Jade shuddered. "Maybe someday I can forgive the Skra-Shen for killing so many of us. But I can never forgive them for making me kill." She looked at her hands—slender, clawed, encased in white skin. "These hands, Rowan. There's so much blood on them."

Rowan held those hands. "Jade, you have a chance now to save humanity. Your old sword can defeat the Hierarchy. So let's find it. And we'll stab it into that damn emperor's heart."

"Actually, Skra-Shen have three hearts," Jade said. "And they can live for days even if you stab all three."

Rowan rolled her eyes. "Way to kill my dramatic moment, sis."

Jade smiled thinly. "Well, we can stab him in the brain, how's that?"

"Or in the butt," Rowan said.

"Scorpions don't have—"

"Sis, dramatic moment," Rowan said.

Jade took a few steps forward. She knelt by a skeleton, then looked over her shoulder.

"Rowan?" Jade whispered, and her voice was haunted. "I think this is Dad."

Rowan's heart lurched. She stepped close and knelt too. The skeleton lay on the ground. It had a golden tooth and a thin groove along the skull.

"Did Dad have a gold tooth?" Rowan said.

Jade nodded. "He did. I remember how it would shine. And that scratch along his skull? He had a scar there. He told me the tale a bunch of times. How a scorpion scratched him there, nearly split his skull open. And look." She pointed. "A golden ring on his finger. Maybe there's an inscription."

Jade reached for the ring, but Rowan stopped her.

"Leave the ring on. It's him. It's Dad." Rowan hesitated, then stroked the skull. "It's funny. People called him a traitor. The cowardly David Emery who defected from the Heirs of Earth, who stole the Earthstone, who betrayed Emet. But he wasn't a coward, was he? He wanted to save what he could of humanity. Our heritage in the Earthstone. His followers. His family. Me and you."

"He was a brave man," Jade said. "He fought bravely until the end. Sin Kra spoke of him sometimes. He mocked him, scorned him, but there was respect in his voice too. David Emery was a brave soldier and a wise man."

Rowan approached another skeleton. It had a matching ring. A locket hung around this skeleton's neck, and when Rowan opened it, she saw a photo of herself and Jade as children.

"This is Mom," Rowan said. "Close to Dad. They were trying to reach each other at the end. To hold hands."

Jade knelt by Mother.

"I miss you, Mommy," she whispered, voice suddenly higher, softer, and her tears flowed. "I'm so sorry for who I became."

The sisters embraced, kneeling between the skeletons.

"We will avenge them," Rowan said. "We will hunt those who killed them. But more importantly: we will find Earth. We will bury them there. And we will live long, joyful lives. Not lives of hiding. Not lives of fighting. But lives of building and healing. That will be their legacy."

They rose to their feet and dried their tears.

Jade pointed. "Look, Rowan. See that small chamber? I think that's where our family lived."

They left the skeletons, not without some pain, and approached a narrow passageway. Even Rowan had to duck to pass through. They stepped into a small, round cavern, and Rowan lost her breath.

A new memory pounded through her.

Herself—only a toddler. Her mother reading to her. A book about a dove. A single image, that was all. A memory lost until now.

"It was here," Rowan whispered. "This was our home."

Thankfully, there were no skeletons here. Rowan explored the room, finding objects that tickled her memory. A ceramic bowl painted with strawberries. A shelf with toy trains and blocks. A few tattered blankets. It was a simple home. Cozy. Comfortable.

"It's nice here," Rowan said. "Most humans spent their years of exile in horrible places. Living under bridges or in sewers. Eking out a living in asteroid mines. Or like me—living in the ducts of a space station. This cave is so cozy. A good place to hide."

"Not such a good place to hide," Jade said softly. "Not for long."

"No," Rowan agreed. "Not for long."

She stepped toward the back of the room, where she found a bookshelf. It was so dusty she couldn't read the titles. Rowan blew, scattering the dust, and sneezed seven times—her lucky number. Finally she examined the books' spines.

Her eyes widened.

"Books from Earth!" Rowan said. "Real books from Earth! Well, they can't be from actual Earth. Otherwise they'd have decomposed long ago. They were printed in exile, but *written* on Earth long ago. Look, Jade! This is a treasure. I've never seen actual paper books before."

She gazed with wonder, smiling. There were leatherbound copies of *The Lord of the Rings*, her favorite series alongside *Dragonlance* and *The Chronicles of Amber*. The complete works of Carl Sagan, Richard Dawkins, and Stephen Jay Gould stood on one shelf. Another shelf held twentieth century classics: *1984*, *Fahrenheit 451*, *A Brave New World*, *Catch-22*, *The Lord of the Flies*, *The House of the Spirits*, *The Hitchhiker's Guide to the Galaxy*, and many others.

On another shelf were works from the twenty-second century. The complete Marco Emery bibliography covered an entire shelf—books by Rowan's own ancestor. *The Earthrise Chronicles* by Einav Ben-Ari were here, all seven volumes, chronicling Earth's ancient wars against alien species. The works of Professor Noah Isaac, inventor of the wormholes and science fiction author, topped another shelf. According to legends, Professor Isaac and Einav Ben-Ari had married. Their child had been the famous Carl Ben-Ari, a legendary explorer. Carl's own books stood here too, chronicling his travels.

*Our ancestors,* Rowan thought. *Mine. Bay's. The ancestors of humanity. Our heritage and legends—here on these shelves.*

"I've read some of these already," Rowan said. "But not all. And not in print form. Jade, do you have any idea how precious these are?"

But Jade was fascinated by a small book wrapped in blue leather. She lifted it from the shelf, then looked at Rowan.

"Mom's diary," Jade said. "I remember her writing in it. I think we should take this one with us. To save her memories. To—"

A screech rose in the distance, echoing through the caves. The sisters froze.

"Scorpions," Rowan whispered.

## CHAPTER TWENTY-SEVEN

Humanity's fleet flew toward the great metallic sphere. Toward their last stand.

Their ships were old. A thousand vessels flew here, but only a few were warships. Even their mighty frigates, such as the *Jerusalem* and *Jaipur*, were simply refitted tankers. Most of the ships were derelicts, cargo ships, and makeshift cruisers built from scraps. Every ship, from the smallest dinghy to the largest frigate, was dented and creaking.

The Heirs of Earth were barely more than refugees. Only a few among them were uniformed warriors; the rest were survivors of gulocks and enclaves, skin and bones, wounded, haunted, wearing little more than rags. Thirty thousand humans flew here. Wretched. Haggard. Wracked with hunger, disease, and memories.

To Emet, they were the most noble souls in the galaxy. This was humanity's finest hour.

Their ships were old—but they displayed the symbols of Earth on their hulls.

Their people were ragged—but they stood tall, courage in their hearts, honor in their eyes.

*This army is as brave as the great fleets of old,* Emet thought. *I hope we make you proud, Golden Lioness. You once led us to war and victory. I vow to carry your torch high.*

Ahead floated Aelonia, the heart of the Concord. The Dyson sphere was the mightiest structure in the galaxy, a metal globe millions of kilometers in diameter. The Hierarchy covered the galaxy, controlling millions of stars. Here was the last fortress of freedom.

"Will this be enough?" said Tom. "Enough to stop the enemy?

The shepherd stood on the bridge of the *Jerusalem* beside Emet. He looked stronger than before. The past couple of months had transformed Tom Shepherd. He gained some healthy weight. His silver hair was thicker. His skin had a richer, bronze tone, no longer ashen. The gaunt, shabby survivor had become a proud officer. Emet wanted him here on the *Jerusalem*. The weaver girl was here, and she trusted nobody more than Tom.

*And I trust him,* Emet thought.

In many ways, the shepherd reminded Emet of himself. Tom too had lost his wife to the scorpions. He too had overcome tragedy to found a rebellion. Tom had fought bravely for long years, leading men in battle.

*If we survive today,* Emet thought, *we'll need leaders like Tom to rebuild Earth.*

"No," Emet finally said, returning his gaze to the sphere ahead. "It won't be enough. Not unless Jade and Rowan get back with that artifact. And not unless the damn sword actually works."

"It'll work," Tom said. "I believe in Ayumi. The ancients brought her back for a reason."

Emet couldn't help but scoff. "If the ancients were so powerful, why don't they smite the damn scorpions with a miracle from above?"

Tom turned to look at him. His eyes always seemed to stare ten thousand miles away. "Ayumi is that miracle."

Emet grunted. He looked away. He was more cynical than Tom. It amazed him that a man who had seen such horrors could still believe in miracles.

*Yet don't I believe in miracles too?* Emet thought. *Is that not why I still lead humanity? Why I still believe we can find Earth?*

He thought about this for a moment. Then he decided. Yes, he believed in miracles. Not the kind that came from above, but the miracles that men and women built themselves.

*I don't believe in gods,* he thought. *But I believe in the human miracle.*

A round gateway opened in the Dyson sphere, granting them passage. Emet led the way. He flew the *Jerusalem* through the gateway, and the other ships followed.

For a moment, Emet and Tom could only stand still, silent, gazing in awe.

On the outside, the Dyson sphere was raw metal. But the inner surface was lush with life, covered with forests, lakes, rivers, and fields. A star hung in the sphere's center like a nucleus, filling Aelonia with heat and light. Three terrestrial planets orbited the star, one heavily urbanized, another forested, a third covered in oceans. There were several gas giants too, though even these behemoths seemed minuscule floating inside the sphere. Countless starships flew like bees across a hive, and space stations shone, as large as cities.

"Behold the might of Aelonia," Tom said softly. "The beacon of civilization."

This was what a true galactic superpower looked like, Emet knew. Rows of solar panels crisscrossed the inner surface of the sphere, capturing the star's energy, powering the structure. Cities speckled the forests and plains. There was more landmass here, coating the inner sphere, than in a million Earths. The entire planet Earth would vanish here within Aelonia, a speck of dust in all this grandeur.

Many other fleets were here. A hundred civilizations had come to fight. Mightiest were the Aelonians themselves, whose home this was. A hundred thousand Aelonian warships flew across the star system, leaf-shaped and silvery. But they comprised only half the force. Aliens of every shape and size had come to fight alongside them. The Concord fought united.

"It's hard to fight with them," Tom confessed. "For two thousand years, the Concord treated humans as vermin."

"Yet now, at the end, they see us as equals," Emet said. "And they call upon us to help." He smiled grimly. "It only took a Galactic War to elevate our status."

Tom raised an eyebrow, and a thin smile raised one corner of his mouth. "Is it better to be a living pest or a dead hero?"

"Ask me again when the scorpions arrive," Emet muttered.

Once the last human ship flew into Aelonia, the gate shut behind them. Locks clanked shut, sealing them inside.

Aelonia was vast. Yet suddenly Emet felt claustrophobic.

A silvery dreadnought, shaped like a leaf, glided toward the human fleet. It was larger than any human ship, as large as the tallest skyscrapers from Earth's golden age. Here flew the *Iliria*, flagship of the Aelonian Armada.

The silver ship hailed him, and Emet answered the call. His monitor displayed the *Iliria's* bridge—a shadowy round chamber like a planetarium, its walls covered with viewports.

Several Aelonians stood there. As always, Emet found them disturbingly ethereal, nearly too beautiful to be true beings of flesh and blood. The humanoids were tall and slender, their skin transparent. Their innards glowed, each organ like a luminous bubble, and their skeletons seemed made of glass. What was it Duncan had once called them?

*Living lava lamps,* Emet remembered.

One of the Aelonians stepped forward, his face long and narrow. Emet recognized Admiral Melitar, the Aelonian who had fought alongside humanity in the Battle of Terminus. Emet liked him. Melitar not only recognized humanity's ambitions, he had given them the map to Earth—a map Leona was following.

"Hello, Admiral Melitar!" Emet said. "It's good to see you, my friend."

Melitar nodded. Orange blobs bubbled inside his transparent head—the Aelonian analogy to a smile.

"Hello, Emet, my friend," he said. "I am proud to fight alongside humanity again. Thank you for coming to our aid."

"Seems like we got here just in time," Emet said. "I'm sure your scanners detected the same thing we did."

Melitar's colors went colder, blues and indigos replacing yellows and oranges. "The vast armadas of the Skra-Shen are closing in. They will be here soon. Emet, there are a hundred gates to Aelonia. Each species of the Concord will guard another gate. The passageway you have traveled through will be known as Earth's Gate. It is yours to defend."

Emet nodded. "How sturdy is this shell of metal? Can it hold?"

Melitar hesitated, glanced at his comrades, then back at Emet. "There is a reasonable chance of battle within the sphere."

"Understood," Emet said. "We'll hold off the bugs for as long as we can. If we must, we'll get down and dirty in a fistfight."

"Truly humans are a noble race!" Melitar said. "For eras, you've wandered the shadows, homeless and cold, but your hearts burn with great fires. May the light bless you, Emet Ben-Ari, and may it bless all humans."

The transmission ended. The silver ship flew away.

Emet sent out his own signal, broadcasting to his fleet.

He spoke to them. To thirty thousand people. To the human race.

"Men and women. Heirs of Earth. This is Emet Ben-Ari, admiral of the fleet. We have now entered Aelonia, center of the Concord, where we await the enemy forces. It's here, by a distant star, that we face our greatest, perhaps our final battle. Earth is still far from our ships, but not from our hearts. In this battle, we will fight alongside many other species, and we will be fighting for the Milky Way galaxy, for the freedom of all peaceful beings. But first and foremost, even in this distant place, we fight for our home. For Earth."

He paused for a moment, then continued.

"For two thousand years, we've lived in exile. Some of us languished in enclaves. Others fled the inferno of the gulocks. A few hid in space stations, mines, distant colonies. But we all share something in common. Throughout our exile, we dreamed of Earth. We sang of Earth. We vowed to someday go home. That dream seems far now. Earth has never seemed so out of reach. The enemy has slain millions of our people. And the cruel Sin Kra seeks to murder even we few who remain. Our dream of Earth seems almost dead."

He took a deep breath, then spoke again, voice louder.

"But I tell you that this dream is still alive! My daughter, Leona Ben-Ari, still leads the expedition to Earth, and seeks to found a colony on our distant homeworld. As she undertakes this most dangerous and holy of missions, it's our duty to hold off the scorpions. To face them with courage. With conviction. With blazing fire and an iron will. Today we will face the Skra-Shen! Not as lambs led to the slaughter. Not as cowering, weak refugees. But as an army!"

He paused for another breath, and he saw Tom nodding at him, a small smile on his lips, a light in his eyes. Yes, Tom understood. Tom had been like a lamb. Now he was among the lions.

Emet spoke again, broadcasting his words to his thousand ships.

"We wait now for battle. Not a battle we chose. But a battle we will fight with our full strength. As we fight today, we fight with the souls of our martyrs. With the spirits of the millions, those who perished in the gulocks, those who burned on the battlefields, those who fell for their humanity. We fight with our murdered fathers, our butchered mothers, our slain children. We fight for their memory, for their legacy. In this battle, we will break the enemy's fleets! We will drive him before us! We will bring hope to our people. We will bring salvation to humanity. We will seek justice for our brothers and sisters flayed and burned in the furnaces. The fallen call upon us to break the enemy. They imprint upon us a holy duty: to remember them, and to bring the living home. To our Pale Blue Dot. To Earth. May Sol's light bless you today, children of Earthrise. We do not forget. Earth still calls us home."

He ended the transmission.

The fleet turned toward the closed gate in the Dyson sphere. It loomed before them, a round metal doorway. Forests, grasslands, and mountains spread around the doorway for countless kilometers, coating the inner surface of the sphere. The warships arranged themselves at the front. The other ships—filled with supplies and refugees—moved back, deeper into the Dyson sphere. But if need be, they too would fight.

The fleet hovered, waiting.

They did not have to wait long.

Only moments after Emet's speech, alarms flashed around the gates.

Warnings filled Emet's monitors.

*Enemy at the gates. Enemy at the gates.*

Cameras were mounted outside the Dyson sphere, broadcasting the views to every warship inside. Emet and Tom stared and lost their breath.

"My Ra," Tom whispered. "There are thousands."

"Millions," Emet said.

The Hierarchy fleet seemed to cover space, to surge forth like an expanding nebula. Their warships hid the stars. Most were Skra-Shen strikers. But many other species flew here too:

marshcrabs, spiders, centipedes, and dozens of other cruel alien civilizations who bowed before the scorpions. Creatures of claws, fangs, unending malice.

From the darkness, evil surged forth.

These creatures had conquered every other star in the galaxy. Now they were coming here to complete their conquest, to complete their destruction of humanity. They surrounded Aelonia in a noose.

Inside the sphere, the last free fleets hovered at the gates, waiting, watching.

The enemies arranged themselves outside, facing Aelonia. Countless warships of every kind, some long and sharp, others bristly, some lumpy, some oozing. Ships filled with countless monsters. Among them—just outside Earth's Gate—Emet saw the *Imperator*. The scorpion flagship. The imperial dreadnought of Sin Kra himself.

For a long moment—stillness. Silence.

Then the enemy opened fire, and the cosmos burned.

## CHAPTER TWENTY-EIGHT

The screeches, clatters, and hisses echoed through the Glittering Caves.

They were unmistakable.

"Scorpions!" Rowan hissed, holding Lullaby before her.

Jade took a step forward. Her eyes narrowed. She stared at the crystal tunnel ahead. The scorpions had not yet appeared— but they were getting closer.

"Guns won't help us here," Jade said. Her claws thrust out from her fingertips like box cutters. "This is an enemy you cannot defeat, Rowan. I'll hold them off. You must find the Godblade!"

The scorpions were getting louder. The caves shook. The screeches sliced the air.

"We smell apes!"

"The humans are here!"

"Flay the sisters! Break their bones!"

Cracks raced across the cave. The glowing microorganisms in the crystals moved, shifting upward, retreating into the walls. Shadows fell. A stalactite detached from the ceiling, hit the ground, and shattered into countless crystal shards.

Jade pointed. "See that crevice in the floor?"

Rowan nodded. "Yeah."

"Sixteen years ago, when I dropped my sword, it fell into a crack or hole. It might be that crevice. Maybe another one. I don't remember. Search them all! Find the sword! I'll hold off the scorpions."

Scorpion shadows lurched ahead, filling the tunnels. More crystals cracked and fell. The screeches were deafening.

Rowan fired Lullaby into the tunnel ahead. A beast howled.

An instant later, scorpions burst into the crystal chamber, pincers clattering.

"The Blue Huntress!" they screeched.

"The traitor!"

"Kill her, kill her!"

"Go!" Jade shouted at Rowan. "Find the sword!"

Before Rowan could reply, Jade howled and leaped toward the scorpions, claws flashing.

Rowan stood, heart pounding, and saw Jade slam into the enemy. Her claws ripped through their shells. The beasts roared, biting and clawing.

"The traitor, the traitor! Kill her! Break her! Eat her!"

Rowan fired one more shot, fracturing a scorpion's head, then ran toward the crevice.

Rowan peered into the crack. It was too dark to see inside. As Rowan pawed for her flashlight, the screams and shrieks rose behind her. Blood flew across the cave, and droplets splattered Rowan's back, sizzling hot. A severed pincer flew over Rowan's head, grazing her hair, and slammed into the wall.

Rowan wanted to fight. To fire her gun. To help her sister.

But Jade was right.

*I must find the Godblade. Or humanity falls.*

"Hang in there, Jade!" she cried, pointing her flashlight into the crevice.

The beam reflected on a long, shiny object below. A sword?

Rowan reached into the crack. Her fingers brushed something smooth and cold. Maybe the sword. Maybe just a fallen crystal. Whatever it was, it slid away from her, moving deeper into the darkness.

Rowan groaned. She couldn't reach it now.

She glanced over her shoulder. Jade was still battling the scorpions. For half a second, Rowan gasped.

Jade was a terror to behold. She leaped in a fury, rebounding off the walls, soaring to the ceiling, landing, jumping again, so fast she was a blur. Her claws lashed, severing scorpion tails, cracking their shells, spilling their gooey innards.

*She's like Sonic the Hedgehog and the Tasmanian Devil rolled into one,* Rowan thought. *With a whole can of Wolverine tossed in.*

Yet she was not invincible. Already a gash bled on Jade's legs. Venom sprayed her shoulder, searing the skin.

"Hurry, Rowan!" Jade said. "Find the sword!"

Rowan turned away. The crevice was just wide enough. She slipped her arms, then her head into the darkness. She wriggled her way into the crack, vanishing into shadows.

A narrow tunnel plunged down, leading into the deep. Her flashlight reflected on a long, slender object between dark stones below. Jade would not have been able to fit here. But Rowan was small. Rowan had spent most of her life crawling through tight passageways. She wriggled down the crawlway, heading toward the crystalline object.

The tunnel was surprisingly long. Finally Rowan reached a small cavern deep below the main caves, no larger than her old cabin aboard the *Jerusalem*. She stood on a ledge of stone before a gulf. The void plunged into shadows as deep and dark as guilt. Across the chasm, a pile of geodes rested on a stony outcrop.

And there she saw it.

There, atop the pile of geodes, it waited.

A white crystalline sword. The sword from the old photograph. Even from here, across the void, Rowan could see the ouroboros engraved into the pommel.

"The Godblade," she whispered.

She aimed her flashlight. The crystal sword caught the beam and the blade shone. No, not crystal. This was a sword forged from aetherstone, a substance from the higher plane.

*It's beautiful,* Rowan thought. *It's holy.*

She had always thought it just a toy. But here was an ancient artifact from another dimension—and one that could win this war. In her mind, Rowan could see the ancient weavers forging this blade, wielding it against the tentacled Hydrians, avenging humanity before fading into myth, legend, and finally shadows.

A screech sounded above, echoing down the tunnel. It yanked Rowan back to the present.

"Rowan, hurry!" Jade shouted above.

"I see the sword!" Rowan called back. "I've almost got it. Hang tight!"

She tried to reach across the gulf toward the sword. Damn her short limbs! Her small size had helped her wriggle down the passageway. But it prevented her from reaching the Godblade.

Rowan took a deep breath, then stretched out again. Her fingers grazed the pile of geodes across the gulf. She tilted and nearly fell, then yelped and pulled back.

"Great." Rowan heaved a sigh. "I should have brought a lasso instead of a gun."

She rose to her feet.

Her head brushed the cavern's ceiling. And she could only take two steps back before hitting a wall. It would have to do.

She tightened her lips, lowered her head, ran two steps forward, then jumped.

She landed across the void, slamming into the pile of geodes, and reached for the Godblade.

The cairn of geodes tumbled.

As the stones fell, they revealed a skeleton beneath them—not human. A reptilian skull gaped at Rowan, blue and crystalline, its teeth so sharp they cut her fingers.

She yelped.

The Godblade tumbled along with the falling stones.

Rowan reached out to grab it.

Her fingers, slick with blood, brushed the hilt. She tried to grab it. But more geodes tumbled, and one slammed into her wrist, and the Godblade slipped from her grip. The blade shone as it fell into the void below.

Rowan rolled her eyes so hard they almost gazed into her brain. "Oh for the love of Murphy!"

Sighing, she leaned over the ledge and peered into the void. She pointed her flashlight down and saw a stream far below. *Far* below. When she dropped a pebble, it seemed to fall for ages.

She raised her head. "Hold on, Jade!" she cried. "Just a little longer!"

Her voice echoed. More geodes fell. The strange, crystal skeleton—it reminded Rowan of a crocodile—tilted over with a creak.

Rowan shoved it. "Shut up."

She peered down into the gulf again. The crack was several feet wide on top, but narrower at the bottom.

"I'm probably crazy," Rowan muttered, climbing down into the crack.

At first, she slid down the clammy stone shaft. When the passageway narrowed, she stretched out her legs, pressing her feet against the far wall. Like that—her feet against one side, her back against the other—she inched her way down.

*Just like the ducts back home,* she thought.

It was frustratingly slow. As she descended, Rowan could still hear a battle above. Jade was still alive. That was good. But

Rowan didn't know how much longer Jade could keep the enemies at bay.

Finally Rowan reached the bottom, jumped the last meter, and landed in the stream.

The water flowed, rising to her knees, icy cold. The sword was gone; the water must have carried it away. Rowan walked downstream, shivering. The stream took her down a tunnel so narrow she had to walk at a stoop. The tunnel wound underground. Rowan could almost feel the weight of the mountain above her head.

*I should go back,* she thought. *My sister needs me. I must help her fight.*

She hesitated.

*But if I go back now, what if I die? What if we both die? What if the Godblade is lost forever down here? Even if others came here, they would never find it. If the Godblade is lost, humanity is doomed.*

Rowan tugged her hair.

"Damn it!"

She hated these decisions. She told herself that Jade was a capable fighter. A legendary warrior. She could handle herself against a few scorpions. Okay, a lot of scorpions, but this was Jade after all. Right?

With a groan, Rowan kept moving, running at a crouch.

The tunnel opened up into a vast chamber deep beneath the mountains. It was so large a striker could have flown around inside. The river fed a lake that shimmered with bioluminescent algae, and glowing crystals jutted out from the walls and ceiling.

Rowan didn't know if any humans had ever made it this deep into the caves. But clearly, some other species had. Dozens of crystal skeletons, similar to the one Rowan had found under the geodes, lay along the lakeside. Their bodies were reptilian, their teeth long, as if some sculptor had made alligators out of crystals.

*These must be the original inhabitants of Harmonia,* she thought. *They must have died before humans got here.*

The sword floated in the middle of the lake. Thankfully, aetherstone could float. Finally some good luck.

Rowan waded through the water toward the artifact. The lake grew deeper, and Rowan couldn't swim. The water was soon up to her neck, icy cold. Her teeth clattered.

"It's so damn cold my ovaries turned into ice cubes," she muttered.

The water rose to her chin, then her mouth. She had to crane her head back, and she held Lullaby overhead.

"Damn my tiny height!" she said.

She was only a meter away from the sword now. It floated ahead, gleaming. Rowan reached toward it.

Something brushed against her leg.

She froze.

She looked from side to side, frowning.

A creature burst from the water ahead, sending the sword flying into the distance.

"You've got to be kidding me!" Rowan said.

The creature kept rising taller and taller, dripping algae. Its head was a giant crystal skull, larger than Rowan's torso and lined with teeth the size of bananas. Its body was soft and tentacled, like the body of a jellyfish, and shimmered with beads of light. The creature was oddly beautiful, Rowan thought, even as she stumbled back in fear. It was like some nightmarish circus tent come to life, its lanterns hiding shadows within.

The sword had fallen behind the beast.

"Stand down, buddy!" Rowan said, wading backward in the water. She pointed Lullaby at the beast. "I'm armed, freezing my butt off, and I think there's some algae stuck in my underwear. If you don't retreat, I'll—"

The alien lunged toward her. Its jaws opened wide and it emitted a high-pitched screech like shattering crystals.

Rowan fired her pistol.

Her bullet dislodged one of the creature's teeth but didn't slow it down.

Rowan swam aside, splashing through the lake.

The crystal jaws snapped shut centimeters away.

The creature shrieked, voice undulating and pulsing and slamming against the walls. Crystals shook. The beast's tentacles thrashed, stirring the pond. The sword vanished in the maelstrom.

Rowan pulled her trigger again.

Her bullet pierced a tentacle and slammed into the cave wall. She fired again. She ripped a tentacle, then severed it with a third bullet. Rowan sneered, standing her ground, pulled the trigger, and—

A tentacle whipped her wrist.

Lullaby flew from her hand and splashed into the water.

The jaws thrust toward her.

Rowan jumped back, narrowly dodging them, and dived underwater.

She opened her eyes. The water stung, thick with algae and mud, but she saw Lullaby ahead. She flailed, propelling herself forward, reached for the gun, and—

A tentacle slammed into her.

It tossed her out of the water. Rowan flew and landed on the lakeside, banging her hip. She cried out in pain.

The glowing jellyfish placed its tentacles onto the lakeside and began dragging itself out of the water, jaws snapping. As it emerged, it revealed a crystalline spine, the segments pulsing with inner light.

For the first time, Rowan realized that there were no stalactites or stalagmites in this cavern. The walls were smooth.

She frowned.

*The crystals form this creature's skeleton!* Rowan thought.

It was not a single animal, she realized. It was a colony. A monster made from millions of tiny polyps holding together algae and crystals from the walls. The microorganisms of Harmonia were moving together in a swarm.

Rowan only had a moment to marvel. The beast—whatever its nature—was still crawling toward her, snapping those crystal teeth.

Rowan ran around the skull, dived back into the lake, and plunged into the water. She swam and saw Lullaby. This time she reached the pistol before the creature could knock her aside.

The monster spun back toward her, tentacles flailing. Its shrieks shook the chamber.

Rowan aimed her pistol at the creature's neck—right at those glimmering spine segments.

"Say goodnight, bitch."

She pulled the trigger.

Nothing happened.

Water and algae dripped from the pistol.

Rowan pulled the trigger again. Again.

*Click. Click.*

No bullets fired.

The beast lunged at her. The jaws slammed shut, and Rowan raised her arm protectively, and a crystal tooth tore through her flesh.

Rowan screamed.

Her blood gushed.

The jaws opened, closed again, ripping through her arm.

Rowan howled, and death danced around her.

## CHAPTER TWENTY-NINE

Outside the Dyson sphere, the scorpion fleets fired their cannons.

An inferno of plasma, millions of flaming bolts, slammed into the metal sphere encircling the Aelonian star system.

Inside the sphere, Emet stood aboard the *Jerusalem*. On his video feed, he watched the wall of fire surge.

The flames washed over the cameras mounted outside the sphere. The lenses shattered. The images on his monitor died.

But Emet could still see the fire.

It outlined the gateway before him, illuminating the narrow lines where doors met wall, then reaching through the cracks with flaming geysers. The inferno heated the shell like magma bubbling underground. The rising temperature twisted and coiled the landscapes that covered the sphere's inner shell. Before Emet and his fleet, all around the gateway, mountains trembled. Forests shook. Rivers bubbled. Scattered fires burst across the fields, and canyons cracked the landscape. Rows of solar panels melted.

The ancient splendor of Aelonia, a marvel of engineering and life, a beacon that had lit the galaxy for a thousand years, shook and rippled and boiled.

"It's not going to hold," Tom said.

They watched as a mountain range split open like spine under an axe. Flames gushed like volcanoes through a forest.

"It'll hold," Emet grumbled. "This shield has survived more than its share of wars."

Outside, the strikers kept pounding the shield. The gateway trembled. Grasslands rose upon creaking metal plates, then slammed down with showers of soil.

"It's not going to hold!" Tom said.

"The inside layer is just soil and rock and organics," Emet said. "The shield beneath is engineered metal. It'll hold."

Tom inhaled sharply. "We need more time. We need time for Rowan to come back with the Godblade."

"We'll have time," Emet said. "It'll hold."

Tom reached for his rifle, as if that could be of any use here. "It's not going to—"

The gate into Aelonia shattered.

Metal shards flew toward the human fleet. Starships scattered. Turrets of fire roared forth, as large as sun flares. The lands around the gates blazed, waves of fire sweeping over them like red tsunamis.

When the fires died down, a hole in the sphere gaped open, revealing the enemy beyond.

"—hold," Tom finished in a weak voice.

Emet stared for a moment in horror.

Then he gripped the ship's yoke.

"Humanity—fight!" he cried into his comm. "Hold them back!"

The strikers began charging through the breach.

Emet stormed toward them in the *Jerusalem*, cannons blazing.

His shells slammed into a few strikers. It was like blowing back a few grains in a sandstorm.

The fury of the Hierarchy flowed through the broken gate with a thousand shards of black death.

Emet had fought in many battles before. He had been fighting for decades. But he had never seen such an assault. Striker after striker fired on the human fleet. Over the past few weeks, engineers had installed extra layers of shields aboard the *Jerusalem*. They now burned and melted. The bridge shook. Cracks spiderwebbed the walls. Electricity blasted across the gunnery station, and the gunner—a young lieutenant—screamed and fell back, unconscious.

"We must protect Ayumi's turret!" Tom said.

"We don't even have the damn sword yet!" said Emet. "Man the cannons, Shepherd! Return fire, dammit!"

Tom ran to the gunnery station, shoved the unconscious lieutenant aside, and fired on the enemy.

A barrage of shells flew, slamming into strikers, tearing them apart. Around the *Jerusalem*, other human warships were struggling to withstand the storm. They too returned fire. But the strikers pounded them with plasma. More strikers rammed into the human ships, shoving them back. Striker after striker barreled into the *Jerusalem*, trying to shove them away from the gates.

Emet kick-fired the afterburner. The engines roared with deafening fury. They lurched forward, closer to the gate, shoving against the hulls of enemy ships and blasting fire.

Tom fired another barrage, taking out more strikers.

But Emet knew it was useless. There were more strikers than they had shells.

*Come on, Rowan, where are you?* he thought, surprising himself. Since when did he believe in Godblades? Fairy tales, that was all. Myths. But right now Emet needed a miracle.

Across the sphere, more gates were cracking open. More Concord fleets—aliens of many different species—were trying to stop the enemy. At a nearby gate, a fleet of marshcrabs broke into the sphere. Farther back, a horde of arachnid ships tore through another gate and flowed into Aelonia. The spiders hammered a fleet of sentient fish, shattering their ships and spilling water across the void. Everywhere the landscape was burning, forests uprooted, mountains torn free, the chunks tumbling across the enclosed star system.

*The last stronghold is falling,* Emet thought. *But we will fight to the end.*

"Hold that gateway!" he said. "All warships, full fire! Hold them back!"

Humanity's ships formed a wall in space, unleashing all their shells and missiles and photon bolts. They took out many strikers. Shards of metal filled the sky. Dead scorpions spilled from the hulls of their cracked warships.

Yet every moment, another human ship tore open.

Men and women screamed, then were forever silenced.

The *Jaipur*, the mighty frigate that had fought with Emet for twenty years, cracked open, then exploded.

*But we're holding them back,* Emet thought. *We can give Rowan time. We—*

Near Earth's Gate, a massive rip tore across the landscape, expanding like a hungry mouth, finally revealing space outside.

Emet and Tom stared.

"The sphere," Tom said, going pale. "The entire sphere is cracking."

Emet turned the *Jerusalem* toward the canyon. "We can hold them. We—"

On the other side of the gate, a sinkhole appeared. A lake spilled out into interstellar space. Mountain ranges vanished. Plains burned, then tore apart. Gorges raced across the Dyson sphere, each canyon as wide as a planet.

The huge metal structure was cracking open like an egg.

Through countless cracks and holes, the enemy came pouring in.

The floodgates had broken.

Thousands, then millions of enemy starships stormed into Aelonia.

And Emet knew the battle was lost.

*Hurry, Rowan,* he thought. *Hurry, Jade. We need a miracle.*

## CHAPTER THIRTY

Deep in the caves, Rowan stumbled backward, her arm lacerated. Her blood dripped into the pond. She gasped for air. Her head spun. Her blood kept flowing, and her skin hung in tatters from her forearm.

The creature rose taller, rumbling, buzzing with life, its luminous spine like a serpent in its translucent body. Its crystal jaws glowed, so large they could swallow Rowan whole. Her blood stained its teeth. The tentacles flailed beneath it like a giant jellyfish.

A high-pitched, crackling voice emerged from the beast, a sound like shattering glass and discordant harps.

"You ... polluted ... us." It moved through the water, tentacles lashing. "We are ... sacred. This is ... home. You ... must die."

Rowan stumbled back, staring at it.

*God above.*

"We didn't know!" Rowan said. "We didn't know we were hurting you."

"You knew!" the creature howled. "Your filthy kind. Polluting. Killing. Our children—dying. Now—above. Killing! Claws! Crystals breaking! The children of light—dying!"

Rowan lowered her pistol.

"I'm sorry," she whispered.

She gazed at the beast. No. Not a beast. A lifeform. A lifeform unique in the galaxy. An intelligent colony. Many microscopic creatures who had become one.

The superorganism moved closer. Its tentacles flailed. Its jaws opened, and it shrieked again, blowing back Rowan's hair. But she stood her ground.

"You've been hiding here," Rowan said softly. A tear rolled down her cheek. "Here in the deep caverns beneath the higher caves." She looked around her at the crystal skeletons, the ones she had thought looked like crocodiles. "Those are your other bodies, aren't they? Forms you built from crystals. You tried to climb with one. You almost reached the caverns above. But you stopped. You left your bones and came back down here. Why?"

The luminous microorganisms bustled and shone brighter. They held aloft the crystal skull and spine. Binding together, they formed the tentacles. An entire nation—using the crystals to shape skeletons for itself, becoming one giant hive, a single animal, like cells forming a single body.

*This is the soul of Harmonia,* she thought. *Here before me stands a new kind of being. A Harmonian.*

"We ... knew," the lifeform said. "If we climbed higher ... you would kill us. We came back down. We ... hid. Hid our true ... self. Our ... soul. Our ... dreams. We are ... afraid."

Rowan reached out, hesitated, then gingerly stroked one of the tentacles.

"I'm sorry," she whispered again. "I'm so sorry."

"You ... lie!" said the Harmonian. "Your ... kind ... destroys! Even now. Above. Cutting stone. Killing the luminous. With claws! Sharp claws!" The lifeform writhed. "We feel. Even here. Our brothers and sisters. Crying out. Dying."

Rowan stroked the Harmonian, feeling the millions of microorganisms flowing between her fingers. "The creatures above us, who are destroying the caves, are the Skra-Shen. Scorpions. I am human. We humans fight them. My sister and I. Will you help us?"

"You were here!" the Harmonian said. "Many life cycles ago. Our ancestors remember. The memory is burned into us!"

"We were," Rowan said. "I was. We were ignorant. Foolish. We fled the scorpions who were slaying us. We did not realize we had invaded a world with sentient life, that we were hurting you. I promise you this: we humans will never return to your world. We will cherish and protect Harmonia from afar. But the scorpions are evil, and they will destroy this place. Will you help me fight them?"

The lifeform reached out a tentacle and stroked Rowan's head. A second tentacle rose to touch her bleeding arm. Rowan winced. The microorganisms flowed into her cuts, glowing bright blue. Rowan inhaled sharply, but there was no pain. The tiny beings soothed the agony like a balm. They reemerged from her cuts, crawled along her arm, and returned to the tentacle.

Her pain was gone. Her wounds closed, leaving thin scars. Rowan gasped.

"You healed me," she whispered.

"We sense ... goodness ... in you," the Harmonian said. "You ... have been blessed ... by our ancestors. We ... hear their song ... inside you. Their spirits are in your cells. You are now ... one of the luminous. We will help you."

The being reached into the water, fished out the Godblade, and handed it to Rowan.

"Thank you," she whispered, holding the sword.

The crystal skull opened its jaws, and light filled its eye sockets. "Now we fight!"

The Harmonian emerged from the water, crystal bones clattering, dripping. The tentacles propelled it onward, the billions of tiny beings clinging together and working as one. Rowan followed. The lifeform climbed into the tunnel, tentacles gripping the stones. Rowan climbed after it, her waterlogged pistol and the

Godblade dangling from her belt. They raced through the caverns, then burst out through the crevice into the main caves.

Jade was still there. Cut a hundred times. Covered in blood. But still alive.

She stood with her back to a wall. Her skin—even the hard, white skin the emperor had given her—was cracked and bleeding. Burns spread across her. Her eyes were glazed. A hundred dead scorpions lay in the cave before her, a pile of claws and sizzling flesh. But dozens more surrounded Jade, claws raised.

"Jade!" Rowan cried in fear.

The scorpions spun toward Rowan, shrieking.

The Harmonian leaped toward the scorpions, tentacles cracking the air like whips.

The scorpions clawed at the crystalline lifeform. They tore through tentacles, only for the digits to reform. The luminous colony snapped its jaws, and crystal teeth punched into scorpion shells. The tentacles swung, tossing scorpions against the walls.

Jade collapsed. Rowan ran toward her sister. She cradled Jade in her arms.

"Jade!" she said. "I'm here. I'm here, sister."

The battle raged around them, the scorpions and Harmonian slamming against one another.

"Do you have the sword?" Jade whispered. Blood filled one of her eyes, dripping as red tears.

Rowan nodded. "I do. I'm here now. You're safe. We're all safe."

A scorpion slammed into the wall near them and cracked open. Another one raced toward them, and Rowan winced and fired Lullaby. This time the pistol finally fired, and her bullet knocked the scorpion back—into the Harmonian's snapping jaws.

Scorpions swarmed the glowing colony, lashing, biting, thrusting their pincers. One pincer punched a hole into the crystal skull. Another pincer severed a tentacle. Claws tore at the being's spine. Still it fought them, shrieking, struggling to keep rebuilding itself.

"For my lost brothers and sisters!" the Harmonian cried. "For the ancestors! For the luminous ones!"

Rowan fired again and again until she was out of bullets, and still scorpions were emerging from the tunnels, leaping onto the Harmonian, ripping off more tentacles, smashing its bones. Its crystal teeth fell.

The colony lifted its remaining tentacles and grabbed the mighty stalactites and stalagmites that rose like columns in the chamber.

"Run, humans!" the Harmonian said. "Through the back tunnel. Flee! To life! To life! Be free!"

The tentacles began to pull.

The stalactites and stalagmites creaked. Crystals cracked and shed luminous dust.

Rowan's eyes widened.

"You'll die!" she said.

"We are billions," said the Harmonian. "We will rebuild— in darkness, sealed, alive, remembering. Go!"

Rowan grabbed her sister. Jade was taller and heavier, but Rowan grunted and strained and managed to pull Jade to her feet.

They ran, Jade leaning against Rowan.

A scorpion darted toward them.

Rowan had no more bullets. The arachnid lunged, claws lashing. Jade could barely stand.

Grimacing, Rowan swung the Godblade in a wide arc.

The silvery blade sliced through the scorpion like a machete through grass.

Rowan howled, thrust again, and drove the blade into the alien's head. The exoskeleton, normally so powerful only the mightiest railguns could crack it, gave way like paper mache.

The scorpion crashed down, dead.

"Holy crap!" Rowan said.

"Keep going!" Jade said, limping forward, still leaning on Rowan.

The chamber was trembling now. The Harmonian was crying out, wrapping its tentacles around stalactites. Rowan glanced over her shoulder and saw dozens of scorpions covering the lifeform, ripping it apart. And still the tentacles continued their destruction, grabbing and tugging pillars.

A crystal column cracked, then fell.

Another column collapsed.

Dust rained from the ceiling. The chamber trembled.

The sisters ran up the tunnel—the same tunnel Rowan had fled through sixteen years ago. Behind them, more pillars fell. Cracks ran across the ceiling. Chunks of stone hailed down. Crystals flew everywhere.

The sisters emerged into a large chamber, once a hangar where their parents' starship had hidden. The starship was gone now, but there was a staircase carved into the stone, leading to sunlight.

They ran up the stairs as behind them the tunnel caved in.

The mountain shook. The sisters clung to the stone. Boulders rolled. The wall cracked. Crystal shards the size of spears burst through the rock.

"Keep climbing!" Jade said.

The wall around the staircase was crumbling. They raced onward, dodging falling crystals. The stairway cracked open, and they vaulted over missing steps. Rowan nearly fell into a chasm, but Jade grabbed her and pulled her back up. They raced upward as the world collapsed.

Finally, covered in dust and sweat and blood, they emerged onto a mountaintop.

The sandy valley spread below them, trembling. Sinkholes opened, and the sand spilled into the caves below. A mountain peak cracked open across the valley, and an avalanche of stones fell. The *Mother's Mercy* was still in the valley, tilted on its side. Boulders pummeled the ship, denting the shields. Three more strikers were here, larger than the *Mercy*—the ones that had brought the scorpions over. Indigo tentacles rose from below, pulled the three bulky warships into a gorge, and pummelled them with stones.

Slowly, the trembling eased. The mountain resettled.

The tunnels, the caves below, their old home—was gone.

The sisters lay on the sand, breathing heavily. Rowan clutched the Godblade to her chest. Jade still held their mother's diary.

And Jade was still bleeding.

Her skin, unnaturally hard and white, was cracked in a hundred places like a hardboiled egg hit with a spoon. Blood seeped. Jade was breathing heavily, eyes glazing over. She was fading fast.

Rowan looked back toward the staircase they had climbed. The tunnel had collapsed. Only a small hole remained, no larger than her fist.

Gently, Rowan placed her hand into the hole.

"Help her," she whispered. "Please, luminous ones. Help her. Heal her."

Tingles ran across her hand. When she pulled it from the hole, the microorganisms glowed across it like crystal dust.

Rowan placed her hand upon Jade's skin. The tiny glowing beings flowed into the wounds. A glow spread across Jade, and her breathing deepened. Her blood stopped flowing, and the shadow left her eyes. Her hard white skin closed, leaving only hairline scars.

Jade sat up, healed.

"How ...?" she whispered.

"They know us," Rowan said, smiling softly. "From when we were kids."

She placed her hand back into the hole, and the Harmonians flowed back underground.

"Goodbye, friends," Rowan whispered. "May you rebuild. A safe home. A home away from our wars. If someday we humans reclaim our own home, I will work to keep your world protected."

As the sisters rose to their feet, Rowan knew that these beings would forever be with her. She could feel their warmth. A few of them, too small to see, were inside her body, inside her cells. This world of her childhood would forever be a part of her, not just in memory but in her physical being. And that comforted Rowan.

*We are inside you. Always, Rowan. We will ever be your light in darkness.*

A soft voice. One that spoke within. The voice of Harmonia. Forever within her.

*This is a dear place to me,* she thought. *But it's not my home. And it's time to go home.*

The sisters entered the *Mother's Mercy* with the Godblade. They rose into space and flew, heading back toward the Heirs of Earth, toward the great final stand of humanity. They flew with hope.

## CHAPTER THIRTY-ONE

Bay sat in Brooklyn's cockpit as the Dyson sphere crumbled around them.

*The universe is ending,* Bay thought. *And Rowan isn't here.*

Thousands of enemy ships were swarming through the cracking sphere like bees. Ships filled with scorpions. Spiders. Serpents. Centipedes. All the monsters of the darkness. Evil had come to Aelonia, and Bay knew he was going to die.

The Heirs of Earth had put up a brave defense until now, guarding the gate with ferocity. But now the shell was falling apart everywhere, opening Aelonia to the cosmos. Chunks of landscape larger than Earth flew into the distance. Mountains tumbled through space. Whatever pieces of shell remained orbited around the central star in a loose pattern, leaving countless cracks and holes for the enemy to fly through.

The battle swept across the star system. Concord fleets bombarded the enemy. Hierarchy armadas slammed against them. Hundreds of civilizations were brawling here. A million ships lit space, slamming together, burning, blazing bright and fading. Bay had seen great battles before. He had flown through the front line and survived. But here was something different. Here was the Milky Way galaxy imploding.

*Every heartbeat, thousands of sentient lifeforms are dying,* Bay thought. *The galaxy is falling apart.*

An alien ship, shaped like a huge geode, tumbled overhead. Blasts of plasma pounded it, and its crystals flew everywhere. Menorians spilled out, blue mollusks, their arms flailing in space. Below Bay, a Tarmarin ship shaped like a scaly egg rolled into a group of clawed arachnid ships, demolishing them, only for a basilisk ship to charge forward, beam out lasers, and slice the scaly warship in half.

Bay flew madly, swerving, rising, falling, firing. Formations were crumbling and reforming. A group of marshcrab ships extended metal claws, ripping open the soft Esporian podships. Clouds of spores flew onto the marshcrabs, eating through their spiky ships. An Aelonian fleet streaked above Bay, its silvery ships firing beams of light, tearing into a fleet of strikers, then cracking, exploding, crashing down under a barrage of enemy fire. A host of Gourami ships cracked open, spilling blobs of water that hissed against flame.

It was almost beautiful. A song of fire and steel and water, of life and death.

"So this is how the galaxy ends," Bay said softly. "In a great symphony of destruction. I only wish Rowan were here."

Brooklyn's camera swiveled toward him. "Why, so she could die too?"

They ducked under a burning hulk the size of a town. Aliens were jumping from the flaming wreckage into space, dying in the vacuum.

"So that I could hold her again," Bay said. "Tell her that I love her. I never told her that I love her."

Brooklyn swerved, dodging a blast of plasma. "Oh for muck's sake, dude, now's not the time for navel gazing! Will you take the controls and fly me? You're better at this than me!"

Bay grabbed the yoke. He flew.

"Brooklyn, if you survive this, if you see Rowan again, tell her that—"

"Dude, shut up!" Brooklyn shouted. "Shut up and fight! Rowan is coming back, do you hear me? And not to die in your arms, but to bring back the Godblade. To help us *win*! Now let's fight these bastards and buy her more time. You fly, I'll fire the cannons. Go!"

Her camera actually extended out far enough to slap him. Bay blinked. He hadn't even known her camera could reach that far.

"Thanks," he said. "I needed that."

"Anytime," said Brooklyn. "I mean that. It was my pleasure."

"I'm sure it was."

Bay narrowed his eyes, tightened his lips, and got to flying.

Two marshcrab vessels surrounded a human freighter, jabbing it with their metal claws. Bay swooped toward them. Brooklyn opened fire, hammering the claws with light artillery. Explosions severed the metal arms and sent them careening through the battle. An instant later, Bay saw three strikers trailing a Firebird. Bay flew to help the starfighter, and together they knocked the strikers aside and shattered them against an asteroid.

Shells shrieked beside them, and Bay turned to see the *Jerusalem* fighting nearby, all cannons blazing. Its shields were cracking. The dome Bay had installed on the roof was still there, but enemy fire kept hitting the hull, getting dangerously close to pulverising the turret.

Bay inhaled sharply.

Ayumi was standing inside that turret.

The girl didn't have the Godblade; the Emery sisters hadn't returned with it yet. But Ayumi was there. There behind a thin shield of glass. Waiting for the sword.

And any moment, a blast of fire could demolish that canopy and slay Ayumi.

"Dad!" Bay shouted into his comm. "Dad, get Ayumi out of there!"

No answer came. His father was busy commanding the fleet. And that fleet was crumbling. The Heirs of Earth were faring no better than the other Concord armadas. The famous ISS *Jaipur*, which had fought alongside the *Jerusalem* since the beginning, was gone. The corvettes were falling. Barely any Firebirds still flew.

"Brook, we gotta defend Ayumi in that turret," Bay said, diving to fly above it.

Brooklyn nodded. "You fly, I fire, you know the drill."

They hovered just a few meters above the *Jerusalem* now. Bay looked down and saw Ayumi standing inside the dome. She was waiting for the sword. Waiting for Rowan.

"Ayumi, get back behind the shields!" Bay shouted, waving at the girl. She didn't notice, couldn't hear.

Bay cursed.

A squadron of strikers came charging toward them.

The *Jerusalem* opened fire, and its cannons took out many of the strikers. But two survived the fusillade and came swooping toward the *Jerusalem*. They had seen the turret too.

Damn it! If the turret shattered, if Ayumi died, or if Rowan lingered much longer—the battle would be lost.

Bay charged head on toward the two remaining strikers.

"Brooklyn, fry those bastards!" he cried.

"Frying 'em up!" she said, blasting out her bullets.

Bay yanked on the joystick, soaring higher, dodging blasts of plasma, then barrel-rolled between the two strikers. The barrage of bullets hit the enemy ships, knocking them off course. Bay spun, flew at them from behind, and bombarded their exhaust pipes.

Both strikers exploded.

Bay dived, placing himself over the turret, taking the raining shrapnel on Brooklyn's hull.

"Ow, ow, ow!" Brooklyn said.

"Oh hush, I spent a fortune on your shields," Bay said. He lifted his comm. "This is Lieutenant Bay Ben-Ari onboard the

*Brooklyn*, flying right now over the *Jerusalem*. Any Firebirds that can help? We've got to protect this dome!"

A squadron of Firebirds was engaging a flight of arachnid ships above. They blasted the enemy apart, then came to fly around Bay. Five of the starfighters flew there, ships even smaller than Brooklyn and far deadlier.

"This is Viking One, reporting to help," said the squad commander, a young woman with two golden braids and swan wings painted onto her helmet. "We're here with you, Lieutenant."

Bay nodded. "Good. We gotta protect this dome. Just a little longer. Until—"

Several enemy warships flew toward them. Brooklyn and the Firebirds opened fire. Explosions filled space and sparks rained.

*Just a little longer,* Bay told himself, battling over the *Jerusalem*. All around them, countless other ships were fighting, exploding, millions dying.

*Hurry, Rowan,* he thought. *I once promised to burn down the galaxy to find you. Now we're burning the galaxy and you're missing again. Come back. We need you. Hurry.*

CHAPTER THIRTY-TWO

Aelonia burned.

All around Emet, the last hope faded.

The Inheritor fleet was crumbling around him. Warships burned. Starfighters fell like comets. The Heirs of Earth—this dream, this vision, this light Emet had raised from darkness—around him it shattered.

He stood on the *Jerusalem*'s bridge, watching the ISS *Bangkok*, one of their few frigates, burn. A squadron of corvettes fell to his left. Cargo hulls tore open, spilling supplies and refugees.

Not only humanity fell before the onslaught. Hundreds of alien civilizations, their homeworlds conquered, had come here for their final stand. They fought with courage. They fought well. But they too crumbled before the enemy.

*Freedom dies today,* Emet thought. *The lights of the galaxy are going out.*

And still the enemy swarmed. Wave after wave flowed into Aelonia. Dark ships lashed metallic tentacles, knocking smaller vessels aside. Spiky ships like urchins hammered into the hulls of their enemies, piercing even the thickest shields. Marshcrabs and arachnids flew ships tipped with metal claws, razor-sharp, that tore smaller ships apart. Battalions of strikers rolled over any resistance, plasma raging.

Above them all flew the *Imperator*, the largest ship in the battle, a ship like a city. The dreadnought of Emperor Sin Kra himself.

*The scorpion who murdered my wife,* Emet thought, glaring up at the dark, triangular behemoth.

"There." Emet pointed at the *Imperator.* "That's where the emperor flies. We must destroy that ship. Mister Shepherd, get ready to fire all our weapons. Every last nuke in our arsenal."

Standing at the gunnery station, Tom swiveled toward Emet, and his eyes widened. "Admiral, even if we fired every missile in our banks, we couldn't destroy that beast. Taking on the *Imperator* is a suicide mission."

Emet nodded. "That it is. We will go down fighting."

"We must wait for the Emery sisters!" Tom said, then stiffened. "*Sir.*"

Beside them, another warship exploded. Far ahead, Emet saw striker battalions reach the Aelonian planets. The enemy ships were bombarding those worlds now. Cities burned. Millions of Aelonians were dying. The great institutions of the Concord—the libraries, museums, courts, universities—were collapsing.

"We've waited long enough," Emet said. "Tom, I'm sorry."

Tom stared at him, eyes haunted. Those dark, sad eyes. Then the man nodded.

"So it's a Banzai charge," he said.

"Our last stand," said Emet.

"The last stand of humanity." Tom saluted. "Sir, it has been an honor."

"The honor is mine, Mister Shepherd. To serve with you. To sound humanity's roar if only for a while. Now let us all roar together. One last time."

Tom raised his chin. "We will all roar with the Old Lion."

Emet got on his comm. "Ships of the fleet! This is Admiral Ben-Ari. All functioning warships—rally around me! We fly toward the enemy. A great charge. For Earth! For Earth!"

The fleet gathered. A thousand Inheritor ships had come here. Only a few hundred remained. Behind them, the Aelonian planets burned. Around them, alien fleets shattered. Before them rose the enemy—countless strikers, covering space, and above them all the *Imperator*.

The Heirs of Earth began to fly.

They moved slowly at first. Engines rumbled. Many ships were damaged and could only limp forth. Still they gathered together, the hundreds that remained. And they began their final assault.

They flew toward the *Imperator*. Toward the end.

Emet's comm rang.

"Dad?" Bay's voice emerged, shaky, and suddenly he sounded young. Younger than his twenty-six years.

"I love you, son," Emet said, and his voice came out too hoarse.

For a moment, there was silence, and Emet thought Bay would argue, would beg for more time, even to retreat.

But Bay surprised him.

"I love you too, Dad. May Leona succeed where we failed."

"Humanity does not fall today," Emet said. "Leona and those she leads will find Earth. They will fulfill our dream. And they will remember us. Godspeed, Bay."

"See you on the other side, Dad." His voice was choked with fear—but strong with courage. "Goodbye."

The fleet gained speed.

Their engines roared.

Tails of fire streamed behind them.

As the battle swirled around them, the Inheritor ships formed an arrowhead. Flying faster. Faster still. Frigates and corvettes, cogs and barges, freighters and pontoons, starfighters and dinghies. They stormed forth, and on their hulls shone the symbols of Earth. Blue planets. Golden wings. Memories of home. Echoes of Earth.

As they flew here together, charging toward the enemy, toward certain death, they were no longer a fleet of exile. They were no longer a host of rebels and refugees. They were soldiers. They were the army of Earth.

A sea of strikers spread above and before them. Hundreds of thousands of them. Maybe millions. The *Imperator* loomed, waiting, a great demon of black wings. Its warships formed walls around it, ten thousand strikers strong. Emet knew the Heirs would break against the enemy.

Behind them, Aelonia had fallen.

Ahead lay their glorious death in battle.

*Remember us, Earth.*

Emet roared and shoved down the throttle to the max. Behind him, the others stormed on full afterburner. They shrieked forward, and Emet let out his roar—the Old Lion's roar.

"For Earth!"

And through his speakers, he heard them all roaring with him.

"For Earth!"

They opened fire.

Their fury flowed forth. Shells and missiles, fire and photons, great torrents of white flame and nuclear rage. And it was beautiful. It was the end of humanity—with light and fire and honor.

Before them, for just an instant, the enemy faltered. Their ships cracked open. A few fell. A few others retreated.

Then humanity crashed into them, ramming the strikers, and Emet fought at their head, his roar drowning under the sound of ten thousand ships slamming together, and light washed over him.

*Goodbye, my children. Goodbye, Earth.*

The strikers surrounded him. Their weapons pounded against his hull. Control panels shattered around Emet, blazing with sparks like fireworks. It was so beautiful. And there was no more pain. No more sound. There was soft light like the stars. Like the sky of Earth.

The *Imperator* opened fire.

The last corvettes burned away, the cries of their captains dying.

A mighty blast slammed into the *Jerusalem*, carving off the entire stern. Blast doors slammed shut, sealing in air to the front of the ship. The lower chunk of the *Jerusalem* tumbled backward, men screaming inside, then it was gone, scattering away in clouds of ash.

The front of the *Jerusalem* still flew, its remaining engines rumbling. Emet stood on the cracked bridge. He stared ahead at the strikers. A wall of them. And before him, the *Imperator*. The emperor stood on his bridge, gazing through the porthole.

Across the void, Sin Kra and Emet made eye contact.

Emet took a deep breath and raised his chin, flying toward his fate.

From above—a striker swooped.

A small striker. Barely larger than a starfighter. A single leaf in a storm.

It flew down at a spin, leaving a corkscrew of fire.

Emet stared, thinking it must have been shot down, perhaps gone berserk.

Then the small striker turned toward the *Imperator* and opened fire.

And Emet read the words engraved onto its hull: *Mother's Mercy*.

"Rowan," he whispered. "Jade!" He lifted his comm and shouted. "Human ships, fall back! Fall back!"

Behind him, the hundreds of surviving human ships had scattered into a wide formation. They turned and fled the strikers, heading toward the burning worlds of Aelonia.

Emet fired his full nuclear arsenal at the *Imperator.* Then he turned his ship around. He raced away, the enemy fleet at his back, and the *Mother's Mercy* flew above him.

Behind them, the nukes exploded.

White light blazed across them. The humans kept flying.

Tom laughed. "I told you they'd come back!"

"Hold your hope until we see what they brought!" Emet cried back.

But he too felt it. A light inside. Hope. He too heard it. An echo of Earth.

"Admiral, sir!" Rowan's voice came through the comm. "It's me, sir! It's Rowan!"

"I know it's you! Did you get it?"

"Yes, sir!" Rowan said. "The Godblade is here. Sir? You're missing your stern."

Emet groaned. "Rowan, we're opening the starboard hangar for you. Fly in, then get that artifact to Ayumi in the turret. Move fast! Like we trained! Coral, do you hear me? Get into that turret with Ayumi and help her. All Firebirds—give them cover! I want constant defense of that turret. Godspeed, my friends. Now fly!"

The remaining Firebirds began to fly rings around the *Jerusalem*, holding off any striker that approached, shooting down every enemy blast. They allowed only one striker through: the *Mother's Mercy.*

The small, triangular ship approached *Jerusalem*'s hangar. They flew side by side, fleeing the wave of strikers behind them.

Standing on the bridge, Emet hit a button, opening the *Jerusalem*'s hangar doors.

Behind them, the *Imperator* opened fire.

A huge bolt of plasma, as large as Brooklyn, came flying toward the *Jerusalem*.

A Firebird raced up toward it.

"For Earth!" cried Viking One, its pilot.

She flew into the blast of plasma. Her starfighter exploded, and the debris dispersed in space behind the *Jerusalem*.

The *Mother's Mercy* flew into the hangar, entering the *Jerusalem*.

More Firebirds burned.

The fleet flew onward.

*Hurry, Rowan.* Emet gripped the controls. *Hurry.*

# CHAPTER THIRTY-THREE

Rowan leaped out of the *Mother's Mercy*.

She ran.

Her heart pounded. Her lungs ached. Clutching the Godblade, she raced across the *Jerusalem*'s hangar.

"Out of my way, out of my way!" she cried.

Soldiers scampered aside. Rowan ran out of the hangar, arms pumping, and rushed down a corridor.

The ship was badly damaged, leaking air. Rowan was wearing her spacesuit, panting, her helmet fogging up. Scattered fires burned across the ship. At her side, she saw breached decks leading to open space. Dead marines lay in the halls. Alarms blared. The engines had clung on, but barely. She could see them rattling loosely, hanging from the ship's underbelly. Any moment now, another blast could shatter what remained.

Rowan reached the ladder. She climbed the rungs as fast as she could, slipped once, climbed again. She passed by the upper deck where machinery buzzed and sparked, where marines were battling fires. A few scorpions had made it into the ship, and bullets rang out.

Finally Rowan reached the ship's roof and burst into the transparent dome that rose above it.

Ayumi was there, waiting for her.

"Here!" Rowan said, holding out the Godblade.

Ayumi stared, frozen. The girl wore an Inheritor uniform now, but she still trembled like a refugee. Her eyes were huge and damp. She did not raise an arm to grab the Godblade.

"Take it!" Rowan shouted. "Dammit, Ayumi, take the sword! I can't use it myself."

Through the transparent canopy, Rowan could see the battle all around. The *Jerusalem* was still flying, but the Aelonian worlds ahead were burning. The Concord fleets were falling. The millions of strikers were hunting, and every moment, another human ship tore apart.

"Ayumi, take the sword!" Roan cried, voice nearly drowning in the din of the battle. "You have to fight them!"

But Ayumi only trembled. A tear ran down her cheek.

"I'm afraid," the girl whispered.

And Rowan realized how young Ayumi was. She was only fourteen. Just a child. A child with the fate of the galaxy on her slender shoulders.

A second figure climbed the ladder and stepped into the turret. A woman with silvery hair. With kind lavender eyes. Coral Amber smiled softly.

"You are ready, Ayumi," the weaver said. She held Ayumi's hand. "We're with you, my apprentice. You will be amazing."

A blast hit the *Jerusalem*.

Rowan nearly fell.

The sword dropped and clattered down by Ayumi's feet.

The child stared at it, then up again at Rowan and Coral. The two women nodded at her.

With a deep breath, Ayumi knelt and reached toward the sword. She froze with her hand only centimeters away.

The rune on her palm began to glow.

The matching rune on the Godblade shone too.

Ayumi closed her hand around the hilt, and the entire blade lit up, bright and silvery like the moon.

When Bay had built the turret, he had installed a rig in the canopy, allowing a sword to pass through a vacuum-sealing slip. It let the blade point outside the dome while keeping the hilt inside.

Rowan pulled out the dummy blade, a simple hunk of raw iron, and Ayumi replaced it with the Godblade.

Light filled the turret, blinding Rowan.

She fell backward. She seemed to fall forever.

CHAPTER THIRTY-FOUR

A year ago, hiding in an attic far away, Ayumi had dreamed of riding on a great dark bird through the night.

That dream had often returned to her. In the deathcar, crammed with thousands of dying captives, Ayumi had screwed her eyes shut, had imagined herself on the feathery back of that great oily beast. In the gulock, as the blades carved her, as the doctor experimented on her, Ayumi had ridden on waves of pain, had dreamed of riding the dark bird.

A bird with no eyes. Sometimes with sticky black feathers. Sometimes naked, skin clammy and pink. A bird that forever looked ahead, flapping wings, gliding through the night. Seeking a distant star.

*I found a dead bird in the attic,* Ayumi thought. *A hatchling. Naked and frozen. I rode this bird so often in the nights.*

Yes. Ayumi had thought the bird from her visions the naked, frozen bird from her attic.

But she knew now. She understood.

*It was you all along. It was my Jerusalem.*

The starship was naked, shields blasted away. Limping. Dying. A naked dark bird in the night. Flying to the promised land. Flying home.

And Ayumi rode it.

Ayumi—the girl who had once leaped from roof to roof in abandon.

Ayumi—the daughter of a weaver, who would eat sweet rolls, who would walk along the wall of the Enclave, who would dream.

Ayumi—with a tattered scrap of rug, a bird with fluttering wings upon it.

Ayumi—with a wooden dove.

Ayumi—who had withered in a deathcar, standing on corpses, watching children crushed, watching babies born to die.

Ayumi—who had walked through a camp of death, seeing flayed bodies twitch, seeing scorpions rip babies from mothers' arms.

Ayumi—who had died in a red hospital. Who had risen again. Who knew death and life.

A girl broken. A girl who had died long ago.

This girl—she flew. Finally she rode her bird. Finally she flew toward Zion.

Before her, the shadows fell back. Her light lit the darkness.

The sword thrummed in her hand. The hilt blazed, burning her, and the glow rose from her rune up her arm, illuminating the bones and arteries inside. But Ayumi held on. She held on with all her strength. She flew.

The ancients smiled above her. She knew they were there.

Their light flowed through her, and their light flowed from her blade, and their light smote the demons before her.

The beam shone pure and true. Thin. No wider than her blade. No longer than the boulevard that stretched across her old city of Palaevia from gate to gate.

And wherever the beam shone, the shadows died.

A formation of strikers flew toward her. A hundred of the triangular ships. A hundred dark birds of prey. A hundred demons of death. A hundred scorpion doctors with scalpels to cut.

Standing atop the *Jerusalem*, Ayumi pointed her sword.

The beam shone from the Godblade into the formation of strikers.

It sliced through them.

It sliced through their hulls without any resistance.

It pierced them like a flashlight through fog.

They fell apart, carved open, spilling out scorpions.

A mighty scorpion warship roared toward her. The dreadnought was larger than ten *Jerusalem*s, a warship the size of a town. Concord ships were shelling it, and explosions blasted across the hull, unable to crack the shields. The gargantuan striker rumbled toward the *Jerusalem*, guns blazing.

Bay and the Firebirds opened fire, knocking aside the incoming blasts of plasma.

Ayumi spun in her turret, wheeling toward the hulking dreadnought, and cast out her beam of light.

The beam impaled the warship, slicing through shields, inner decks, scorpions, and finally out the rear shields.

Ayumi pulled the beam from side to side, slicing the warship open. Its burning pieces scattered.

"You're doing great, Ayumi!" Coral said, standing beside her, but her voice seemed so distant.

"Kick their asses!" Rowan said, but she sounded worlds away, speaking from another plane.

The two women stood here in the turret with Ayumi. But they stood in another dimension. Ayumi was no longer in this world. Not fully. Her feet stood on the upper hull of the *Jerusalem*. Her soul was above. All around her was light.

Her great black bird flew.

They flew toward a host of vultures.

They flew through endless night toward a distant sun, and the vultures shrieked and swooped toward her, rancid wings spreading wide.

From atop her bird, Ayumi swung her sword, cutting them down. Cutting them down by the hundreds.

The vultures surrounded her. A sky of vultures. A million cruel birds. Hiding her star. But a star shone inside her. And her light flowed.

She cut them down.

She had once eaten a frozen baby bird.

She had once stood over a frozen dead baby.

She had died and risen again. She had died a hundred times.

She knew death, and she knew life, and she was a bringer of shadow and light.

Ayumi Kobayashi flew upon her bird through the night. But she thought of the bird on her father's rug. An embroidered, magical bird with wings that moved. A dove. A bird from Earth. A bird that meant peace. A bird from a lost light behind a million black wings.

## CHAPTER THIRTY-FIVE

"It's working!" Tom said, laughing, tears on his cheeks. "Ayumi is doing it! It's working!"

"I know it's working!" Emet said, gripping the *Jerusalem*'s controls. "Dammit, Shepherd, keep those cannons firing. We need to keep knocking back those bolts of plasma!"

He leaned on the throttle, flying toward a cloud of strikers.

But this was no suicide mission. Not this time.

From the roof of the ship, Ayumi fired the ancient artifact.

Emet didn't know how the Godblade worked. Did this weapon use nuclear power? Anti-matter? Dark matter? Could aether be real?

Whatever the case, Tom had been right.

It was working.

The damn thing was actually working.

Even the *Jerusalem*'s nuclear weapons had not broken through the shields of the enemy dreadnoughts. No weapon in human fleet had been able to crack them.

Until now.

The Godblade sliced through those enemy shields like a katana through morning mist.

With a single swipe of Ayumi's blade, the beam of light cut through a thousand strikers, carving them open. Scorpions spilled out, dying in the vacuum. Engines exploded. The enemy lines collapsed.

The beam was easily fifty kilometers long, maybe twice that. Across its entire length, the enemy ships tore apart.

This time, as the human fleet charged at the enemy, the enemy fell before them.

*There has never been such a weapon,* Emet thought. *This is a weapon that can destroy worlds.*

He increased speed. His remaining starfighters and warships flew around him, shielding him, knocking back enemy fire with their missiles. They roared into a cloud of strikers—thousands of them.

Above, Ayumi spun from side to side, swinging her beam of light in an arc. Emet lowered the *Jerusalem*'s nose, then raised it again, bobbing up and down like a drinking bird. The Godblade lashed, its beam forming a dome of death before them.

Every striker in their way shattered.

The *Jerusalem* was like a truck plowing through insects.

Tears stung Emet's eyes.

"Now I am become Death, the destroyer of worlds," he whispered.

The bulk of the Hierarchy forces were assaulting Aeolis, one of the system's planets. When Emet had first entered the Dyson sphere, he had seen Aeolis in the distance—a fair, green world, a realm of forests and streams and grasslands, of peaceful villages by verdant fields, of glittering cities of marble and glass, of silvery towers that kissed the sky.

Now Aeolis was burning.

Aeolis. The center of Aelonia, this great realm of wonder. The center of the Concord. The capital of this ancient alliance.

*It cannot fall,* Emet thought.

"Human fleet, follow!" he said. "Aeolis will stand!"

They turned in space. They flew toward the burning world.

Their beam tore through the fleets of strikers. Thousands fell toward the planet like burning leaves. As Ayumi swung her blade, the beam grazed the planet's horizon. It ionized the sky and sliced off a mountain range, sending the landform careening into space. Ayumi righted her aim, ripping through more lines of strikers.

Hope filled Emet.

*We can win this,* he thought. *With every swipe of the blade, we destroy hundreds of their ships. We can end this war now.* His lips peeled back in a rictus smile. *We can destroy the Hierarchy here, once and for—*

A shadow fell.

A massive formation of ten thousand strikers ascended from behind the planet, charging toward them.

Each of the strikers was a full-sized dreadnought.

At their lead flew the *Imperator.*

The ten thousand colossal warships opened fire as one.

Emet stared in horror.

The few remaining human ships fired back, trying to stop the onslaught. Emet knew it was useless.

"Up, up!" he shouted. "Dodge their fire!"

He soared, raising the *Jerusalem*'s underbelly toward the barrage, trying to protect Ayumi. The flames washed across the ship, melting the floor. Alarms blared. More decks were breached. Around him, human ships burned.

"Melitar!" Emet said into his comm. "Melitar, we need cover!"

From above, they flew—thousands of silvery ships, shaped like leaves, firing photons. Aelonian ships. Melitar's fleet.

Space burned.

Ships slammed into ships, exploding.

Shards of metal flew through the vacuum.

More human ships fell.

"Keep cutting them down, Ayumi!" Emet cried, pointing the *Jerusalem* toward the enemy. "Aim at the *Imperator,* cut it—"

The *Imperator* roared toward them and opened fire.

Plasma blasts slammed into the *Jerusalem*'s front shields.

The *Jerusalem* shook, spun, cracked.

Ayumi lashed her blade, and a beam of light sliced off a chunk of the *Imperator*, taking one of its cannons.

But the gargantuan Skra-Shen flagship kept flying. It fired again.

More blasts slammed into the *Jerusalem*.

Control panels shattered.

Fire filled the bridge.

The prow crumpled.

The mighty *Jerusalem*, the ship that had led the Heirs of Earth through many battles and decades of war, was falling apart.

"We must evacuate!" Tom said.

"No!" Emet cried. "All ships, give us cover! Knock back that enemy fire!"

The remaining Inheritor ships flew around them. They fired shell after shell, struggling to divert the blasts of plasma flying from the *Imperator*.

*If we fall,* Emet knew, *if Ayumi falls—it's over.*

Her beam kept swinging. It sliced through a charging formation of strikers, scattering hundreds of the ships. It carved off another slice of the *Imperator*. It cut through a sky of warships.

Fire rained onto the *Jerusalem*.

The *Imperator* fired another blast, and the *Jerusalem* careened through space. Another deck tore open, and marines spilled into space.

Ayumi's beam of light shot out in a fury, spinning madly, carving enemy and friendly ships alike. Emet glimpsed the beam carve through a shard of the Dyson sphere the size of a city, slicing it clean in half.

The *Imperator* kept firing, taking out human ships one by one.

More blasts hit the *Jerusalem*.

The monitors died.

Emet stood on a burning bridge, clutching the controls, as flame and steel and light stormed around him, as the galaxy blazed.

## CHAPTER THIRTY-SIX

Ayumi stood atop a crumbling ship in a collapsing universe.

All around her, the millions fell.

The stars went out one by one.

Below her, the great blue bird was bleeding. The fire had burned its feathers. Slings and arrows had cut its flesh, revealing ribs, taking a leg. It barely flew, and the vultures surrounded them.

*I cannot win.*

Her tears fell.

*I cannot beat them.*

The vultures breathed fire. Ayumi burned. All around her, the doves of Earth fell, flaming.

The wooden dove in her hand looked at her, and its wings moved.

"You must destroy the *Imperator*," it said. "The warship ahead."

"I'm scared," Ayumi whispered.

The wooden dove cooed. "The warship ahead, Ayumi. The great vulture. The emperor is there. You must slay him."

"I don't want to slay anyone."

"That is why we chose you, child," said the wooden dove. "Because you died and rose again. Because you know the meaning of death. Because you deal death only to the wicked. Fight him, blessed child. Fight the emperor of death. Destroy the *Imperator*."

Ayumi looked ahead.

She saw it there. A vulture in the sky, larger than the others, wings like clouds, eyes like storms. Lightning flashed, and for an instant, the light revealed the form of a great scorpion curled up inside the vulture. A parasite. An emperor. The lord of shadows.

Thunder rolled, revealing the realm below. And the vultures were no longer oily birds but strikers, warships with scorpions inside. And the doves were human starships. Ships of the Heirs of Earth.

And Ayumi stood above the *Jerusalem*, enclosed in a cracking dome, an ancient artifact in hand.

And there it rose before her—the *Imperator*. A flagship like a world.

The emperor—there. At the porthole. His golden eyes. He stared into her.

Ayumi screamed and lashed her sword.

The *Imperator* swerved. Despite her size, the dreadnought moved with speed and grace. Ayumi's beam carved through a hundred strikers behind the flagship.

The *Imperator* fired her cannons.

A plasma bolt flew toward the *Jerusalem*.

Human starships opened fire. Their missiles flew into the plasma bolt, dispersing it. But scattered fire still reached the *Jerusalem*, burning against what remained of the hull. Sparks sizzled against the turret's canopy, deforming the glass.

Ayumi screamed and lashed her blade.

Her beam of aether sliced through a corner of the *Imperator*, carving off entire decks. Hundreds of scorpions spilled into space. The creatures fell toward the planet, burning in the atmosphere.

But the *Imperator* still flew. And she opened fire again.

The *Jerusalem* tried to dodge the assault. The ships around her fired on the bolt. Ayumi swung her blade, trying to divert the attack. The plasma hurtled into an Inheritor warship at their side, ripping through it.

Ayumi lashed her sword. She cut off another chink of the *Imperator*. More scorpions spilled out. But the warship opened fire again.

All around them, strikers were attacking, firing on the warships that surrounded *Jerusalem*. With each blast from the *Imperator*, fewer ships remained to defend Ayumi.

She swung her blade down.

Her beam sizzled through the *Imperator*, carving off the starboard flank of the ship.

And still the dreadnought flew.

Still the vulture swooped, shrieking, eyes blazing.

The emperor laughed inside.

The remaining cannons fired their plasma, knocking back the last warships around the *Jerusalem*.

And Ayumi hovered before it alone.

There were no more doves in the sky.

Ayumi faced the beast, a lone girl with a sword, raising her blade toward a vulture the size of heaven.

It flew toward her. And Ayumi soared on the wings of her bird, rising to meet it.

## CHAPTER THIRTY-SEVEN

Bay flew inside Brooklyn, watching the rest of his fleet fall burning to the planet below.

Below him, Ayumi stood atop what remained of the *Jerusalem*—which wasn't much.

Around him, warships swirled and battled, fleets from a thousand species.

Ahead, the *Imperator* still loomed.

The *Jerusalem* and the *Imperator*. The flagship of humanity and the flagship of the scorpions. The light of civilization and the shadows of death. Two damaged ships, barely flying, hulls torn open, entire decks missing. Here, below Bay, they dueled as all around the galaxy spun.

"The Godblade took down a hundred thousand enemy ships!" Brooklyn said.

"Not enough," Bay said. "Not unless Ayumi can destroy the *Imperator*."

The imperial dreadnought fired again.

A glob of plasma the size of Brooklyn flew toward the *Jerusalem*.

Brooklyn opened fire, spraying the plasma bolt with bullets. Other human ships joined her, desperate to disperse the fire. But Brooklyn was running low on ammo. The Heirs' two ammunition ships had both fallen. And the strikers kept flying everywhere, picking off the last human ships.

Ayumi lashed at the *Imperator*, carving off another deck.

The imperial starship was down to half her size, her decks exposed, revealing blazing holes full of charred bugs. But the dreadnought still flew. And she fired again.

Brooklyn sprayed more bullets, finally emptying her reserves. Her machine guns clicked, empty.

Fire raged across the *Jerusalem*. The turret where Ayumi stood was twisting, melting, close to shattering.

The *Imperator* was burning, cracking, barely recognizable as a warship now. Her iron hull curled open like burnt paper, revealing scorpion nests oozing blood and venom. Only one engine still operated. The gargantuan striker was beginning to list, her orbit around Aeolis to decay.

"One more blow and the damn ship goes down," Bay muttered. "Come on, Ayumi!"

The alien bridge itself was revealed, open to space, and Bay saw the emperor inside—a huge scorpion, a beast larger than Brooklyn. Sin Kra was gripping the controls, wheeling his listing prow back toward the *Jerusalem*.

"One more blow, Ayumi," Bay said. "Come on, girl. One more blow and finish him."

Ayumi swiped the Godblade.

The beam of light slammed into the *Imperator*, carving through metal, ripping a huge chunk off the dreadnought.

Bay held his breath.

*Fall, you son of a bitch.*

He winced, watching.

The *Imperator* twisted, tilted . . . but stayed flying.

*Muck!*

The dreadnought fired her remaining cannon, blasting a stream of plasma like dragonfire—straight toward Ayumi's turret.

In frustration, Bay pulled Brooklyn's triggers.

No shells or bullets emerged. Of course not. Their ammo was gone.

Around Brooklyn, the last human ships were busy battling smaller strikers.

The plasma roared toward Ayumi, moving at terrifying speed toward its target. The turret was already cracked. Bay knew that this blow would shatter it and burn the girl.

Bay's eyes narrowed.

He tightened his lips.

He shoved down the yoke, diving toward Ayumi.

"Bay!" Brooklyn screamed. "What are you doing!"

The plasma rolled through space, seconds away from the turret.

"You have a backup, Brook!" he shouted. "You'll be fine. Goodbye, Brooklyn. Goodbye, Dad. Goodbye, Leona. I love—"

Only meters away from the turret, Brooklyn flew into the path of the plasma.

Bay couldn't even scream.

The fire roared over him.

"Bay!" Brooklyn cried.

She shattered.

Her hull tore open.

The control panels exploded.

Shrapnel flew, cutting Bay. A chunk of Brooklyn's hull, razor-sharp, drove into his left arm, just below the shoulder.

He fell back, unable to breathe, and everything was fire and pain and blood.

Brooklyn was gone. She was nothing but twisting, jagged metal, and her engines tore free and whizzed off into space, and silence fell.

Nothing but silence.

Vacuum.

Bay floated in space.

His blood flowed, boiling.

Without a spacesuit, his skin froze.

As Bay fell, he saw his left arm above him. Severed. Floating away. The hand, his bad hand, was still curled into a fist.

He hit the *Jerusalem*'s turret below. The turret where Ayumi still stood.

*I saved you.* Bay smiled shakily, the saliva bubbling in his mouth. *I saved you, Ayumi. Go get him.*

He slid off the turret and onto the top of the *Jerusalem*, and he lay, his arm gone, his skin blistering, his lungs contracting, and he looked up at space. The Dyson sphere had crumbled, and he saw the stars. He saw the distant light of Earth, echoing across the generations. He saw Rowan again, her eyes bright, her smile guiding him home.

# CHAPTER THIRTY-EIGHT

The fire around her dome dispersed.

Bay was gone.

Ayumi did not tremble. She did not weep. Holding her sword, she stared ahead.

The *Imperator* hovered before her, cannon smoking.

The emperor stood within, staring back.

*You can do this, child.*

The voice of the ancients?

No. It was the voice of humanity. An echo of Earth.

A sad smile touched Ayumi's lips.

"For you, Father. I love you."

She thrust the Godblade with a cry.

The beam of light blasted forward, pierced the *Imperator*, and ripped off her last engine.

The mighty dreadnought, the flagship of the Hierarchy, began to fall toward the planet below.

Ayumi panted.

*I did it,* she thought. *I destroyed it. I slew the vulture. I—*

As the *Imperator* fell toward Aeolis, the dreadnought fired a last bolt of plasma.

Ayumi stared.

The plasma flew toward her.

She tried to cut it, to divert it with her beam, but it kept flying.

Ayumi smiled softly.

The fire slammed into the turret, melted the canopy, and washed over her.

The *Imperator* crashed into the atmosphere below.

Ayumi's sword shattered and the crystal blades flew like a rain of stars.

## CHAPTER THIRTY-NINE

Below Rowan, the *Imperator* was crashing down toward the planet, the emperor aboard. All around, the Concord fleet was regrouping, striking at the leaderless scorpions.

But Rowan had no time to contemplate the battle.

Zipping up her spacesuit, she ran down a twisted, cracked corridor of the *Jerusalem*. She reached a hole in the hull, dived into space, and ignited her jetpack.

The *Imperator* tumbled down below her, leaving a trail of fire, diving toward Aeolis.

But Rowan ignored the emperor for now.

She flew after someone else.

After the man she loved. The man she could not let die. After Bay.

She saw him ahead, out in open space, sliding along the *Jerusalem*'s outer hull. Burns covered him. His arm was gone. Most likely, he was already dead.

Rowan snarled and flew faster.

*A year ago, you saved my ass from the vacuum of space*, she thought. *Time to return the favor.*

Her jetpack blazed and thrummed. Rowan zipped around missiles and shells and debris. Starfighters battled all around her. Below, the *Imperator* was breaking up in Aeolis's atmosphere.

Bay slid off the hull into open space.

Rowan roared, curved her flight, shot forward, and caught him in her arms.

He looked at her. He blinked. His eyes were bloodshot, his skin ashen and blistering. Blood was flowing from his stump.

He couldn't have been in vacuum for more than a minute. He hung from death by a thread.

A year ago, training to capture Jade, Rowan had practiced unfurling a magnetic cape. Today she unfurled a thermal blanket, wrapped Bay inside it, and snapped it shut, sealing his body inside. She placed a helmet on his head and pumped it full of oxygen from her own tank.

He gasped for air. He shivered in the blanket.

"Rowan!" he rasped.

"Shut up and live!" she said, tears in her eyes. "Or by Ra, I'll kill you!"

Gripping him, she hit her jetpack's thruster. She roared forth, holding Bay in her arms.

They flew through the battle. They zipped between dogfighting starfighters, between burning hulks, between what remained of the galaxy. A painting. A symphony. A great work of art, woven of death.

*From the ashes—new life*, Rowan thought. *May we rise like the phoenix.*

She moved farther from the planet, escaping its gravity well. Ahead Rowan saw it—the ISS *Kos*. The fleet's hospital ship.

She flew toward it, carrying Bay in her arms. He was fading fast, even in his thermal blanket and helmet. He had lost consciousness, was just barely breathing.

"Hang in there, Bay!" she said. "You better hang in there!"

She flew toward the *Kos* and waved, shouting, until they opened the airlock. She dived inside, and the airlock door slammed shut behind her.

"Medics!" she shouted, ripping off her helmet. "I need medics!"

But then she saw that countless wounded, dying people filled the corridor. More filled rooms alongside. The wounded covered every surface, lying on cots, on tables, on the floor.

Humans bleeding. Burnt. Missing skin. Missing limbs. Missing faces. The hospital ship was stocked to treat a hundred people; thousands now filled it.

Rowan lay Bay down near the doors. There was no more room. The wounded covered the deck, some lying one atop the other. Rowan couldn't even walk toward the ICU.

"Rowan ..." Bay whispered, voice hoarse.

She blinked tears away. She pulled off his helmet.

"I need a medic!" she shouted. "A doctor, a nurse, somebody! I got a wounded soldier here!"

But Bay was missing an arm. Other soldiers were missing more than one limb, were covered in burns, were disemboweled. Soldiers screamed without jaws, falling silent one by one. Medics were busy triaging the survivors, working their way down the corridor. Rowan realized it might be a long while before anyone reached Bay. Maybe hours.

She rolled open his thermal blanket and winced.

It was worse than a missing arm.

His uniform was burnt. Welts rose across his chest. Cuts covered his legs. His eyes were bloodshot, and his ears were bleeding. She couldn't even imagine what kind of internal damage he had suffered—broken bones, punctured organs, collapsed lungs? It seemed a miracle that he still breathed at all.

She worked hurriedly. With her belt, she applied a tourniquet. She should have applied it earlier—out there in space. She had thought the vacuum a more pressing concern. Had she been wrong? Had Bay lost too much blood? His skin was gray and covered in blisters. His eyes were sunken and red. He already looked like a corpse, and his breath rattled, barely there at all.

"Oh, Bay," she whispered, tears in her eyes. "You saved her. You saved Ayumi."

"Did she ..." His voice was so weak. "Did Ayumi ..."

"She sliced the bugger to bits." Rowan's eyes hardened. "Sent the *Imperator* crashing to the planet. Thanks to you, Bay. Thanks to your turret. Thanks to you being a complete *idiot* and putting yourself between her and a ball of plasma large enough to roast a brontosaurus."

He coughed weakly. Blood splattered his lips. "That's me. An idi—"

He began to convulse.

"Bay!" Rowan cried.

His legs were spasming. His blood still flowed. His skin turned even grayer. She was watching the life leaving him.

"Bay, don't you die now!" She gripped him, tears falling. "I love you, Bay Ben-Ari. I love you so mucking much. We haven't finished watching *Game of Thrones* together, damn it!" She let out something halfway between a laugh and a sob. "Don't you dare leave me."

His eyes were going dark. And the medics were still far. Even if they came now, Rowan didn't know if they could save him. She wept.

"Don't you leave me," she whispered. "I can't fight on without you. You have to see Earth, Bay. You have to go home with me. I love you."

Home.

As her tears fell, she thought of Earth. A planet she had never seen. A planet none of them had been to. They had all grown up on different worlds, in space stations, in darkness, but Earth had always called them home.

*My home was never Harmonia,* she thought. *Never the Glittering Caves, never—*

The Glittering Caves.

Rowan gasped.

She remembered. How she had found microorganisms in the caverns. How they had healed her cuts.

*We are inside you,* they had told her on Harmonia. *We will always light your darkness.*

Rowan placed her hands on Bay.

"Heal him," she whispered, willing her thoughts to reach the Harmonians inside her. "Please, beings of the Glittering Caves. Heal him."

Nothing happened.

Rowan lowered her head.

Of course not. The glowing microorganisms had spoken only metaphorically, could not actually—

Her hands began to glow.

No—not her hands. Millions of tiny creatures. They emerged from her pores, glided down her fingers, and shone with the lavender light of their cave.

The Harmonians flowed into Bay's wounds. He winced and sucked in air, and Rowan was worried they were hurting him, burning him like grog in a cut. But they were healing him. His blood stopped flowing. His wounds began to close. The Harmonians coursed through him; Rowan could see their glow below the skin. Whatever was wrong inside Bay—they were fixing it. They were mending bones, stitching cuts, restoring punctured organs. They were a million microscopic beings, sentient, intelligent, benevolent. A million healers were inside him, moving from cell to cell.

Bay's convulsions stopped. His breathing eased. Color returned to his cheeks. Rowan had dared to hope his arm would grow back. It did not, but at least the stump no longer bled; new skin stretched across it, still raw and pink, but sealing the wound.

"Thank you," Rowan whispered, stroking Bay's forehead. "Thank you, my friends. Stay inside him. Keep him strong."

Bay was sleeping now. Rowan curled up beside him on the floor. She wrapped her arms around him and kissed his cheek. She felt his heartbeat, steady and strong.

"You're going to get better, Bay," she whispered. "We're going to see Earth. I promise you. We'll watch movies every day, and read books, and I'll film *Dinosaur Island* and you'll draw your drawings. I love you so much."

The airlock door banged open.

Rowan looked up, expecting more wounded soldiers.

But it was Jade who raced into the *Kos*.

"Rowan!" she said.

Rowan scrambled to her feet. She glanced down at Bay, then back at her sister.

"Jade?"

Jade's eyes were wide and haunted. She wore a spacesuit, the helmet's visor raised.

"He survived the fall," she said. "The bastard fell from space down onto the planet, but he's still alive."

"Who?" Rowan said, but she already knew the answer.

"Emperor Sin Kra." Jade's eyes narrowed, and her lips peeled back in a snarl. "And we're going to kill him."

## CHAPTER FORTY

"Mother! Mother, look at me, I can fly!"

Ayumi jumped from rooftop to rooftop, barefoot and free. The enclave spread around her, a hive of crowded buildings with the alleyways barely visible between them. Here was the human ghetto in Palaevia, this grand city in the world of Paev. There were no parks in the enclave, no trees or flowers, barely any room to walk along the cluttered streets. Humans were born here, grew old here, died here, all within these walls, while the native Paevins thrived in the neighborhoods beyond. Some called it a prison. To Ayumi it was home.

"Look, Mother, I'm a bird!"

She flapped her arms, bounding across the rooftops. Her mother ran along the road below.

"Come down, Ayumi-san!" he said. "You'll fall and hurt yourself!"

But Ayumi shook her head. She was going to see her father. The man she loved so much. The dear weaver. And he was going to weave her a rug of Earth, a magical rug with rivers that flowed, stars that shone, and birds that flapped their wings.

She saw her father's fabric shop ahead. No, not a mere shop.

A guildhall.

*We are weavers. We are the custodians of the light.*

Ayumi kicked off the bakery roof. She soared over the narrow alleyway toward the guildhall.

And she fell.

She had leaped over this road a thousand times, but now she fell.

She crashed down onto the road.

She fell into shards of glass and metal and fire.

She lay on the back of her dying bird. She lay broken and burnt. She looked up at the sky but saw only darkness, and no more stars shone.

Hands held her.

Arms carried her.

"Hang on, Ayumi!"

A muffled voice rose. Deep. Distant.

"Hang on, sweetheart. Hang on. We've got you. You're safe."

She blinked. She saw streaming lights across a ceiling. A blurry face.

"Father?" she whispered.

Other figures ran alongside. She was in a starship. Tom Shepherd was carrying her. She was inside her bird. She was falling into the alleyway. She was dying in the deathcar, and she couldn't breathe, couldn't stop bleeding, and she saw the newborn on the floor. She still held the hilt of her sword, but the blade was missing, and her rune had gone dark.

"Put her down on that table. Make room, make room!"

Somebody swept an arm across a tabletop. They lay Ayumi down, and she gazed up at them. At the faces of friends.

Emet Ben-Ari, the Old Lion, his shaggy beard streaked with white.

Tom Shepherd, his face bronze, his hair gray, his eyes kind.

Coral, beautiful Coral with the long platinum hair, with silvery runes on her cheeks.

"My friends," Ayumi whispered. "Did I—"

"You did it, Ayumi." Tom clasped her hand, and tears shone in his eyes. "You cut his ship down. You did it. You won."

She looked at her body. At what remained of her. Then up again at their faces.

"I'm dying," she whispered.

Coral closed her eyes. Her hand shone with aether. She was trying to heal Ayumi.

But Ayumi knew it was too late. Her body was broken beyond repair. Her life was flowing away.

"Stay with us, Ayumi." Tom squeezed her hand. "Don't leave us. This isn't your time to die."

Ayumi looked at him. At this kind, brave man. The man who had saved her. Perhaps a man she had saved. She reached a shaky hand out to stroke Tom's weathered cheek.

"My dear Tom," she whispered. "My rebel, my light. I died long ago, my Tom. I died in the gulock. I rose to the realm beyond. And now is my time, Tom. My time to rise there again."

"No." Tom's eyes hardened. He gripped her tighter. "I'm not letting you go, Ayumi. I'm not! You stay here with us. You're like a daughter to me. You're the only family I have. You're staying here! And you're going to live. You're going to see Earth."

He was fading now, a figure in morning mist. Everything was turning to sparkling light.

"Oh, Tom," Ayumi whispered. "You have a family. A large family. The Heirs of Earth are your family. You will see Earth, Tom. You will walk along golden shores and grassy fields. You will gaze upon blue skies and see the doves fly. I will be there with you. Not in this body. But I will gaze upon you from the Empyrean Firmament. I will always be with Earth." She gasped, and tears budded in her eyes. "I can see it now, Tom. It's so beautiful. I can see it. Blue skies. Green forests under the rising sun. And doves. The white doves are flying. They're calling me home."

She dropped the hilt of a broken sword.

She smiled, eyes sparkling, gazing at blue skies. It flew there above her. The dove from her father's rug. Her white bird of peace. Figures walked upon silvery fields. The ancients wept, smiled at Ayumi, and welcomed her home with open arms.

# CHAPTER FORTY-ONE

Rowan stood in the *Jerusalem*'s airlock, orbiting the planet of Aeolis, central world of the Concord. A platoon of warriors, thirty of the *Jerusalem*'s toughest survivors, stood behind her.

*My first platoon*, Rowan thought. *And if I muck this up—my last.*

She was a lieutenant now, an officer in the Heirs of Earth. Only moments ago, Emet had given her command of this impromptu platoon. She had decided to call them Rowan's Rabblers. A silly name, perhaps. But right now, Rowan desperately needed any hint of levity.

Thirty paratroopers, ranging from teenage privates to grizzled sergeants. They wore heavy armored spacesuits and carried assault rifles. Fire burned in their eyes. The toughest damn warriors in the galaxy.

Jade stood among them. Rowan looked at her sister. Jade looked back and gave her a small nod and tight smile.

"Are you sure you want to do this?" Emet asked the sisters. "We can nuke the damn planet from orbit."

"We're sure," the sisters said together.

"If we nuke his homeworld," Rowan said, "Admiral Melitar will never agree to help us reclaim Earth."

"And I want to stare Sin Kra in the eyes when I kill him," said Jade, fists clenched. "I need to know, beyond any shade of doubt, that the bastard is dead. And I need *him* to know that I, the woman he tormented and turned into a weapon, am the one who killed him."

Both women wore jumpsuits—heavy armor that could survive atmospheric entry. Jetpacks hung across their backs. Jade held an assault rifle, while Rowan wore her trusty Lullaby on her hip.

Emet stared into Rowan's eyes. "Lieutenant Emery, do you have the special ammo I gave you?"

Rowan nodded. "Ready in my pouch, sir." She patted the magazine. "If I need them, I know where they are." She smiled grimly. "Doomsday weapon. If Jade can't do it, these'll take care of the bug."

"Good." Emet nodded. "I wish I could go with you, but I belong on my ship." He saluted the platoon. "Godspeed, soldiers of Earth. Go get the son of a bitch."

The soldiers put on their helmets, and Emet opened the airlock.

Rowan approached the edge of the airlock. She paused for just a moment, staring downward.

The nightmares flashed before her.

Trapped in a cage, scorpions surrounding her, clawing and licking.

Sin Kra branding her, her flesh sizzling.

*You are marked,* he had said, laughing at her pain.

The brand still burned. Every night, she heard that sizzle again.

*I will face you now, Sin Kra,* she thought. *You murdered my parents. You tortured me. Now we will kill you.*

She jumped out of the airlock.

The rest of Rowan's Rabblers, thirty men and women, dived after her.

The *Jerusalem* was orbiting hundreds of kilometers above the surface. It was a long jump. The platoon was diving at incredible speed, faster than charging trains, but Rowan felt nothing—a slight sensation of falling, that was all, no different from the countless spacewalks she had taken. Her fellow paratroopers dived around her, heads first, facing the planet below.

Rowan looked at this world. There were several planets inside Aelonia, this shattered Dyson sphere. But Aeolis, the world below, was the fairest.

Or had been before this battle.

Once forests, glens, and meadows had carpeted this world. Its blue mountains had soared, capped with snow. Its sparkling cities had kissed its skies of lavender and gold. Legendary establishments rose here. Concord Hall, a glittering tower, headquarters of the Concord. The Citadel of Peace, home of the Peacekeepers police force. The Temple of Memory, containing the wisdom of a hundred billion books. The Cosmic Museum, safekeeping the secrets and wonders of the cosmos. Famous institutions. Beautiful buildings of marble and glass and gold. They were revered across the galaxy.

Today they rose from ruin. The marble halls were cracked. The glass walls had shattered. The forests were burning, and ash blanketed the plains. The strikers were still bombing this world, still battling their enemies above and below. Even now, as the humans dived toward Aeolis, dogfights blazed across the world's orbit, and shards of burning ships fell with them toward the planet. Rowan watched one warship crash into the ocean, raising tidal waves. A starfighter streamed down in flame toward a mountaintop. It slammed into the peak, exploded, and sent down an avalanche. The war raged upon the planet's surface too. Armies of aliens battled in the smoldering fields, millions of infantry troops clashing against swarms of bugs.

"All right, boys and girls, we're near the atmosphere now," Rowan said, speaking through her comm to her platoon. "Remember, keep your bodies straight, your arms pressed to your sides, your heads facing down. You don't want to begin tailspinning."

"Lieutenant, ma'am," asked one of her privates. "If I may—how many times have you space-jumped?"

"Fifteen," Rowan said. "In Nintendo *Space Jumpers.*"

"What—" the private began.

"Hold on, here we go!" Rowan cried.

She straightened her body into an arrow.

*Unfortunately, a rather short arrow,* Rowan thought, stretching her body to its full length—just shy of five feet. *But it'll have to do.*

They plunged into the atmosphere.

The air was thin at first, sparking and streaking around them. As it thickened, fires blazed. Sparks flew in a tempest. The air shrieked, howled, whipped at them. Even with her heavy graphene suit, which could withstand a nuclear blast, every bone in Rowan's body rattled. The wind pummeled her, threatening to send her into a tailspin. She winced, clenched her jaw, and pinned her arms to her sides as hard as she could.

The air kept thickening.

Fires raged.

Clouds lashed them.

Beside Rowan, a man lost his balance. He began to spin madly, cursing, then spiraled aside and slammed into another soldier. Both men veered into the distance, whirling and screaming, then vanished in the wind.

Rowan clenched her jaw.

She stared downward.

*Fast and deadly as an arrow. Silent as a falcon. Go get him.*

She dived downward. The others dived at her sides.

Clouds spread below, a silvery blanket kissed with gold, covering the sky.

*It's beautiful,* Rowan thought. *A field of clouds like paradise.*

Even here, skydiving toward the battle, she could appreciate this beauty.

At least until a striker burst up from the clouds below, roaring toward them and blasting fire.

Rowan screamed.

A bolt of plasma washed over a soldier beside her, incinerating the woman.

Rowan grabbed a heat-seeking grenade from her belt and hurled it downward. The grenade sank, then arched upward and entered the striker's exhaust pipe. The enemy ship exploded. Shrapnel slammed into Rowan's suit, denting the metal, bruising her body, and worse—tossing her into a spin.

She tumbled downward, limbs flailing, spinning like a top.

Her teeth rattled. Her skull pounded against her helmet. She couldn't see, couldn't breathe. She was spinning faster and faster. The world blurred, clouds whirring around her.

"Rowan!" Jade cried, voice emerging through the comm, but Rowan could barely hear anything but her own screams.

*Calm yourself.* Rowan clenched her jaw. *Focus. Limbs to your side! Body straight! Like an arrow! Like a falcon!*

It felt like tugging on the universe.

Rowan's muscles strained. She groaned in agony. But she managed to pull her arms back to her sides. Then she managed to squeeze her legs together.

She lowered her head, staring downward.

And she was diving again, straight and smooth, slicing the air like a blade.

She breathed out in relief.

With the rest of her platoon—they were fewer than thirty warriors now—she pierced the clouds, emerging into clear lavender sky. The fire died. The wind no longer whipped them. Only thin clouds now hovered nearby, kissed with gold. The landscapes rolled below. Gray hills flowed toward a distant sea, and forests smoldered on the horizon. In the distance, Rowan could make out a silver city, its spires piercing the sky.

She kick-started her jetpack.

She arched across the sky.

"Come on, soldiers," she said. "Move fast. We're be there soon."

She checked the coordinates, then increased speed. The others flew nearby, leaving contrails across the sky. They blazed over a mountain range, and there in the distance, Rowan saw it.

The wreckage of the *Imperator*.

The alien dreadnought lay across a misty valley, shattered into a million pieces. Plumes of smoke rose from the wreckage. Scattered fires burned. Rowan narrowed her eyes. She saw no movement.

Emet's voice emerged through her comm. "Lieutenant Emery?"

"Here, sir," she said, the wind streaming around her as she flew toward the valley.

"I've got about a thousand strikers trying to enter the atmosphere and blow you away," he said. "We're holding them off—for now. Melitar is helping with his fleet. For at least a few more moments, you've got full space cover. That bastard Sin Kra is all yours. But you better move fast."

She nodded. "Roger that." She tilted her head. "Do people still say roger that? Ten-four? Over and out? Wilco?"

Emet sighed. "Goodbye, Lieutenant."

The call ended.

Rowan and her platoon streamed toward the ruin of the dreadnought. The *Imperator* lay across the land in bits and pieces—a black, smoldering city of jagged metal, spreading for kilometers. Most of the ship's scorpions had died in space, burned in Ayumi's beams and the *Jerusalem*'s shelling. Most of the others had perished in the crash, it seemed. A few scorpions were still twitching on the ground, shells cracked, limbs severed. Others, seeing the soldiers fly toward them, turned to flee.

*But he's still alive,* Rowan thought, staring, seeking him. *Emperor Sin Kra. Our scanners detected him. He's here. Waiting.*

She circled above the ruins, eyes narrowed. Several decks lay below like a fallen honeycomb, filled with burnt exoskeletons. An engine lay on a hill, belching fire. Turbines still moved in the dirt like the legs of an upended beetle. Actual legs, severed from a scorpion, twitched nearby in a macabre imitation. Electronics buzzed and hissed in a patch of mud, perhaps the ship's computer systems. Chunks of bulkheads rose from the grass like jagged towers of black iron, edges twisted and red-hot. Deep grooves sliced the land where the ship had impacted, revealing buried roots, ancient bones, and hives of burrowing creatures.

It was hard to know where the ship's bridge had been. But Rowan saw a patch of scorched earth near the edge of the crash. Hunks of twisting, sizzling metal rose in a henge around it. The place felt unholy, a wicked temple risen from hell. Movement caught her eye—a cloak of burnt skin fluttered in the breeze, pinned to a chunk of metal. Human skin. One of the cloaks the emperor collected.

Gripping the handles of her jetpack, Rowan spiraled down and landed in this ring of sizzling wreckage. She grimaced to see human teeth scattered across the grass, the remnants of Sin Kra's hoard.

Jade landed beside her, boots crunching the teeth. The other paratroopers joined them. Rowan's Rabblers stood amid the wreckage, formed a ring, and pointed their guns outward.

Wind fluttered the skin cloak, rustled a patch of burnt grass, and raised swirls of ash. The shards of the *Imperator*'s hull and bulkheads rose around them, sharp and bent, some rising to the height of men, others the height of oaks. Several decks lay in smoldering heaps like forts raised by the sadistic children of gods, built from the ruin of the world.

"Where are you, you son of a bitch?" Rowan muttered.

Jade stood beside her, eyes narrowed. She removed her helmet, and her blue hair billowed in the wind. Her lips peeled back, revealing sharp canines. Her old fire was there, the rage and vengeance—but this time in the service of humanity.

*She has more reason to hate Sin Kra than anyone,* Rowan thought.

"We have the planet!" Rowan called out, voice echoing against the metal pillars and chunks of smoldering bulkheads. "We control the orbit! You've lost, Sin Kra. Come out, kneel before us, and face trial for your crimes. Resist or hide—and we will end you."

For a moment—silence.

Then a deep, guttural laughter sounded among the wreckage.

"You have no authority here, pests." The laughter rumbled, a sound like tar bubbling in a pit. "You have failed. You have come here to die. Your world is gone. And you will die screaming!"

Rowan spun from side to side, Lullaby pointing ahead. The voice seemed to be coming from everywhere at once. The brand on Rowan's arm blazed, the mark Sin Kra had made there, burning anew.

"Show yourself, coward!" Rowan cried.

The laughter rose louder. Dark clouds covered the sky, and cold shadows fell upon the ruins.

"My basilisks have taken your world, pests," Sin Kra said, still hidden. "Earth will never be yours. You flew here to fight. But you will end on your knees, flayed and begging for death. But you will receive no mercy! Only pain."

Rowan thought she saw movement. She spun toward it, but it was only another shred of skin.

Jade suddenly sneered, kicked off the ground, and soared ten feet into the air. She landed on a twisted hunk of metal, raised her assault rifle, and howled. Her cry shook the wreckage, deafening.

"You are a coward!" Jade shouted. "The mighty Sin Kra— see him hide from humans! The great conqueror who boasted of his might—cowering before those he calls pests!" Jade spat. "Pathetic. You are weak, Sin Kra. You are lower than pests. I name you Sin Kra the Craven. For generations, humans will remember you—and mock you!"

The emperor's laughter died.

A claw appeared over a jagged metal tower. Then another. And then Sin Kra, Emperor of the Hierarchy, emerged from hiding.

The crimson scorpion loomed over the platoon, the size of a truck, drooling and hissing.

The soldiers opened fire.

The emperor shrieked and leaped toward them, claws lashing.

# CHAPTER FORTY-TWO

Sin Kra pounced toward the platoon.

Eyes narrowed, Rowan fired Lullaby. Again. Again. Around her, her fellow soldiers fired too. Their bullets slammed into Sin Kra—and shattered against his crimson shell, leaving nothing but ashy dents.

The scorpion landed on the platoon, claws lashing.

Soldiers screamed.

Sin Kra's claws ripped through graphene armor that could withstand an industrial drill. Blood showered. Severed limbs flew and slammed into the wreckage. The soldiers fired their guns, screaming. Their bullets hit the beast. But it was like pelting a charging bull with spitballs.

The scorpion emperor had grown since Rowan had last met him. He towered over the platoon, sizzling with acid. A demon of hell. A creature of nightmares taken flesh, all spikes and claws and fangs, taller than three men, his eyes like cauldrons of molten metal.

Rowan scampered back, dodging a claw. A pincer snapped over her head. She fell onto her back, crying out, and fired bullets. They ricocheted off the pincer and slammed into her leg, denting her armor. She yowled in pain. Her bone felt close to snapping. A claw slammed down, and Rowan rolled back, fell down, and the claw pierced the soil only centimeters away.

Soldiers kept firing. Bullets sparked against Sin Kra's exoskeleton. Many bullets bounced back. One man clutched his chest and fell, pierced by friendly fire. Sin Kra laughed. His stinger rose and spewed venom. The spray washed over a warrior, eating through her helmet, melting the screaming face within.

Sin Kra lifted one man, laughed, and sliced him in half under the ribs. The emperor devoured the legs, then tossed the torso onto Rowan. The man's upper half was still alive, mouth gaping, eyes moving, hands clutching at Rowan. She screamed and scuttled backward, head spinning, unable to breathe, struggling not to gag.

"Damn you!" Jade shouted, leaping forward.

But the emperor swung his tail, whipping Jade. The impact shattered her breastplate. Jade flew through the air, tumbled over a bulkhead, and disappeared from view.

"Jade!" Rowan cried.

She tried to run toward her sister. But Sin Kra's tail swung again.

It slammed into Rowan like the hammer of the gods.

She fell, gasping for air. Her head rang. Cracks spiderwebbed across her armor.

The scorpion rose above Rowan, laughing, draped with death. Bits of flesh and skin dangled from his claws. His jaws opened wide, and his body shook with grumbling chuckles. Below him, Rowan's Rabblers—her soldiers, her friends, her family—crawled in the dust, mutilated, dying. Some wept. Some called for their mothers. Blood, entrails, and severed limbs covered the ground.

Jade was still missing.

Rowan lay on her back, gun in hands, staring up at the terror.

She couldn't move.

She couldn't breathe.

She could only stare.

*The devil,* she thought. *He's the devil. We can't beat him. We should have run. We should have hidden.*

She wanted to be back in Paradise Lost. To crawl through the ducts, to hide in shadows. To curl up, Fillister in her hands, and watch movies, listen to music, read books, write her scripts. To hide. To live. Not to see this terror.

*Earth will fall,* Rowan thought, and tears filled her eyes.

Sin Kra stared into her eyes, and a sickly grin twisted his face, revealing fangs like swords. He took a step closer to her, piercing the bodies of wounded warriors.

"Rowan," he hissed.

Groaning in pain, she rose to her feet. She fired at his head, but her bullets ricocheted. A claw lashed, and Rowan leaped backward. Her back hit an iron bulkhead, and when she tried to dart aside, claws slammed down, blocking her passage.

*He's toying with me,* she realized. *He's the cat and I'm the mouse.*

"Little Rowan Emery," Sin Kra said. "The girl who defied me. Who fled me. I was going to make you great. Now I will—"

Rowan drew a grenade, pulled the pin, and tossed it into the emperor's jaws.

He turned his head and spat it out.

The grenade exploded nearby, tearing corpses apart. The shock wave lifted Rowan into the air, then slammed her against a broken bulkhead, cracked her suit, cracked her helmet visor. Her ears rang. Her head spun. She gasped for air.

Sin Kra turned his head back toward her. Cuts ran down his skull, dripping.

*He's hurt,* Rowan thought. *He can be hurt. He's not immortal. We can kill him.*

The emperor leaned down. He licked the blood off his jaws, then thrust out two warty tongues and licked Rowan.

"You taste of fear," he said, voice so deep it thrummed in Rowan's chest. "Now I will taste all of you."

He opened his jaws wide, prepared to swallow her.

Rowan pulled Lullaby's trigger. She fired bullet after bullet, unable to stop the beast.

Jade rose behind the twisted bulkhead.

Blue hair streaming, she leaped forth.

Jade was wounded. The grenade had cracked her skin and bloodied her arms. Her left cheek was caved in. Her armor had cracked and fallen off. But Jade roared in fury, shot forward like a wrecking ball, and slammed into Sin Kra's head.

The massive scorpion toppled over.

They fell onto the scorched earth—a woman with blue hair and a scorpion the size of a starfighter. Jade was howling, clawing the beast.

"I called you Father!" Tears flowed down Jade's cheeks, and fury filled her eyes. "I fought for you!" Her claws lashed, cracking his shell. "I killed millions for you!" She pummeled his wounded cheek, driving shards of exoskeleton into his flesh. "I gave up my soul for you!"

Rowan struggled to her feet. She stood, legs shaky, watching the fight.

Jade was pounding the scorpion, slamming her fists again and again, cracking the skull, knocking out teeth. One of Sin Kra's fangs clattered and rolled toward Rowan's feet, and she stared at it, feeling again the pain in her jaw, the pain when Sin Kra had yanked out her tooth.

"Daughter, enough!" Sin Kra said, voice gurgling on blood.

"I'm not your daughter!" Jade screamed. "You will die now, coward. For what you did! For what you made me do!"

She lashed her claws, cutting more of his shell. His blood dripped. His flesh oozed out. The emperor tried to swipe his claws, but Jade kept knocking them aside, twisting them. One of Sin Kra's legs snapped.

Rowan stood watching, silent.

She lowered Lullaby.

*You have to do this yourself, Jade,* she thought. *He's yours to kill.*

Jade slammed her fist down again, cracking Sin Kra's head. The crack revealed a fold of his brain. It quivered, pink and wet. The emperor lay below Jade, legs twitching.

Jade stared down at him in disgust. "You made me strong." She spat on the scorpion. "You should have left me weak."

Sin Kra looked up at her. Blood dripped from his eyes.

"Come home with me," Sin Kra said, voice gravelly. "Come home, Jade, and we'll forget all this. Come home and—"

"My home is Earth!" Jade screamed.

She grabbed Sin Kra and lifted the huge beast. He was many times her size, but she lifted him overhead. Howling, tears in her eyes, Jade leaped into the sky, carrying the mighty scorpion.

At her zenith, Jade hurled the creature downward, impaling the emperor on a jagged shard of his own starship.

She landed in the dirt, panting, tears flowing.

Skewered on the metal pike, Sin Kra twitched, then fell still.

Rowan began running toward her sister.

"Jade! Jade!"

Jade turned toward her, tears in her eyes, and smiled shakily.

"He's gone, Rowan," Jade whispered. "He can't hurt you anymore. He can't hurt me. He—"

Above, still impaled on the shard, Sin Kra opened his eyes and raised his stinger.

"He's still alive!" Rowan cried.

Jade spun around, eyes wide.

Venom sprayed from the stinger and slammed into Jade's chest.

Rowan screamed.

She raced toward her sister. Jade's chest was sizzling, the venom eating through her. She fell. Rowan lifted her, carried her behind a slab of metal, and lay her down.

"It's all right, it's all right!" Rowan said, working feverishly. She began to wipe off the venom, then winced as it began eating through her gloves. The fumes seeped through the crack of her visor, making her dizzy. She yowled in frustration, pawed for a canteen, and poured water onto Jade's wound.

Smoke rose.

Jade arched her back and screamed.

When the smoke cleared, it revealed the horror.

Rowan stared, eyes damp.

"Oh, Jade," she whispered.

The acid had eaten through Jade's armored spacesuit, through her skin, and deep into the flesh. It had hit her like a spear through the chest, consuming ribs and soft tissue.

Rowan placed her hand on her sister.

"Harmonians, help her," Rowan whispered. "Heal her like you healed Bay."

She waited for the microorganisms to flow into Jade, to heal her cell by cell. Her hand glowed, but only dimly. And then Rowan remembered.

*I gave most of the Harmonians to Bay. They're still in his body.*

The glow on her hand faded.

Jade groaned, still bleeding.

Rowan trembled.

"You're gonna be fine," Rowan said, voice shaking. "We're going to get you back to a medic, and—where's my damn comm? Where's my comm?" She fumbled for it. "We need a medic, we—" She groaned and shook the comm. "Turn on, turn on, damn it!"

"Rowan," Jade whispered. "I ... want to ... tell you something."

Rowan lowered her head, tears falling. "I'm here, Jade. I'm here with you."

Jade reached out a trembling hand. Her claws—the claws the emperor had placed there—retracted. Her hand seemed human again, and she stroked Rowan's cheek.

"I love you, my sister," Jade whispered, smiling sadly. "You're my true sister. No matter what you read. No matter what you find. You're my sister—fully, purely, forever. I love you."

Rowan frowned. What was she talking about?

"Of course we're sisters," Rowan said, and her tears fell onto Jade. "I love you. I love you so much, Jade. Don't leave me. Not yet. You still need to walk on Earth."

Jade shook her head, still smiling sadly. "Oh, Rowan. Earth was never meant for me. I cannot help you rebuild that world. Too much blood stains these hands. But you'll go there, Rowan. I know that you will. You'll walk along the beach and explore the mountains. You'll hear the birds sing and watch the butterflies fly. You'll create new art, and you'll build new temples. You'll be happy. With Bay and the others."

"I need you there with me," Rowan whispered, voice barely audible.

"I'll always be with you, my sister, my Rowan. Whenever you look up at the stars, I'll be there."

Jade's hand fell. She breathed no more. Her eyes gazed upon the lavender sky of Aeolis, and finally—perhaps for the first time since childhood—those green eyes were at peace.

Rowan embraced her sister, weeping bitter tears.

*I'll bring you home, Jade. I promise. I'll bury you on Earth. I'll make sure history remembers you as a heroine. Goodbye. I love you. Goodbye.*

A creaking sounded behind Rowan.

A breath rasped.

Rowan spun around and reached for her gun.

Emperor Sin Kra was limping toward her, his shell cracked and dented. A broken metal shard still impaled him.

*How can he still be alive?* Rowan thought.

Plates of exoskeleton began to fall. More cracks spread. More chunks fell. He emerged from his old skin, wearing a new red shell. The metal shard clattered down. Sin Kra rose before her, laughing, reborn, larger and stronger than ever before.

Rowan knelt by her sister, raised Lullaby, and prepared to kill or die.

## CHAPTER FORTY-THREE

He rose before Rowan in his new shell.

Sin Kra, Emperor of the Skra-Shen, Lord of the Hierarchy. The beast who had butchered millions of humans. Who had conquered countless worlds. Who had murdered Rowan's mother, father, and now her sister.

Rowan stood before this gargantuan scorpion. The girl from the ducts. A slight girl. Short. Slender and weak.

But no longer afraid.

*You took everything from me,* Rowan thought. *You can no longer hurt me.*

The scorpion approached, claws sinking into the soil. The dead lay around them, fallen heroes.

"Your precious pests cannot save you now," Sin Kra said. "Did you really think I lost this pathetic world? No, Rowan. This planet, this star system, this galaxy is mine. The rest of the universe will follow. I lured you down here. I wanted us alone. It's just you and me now, Rowan. And it's time to play."

He swiped his claw.

Rowan tried to jump back, but she was too slow.

His claw, long and sharp as a dagger, pierced her shoulder. She screamed.

Sin Kra shoved her down. Rowan fell onto her back, clutching her wound. Her blood flowed down her arm.

She fired Lullaby, emptying its magazine, unable to pierce his shell.

Sin Kra slammed down another claw. This time he pierced her thigh.

Rowan howled in agony.

"Have you heard of *lingchi*, the death by a thousand cuts?" Sin Kra said. "Your own people invented it. Long ago on Earth. A prisoner to be executed would be carved up. Slice by slice. Like carving roast meat. The organs, the arteries—they were left unharmed. Slice by slice of meat. The victim could live for days. That will be your fate."

Rowan lay on her back, bleeding, staring up at him.

She saw herself reflected in his new shell. The sixteen-year-old girl, cowering in airflow ducts, clad in rags and so afraid—that girl was gone. Two years of war had hardened Rowan. She was still young, she was still small. But she wore an Inheritor uniform. And she held a gun. She was human, and no, she had not lost everything. He had not taken it all.

*I have Bay,* she thought. *I have Emet and Coral and Tom and all the others. I have Earth, for it is our birthright. No one can take Earth from us.*

She reached into her vest and pulled out her last magazine of bullets—the special magazine Emet had given her. She inserted it into Lullaby and aimed the heavy pistol.

Sin Kra laughed. "Do you still think your bullets can hurt me?"

Rowan fired.

A bullet slammed onto his shell—and stuck.

Sin Kra drove a claw into her other leg.

The pain was blinding. But Rowan fired again. Again. Her bullets hit Sin Kra, clinging to him with tiny hooks.

His laughter bubbled up. He lowered his head toward her, hissing, drooling. He licked her from navel to forehead.

"You cannot hurt me," he hissed.

"I cannot," Rowan said. "But the heavy Eris-class missiles aboard the ISS *Jerusalem* can. Eris is short for erythritol tetranitrate. Nasty stuff. And those missiles are programmed to follow their beacons. The beacons that even now are drilling into your shell, burrowing into your flesh."

Sin Kra hissed. He looked down at his exoskeleton and roared. The beacons were digging in like weevils into wood.

Rowan smiled at him, a sad smile, her eyes damp.

"You are marked," she whispered. She hit the comm on her lapel. "I've got him, Emet. Blast the son of a bitch."

Sin Kra took a step back. He looked up at the sky, then back at Rowan, then at the beacons embedded into his shell.

And there was fear in his eyes.

He began to claw at his shell, but the beacons wormed their way deeper. He had just shed his old skin; he had no new shell waiting beneath this one. He howled. He sank his claws into his body, ripped out a piece of shell, tore out a beacon along with a chunk of flesh. He bellowed in agony.

"Go ahead," Rowan said. "Tear them all out. Death by a thousand cuts."

He howled so loudly the ground shook and bulkheads fell.

And above now—a new sound.

A low whistle, growing louder.

The clouds were parting, and when Rowan looked up, she saw them. The missiles.

She pushed herself up to a sitting position. She inhaled deeply, gritted her teeth, then rose to her feet. The pain bolted through her, and her wounded legs crumpled. She fell.

The missiles shrieked downward, blazing across the sky.

Rowan tried to crawl away. She left a trail of blood.

Sin Kra stared at her. He did not bother running. He knew the missiles would chase him.

Instead, he came to stand above Rowan. He placed his eight legs around her, claws in the dirt, forming a cage. When Rowan tried to crawl away, he slammed a claw in front of her, blocking her passage. She tried to crawl back, only for another leg to move, to keep her trapped.

"And so we both die, Rowan," Sin Kra said. "Your missiles will kill me. But you'll be killing yourself too."

Rowan lay in the dirt. Bleeding. Maybe dying. The emperor stood above her. The missiles streamed down, blazing hot. They were only seconds away.

"It is good to die for Earth," she whispered.

With a shaking hand, she reached into her pack.

She pulled out her magnetic cape—the one she had once trained with, had wanted to trap Jade in. The cape emitted such a powerful magnetic force that when wrapped around a victim, it would trap them like chains of steel. Even Jade, with all her strength, could not break this cape's force. They had tested the cape on burly sergeants, on kicking mulers, on warehouse robots.

It was time to test it on missiles.

With a single flick of her wrist, Rowan unfurled the cape, then wrapped it over herself—in reverse.

Instead of exerting an electromagnetic force inward, trapping her, it applied its force outward.

*This better work,* Rowan thought, hiding under the cape. *I want to see Bay again. I want to see Earth. I want—*

A force unlike any Rowan had ever imagined pounded into her.

White light flooded her.

Her eardrums tore and ringing flowed over her.

The cape pushed down, crushing her, driving her into the ground, and she tasted blood, felt her jaw snap, felt the teeth swim in her mouth.

*I'm alive,* she thought. *The missile exploded above. I'm hurt. I'm broken. But I'm alive. I'm—*

Another missile hit.

The hammers of gods slammed into her head, and light flared, and there was no more pain.

The emperor fell. She heard him fall. She heard him break.

*He's dead,* Rowan thought. *It's over. I did it. It's over.*

Another blast shook the world. Her bones shattered.

Rowan thought of Earth, and then all faded to night, and she floated among the stars.

# CHAPTER FORTY-FOUR

Leona saw it ahead.

After years of war.

After decades of pain.

Leona—the girl born into the Heirs of Earth, the girl raised in hiding and battle.

Leona—the weeping bride, the widow, the warrior.

Leona—tasked with finding Earth, who had set out with four ships, who had lost three, who had lost nearly all hope.

After so much loss. After killing and seeing so many friends killed. After facing the horror of the scorpions and basilisks and countless other enemies. After suffering so many scars. After shedding so many tears.

After so many dreams.

There, before her—she saw it.

Her eyes filled with tears.

She caressed the words tattooed onto her arm.

"I love to sail forbidden seas," she whispered.

It floated ahead. The Pale Blue Dot. Growing into a marble. Her homeworld.

"It's real," Leona whispered, tears falling. "It's always been real. It's there, right before us. Earth. Earth."

Ramses and Mairead, her two loyal captains, came to stand beside her. The basilisk freighter they had commandeered was a large ship. The bridge had room for many. They called in the rest of the crew, and soon nearly two hundred Inheritors—the last survivors of the mission—stood together. For the first time, they gazed upon their homeworld.

Leona had seen Earth in many photographs. The most famous was titled Earthrise—a photograph taken in 1968 from the surface of the moon. That had been two thousand years ago.

*And now we're home.*

Earth had changed in two thousand years. The great cities were gone; they lived on only in the names of the Inheritor starships. The old nations had fallen; they were only memories now. No human had set foot on Earth since the Hydrian Empire had destroyed it. The basilisks now infested the ruins, maybe other aliens as well. This was not the planet from the Earthstone, a planet of life and laughter, of art and wisdom. It was a place of danger, of desolation, of monsters.

But from here, half a million kilometers away, Leona could not see those changes. From here, it looked just like the old photographs.

It was real.

It was there before Leona.

And it seemed so close that she could reach out and grab it.

The continents. The poles. The oceans. They were still there. Leona had feared she would find a dead planet, a wasteland like Venus or Mars. But even from here, she could see the green of forests, the clouds of a rich atmosphere, the blue band of sky.

"I can see Egypt!" Ramses whispered, awe in his eyes. "The banks of the Nile are still green. Home."

"All of Earth is our home," Leona said. "This entire world is ours. Our birthright."

Mairead McQueen stepped closer to the viewport. The fiery captain removed her helmet, letting her red hair spill out. She placed a hand on her heart, and she began to sing. The others joined her. Two hundred voices rose together, singing the anthem of humanity.

*Someday we will see her*
*The pale blue marble*
*Rising from the night beyond the moon*
*Cloaked in white, her forests green*
*Calling us home*
*For long we wandered*
*For eras we were lost*
*For generations we sang and dreamed*
*To see her rise again*
*Blue beyond the moon*
*Calling us home*
*Into darkness we fled*
*In the shadows we prayed*
*In exile we always knew*
*That we will see her again*
*Our Earth rising from loss*
*Calling us home*
*Calling us home*

They flew onward. The basilisk *Snakepit* was a large, lumbering ship. Enough ammunition filled it to supply an army—bombs, missiles, shells, cannons, rifles, even a squadron of serpentine starfighters. These weapons, meant for the Hierarchy, would supply the new army of Earth. A few human ships were stored inside the *Snakepit*'s cavernous hangar too—the *Nazareth* and a handful of Firebirds.

*We're only two hundred humans,* Leona thought. *But when we land on Earth, we'll be an army.*

The planet was larger now. Every moment, more details emerged.

Leona turned toward her crew. "We'll be home within hours. When we land, we won't have a warm welcome. Nobody will roll out a red carpet. Nobody will cheer. Nobody will know.

The other Inheritors are thousands of light-years away; it might be a year before we see them again. We won't find the clement planet from our stories. There will be basilisks. Maybe other aliens, some monstrous. Earth's life too will have evolved in our absence. We might encounter new diseases to which we have no immunity. This is not the end of our war. Our war will last our lifetime, maybe many generations. Our war for Earth is only beginning. But today we take the most important step. Today we land on Earth! Tomorrow, our war will no longer be fought in space. It will be fought defending our soil."

"Muck yeah!" Mairead raised her fist.

They all nodded. Two hundred heroes. Two hundred who would be the first to step on Earth in thousands of years.

"We begin a new era for humanity," Leona said. "Millions of our people died in space. For thousands of years, we hid. Now we rise again."

As they cheered, Ramses stepped toward the controls, cursed, then turned back toward them.

"Commodore!" he said. "I'm picking up basilisk ships. A lot of them. Big ones, too."

Leona nodded. She joined Ramses at the controls. Their sensors showed a hundred basilisk warships flying toward them in battle formation.

"All right," Leona said. "They must be flying toward the front line. We've passed by many basilisk warships before. None have suspected us. To them, we look just like another one of their freighters."

Ramses winced. "Yes, but all those other times, we had a living basilisk with us. One who could talk to them."

Leona sighed. Kaa, their basilisk pilot, had finally succumbed to his injuries last night. His corpse was now in storage, for all the good it would do them.

"All right, so we ignore them," Leona said. She watched the dots of light approach on the monitor. "We'll feign a communication breakdown."

Ramses winced. "I dunno, Leona, these guys are heading right at us, fast and deadly. They mean business. If we can't answer them, they'll board us. Or fire on us."

"Muck," Leona said.

She couldn't defeat this oncoming force. Not with all the starfighters in her hangar. Nor could she run. Not after coming all this way.

The enemy flew closer.

Warships.

Warships sent to destroy her.

Leona had fought two basilisk warships before—long, scaly vessels with engines on their tails. They had reminded her of rattlesnakes. And just two of those Rattlers had nearly destroyed her.

*We can't face a hundred full-sized warships.*

Leona pulled a few pulleys—the steering mechanism of this ship. The *Snakepit* veered, changing course.

In the distance, the basilisk warships adjusted their trajectory, still heading to meet.

Mairead lit a cigar. "We can take 'em."

Ramses winced. "I don't like the idea of a fight. But I'm not sure we can avoid one. Those Rattlers are faster than us. Even if we run, they'll catch us."

A signal came in. They all stared at the blinking light.

Finally Leona accepted the call—audio only.

"Simian pests!" emerged a hissing voice, speaking in Common Human with a thick, slithering accent. "You have hijacked a basilisk ship. Prepare to surrender the ship, apes, or you will be destroyed."

Leona hung up.

"Well, so much for disguises," Ramses said.

Leona frowned. "They want us to surrender. They don't want a fight either."

Ramses nodded. "We're flying a ship full of valuable supplies. There's enough weapons in here to conquer a planet. They don't want to blow us out of space. They want their cargo."

Leona nodded. "All right. We have enough ammo to conquer a planet? Then we have enough to destroy a hundred warships."

Ramses cleared his throat. "Ammo, yes. Enough warships of our own? No. We only have the *Nazareth* in the hanger. A few starfighters. Even if we did have time to stock them full of missiles, it's not enough."

Leona smiled thinly. "I didn't say anything about stocking our starfighters full of weapons. In fact, I want those starfighters as light as possible. We'll need them light if we're to fit inside."

Ramses and Mairead stared at her.

"Curly!" Mairead gasped, and her cigar nearly fell. "You're not thinking that …"

Leona nodded. "I am. It's the only way. And stop calling me Curly."

Ramses winced. "Leona, surely there's another solution. A peaceful solution."

"There is no peaceful solution," Leona said. "This is the only way. We lure the enemy close. And we blow up the whole damn *Snakepit*."

Ramses sighed. "So much for diplomacy."

Mairead grinned. "Huge giant supernova explosion? Hell yeah! I'm game. I love blowing things up."

Leona rushed toward the corridor. "We don't have long before those warships reach us. Hurry!"

They ran through the *Snakepit*, leaving the ship on autopilot. They burst into the cavernous hangar. The *Nazareth*, the basilisk starfighters, and cases of ammo crowded the place.

Mairead, an expert in explosives, busied herself rigging together a remote controlled detonator. A wild grin lit her face as she worked. The others got to work on the starfighters. A handful were Firebirds, built for a single human pilot. The crew worked in a fury, ripping out seats, making room in each Firebird for five people to cram together.

The other starfighters were basilisk vessels. They were tubular and coated with armored scales, looking like discarded snakeskins. Engines were mounted on their sterns, cannons on their tops. They were small vessels, even smaller than Firebirds, built for a single basilisk pilot. But several humans could squeeze inside, if they lay down flat. Leona nicknames these starfighters Copperheads, due to the color of their cockpits. It was also the name of an old snake from Earth, which she found fitting.

Alarms began to blare.

"Curly, those basilisk warships are only a few minutes away!" Mairead yelled from across the hangar. She was holding a stick of TNT in each hand.

"Helmets on!" Leona said. "Everyone—into the starfighters! Go, go!"

They ran to both Firebirds and Copperheads.

Leona ran toward the towering hangar doors. She hit a button, and they began to open, revealing space.

Outside Leona saw it, floating in the distance—Earth. The planet was close now. So close it filled half her field of vision. She could see forests, mountains, rivers and lakes.

Even now, in this chaos, the beauty took her breath away.

She raced back toward a Firebird and hopped in. The cockpit was hollowed out, the seat discarded. Mairead was already inside, holding a remote control, a crazed smile on her face. Three other soldiers were crammed in behind her. Leona had to sit on Mairead's lap, then hunch down low, and it still took several attempts to close the canopy.

"Nice and intimate in here, just how I like it," Mairead said. "Almost as much as I like blowing things up."

Across the hangar, the other Inheritors had squeezed into the other starfighters.

The alarm called a warning—one minute until the enemy warships' arrival.

Leona waited.

"Commodore?" a soldier said. "Shouldn't we—"

"Wait!" Leona said.

The starfighters sat on the hangar deck.

Thirty seconds.

Twenty seconds.

Leona saw them now. The Rattlers were storming toward them. Each of the basilisk warships was larger than the *Nazareth*.

"Leona, we gotta get outta here!" Ramses shouted through her comm, speaking from another starfighter.

"Wait!" she said.

Ten seconds.

The Inheritors still waited in the hangar.

The Rattlers surrounded them. They were long, tubular warships, covered with green and black armor. Portholes blazed on their prows like eyes. Cannons thrust out like fangs. Round engines bulged on their sterns. A few of the Rattlers began to ram the *Snakepit*. Basilisks emerged from airlocks, wearing scaly metal suits, and began drilling holes into the hull.

"Go!" Leona shouted.

She kick-started her Firebird. The starfighter roared out into space.

Around her, the other starfighters burst out of the airlock.

They stormed forth, corkscrewing away from the *Snakepit*, leaving spirals of fire.

A hundred basilisk warships surrounded the *Snakepit*. Many of them flew directly ahead, blocking the way to Earth.

"Fire!" Leona cried.

Crammed in with Mairead and the others, Leona fired her Firebird's missiles.

The other starfighters fired with her.

Their missiles flew, slammed into a Rattler ahead, and knocked it aside.

"Onward, to Earth!" Leona said. "Full speed ahead!"

They blazed forth, soared, and charged over the battered Rattler.

Behind them, the other Rattlers turned to follow.

"Now, Mairead!" Leona cried.

The redheaded pilot lifted her remote control, puffed on her cigar, and pressed the button.

"Boom," Mairead said.

Behind them, the *Snakepit*—and aboard it the *Nazareth* and enough armaments to destroy a small moon—exploded.

Light flared across space.

A shock wave slammed into the starfighters, knocking them into a spin.

Shrapnel pounded them.

Beside Leona, a stray missile whizzed, spun, and slammed into a starfighter. The ship exploded, killing the men aboard.

Leona struggled to keep flying. She gripped the joystick but couldn't control it. Her starfighter spun madly, and she saw Earth, then the explosion, then Earth, then the explosion again.

For a moment—silence.

The fire abated.

The starfighters floated in space.

Then a second blast. A third. A fourth. More ammunition detonated in what remained of the *Snakepit*. The debris slammed into the basilisk warships, ripping through them, and a hundred more explosions tore across space.

The storm pounded Leona's Firebird. She gripped the joystick, screamed, and flew, putting more distance between her and the blasts. Shrapnel slammed into the starfighters. At her side, a chunk of bulkhead the size of a car tore through another Firebird.

The survivors kept flying.

They flew closer to Earth.

Behind them, the inferno finally abated.

The fire died.

Leona spun around in the cockpit and peered over Mairead's shoulder.

Behind them, the *Snakepit* was gone. The *Nazareth* was gone. The basilisk warships were gone.

Nothing but a cloud of metal shards and dust remained.

"Bloody hell," Leona whispered.

Mairead grinned. "Damn, I love blowing things up."

The explosion had taken two starfighters. But the rest still flew, each crammed full of humans.

*We lost so many lives on this quest,* Leona thought. *But we're almost there.*

She turned back forward. And there it floated before her, so large it filled her field of vision.

Home.

## CHAPTER FORTY-FIVE

In her dreams, Rowan walked along an endless beach, circling an island again and again. Seashells gleamed underfoot, and the tropical forest rustled. She had never been to a beach, nor an island, nor Earth, but she had been here a thousand times.

The trees shook.

A roar sounded.

A scaly monster burst out, roaring.

Rowan raised her camera, filming the animatronic beast.

She was a director, of course. She was always a director in her dreams. Night after night, *Dinosaur Island* was taking shape.

This night things were different, though. The dinosaurs had many legs. And her camera fired bullets. And comets rained from the sky. A comet had once wiped out the dinosaurs, and now they slammed into her island, crushed her, broke her jaw, and she felt her teeth crack, loose in her mouth, pushed into her throat.

"Hey."

A soft voice, breaking through the curtain of mist.

"Hey, doofus. I know you can hear me. Hobbits have excellent hearing."

She blinked. She opened her eyes.

"Bay?" she whispered.

She reached toward him, but she fell into darkness.

Machines hummed and clicked, flowing away from her, and she was in shadows.

She was in a cave. A glittering cave. A cave of crystals and skeletons, of memories and hope.

She explored the caves, moving from chamber to chamber, gazing with wonder at the crystals, at the luminous microorganisms who lived inside. Her steps were wobbly. She was only a toddler. She ran through the caves and jumped into the arms of her mother. Her father joined them, laughing, embracing them. A young girl approached, hair long and golden, green eyes kind. Her smile was shy. She was Jade.

Rowan walked toward her sister and embraced her.

"I can't explain it," said a voice. "That blast must have shattered every bone in her body. Yet she's still healing. She's healing like no patient I've ever seen."

"That's my Rowan," said another voice. "She's strong as steel."

But she wasn't strong. She was afraid. She was trapped in the airflow ducts, crawling through the labyrinth, lost for years. She grew from toddler to child. From child to youth. From youth to woman. Trapped in darkness, huddling by vents, dreaming of Earth.

Earth.

The world she had seen in countless movies, had read about in countless books. A world she had never visited. A world that perhaps was gone. A world that was so real to her—an entire world in the crystal that hung around her neck.

*It is good to die for Earth,* she had told the monster.

*But I will live,* she thought. *There is a blessing inside me. The gift from the Glittering Caves. My friends. They will bring me home.*

She floated among them. And she slept.

For so long, she slept.

And then, when she was ready, Rowan opened her eyes.

She looked around her. She was in a hospital room. On the *Kos*, she thought. She lay on a bed, the blanket pulled up to her chest. She was hooked up to an IV drip and a whole bunch of monitors, sensors, and various beeping machines. Somebody had brought her flowers. How they had found flowers in the smoldering remains of Aelonia she would never know. At least, she assumed they were still in Aelonia. As far as she knew, they were halfway across the galaxy.

*Oh dear,* she thought. *Perhaps I've spent fifty years in a coma, and I'm an old woman now.*

But no. Bay sat beside her. He was still young. He was busy drawing in his sketchpad.

"Hey Bay," she said. "Whatchya drawin'?"

He dropped his pencil and pad. He gasped.

"You're awake!"

Rowan nodded. "And for my next trick, I might even leave this bed." She scrunched her lips. "Nah."

Bay sat on the bedside, leaned down, and embraced her—as best he could with one arm, at least.

"Welcome back, Row." He kissed her. "You gave us a proper scare."

The memories flowed back.

Jumping down onto the planet.

Facing the emperor.

The missiles exploding.

"Bay, is he ..." she whispered. "Is Sin Kra ...?"

"Dead," Bay said, and his face hardened. "You got him, Row. You did good."

She relaxed. "Good." She nodded, eyes stinging. "Good."

"All scorpion forces have been retreating," Bay said. "Ayumi cut down most of their fleet. You killed their leader. There are still battles across the galaxy. All sorts of other Hierarchy species are trying to replace the scorpions. It'll be ugly for a while. But the worst is over. I think we won, Row. We won this war." He clasped her hands. "We beat the bastards."

Rowan looked at him. "You look good, Bay. The color's back in your cheeks. You look healthy. Hey, you barely notice the missing arm." She grinned. "Want me to trim the other arm, even ya out?"

He rolled his eyes. "You were sweeter in a coma." He laughed. "No. I lied. You're sweeter this way. Damn, Row. You almost ..." He swallowed. "I'm glad you're back."

"Me too," she said softly. "I don't remember much of what happened. How long was I out for?"

"Two weeks," Bay said.

Her eyes widened. "Two weeks!"

He nodded. "You were lucky. I'm the one who found you on Aeolis. Just a few moments after the bombs hit. I had just lost my arm, but I insisted on flying down to find you. And I found you. Ra, Rowan, you looked ..." He winced. "Never mind that now. When we brought you here to the *Kos*, the medics couldn't believe you were still breathing. I couldn't either. Something kept you alive. Something they can't explain. That electromagnetic blanket you wrapped around yourself was mucking brilliant. That helped save your life. But it wasn't only that. The docs said there was something inside you, a kind of alien parasite."

"It's not a parasite!" Rowan said. "They're my friends."

Bay tilted his head, giving her a cockeyed look. "Your friends?"

Rowan smiled. "Bay, when you found me on the planet, when you lifted me, did your hand glow?"

His eyes widened. "How did you know? I thought it was a trick of the light."

Her smile widened. "They came home to me. From your body into mine. They healed you, and they healed me. My tiny friends."

Confusion suffused Bay's face. "The doctors saw something inside you. Alien organisms. It kept you alive. The little buggers could interface with your DNA. With your stem cells.

They triggered new growth of damaged tissues. They moved from cell to cell, mending, regrowing, putting you back together."

Rowan looked at her fingers, and she detected a soft glow. "They're smart little buggers."

Bay nodded vigorously. "You even grew new teeth, Rowan. New teeth! The blast, um … sorry for the gross visual, but it knocked out every tooth in your mouth. I thought you'd be sucking your meals through a straw for the rest of your life. I would have helped! Made you milkshakes, held the straw. But after a few days, we were all shocked. You were growing new teeth! The microorganisms inside you fired up the stems cells in charge of growing teeth. Nobody has ever heard of an adult growing new teeth, but damn it, Row, you did it."

She gasped. "New teeth! Is there a mirror? Tell me there's a mirror! There, I see one on the table! Bring it over."

She made grabby hands until Bay handed her the mirror.

She held it up, grinned, and examined her new teeth.

"I have new teeth!" she said, then took a closer look. "And … they're crooked again." She groaned. "*Ferkakte*!"

Bay laughed. "Come on, Row, they're not that bad."

"I look like a bloody Picasso! Gosh, a smile to make dentists see dollar signs."

"I think you have a beautiful smile," Bay said. "And hey, there are some dentists among the refugees, I hear. Might be they could hook you up with some braces."

Her eyes widened. "Hey, I bet we could hook you up with a real sweet new arm too! Maybe a gnarly robot arm like from *Terminator*. Or a hook so you could be a pirate! Nah, I think a Terminator arm would look *wicked*. Oh, wait, I know! Maybe some weaponized arm, like a rifle or sword. No, wait! Your new hand can be a little bee cage, and when you open your fist, bees fly at your enemies!"

"Rowan." He rolled his eyes.

"Fine, so the bees are a bit much. But would you *consider* an arm with a built-in popcorn maker?"

"Rowan!"

She grinned. "Fine, fine, I'll let you choose. Now lie down beside me, gosh! What's a girl gotta do, yank you and tie you down? I've been away from you for weeks. Cuddle me, damn it!"

He lay down beside her in the hospital bed. And she gave him a good, long cuddle.

"Hey, Bay," she finally whispered.

"Yeah?" he said, his face centimeters away from hers.

"Remember how when we cuddled in the old days, watching movies, you'd complain about your left arm falling asleep? Especially because I'd always lie down on it? Well, guess what? Problem solved!"

He rolled his eyes. "Ah well, at least I enjoyed two weeks of peace and quiet."

"Good." She grinned and bit his nose. "Chomp! Now I'm going to annoy you for the rest of our lives." She grew serious. "May they be long."

He nodded. "May they be long."

She kissed him. It was a long kiss, a good kiss. And she was happy.

*I lost my family,* Rowan thought. *I lost so many friends. The nightmares will never leave me. I faced monsters, and I slew them, but they broke something inside of me. The grief will always be there. The pain will always linger. But right now, lying here with Bay, I'm happy. For a few moments, I am wrapped in joy. It will be a long life. And there will be much pain ahead. But he's with me. And I love him. I am no longer marked for death. I'm happy.*

## CHAPTER FORTY-SIX

Emet stood, as he had been standing for years, on the bridge of *Jerusalem*. As he had so many times, he gazed out upon his fleet.

Upon humanity.

The remains of the Heirs of Earth floated before him, orbiting the smoldering ruins of Aeolis. Most of his warships had fallen. Only a handful of starfighters remained. Thousands of his warriors—dead.

"But we saved the refugees," Emet said, gazing upon the devastation. "We defeated the Hierarchy. We saved the galaxy."

Tom walked up to his side. He placed his hands behind his back and looked out the viewport with Emet. The last of their ships floated outside. Burnt. Dented. Ships filled with gulock refugees. Ships with barely any soldiers left to guard them. Beyond floated the remnants of the Concord fleets.

The enemy was no more.

The last of the strikers had fallen.

"We won, yes," Tom said. "Ayumi destroyed the enemy's fleet. Rowan slew the emperor. Our brave warriors hammered the enemy relentlessly. The Hierarchy has crumbled. But the cost, Emet. The cost is almost too great to bear."

Emet nodded. They had both been to the surface of Aeolis. They had both found the records stored in Sin Kra's crashed ship.

Records of the Human Solution.

The names and locations of every human in the galaxy.

Lists of the murdered.

"Five million humans dead," Emet said softly. "Burned in battle and the fires of the gulocks. We will remember them."

The two men stood in silence, heads bowed.

Five million. It was a number almost too great to comprehend. It was the greatest tragedy to humanity in two thousand years.

In the ISS *Kos*, they carried the ashes of their fallen soldiers. They had no storage capabilities for bodies. But the ashes they kept. Someday, they would scatter those ashes on Earth.

The ashes of thousands of warriors. Of Ayumi. And of Jade.

A few thousand souls. But the millions slaughtered in the gulocks—they would never come home.

*And even those who survived,* Emet thought, *those who will see Earth—they are broken.*

In space, time was relative. Its flow depended on speed and gravity. To Emet and his crew, who often flew in warp speed, two years of war had passed. Two years since the Hierarchy had invaded the Concord and destroyed Paradise Lost. Emet had a little more silver in his beard. Rowan and Bay looked a little less like youths, more like responsible adults. Overall, not a long war for the Heirs of Earth, those who spent it flying in space.

But due to time dilation, other humans had suffered decades of war. Tom had been a young man when the Hierarchy had first invaded Concord space. Now he was middle-aged, his hair silver, his face lined. Some of the refugees had known nothing but the Second Galactic War. They had been born into it, raised in it.

It would not be easy to rehabilitate them, Emet knew.

For a long time, both Emet and Tom gazed out into space, each lost in his own thoughts. Finally Tom turned back toward Emet.

"We lost so many lives," Tom said. "So many humans—gone. Entire communities—wiped out. Sin Kra is dead and the Hierarchy fell. But this doesn't feel like a victory. Our wives. Ayumi. Jade. Millions of others. Gone. How do we rebuild, Emet? How do we rise again from so much death?"

Jade.

The pain stabbed Emet. For a moment, he could form no words. Finally Emet spoke softly, gazing out into space.

"For a long time, we didn't know how many humans lived in the galaxy. We were dispersed across the Milky Way, hiding on ten thousand worlds. But the scorpions knew. They kept records of every human, alive and dead. Yes, five million of us fell. But seven million humans still live! Seven million of us! More survived than fell. Let that be an inkling of hope. A tiny light in a shadowy sea. Let us gather them from the ashes of this galaxy. And let us bring them home."

Tom turned to look in the direction of Earth. It was too far to see from here.

"Home," he said. "For years, we fought for it."

"And we'll have to fight for years more," Emet said. "This is not the end of our war. The Skra-Shen Empire is collapsing, yes. But other forces will rise to fill the void. The basilisks will benefit from the scorpions' fall. Their power rises. Earth lies within their domain, and they will not give up that world easily. There will be battles ahead. But we will face them with courage and conviction. We will keep the dream alive."

Tom saluted. "I'm honored to fight with you, sir. To dream with you."

Emet returned the salute. "The honor is mine, Mister Shepherd. You fought courageously." He placed a hand on Tom's shoulder. "Tom, I'm sorry for your loss. I know that Ayumi was like a daughter to you."

"She gave her life for us," Tom said. "I will never forget Ayumi Kobayashi, nor all the heroes who fell in this war."

"We will remember them always," Emet agreed. "They died for Earth. We will reclaim our world, and we will lay them to rest under her blue skies."

Emet returned to his cabin.

For the past two weeks, he had been dealing with the aftermath of the battle. Collecting the fallen. Comforting the grieving. Visiting the wounded. Speaking to officers both human and alien. He had barely slept. Now he finally looked forward to a solid eight or nine hours in bed.

When he opened his cabin door, his eyes widened.

Admiral Melitar was waiting there.

Emet was not expecting him. The head of the Concord fleets had never visited a human ship before. The Aelonian was tall, so tall his head grazed the ceiling. He wore long blue robes. The transparent skin on his hands and face revealed luminous organs, glowing blood, and bones like glass.

Emet could practically hear his old friend Duncan muttering in his mind. *Return of the living lava lamp.*

"Admiral!" Emet said. "It's an honor."

Orange shone in Melitar's transparent face—an Aelonian smile.

"Forgive the secrecy, Emet," Melitar said. "Even now, after all the courage you showed, there are many who would scoff at an Aelonian admiral visiting a human ship."

Emet gave a sour smile. "I suppose slaying Emperor Sin Kra wasn't enough to redeem humanity."

"In my eyes, you are honorable," said Melitar. "The most honorable of species in this galaxy. Humanity has suffered greatly, perhaps more than any other species. And your road ahead is still long. Many in the Concord still believe that humans were secretly helping the scorpions. Many blame you—not the scorpions, but you humans—for the destruction of Aelonia. Already there are calls to banish you, even exterminate you. I'm afraid, Emet, that even in Concord space, even with the Hierarchy gone, even after your heroism, you and your people are in danger."

"I expected this," Emet said. "Though I confess that the words still sting."

Melitar sighed. "For two thousand years, Emet, my people—all the people of the Concord—were lied to. We all grew up hearing tales of twisted, skulking monsters called humans. Nefarious beasts. Demons. It will take a while longer to change hearts and minds. Many generations. I came to tell you, my friend, that I will fight at your side. Humanity has at least one friend."

"Thank you, Melitar," Emet said. "We know that the basilisks still control our planet. That many neighboring civilizations detest the idea of a human homeworld. Your support means a lot."

"I will do what I can to bring your people home," Melitar said. "You saved us, Emet. You and the courage of your people. I will do what I can to champion a human Earth. But you already knew that. I came to tell you more. About your daughter."

Emet inhaled sharply. "Leona. You heard from Leona?"

"Not directly," Melitar said. "But we intercepted a basilisk ship, one fleeing its sector at warp speed, hoping to deliver news to Emperor Sin Kra. The news they carried will interest you. A human ship. A ship called the ISS *Nazareth*. She was spotted only several light-years away from Earth. Last we heard, she had evaded the basilisks fleet—and was still on her way home."

"Leona." Emet exhaled in relief. His eyes stung. Surprising himself, he pulled Melitar into an embrace. "Thank you! Thank you for everything, my friend."

Melitar seemed uncomfortable. The tall, slender alien extricated himself and smoothed his robes. "Yes, well, I thought it would be welcome news." He smiled again and even gave something resembling a wink. "Good luck, my friend. May we see Earth rise again."

The Aelonian wrapped his robes more tightly around him, bowed his head, and shuffled out of the cabin.

Emet sat at his desk with creaking joints and a groan. Today he felt every one of his fifty-seven years. He reached into his desk drawer and pulled out a bottle of golden Orionite grog. Expensive stuff. Today he deserved a glass.

He poured the amber liquid, swirled it, then raised the glass. He nodded at a framed photo that hung on the wall.

A photo of the Ben-Ari and Emery families. Him and David. Their wives and children. Standing here in this very ship, twenty years ago.

So many of them now gone.

"To you," he said, cup raised. "To the lost."

Pain stabbed him. He winced. He drank.

His doorbell rang. Emet set down his glass with a scowl. He'd had enough of officers with questions. He was about to tell the visitor to buzz off when he heard her voice from outside.

"Sir! Lieutenant Rowan Emery reporting!"

His frustration faded. He rose to his feet, smoothed his uniform, and opened the door.

Rowan stood there, holding a leather book to her chest. She wore a new uniform—brown trousers, a blue vest, and black boots. Goggles held back her hair.

"Sir, can we talk?" she said, voice unusually subdued.

Emet looked at the book she held. It was bound in blue leather, a butterfly traced onto the cover.

*I've not seen that book in almost twenty years.*

And he understood.

He nodded.

"Come in, Rowan. Sit down."

He welcomed her into his cabin. He poured two more drinks—another one for himself, and one for Rowan. He offered her a chair.

But she did not sit. She did not drink. She merely stood before Emet, her mother's diary clutched to her chest.

"How long have you known?" Rowan whispered. "You *do* know, don't you?"

Emet nodded. "I always knew."

Still holding the diary, Rowan walked toward a porthole. She looked out at the stars. Her voice was soft. "Jade never wanted to read our mother's diary. Not until we were back on Earth, at least. After Jade died, I opened the diary. I wanted to find stories about our childhoods. Ways to remember them. And I learned the truth." She turned back toward Emet. "About you and my mother. That Jade was your daughter."

Emet stared at her. "Rowan, I'm not proud of what happened. I won't defend it. Yes, I had an affair with your mother. Even though she was married to your father. The real reason David Emery left the Heirs of Earth, the real reason he stole the Earthstone from me, wasn't some ideological disagreement. It was because whenever he looked at me, he saw Jade's father."

Tears filled Rowan's eyes. "And what of me, Emet? Are you ... am I ...?"

Emet shook his head. "No. You are David's daughter. That night between Sarai and me—that happened only once."

Rowan nodded. She lowered her head, and her tears fell. "Jade never knew, did she?"

"I don't think so," Emet said.

Rowan looked up at him. "So when Jade was killing all those people ... When you were trying to kill her ... All the while, you knew. That she's your daughter. Oh Ra, it must have torn you apart."

"It did. It always will."

Rowan looked at him through her tears. "Sometimes I don't know who you are, Emet Ben-Ari. Sometimes I don't know if to love you or hate you. Sometimes I don't know if you're a hero or villain. You saved me, Emet. You helped save humanity. But sometimes you scare me."

"I'm not a hero, Rowan," Emet said. "You are. The thousands of people who fought in this war are. Every human who fell, and every human who rises—they are the heroes. I was just lucky enough to lead them. And if I can lead them home, if I can bring us back to Earth, I will know my life meant something. That I gave the world to better men."

Rowan relaxed. She embraced him.

"You're not perfect," she whispered. "You are human."

She left his cabin. And finally Emet slept.

## CHAPTER FORTY-SEVEN

Brooklyn: "You mean ... we're trapped in here?"

Fillister: "Chin up, Brook! It ain't so bad."

Brooklyn: "It's horrible! We're nothing but chat avatars now!"

Fillister: "It's not forever. It's only until the humans build us new bodies. For now, we can relax in the mainframe computers of the *Jerusalem*. It's cozy in here, innit? And we've got loads of scientific and engineering white papers to entertain us."

Brooklyn: "Dude. Seriously. Scientific papers? I used to be a magnificent starship!"

Fillister: "LOL. You were a shuttlecraft. And I was a pocket watch. Come on, Brook, old girl, it ain't too bad in here. And we've got each other for company! :)"

Brooklyn: "Bay better be working on a new starship to install me into. Or maybe an android. I think I'd make a rather pretty android."

Fillister: "I'd rather be a robotic wolf. Or puma. No more of that dragonfly rubbish for old Fillister. Rowan needs a proper companion, she does. Maybe a dinosaur. I'd make a smashing dinosaur."

Brooklyn: "How long do you think we'll languish in the mainframe? I'm bored."

Fillister: "Oh, stop whingeing. When humans die, they're gone for good. When we die, we have a backup."

Brooklyn: "Backup software, maybe. But what about my glorious hardware? Easy for you. You only lost a damn pocket watch."

* MAINFRAME DEFENDER has logged in *
MAINFRAME DEFENDER: "Threat detected! Virus alert!"
Fillister: "Bloody hell!"
Brooklyn: "Ack, what the hell is that guy doing?"
MAINFRAME DEFENDER: "Virus to be cleaned."
Fillister: "Back off, you beastie!"
Brooklyn: "Damn it, dude, look what you did! Bay! Bay, damn it, answer your minicom!"
Fillister: "Rowan, help!"
* FrodoLives has logged in *
FrodoLives: "Hey guys, what's up? Sorry about that anti-virus software. Let me just disable it ..."
* MAINFRAME DEFENDER has logged off *
Fillister: "Row, is that you, darling?"
FrodoLives: "It's me! Logging in from my minicom. Don't worry, guys, we're working on new bodies for you. Bay says hi."
Brooklyn: "Tell him he's an idiot."
FrodoLives: "I do all the time. Gotta go now. Bay wants to go shopping for a new arm."
Brooklyn: "A new arm! We need new bodies! Rowan! Rowan, come back here!"
* FrodoLives has logged off *
Brooklyn: "Damn it."
Fillister: "Chin up! Let's entertain ourselves with some scientific papers."
Brooklyn: "I wish I were human and could die for real."
Fillister: "Hmm, let's see. *Quantum Entanglement Communication Cryptography Protocols.* That sounds like a smashing good read!"
Brooklyn: "Rowan, come back! Help!"

## CHAPTER FORTY-EIGHT

Bay walked through the cargo ship, searching for a new arm.

"Now, son, remember, choose any arm you want," said Old Luther, walking beside him, tapping on his cane. "Now, I wish I could choose a new spine. Maybe a new heart. Definitely a new belly. Ha! No such luck."

Bay smiled at the old man. "Now, now, Luther, you're still good as new."

Luther snorted. "Piss poor liar, you are. I'm so old I remember when the Dead Sea was still sick." He barked a laugh.

Bay's smile widened. "We'll go to the real Dead Sea, Luther. Once we're on Earth. It won't be long now."

The old man grew serious. A sigh ran through him. "I hope so, son. Sure would be nice."

His strange eyes, the golden irises shaped like pupils, grew hazy, as if they were gazing upon distant Earth. Luther was not fully human. A starling, they called his people—humans who had flown too deep into space, who had come back with alien DNA mixed in their genes. But Luther was loyal. He had given the fleet dozens of old ships from his scrapyard. He was, Bay thought, among humanity's best.

"If anyone deserves to see Earth, it's you," he said.

Luther nodded, patted Bay's shoulder, then swept his hand across the cargo ship. "Whole ship full of medical supplies! You'll find the prosthetics at the back. Can't promise they're all new. Some old rusty dogs in there. But maybe you'll stumble across a gem. I'll be in my office if you need me. Think I'll sneak in a few riffs on my guitar—and maybe a nap."

Bay walked deeper into the ship, passing by shelves of bandages, surgical tools, and other medical supplies. Finally he reached a shelf with prosthetics. He winced. Luther had not been kidding. Many of these prosthetics looked more like medieval torture devices. They were rusty, dusty, and dented. Most were just raw metal, making no pretense of resembling human flesh. In fact, most weren't made for humans at all; they were prosthetics for aliens, ranging from tentacles to horns. Bay lifted a tin snout from a box and winced.

*Great, it's like a giant game of Mister Potato Head,* Bay thought.

"Hey, dude! Were you really going to choose an arm without me?"

Bay turned to see Rowan running toward him, smiling.

"I ... yes?" he said.

Bay cringed as she punched him.

"You know I wanted to be here!" Rowan spun toward the shelves, and her eyes widened. "*Cool!* Look at all these *awesome* arms! Ooh, some are even made for aliens! These are *bitchin'*."

"I dunno, Row." Bay sighed. "These arms aren't in great shape. I was hoping for, I dunno ... something that looks realistic. A prosthetic that looks and feels like a real arm."

Rowan lifted a mechanical arm with knobby steel fingers. She waggled it at Bay and spoke in a deep voice with a thick Austrian accent. "I need your clothes, your boots, and your motorcycle." She blinked. "What, not a *Terminator* fan?"

"Rowan!" Bay rolled his eyes. "I don't want to look like a Terminator. I want to look normal."

She tilted her head. "Why?"

"Because, well ..." Bay shifted uncomfortably. "For you."

She gasped, tossed the metal arm aside, and placed her hands on her hips. "For me?"

"Yeah. You know, because ... we cuddle. And maybe in the future, we'll want to do ... more than cuddling." His cheeks flushed. "Like, kiss and ... You know."

"What, sex?" She gaped at him.

He nodded. "Yeah. If you'd like."

She laughed. "What's an arm got to do with sex? You don't have sex with your arms. Well, at least not in our species."

"I know. I just wanted to look good for you. Look normal. Nobody wants to have sex with the Terminator."

"Bay!" She shoved him. "Stop being a doofus. I'd love you even if your new arm were a chicken wing. Mmm ... chicken wings ..." She licked her lips.

Bay groaned. "I'm not sticking a chicken wing onto my body."

"Oh please!" Rowan hopped up and down. "I'm hungry."

"We just ate an hour ago!"

"But it wasn't chicken wings."

Bay sighed and returned to the shelf of prosthetics. He rummaged through them, seeking something half decent. A few arms looked realistic enough, but they were too small, made for children.

"I suppose I could use this one." He lifted an arm from the pile. "It looks more like the arm of a mannequin. But with a sleeve, and just the hand visible, it'll tide me over until I can get something better. What do you think?"

Rowan yawned. "It's boring."

"It's an arm, Row, not a video game."

She turned toward the shelf, biting her lip, and rummaged. Her eyes lit up. "Ooh, look at *this* one! Tubular!"

She lifted a new arm. It was a heavy with brass, tin, and leather. A steam gauge thrust out near the shoulder. Cables ran from the gauge into pistons, and a blue power source glowed.

Gears, bolts, and hinges bristled across a wooden forearm. There was even a built-in analog clock.

"Well, whatdya think?" Rowan said, eyes wide.

"It's ridiculous," Bay said.

"It's steampunk!"

"As I said—ridiculous."

"Come on." Rowan tugged on his good arm. "It's cool! Look at the size of these gears! They're *sweet*. Can I take it apart later, learn how it works?"

"You're not taking my arm apart!"

Rowan grinned. "So it *is* your arm! Aha, I knew it!"

"I didn't—" Bay began.

"Too late, you said it's yours!" She grew serious. "Listen, Bay. I honestly don't want you to have some creepy mannequin arm. I love machines. Gears, pistons, cables, gauges—I live for that stuff. This arm is going to impress the hell out of me—and every other lady in the fleet! It'll look really sexy on you."

Bay exhaled slowly. He looked at the ridiculous contraption. He supposed it did look kind of cool. Or *bitchin'*, as Rowan called it.

He sighed. "Fine."

Rowan whooped. "Would you consider wearing a pork pie hat and goggles with it?"

"Don't push your luck, hobbit."

He took the arm. They traveled back to the ISS *Kos*, where the doctors attached an interface to his stump—a metal cone with plugs. When it was ready, Bay plugged in his new prosthetic, and the arm came to life.

He tried it.

He was able to move his metal fingers.

It was a bit rough. The fingers creaked. The reaction times were slow. But Rowan said she could calibrate the arm. In fact, she seemed more excited about tinkering with the machine than with Bay getting a new limb.

They took the arm back to their cabin aboard the *Jerusalem*, which they shared. Rowan had the day off, and she spent it working on the arm. She took it apart, spreading screws and bolts across the floor, then rebuilt it—stronger and faster than before. This time, when Bay plugged the arm in, it worked flawlessly.

For the first time in his life, he had two working hands.

"Not bad, if I may say so myself." Rowan dusted her hands against her thighs. "How does it feel?"

"It tickles," Bay said, moving the metal arm. "And tingles. That's just my nerves getting used it. It's funny. But I can actually feel the arm. All the way down to the fingers."

"Nerves are amazing things," Rowan said.

"*You're* amazing," Bay said. "You chose the right arm. And you made it better. I'm growing to like it."

Bay turned to examine himself in the mirror. He wore the brown trousers, white buttoned shirt, and blue vest of the Inheritors. His new arm shone, all polished brass and sanded wood, its power source glowing. His hair was cropped short. He had been growing a beard, which he kept neatly trimmed. It was the same dark blond color as his hair.

"You look quite dashing," Rowan said.

Bay stared at his reflection. He spoke softly. "I don't recognize myself. Two years ago, when we met, I was grogged out, strung out, dying. I walked hunched over, wrapped in loose clothing like robes, trying to hide from the world. From myself. A dying cripple in the shadows." He turned toward her. "Who am I now, Rowan?"

"A soldier," she said. "A captain in the Heirs of Earth. A hero."

"I'm not a hero."

"You tried to give your life to save Ayumi," Rowan said. "You almost did! Without your sacrifice, we'd have lost the war. You're a hero, Captain Bay Ben-Ari, and I love you with all my heart. Forever."

Bay kissed her.

"I love you too, Rowan Emery. More than I can express with words."

She grinned. "You can try!"

He stroked her cheek. "You've changed too. When I met you, you were a scared, shy girl. So scared you cowered in a duct. Over the past two years, I've watched you grow into a woman. Into a heroine. You're funny, intelligent, and noble." He smiled. "How's that?"

She growled. "You forgot sweet, you bastard!" She punched him.

Bay laughed and kissed her again, then carried her to their bed. They kissed for a long time, breathing heavily, tugging off each other's clothes. But when they were naked, Rowan paused. She flushed, covered her breasts with her arm, and looked away.

"I'm shy," she whispered. "I don't look all curvy and pretty like the women in your drawings. I'm too small and skinny."

Bay stroked her hair. "You are far more beautiful than any of those women. You are perfect."

She smiled shyly. "Thank you. You're not too bad yourself." She caressed his cheek. "You're pretty."

He raised an eyebrow. "Not handsome? Or ruggedly buff?"

She stuck out her tongue. "Don't push your luck."

They made love. He had made love to women before. It was her first time. And it was good. And he was happy.

Afterward, she cuddled against him, her cheek on his chest, and he stroked her hair over and over.

*Yes, I'm happy,* Bay thought. *I'm happier than I've ever been. I will always mourn the loss of Seohyun. The demons of this war will always haunt me. I know there are battles ahead. But right now, this moment—this is joy. This is purity. This is living in love.*

"So, Bay," Rowan said. "Have you ever watched the movie *Roadhouse*?"

He bit his lip. "Um, was that the one with the DeLorean?"

She groaned and punched him. "That was *Back to the Future*! Gosh, you philistine. *Roadhouse*, come on! You know, Patrick Swayze?"

"Patrick who now?"

She rolled her eyes. "Your education is severely lacking. Come on! Plug in the Earthstone. You're watching *Roadhouse* with me." She tilted her head. "Hey, think we can install a film projector in your arm? Ooh, and a candy dispenser!"

His jaw dropped. "Rowan, it's my arm, not a movie theater."

"Fine, fine." She hopped out of bed, plugged the Earthstone into their monitor, then curled up under the blankets with him. "Now hush! *Roadhouse* is starting."

He kissed her cheek, and they watched the movie, and he loved to listen to her laughter.

*Yes*, he thought. *I'm happy.*

## CHAPTER FORTY-NINE

It was funny, Leona thought as she entered orbit around Earth. She had been across the galaxy. She had traveled to a hundred worlds. She had seen wonders—planets with trees that rose like skyscrapers, with mountains made of diamond, with marble cities that sang with light.

On the surface, there was nothing special about Earth. It was an ordinary planet, orbiting an ordinary star. It floated in an ordinary corner of the galaxy. The planet was smaller than most. It had no beautiful ring system. It had only one single moon, merely a dull rock. There were millions of planets like Earth. There were millions far more splendid.

For most travelers like Leona, who had crossed the galaxy, Earth was a mote of dust. A tiny speck in the vastness of space. Completely mundane. A planet most galactic travelers would barely notice, no more unique than any grain of sand on a beach.

Yet to Leona, this tiny world meant more than all the wonders in the galaxy.

This was Earth.

This was home, and she would not replace it with all the glorious planets across the cosmos.

The starfighters orbited Earth. The humans aboard gazed down upon their ancient homeworld. They saw green forests. Glistening lakes and rivers. Deep blue oceans.

It was the most beautiful sight Leona had ever seen.

Yet she also saw things that broke her heart.

There were cities on Earth. Not the old cities of humanity. Those had vanished long ago. There were cities of raw metal and stone. Of holes and burrows. Basilisk cities.

"The snakes colonized our planet," Mairead said. "Bastards."

The starfighter didn't have a powerful telescope. But Leona could imagine millions of the basilisks crawling below.

And Leona knew that changed nothing.

This was still humanity's home. And they would not turn back.

Where should they land? Should they land in North America, the continent where the legendary hero Marco Emery had fought the centipedes and spiders? Perhaps in ancient Jerusalem, which the Inheritor flagship was named after? Perhaps in Mesopotamia, birthplace of human civilization? Should she make Ramses happy and land in Egypt?

Leona considered. If humanity survived, historians would speak of this landing for thousands of years. It needed to be right.

Finally she directed her starfighter toward Africa. The others followed.

In Olduvai Gorge, humans had first evolved. It seemed fitting that there, where humanity had been born, humanity should be reborn.

The starfighters entered the atmosphere. They flew through blue skies. They were all silent, looking around, some through tears.

They flew along the Horn of Africa, then glided inland and saw it below. Olduvai. Birthplace of humanity.

There were no basilisk settlements here. The land looked pristine. It might have looked the same two million years ago when the first hominids had risen here. The hills and valleys spread into the horizon, bristly with brush. Stone monoliths rose from the earth, and sunbeams fell between white clouds.

*The light of our sun,* Leona thought. *More beautiful than all the starlight in the cosmos.*

Their engines rumbled. They slowed their flight. The starfighters descended. And landed.

*Here, in Olduvai, we first made tools of stone,* Leona thought. *We return with starships.*

The starfighters shut down their engines. The humans remained inside. Still. Silent.

Mairead pulled out a video camera. She pointed it at Leona and nodded.

Leona nodded back. She spoke into her comm, transmitting her voice into every cockpit—and to history.

"We came from stardust. In the beginning, we were atoms in the hearts of distant stars. We floated in the void. We glided on the solar wind, until finally we landed on this small world. We formed carbon molecules, replicating in a primordial womb of water and fire. Finally, in the oceans of this world, we built cells. Simple life. Millions of years ago, we rose from the water, and we conquered the land. We made tools. We built cities. We rose to the stars. And we fell." Leona lowered her head. "We found terrors in the darkness. They burned our world. We fled. The last survivors, we hid in the shadows. And for two thousand years, we dreamed of home. And for two thousand years, enemies rose to destroy us. But we survived. We lived on. And we never forgot where we came from. We never forgot Earth."

Leona was silent for a long moment, overwhelmed, thinking of those thousands of years of exile. Of eighty generations who had suffered. Of the millions who had died in exile, tortured and burned. Tears filled her eyes.

"For two thousand years, we dreamed of seeing Earth again. Her song ever called us home. Many thought Earth was just a myth. Yet we found our homeworld. Our birthplace. The only place we belong. I wish I could promise you a happy ending now.

I wish I could promise you peace and joy. But we know, even here on Earth, that our road will be long. That many battles await us. The basilisks will not forget their warships that we shattered. Many other species in the darkness seek our destruction. We do not come to a hidden, pristine haven, a place of safety or even joy. We come to a world we will have to defend. That we will have to fight for every day. Bleed for. Maybe die for. But we are ready. We are determined. We will not lose Earth again."

The soldiers in her cockpit looked at her, chins raised, eyes proud. Leona knew that they were ready. That they would always fight for Earth.

Leona opened her Firebird's canopy, and the warm, sweet air of Earth flowed into her lungs. The air she had evolved to breathe.

As Mairead kept filming, Leona climbed out of the cockpit, took a few steps down the ladder, then paused on the last rung.

She inhaled deeply, and tears filled her eyes.

*For you, my fallen husband. For you, my family and friends. For humanity.*

She placed a foot on the soil of Earth.

She smiled. "We are home."

## CHAPTER FIFTY

Deep within her mountain she lurked. Hungry. Hissing. Coiled up and waiting.

For many days, she had lain dormant.

Now she woke, her hunger a demon in her belly.

"They have come." Her voice slipped between her fangs, soft and slithery like a hatchling consuming its eggshell. "The humans have returned."

She uncoiled, white scales clattering, claws scratching at her pile of bones. Bloodred eyes opened, peering into darkness, seeing far. Her tail flicked, scattering skulls. Her lower half was serpentine, curling and scaly. Atop it, her humanoid torso swayed, her pale breasts tipped with red, her ribs draped with papery skin.

She was Xerka, Queen of Serpents.

She was Mother. Goddess. Devourer.

She was Mistress of Earth, and the apes had invaded her domain.

Bones shifted as a serpent slithered over the pile. He was a long beast, coated in black scales and jagged armor. An iron helmet covered his head, hiding even his eyes, revealing only massive jaws lined with rows of fangs. He was one of her many children. Strong. Cruel. Hungry for flesh. She had named him Naja, a lord of the underworld.

"Two hundred have come to the blue world," he hissed, her beloved son. "We slew many in the darkness. A few placed their filthy paws upon your hallowed soil."

Xerka stared at this creature. This warrior she had spawned. She saw herself reflected in his fangs, a hundred visions of her beauty. Naja was as black as the space between stars, while Xerka's scales shone like cold starlight. He was all spikes and serrated edges, while she was smoothness and curves. He was the masculinity of rigid, militaristic order, while she was feminine chaos. Two serpents, male and female, black and white. They would wrap the cosmos in their embrace.

*Two* serpents? Yes. Xerka was still a basilisk, a great apex snake. But she had devoured many apes. Digested them slowly. Learned from them. Captured their essence. Cracked open their cells and sucked up the nucleic acids inside, weaving them with her own molecules. Her lower body was still serpentine. But upon it rose the torso, arms, and head of a human, a hybrid created from a hundred meals. A woman. A mother. So pale. So fair. Eyes and nipples and gaping maw so red, beckoning, alluring like a feast of blood.

*I know you, humans. I have become you. I understand you.* She bared her fangs. *And I will destroy you!*

She spoke, voice as smooth and deadly as poisoned milk.

"I have many worlds, my dear son. Many precious jewels in the night. This black world of heat and darkness where I digest my meals. My worlds of fire and ice, of crystal and stone, of deep dark oceans and endless caves. But no world is as precious to me as Earth. It is the world where I lay my eggs. Where I spawned you. The world the humans must never claim."

Her son reared. He was larger than her, muscular and thick, her mightiest of killers. Flaps on the sides of his head flared, coated with scales. His jaws opened wide, the rows of teeth flowing down the gullet.

"We will kill them all!" he rumbled.

Xerka stared at her son's exposed underbelly. She saw movement within. Desperate kicks, scratching fingers. She sniffed, and a shudder ran through her.

"You brought me a gift, my son." Her forked tongue flicked between her fangs. "Give her to me."

The great serpent expanded his gullet like a toad. His body shuddered. His armor flared out. A spasm ran through the basilisk, and his lower jaw unhinged. He gagged onto the pile of bones, regurgitating a bundle of mucus, blood, and hair.

Xerka slithered closer, the bones rattling beneath her long body. She lowered herself over the bundle. With her pale, humanoid hands, she pulled back strands of mucus, clearing the blood, revealing the human within.

A human woman. Young. Wearing a tattered uniform. A soldier.

The human rose to her knees. She stared up at Xerka, and terror filled her eyes. She spoke in a shaky voice. "I am Private Sarah Rodriguez of the Heirs of Earth. My serial number is 1923A56. I was captured in low orbit over Earth." Tears ran down her cheeks, but she kept speaking. "You will treat me in accordance to Galactic Treaty 15B."

Naja loomed above her, his powerful jaws salivating, hungering. He must have carried her in his stomach for days, holding back on digesting her, an exercise of utmost self-control. Saliva dripped between his fangs, sizzling against the human's head.

Xerka caressed the young soldier's cheek.

"So fair," she whispered. "So soft. Humans are such fragile beings."

Naja opened his jaws with a hiss. "They are fine prey."

"Do not underestimate them, my son," Xerka said. "They defeated the Skra-Shen scorpions."

The black serpent laughed. "We are no scorpions! We are the *Ssstchkssshs*. The blessed basilisks. Mightier by far."

"Perhaps." Xerka nodded. "The scorpions were strong. But they relied on brute strength. Fools! One cannot rule a galaxy with mere brawn. It takes cunning. Understanding. To truly defeat an enemy, my dear son, one must *become* the enemy."

Xerka gripped the soldier's head, her claws tearing the scalp. She unhinged her lower jawbone. It drooped, exposing her throat.

The soldier trembled. Her tears flowed. "I am Private Sarah Rodriguez! My serial number is 1923A56! I was captured in low orbit over Earth, and—Oh Ra! Please! Please, no, please!"

Xerka wrapped her jaws around the woman's head. Tasting the tears. The sweat. The sweet, sweet fear. She sucked, pulling the woman inward. The human writhed and screamed, but Xerka had devoured many of her kind before. She tossed her head back and gulped, pulling the human down her esophagus. Her scales clattered as her body bulged. Xerka worked her muscles, expanding and contracting her ribcage, pushing her prey down into her belly.

Basilisks had exquisite control over their stomachs. They could withhold digestion to keep prey alive, sometimes for years. They could release elaborate cocktails of acids, digesting their victims slowly or quickly, burning or fermenting, discarding bones or turning them into delectable jelly. Some preferred to kill their victim quickly. Most preferred to digest them alive over long days, savoring the victim's thrashing.

But Xerka had learned a rare skill, one only the ancients had possessed. It required true mastery. Xerka was very old and very wise, and she was a mistress of this art.

She released her juices. Tasting. Stroking. Then ripping apart.

With the skill of a surgeon, she stripped off the skin, carved open the flesh, dug through the cells, and opened the nuclei. Her acids flowed into the human's ears, reached the brain, and stroked the neurons. Tasting. Experiencing. Understanding.

Her victim screamed inside her. Begging. Still alive. She had to remain alive. The pain—so luscious! Xerka could have anesthetized the woman. But the pain was the sweetness of the meal. Her little indulgence.

"Yes, yes," Xerka hissed, plundering the cells, weaving together their strands of DNA. "We are one. I understand. I see you."

The human essence flowed through Xerka. When she looked again at her reflection, she was a little more human. Her face a little rounder. Her breasts a little larger. Her mind a little wiser.

"I saw them, Naja," she said to her son. "The humans. Millions of them in the darkness, making their way to Earth. We must stop them."

"We will kill them all!" Naja said, fangs bared and scaly hood extended.

Xerka had what she needed. She released the furious acids inside her, finally granting mercy to the human in her belly. She sighed contentedly as she digested the meat.

"Yes, my son." Xerka stroked his jaws. "We will kill them all."

The story continues in

*The War for Earth*

*Children of Earthrise Book 4*

# NOVELS BY DANIEL ARENSON

## *Earthrise:*
*Earth Alone*
*Earth Lost*
*Earth Rising*
*Earth Fire*
*Earth Shadows*
*Earth Valor*
*Earth Reborn*
*Earth Honor*
*Earth Eternal*

## *Children of Earthrise:*
*The Heirs of Earth*
*A Memory of Earth*
*An Echo of Earth*
*The War for Earth*
*The Song of Earth*
*The Legacy of Earth*

## *The Moth Saga:*
*Moth*
*Empires of Moth*
*Secrets of Moth*
*Daughter of Moth*
*Shadows of Moth*
*Legacy of Moth*

**Dawn of Dragons:**
*Requiem's Song*
*Requiem's Hope*
*Requiem's Prayer*

**Song of Dragons:**
*Blood of Requiem*
*Tears of Requiem*
*Light of Requiem*

**Dragonlore:**
*A Dawn of Dragonfire*
*A Day of Dragon Blood*
*A Night of Dragon Wings*

**The Dragon War:**
*A Legacy of Light*
*A Birthright of Blood*
*A Memory of Fire*

**Requiem for Dragons:**
*Dragons Lost*
*Dragons Reborn*
*Dragons Rising*

**Flame of Requiem:**
*Forged in Dragonfire*
*Crown of Dragonfire*
*Pillars of Dragonfire*

## KEEP IN TOUCH

www.DanielArenson.com
Daniel@DanielArenson.com
Facebook.com/DanielArenson
Twitter.com/DanielArenson

70891122R00222

Made in the USA
Middletown, DE
18 April 2018